NEW
HAMPSHIRE

MASSACHUSETTS

Cambridge

Boston

Worcester

Framingham   Roxbury

Charles River

JOSEPH PATTI

Books by
Robert Newton Peck

A Day No Pigs Would Die
Path of Hunters
Millie's Boy
Soup
Fawn
Wild Cat
Bee Tree (poems)
Soup & Me
Hamilton
Hang for Treason
Rabbits and Redcoats
King of Kazoo (a musical)
Trig
Last Sunday
Patooie
The King's Iron

THE KING'S IRON

Robert Newton Peck

THE KING'S IRON

LITTLE, BROWN AND COMPANY *Boston—Toronto*

FIRST EDITION

T 11/77

LIBRARY OF CONGRESS CATALOGING IN PUBLICATION DATA
Peck, Robert Newton.
   The King's iron.

   1.   Ticonderoga, N.Y.—History—Revolution,
1775–1783—Fiction.   2.   Knox, Henry, 1750–1806—
Fiction.   I.   Title.
PZ4.P3675Ki   [PS3566.E254]   813'.5'4   77–24572
ISBN 0–316–69655–2

Designed by Janice Capone

*Published simultaneously in Canada
by Little, Brown & Company (Canada) Limited*

PRINTED IN THE UNITED STATES OF AMERICA

To Stephanie,
and her fine crop of sons . . .
and to Ticonderoga.

THE KING'S IRON

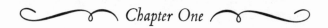

Chapter One

"General Washington will see you, sir."

Despite his two hundred and fifty pounds, Henry Knox jumped to his feet. So quickly that the ladderback chair slid backward on the well-shined parlor floor. Washington awaited him at the top of the narrow flight of stairs.

"I welcome you, Henry."

"Thank you, sir." Knox climbed the stairs two at a step.

"Please don't thank me. You are warming company on a chilly November night." General Washington pulled a bright red blanket more snugly about his shoulders in a bedchamber cold and dimly lit. A candle flickered at his desk.

"You look well, General."

"Then you may require spectacles, young sir, for I am froze from toe to top. And to boot, took a hack of a cough. Damn this Massachusetts weather. I don't know how in hell you people abide it."

"It suits our natures, sir, as it's been oft said that we New Englanders are as hospitable as a clam bed."

"All but you, Henry."

"Thank you, sir." Knox smiled.

"Please take no offense if I ask your age."

"I am twenty-five, General."

"Twenty-five? I think of you as older. Your size matures you. Well, I am forty-three. And unless I return to the sunshine of Virginia soon, I'll not reach forty-four. Let's give this fire a poke or two."

Together they added wood. The bedchamber brightened with firelight. Henry Knox was about to stuff an old bit of newspaper under the front log, as Washington rescued it. "Wait," he said. "I'll not be deprived of reading the words of Samuel Adams in your transplanted Boston *Gazette*. Ah, here it is. I wonder how he'll sign his name."

"As some ancient Roman, as usual. Populus or some such. What think you of our Sam?"

Washington straightened up. His hands tried to clutch one more grasp of the yellow heat before pulling the red blanket more snugly around his tall frame. "I will tell you, Henry. Poor men are often stupid, but not your Samuel Adams. Puny men can be weak, but this fellow is tougher than Carolina tripe. Men sloppy in their attire can be persons who have ceased to care. Yet your Adams cares as deeply for his country as does a mother hen for her chicks. No, that's not accurate enough. Like a she-bear for a cub."

"Sam's a staunch Puritan, sir."

Washington motioned Knox to a seat, and then sat at his paper-strewn desk. "Yes, a Puritan, but a pure one. I would pick his company to his pudge of a cousin. John's a man of New England nature." The general smoothed out the scrap of newspaper with his fingers. "But getting back to Sam Adams, I can always tell his writing. Witless, heavy and hot. Direct as an indian arrow. And seems to hiss in like manner with its own ire. I tell you, Knox, I'll drive the British from Boston if only to save his scrawny neck from the noose."

Henry Knox laughed.

"Tell me, are you also a Puritan?" asked Washington.

4

"No, sir, I think not. A Presbyterian is what I am. The Puritans smile every decade, but we grin once a year."

"Cleverly said, lad. Say, I can feel the fire, if your oxlike person does not soak up all the baking. No wonder all your northern Puritans are such a sour lot. Can't ask a frozen face to smile, especially one from Massachusetts. If you folks could come just once for a week in Virginia, you'd all thaw a bit. I can just see the Adams boys skipping around the ball floor with one of our comely ladies." Washington threw back his head, loudly laughing. "If John ever smiled, he'd break both knees."

"It's so good to see you laugh, General Washington."

"Is it? Well, my good lad, best we store some mirth into our ribs now, for it could be a long war. And for scores of our fair sons, a short one." General Washington searched his desk, finally discovering the folded paper that he sought. "This," he said, "is a letter that arrived this day from Benedict Arnold."

"A good soldier, sir, as I hear of him."

"The best. You shall never know how often I wonder why he is not Commander-in-Chief and not I. Methinks he wonders the same. And that is the thought that sobers me to shoulder the command. I may doubt myself, Henry, but no other shall doubt me."

"How do you mean, sir?"

"Twenty years ago, General Braddock taught me one thing, my dear friend. He taught me how to whip a British army."

Henry Knox stared at the Virginian. This was not one of Washington's jests, thought Knox. The general was serious. Or insane. This arrogant Southerner really thinks he can do it.

"Whip a British army," Henry said softly. "A boast that sounds as unlikely as riding a goatcart to the moon. But I'll give you this much, sir. You could convince me that you can."

Washington sighed. "That's the nut of it, Henry. You point out with your usual Presbyterian precision what my job is: to warp the young wills of clerks and farmers enough to convince them that *they* can whip a British army." General Washington nodded toward the window that looked over the fires of his encamped army.

"Indeed we must," said Henry Knox.

5

"Our troops never see me shivering in this red quilt. Nor will they. I make sure that I review our lads on a white horse with my boots polished and my sword as clean as cold steel can be. Little do they know my feet are just as cold. They believe what they see. And it's my job to show them a leader, a man to follow and to obey. Yea, even as do the English their King George."

" 'Tis true, sir. Such is called for."

"Flog me if I am wrong, because I'll have a heap of bleeding boys at my feet, and their poor souls upon my conscience. You cannot show a soldier what God looks like, or paint him a portrait of independence to hang on his cabin wall for a battle trophy. But I can show our boys a general . . . Yet is it enough to be some parading popinjay on a white steed? Vain hope. So I thank the Lord who made me that I rode at Braddock's hip. Believe me, Knox, I truly believe we can stomp on all the red ants."

"How?"

"We don't ever make the mistake of thinking we're as good as they are and charge them like a bull. They'll kick our teeth in."

"Then how do we fight those Lobsterbacks?"

"We sting, and slap, and throw grit in their eyes and sand in their powder. Like wasps, we strike and fly away to later sting again. But we shall not cross bayonets. For if we do, they shall surely slice us to bacon."

"You would persuade even a deacon to enlist, sir," Knox said.

"Spare me that. The trouble with our army is the same as in our churches. We have more deacons than parishioners. And we have more officers than we do infantry. Half the plantation owners I know in Virginia already strut about in uniforms their ladies designed for them, tripping on sabers long enough for lances. Perhaps I appear as foolish as they."

Henry Knox smiled. "Not true, sir. You look proud to us. You do not play the clown. I am sure you must realize, sir, that few of us here in Massachusetts have ever set eyes on a Virginian, much less been led by one."

Washington rose from his desk, still clinging to his red blanket. " 'Tis true, Henry, that all living things tend to flock among their own kind. Birds, bugs, and beasts. Fish or fowl or flowers. I know, to most of you New Englanders, that a Southerner is looked upon with disfavor."

"No, sir, I would not say . . ."

"Hear me out, lad. It troubles me not. You cannot change nature nor human nature. I accept the phenomenon, as I would choose the company of Virginian affability to Bostonian starch. Although you are a warm friend, Henry."

"I am, sir."

"That's why I share with you these confessions. God, I have to own up to someone, or go mad. So I admit to you, my dear Knox, that never in my forty-three years have I ever met such a herd of self-righteous bastards as you Bostonians. Be you Puritan or Catholic, be you Presbyterian or Baptist or Congregational or Episcopal, I find the town of Boston full of pompous jackasses who can compromise less even than they giggle."

"Indeed, we lack your humility, General."

Washington smiled. "Well called, Henry. I shall always welcome the spice you can add to our cupboard of conversation. Yet here I am in Cambridge, trying to crack a hard nut. I must rescue a town that I detest from being burned or bludgeoned by the British. I know why I am here; and furthermore, why they are." Washington now sat again and studied the face of Henry Knox.

At length, he spoke. "Knox, I find you fair of nature and, to boot, high of mind and spirit. You pretend not to be a soldier, but despite your protestations I see you as one. Nay, as an officer of field rank. Until a while ago, Colonel Richard Gridley was my chief of artillery."

"What artillery? We have none, sir."

"Patience, young man. Gridley fought the French, years back. Experience? Yes, and a-plenty. But he is aged fifty-four and in frail health. And that is why, as you must know, I have asked Congress to approve your commission as Commander of Artillery."

"I have heard it spoken of, and I would do your bidding."

"Well, they approve. They offer the rank of lieutenant colonel. You will accept, of course."

7

"No, sir, I will not."

"Explain yourself." There was no warmth in Washington's eyes, and his words were a command.

"I refuse the rank, sir. If I aim the Continental artillery, spare though our cannon may be, I shall wear a colonel's rank or none at all."

"For what devil of a reason?"

"If Gridley was a colonel, then I will be also. My mind is made up, sir. And I mean no disrespect."

"Your mind is about as genial in this matter as a Georgia mule."

"Or a Scotch-Irish Presbyterian?" Knox asked.

"One or the other, as they could flank a wagon tongue and pull as a team."

"What does it matter? We have no artillery," said Knox. "I might as well be in charge of a battery of men who bend their backsides to British warships . . . and fart."

"We have cannon, Henry."

"Sir?"

General Washington lifted the letter that he held, gesturing lightly to Knox. " 'Tis a letter from Ben Arnold to Schuyler, who did forward same to me. Since last May, all credit to our wily Benedict and to Ethan Allen and his Verdmont plowmen, we have had row upon row of British cannon in our keeping at Ticonderoga. Your job, Henry, is to bring the mountain to Moses. I want you to get yourself north and bring that iron to Boston. Can you do it?"

"You must believe I can, sir. Else you would not ask. Yet it is a sobering proposition at this season of the year."

Washington lifted the lamp from his desk. Three strides took him to a map on the wall. Its upper right corner was torn; New Hampshire was missing.

"Here!" said Washington. "Here is Fort Ticonderoga. You will haul the iron south to Saratoga, to Albany, then cross the River Hudson bearing south through Dutch country to Claverack. Thence, with God's help, you will traverse the Berkshire Mountains. And so at last to Boston. It is a frightful task, Henry. But you must be master of the mission."

8

"I thank you for the order, sir. But come, my dear General, let me at least stitch a colonel's eagle on my cape ere I wish for a star."

"Well said, my hearty lad. And so it shall be. But realize that as of late, I have formed a shabby habit. I offer rank for favors, as I would throw a bone to a cur, in order to keep our army . . ." Washington smiled briefly . . . "afloat. I must have those cannons, and so I dangle a star before you like a carrot to a mule. Come, Colonel, we'll stretch our legs, and draw a few deep breaths of night air from the foggy bogs of Massachusetts."

The general tossed his red blanket at the bedfoot and donned a blue cape, with a red and cream trim. Then setting a black tricorne upon his wig and buckling on his sword, Washington was ready. Knox went first down the narrow stairs. The two left the house to walk out into the November night.

Outside, two young Virginians huddled against a tree, no doubt hoping their relief would soon come. Seeing their general, they snapped to attention. Knox observed the general's greeting to them. No longer was he a perplexed old man, warming himself under a red blanket. Instead, he was a man of war, confident without swaggering, his walk more like that of an English poet than a soldier. Sir John Suckling, thought Knox. Our dashing cavalier from Virginia come north to charm Billy Howe as well as all of Boston society.

"Nippy night, lads." Washington's voice was quiet.

"Yes, sir, and more," a corporal drawled.

"Well, be glad for it. Welcome it. Hot nights will turn us tender. Soften our vigilance. But a crisp night, Corporal, will keep us all alert and not back on our heels."

"Yes, sir."

Together they passed a larger group of uniformed Continentals. As the group saw Washington, they also stiffened and saluted.

"Carry on, boys." Washington did not stop.

"Do you ride, Henry?"

"Very little, sir."

"Ofttimes, as a mount is on the brink of a stumble, a good rider can pick up his head and save a spill. The same for soldiers. If we can heighten the spirits of a company of foot or artillerymen who watch us pass, we should."

"I agree, sir."

"Show them a general, Henry. Remember that."

"Aye, sir. That I will."

There were shouts ahead, near a campfire that divided two long rows of tents. Men seemed to be fighting. Washington quickened his pace until both he and Knox were among several score of men. A young boy was being stripped of his shirt. Two men were lashing his wrists with thongs to a crossbeam that seemed to exist for purposes of discipline. Nearby, a third man who wore the insignia of a sergeant held the handle of a hot branding iron, and its D glowed red-faced in the night.

"Good evening, Sergeant."

"Sir." The sergeant braced to attention. Most of the others who watched did more or less likewise, despite their obvious lack of military training.

"What's his offense?" asked Washington.

"Desertion, sir. Stole a horse, he did, and we caught him headed for home. He deserves the brand, sir."

"How old are you, lad?" Washington asked the boy.

"Seventeen, sir." The boy was so cold in his half-nakedness that his lips could barely chatter a response.

"Heading home, eh?"

"Yes . . . yes, sir."

"Son, if I had my way, I'd have you steal a team so I could duck, too."

The men roared a laugh.

"Sergeant."

"Sir."

"Tell me true, Sergeant. Do you have the belly to return this pup to his mother with a brand on his chest?"

"I don't relish it, sir."

"Nor do I. If we are to hurt anyone, I say we tack a few bumps on the British."

"You mean let him loose, sir?"

"Son," the general addressed the deserter, "what is your father's occupation?"

"He's a farmer . . . , sir."

"And if you were not home for evening chores, how did your good old dad treat you?"

"He'd give me a smarting, sir."

"Sergeant, give our runaway a smarting. Make the lash sting, but do not cut his flesh. Hear?"

"I hear, sir."

"And if he runs away again . . ."

"Yes, sir?"

"Brand his bum."

The men yelled out their approval of the justice, as Washington tossed his cape over his right shoulder to return the farewell salutes he knew he would receive. Every hand went up, except for the lad's who was bound. Yet Knox read a respectful salute on the young face. The two continued their walk, beyond the sounds of a cracking lash on a yelping and contrite recruit.

"General Howe would have branded a D on that boy's body," said Washington, "as that is the British way. And that, my good Henry, is why we are going to win this war. To stop the stink of sizzling flesh. Discipline is one thing, but cruelty is another. Leadership is based on faith, Henry. It's a hell of sight more prayer than penalty." Washington sighed.

Knox followed him up a short hill and observed how the general looked southeast, toward Boston. He wondered what the Virginian thought. How to get the upper hand of General Howe, no doubt. Suddenly the general turned with a swirl of his blue cape.

"Henry," he said, "get that cannon to Boston."

"I will, sir."

"Bring me the King's iron."

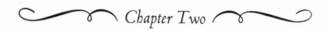

Chapter Two

A crow barked.

Blue Goose reached his hand forward to cover the mouth so his friend would not speak. For the sound that Blue Goose had heard had not come from a crow. The two men sat silently in the canoe to await the next sound, wondering if it would be the hiss of an arrow, a report from a musket, or a scream from an attacking enemy who had suddenly discovered where they hid.

"How many?" the white man with the white hair asked.

Blue Goose counted the noises in the forest, holding up three fingers.

Their canoe floated in place between two great walls of rock that grew up from the lake shore so closely that a man could extend his arms in places and touch both faces of the gray rock. The crack had a strong smell of juniper, given off by the tiny yet determined cedars that seemed to sprout from the heart of the wall. The space between the two rock faces was familiar to both men, a good spot to lodge a canoe. Or to wait inside while other canoes passed by on the lake. Neither the old man nor Blue Goose made a sound; and the drops of water that fell from the blades of their paddles created circle within circles on the silent surface of the black water.

The sun backed slowly away.

Blue Goose wanted to prepare an evening meal, to eat in peace. But these were days of war. And so he waited without movement, telling the dog in his belly not to whine with emptiness nor to whimper in the cold. He sat and listened, waiting for an enemy that was red and not white, thankful that his ears were young and sharp, and that he could listen for himself and for his old white friend, the man whom he thought of as Old Ax but who called himself Durable.

White men were not to be trusted.

Traded with, if it suited their purpose to trade their pelts for food or a warm floor to sleep upon, yet not trusted. Blue Goose had once given a perfect white pelt of an ermine for a jug of hot tea, with sugar. He remembered how he had kept the jug near the orange coals of a cooking fire so that the tea would stay hot. Now his belly almost sang for a swallow of tea, warm and hot and sweet with sugar. So sweet, thought Blue Goose, it would be like drinking from a flower. Blue Goose would be a bee. I must not, he thought, ever think that all white men are like my white man, Durable Hatch. They are not. No, they are far from honest drinks like tea. Rather they are hot drinks of whiskey that warm the belly and then burn the brain.

In the canoe, he sat at Durable's back.

Always it was this way, as the heavier man should ride rudder to let the bow be weighted less and lift over the labor of many days' paddling. He saw the old man's lean hand rest on the hickory handle of the tomahawk that rode his leather belt. Other than a skinning knife, the tomahawk was the only weapon carried by Durable Hatch. Yet he could hurl it, thought Blue Goose, truer than many white men could discharge a musket. Truer than many red men could send an arrow. He wondered the age of Old Ax. Perhaps he was now five all-fingers, or even six.

The crow sound came again. Durable turned slowly so that their eyes met, and his bearded face that was white like morning frost shook once, side to side, to say that he knew it was no crow.

"Where?"

Blue Goose pointed with his eyes, looking upward and then back to the face of Durable Hatch. Again he held up three red fingers. Pulling his small knife from its sheath, he made three gestures, a stab of the air three times. But the old man shook his head no. Waving his arm, he told Blue Goose that perhaps the three would grow tired or hungry or cold and go away. Blue Goose did not believe this. White men would. But not red men, who feel the hunger for war stronger than the thirst for water or a woman. Men who wailed of their hunger for women were weak. Dogs with their tails down. His father had told him that hunger was the fragrance of cooking meat, and that his patience would be another twig for the fire. I wonder, thought Blue Goose, if my father still lives.

Sixteen winters is a long time in Canada.

Now it was dark. Still they waited, saying nothing to one another except for a sign, wondering if the three men were yet among the rocks above their heads, where the two great faces leaned together to touch brow to brow. I am thankful, thought Blue Goose, that the leaves are no longer red on the trees. They are brown or fallen, and there are few bugs to bite our skin. But now the sun leaves the lake, and my back no longer wets from the work of the paddle, so I long for the buckskin shirt that is in my roll. The rock behind us is damp above the waterline. There is a spring there. We may see ice before we see the next sun. My bones tell me this. What matters a Mohawk arrow into a frozen Blue Goose?

The paddle still lay across his knees, but now Blue Goose saw no more shine on its blade. No more drops. The spoon of the paddle was now as dry as its shaft. Silently he unrolled his pack, his hands exploring the blackness until he touched his shirt. Once his head punched through the neck and the laces were tied, the ache of the cold November night left him. But the craving for food and rest still shared their canoe.

Blue Goose heard the scream of the great horned owl, whose talons even the golden eagle respected. The owl was real, not a brother to the crow. A great owl hunts this night, but Blue Goose will not. Blue Goose only waits in his hole like the gray mouse. But yet only by day. The cover of night beckons to the mouse and lends her the heart of the panther and the blood of the bear. Out she comes, to spring upon a beetle. Ah, but does Blue Goose stir? No, he waits. So that he may live and see the town of Boston as Old Ax had promised.

"Old Ax," he whispered, and when Durable turned, he said to the old man, "I take bow up and over rocks, slay three, and then we boil stew." His mouth was close to Durable, and his words were no louder than a breeze through a fern.

"They are three," said Old Ax, "and Blue Goose is only one."

Blue Goose smiled: "Three tongues always talk. But one lies flat in its lair. Blue Goose hear them, but they not hear me."

"Take care," the old man touched his shoulder.

Blue Goose nodded.

The canoe hardly moved as he left it. With a moc on a tiny ledge, his fingers sought a handhold above his head. He thought, I must press my chest close to the rock, being careful not to let my bow clatter against its hardness. Up he climbed; higher, higher, until the rock faces could touch both sides of his body. There was no moon as his leg hooked over the brim of the drop. Due west, the sky held the pink paint of sundown, and through its color he saw one of the men, a Mohawk. My bow? No, my knife on the first two. An arrow for the third.

I wonder, thought Blue Goose, if my white man grows ill with worry for his red friend. Were I in the canoe and he up here, my hands would be wet for his safety. Does he pray? He does not speak of his God to me and yet I know that he has one for he says "God!" when he drops his food into the fire, and repeats the name when his hand burns in trying to retrieve it. Yes, my white man must have a God to worship. I believe all men do, be they of red skin or of white. How could a man think not of a God, unless he has never seen the night sky dusted with stars?

Blue Goose saw the Mohawk wave his arm, as if to summon another brave to his side. Following the glance of the Mohawk chief, he saw two men moving out of the night blanket. The men had spun no fire.

Little was said when the three met. Yet the Mohawk chief made it plain with signs that the other two were to climb down the rock to the north, slip into the water, and swim to the canoe of the red man and white man. Blue Goose was Huron, but he knew that the two braves did not want to enter the water. The lake was cold, he heard one say. Then he heard a hand slap a cheek, and a foot kick a belly. The two went slinking off and over the rocks out of sight. The two would talk to each other, Blue Goose thought, but my white man will be as still as the turtle.

He fitted an arrow into his bow, and waited.

"Hey!"

It was but a whisper, yet Blue Goose knew its source. Old Ax was fretting again or growing impatient. Please be still, old man, and remain like a mouse in your dark hole.

"Hello!"

No, I am wrong. This is not the old friend of Blue Goose who speaks, but rather a Mohawk trick. As the great owl shrieks to cause the chipmunk to run from hiding, so does the Mohawk cry out in Yengeese. I am now happy that the snows of many winters clog the ears of Old Ax, so he knows it is not his friend Blue Goose who yells in the night like bad whiskey.

Blue Goose could not believe his good fortune.

Before his eyes, the Mohawk chief walked toward him. His head was shaved, except for a topknot with two eagle feathers. Around his neck was a necklace of panther claws. Below his naked chest he wore flaps of loin skin; and on his legs were wraps of deerhide bound by thongs. Although a Mohawk, the man was a proud warrior and no doubt his arrowheads had found much meat. Many geese. And no doubt many of our Huron from the north. But I am one goose, thought Blue Goose, that you will not slay.

Thud!

Blue Goose saw the hungry head of his arrow bite deep into the Mohawk's chest, less than the width of a hand below the man's nipple. Falling forward, his kicking body seemed intent to fall over the edge of the rock face and into Lake George, as Old Ax called the water. Pulling him back from the high brink, Blue Goose rolled the dead body on its back.

Let the arrow rest there. Instead he took the topknot of hair.

Blue Goose wanted all Mohawk to see the arrow that grows like a flower from the heart of a Huron's enemy. His father, Tall Face, would nod to his son. Tall Face, who had fought with the French at the side of General Montcalm, felt shame when they retreated north from the Yengeese guns of General Amherst. The French were friends of the Huron, and givers of blankets. The Yengeese were allies of the Mohawk. Kill the Yengeese, all of them, Tall Face had said.

But there were things that Tall Face did not know about a man with white hair, Old Ax, who speaks Yengeese. Tall Face may well think his son Blue Goose is dead, as a musket ball creased my skull, and I was captured by the Mohawk, and beaten. Had it not been for Old Ax, I would be dead. He saw me stretched out on the ground, stripped of my weapons and clothing, my arms and legs lashed to a cross of logs. The Mohawk women and children were beating my face with flaming sticks from the fire, and kicking my belly.

Old Ax bought me then. And I slowly knew that he did not wish to kill me, but to heal my wounds with medicine on a warm poultice, and later set me free. His face smiles little, but his heart is rabbit-soft.

These were his thoughts as Blue Goose crept along the top of the great rock, until below him he saw a Mohawk warrior climbing slowly downward. The moon hid behind a puff of cloudsmoke as if it also felt the wet of fear.

Coiled at his belt, Blue Goose kept a noose of light rawhide: thin as any twig, yet as strong as the twisted deergut of his bowstring. The noose was useful to snare a cooking rabbit. Would it be stout enough to encircle a Mohawk neck, and not break but strangle?

"Up here, dog!" he said. As the warrior turned his face upward, fear whitened his eyes. Blue Goose dropped the rawhide, and the hands of the Mohawk shot upward to claw at the death that silenced his warcries, the death that yanked tighter until he lost his balance to hang himself in the black air of night. As he pulled upward, Blue Goose looped the twine around the tough stump of a juniper. The bough pricked the tops of his hands, but he felt no pain. Only the kicks of a dying Mohawk as the snare cut into his clenched Huron fingers.

"Die," he smiled in silence.

Down he climbed, down beyond the dead Mohawk slowly twisting in the November night, his hands still clutching his throat, and horror frozen on his face. With a quick stroke of his knife, Blue Goose took the second topknot of Mohawk hair as he had the first. He stuffed it inside his shirt to tickle his chest.

Looking below, he could not yet see the stern of Old Ax's canoe. And where was the third Mohawk? Then he heard the sound. It came from the side of the canoe of birchbark as it scraped against the rocky face. You grow careless, Old Ax. Quickly the canoe shot out from under its protection, causing Blue Goose to say strong words to himself in Huron. Do not expose yourself, Old Ax. Not for Blue Goose.

Now he saw all of the canoe. It was empty.

In the center a mound of skins and a blanket appeared to hold a paddle, dragging it in the water, causing the canoe to circle back toward shore again. The old white fox!

A scream above his head made Blue Goose look upward. A body was falling on him from above, and before Blue Goose had time to think, the Mohawk hit him at full force, like a great falling stone. Blue Goose laughed. Both fell from the edge of the rock; down, down, to hit the shock of icy water. All that Blue Goose saw was the silver flash of a knife held in a Mohawk grip, which made him again laugh. The knife tip cut his face as their two bodies sank under the black surface.

Beneath the dark water, the Mohawk seemed more eager to regain the surface than to do battle. His legs kicked the chest of Blue Goose, who reached for his knife. He wanted air, but air would come later. Without life, there would be no air. Lungs breathe poorly when pierced by Mohawk iron. Their faces broke the surface less than an arrow's length from each other, and Blue Goose read the hideous leer on the warrior's face. Once, twice, the blade of Blue Goose invaded the gut of his enemy. But when the Mohawk's face sank slowly forward into Lake George, his back floated upward.

Stuck in his back was a tomahawk.

Splash!

Less than a canoe length from where Blue Goose stared at the third dead Mohawk, the old man hit the water. Beneath the surface, he approached the two. Before rising for air, his knife ripped three times at the Mohawk's side. The water was sticky with blood. As the dead Mohawk sank, Durable retook his tomahawk.

"A good throw, Old Ax."

The old man's white hair and beard trembled in the cold water, his clothes sucking him downward. Blue Goose threw a strong arm across the old man's chest, and together they kicked to the side of their canoe. Old Ax shook with cold.

Later their small fire crackled with joy, as if smelling its own cooking. The dried venison stung their mouths with heat. In a folded pot of bark they heated rum, seasoned from Durable's tiny packet of spice. The hot rum burned away the cold of death and the icy pain of the water. The honey was gone and so they added extra sugar to the rum to build more belly fire.

"Again you save me, Old Ax."

" 'Twas the canoe I fretted on," snorted the old man.

"Our blankets dry. And food. Hides from our traps trade well. Come morning, I dive to take last scalp." Blue Goose held up his two.

Old Ax coughed. Blue Goose did not like the noise, as more than twenty winters ago, Leaf, the mother of his mother, died with a cough. It was a sound he remembered with sorrow.

"You jump off high rock, Old Ax."

"Yes, like a dang fool. To save your worthless red soul."

"And you cannot swim," smiled Blue Goose.

Chapter Three

"Are you asleep?"

"No, my dear. But how did you know?"

"I know *you,* Henry."

"Yes, indeed you do. And I am the richer for knowing you, my Lucy."

"Richer than John Hancock?" She snuggled closer to his big body in their great bed.

"By far." Lifting up his right arm, Henry Knox lowered it gently, bringing her to him, suddenly aware of the sweet nearness of her and all the pleasures she gave him.

"It is so good to have you back home."

"Worcester is not our home," he said. "Boston is, was, and shall be. I was there yesterday, pet."

"Did you see the store?" she asked.

"No, as I couldn't bear to see it closed and with nary a candle to light the window. The best bookstore in Boston without a candle. But you should be spared the sight of Boston now. Houses boarded up. British troops in every nook. Little food, or even none. Red-coated soldiers wenching on the pews of our churches."

"Surely they might find more comfortable places for such amusement. Though 'twould be a welcome change from the Reverend Canver's sermons."

"Lucy!"

She gave Knox a squeeze, and knew he was smiling. "Are you happy?"

"With you? Always."

"But what of the war? What did Washington say? Tell me again."

"He's some fellow, our George."

"You like him."

"Very much. Even though he thinks we Massachusetts boys are a cold lot."

"Then he's never been abed with you," she pinched him, "or with me. . . . But I beg you, tell me more about the general."

"He is our Cromwell, Lucy. There's a book hereabouts on old Cromwell that I would commend to thee."

"Methinks he was a Puritan."

"Yes, a Puritan, as our general is not."

"And perchance a tyrant," she added.

"Nay, not so. Treated his troops in fair fashion. England offered Cromwell the crown. When he did not accept, they made him the Lord Protector."

"I shall read the book," Lucy said.

"Of course. Start it on the morrow, as I will be gone for a few days." As he spoke, Knox felt her pull closer to his side. He touched her hair with his face, inhaling her fragrance, hoping to remember it in the days ahead.

"Where is he sending you?"

"To New York, dear one. Brother William will ride with me. 'Tis no great journey."

"Henry, you speak at moments as though you mistrust even your wife, whose bed you now share."

"The less you know . . ."

"Enough!" Lucy's hand punched the pillow. "If you and William ride off to die for the cause of Massachusetts Bay, then I demand to be privy to it."

"I'll tell you," he sighed. "We ride north to the place called Ticonderoga. . . ."

"Father oft spoke of it. There's a fort."

"Yes, recently captured by . . ."

"Benedict Arnold and others. Six months ago. Is that all you have to tell?"

"We want their cannon, Lucy."

"And so you go to New York and then on to Fort Ticonderoga, returning with such."

"If I can."

"*If?* That's no Henry Knox of mine."

"It shan't be too easy."

"Nothing worthwhile is. But that's why General Washington is sending *you*. No one else could do it. Except for Cromwell. And he's long dead, by your own admission."

"So he is. And so shall be Boston if I fail. We can't arm our young farmers with varmint muskets and ask them to rush at Billy Howe. War is an ill business. How can we order our green lads to cross fire with British Regulars?"

"About a year ago," Lucy said, "I was walking one afternoon on the Common, with Father and Mother, when a disturbance took place."

"Of what nature?" asked Henry.

"Some toughs. Ropers, I think, itching to fist a Tory. Some carried lengths of wood, for clubs."

"Woolder sticks, no doubt. Used by the rope walkers to correct the lay in braiding. What occurred?"

"Pushing and naming at first. Then fisting. I guess they didn't know my father was Thomas Flucker and a friend of General Gage."

"Go on."

"Someone rang an alarm bell, and almost within breathing, a squad of Redcoats came at the hurry, muskets held high. Some rowdy hurled a stone, causing the officer in charge to command that the Regulars affix their bayonets."

"Did they?"

"Yes, and in a trice. Perhaps a dozen British soldiers formed two lines that joined in front like a point. A triangle with two sides."

"A phalanx, I so believe. The ancient Greeks devised it as a battle maneuver. Did it effect?"

22

"As I said, the Redcoats with bayonets pushed back a surly crowd of scores."

"British steel hath tasted every flavor of blood in Europe," Knox said, "and they are the best damn soldiers on earth. General Washington has told me as much."

"War excites you, Henry. Confess it."

"*You* excite me, pet. War only fascinates me. I like to read about it, and I conclude that war is a natural phenomenon. A matter of population, I suspect."

"Population?"

"Well, my Lucy, here we are safe in Worcester, a town which may feel but lightly the wounds of war. But look you at Boston. Fifteen thousand souls. How could it possibly grow bigger? Boston has America's largest concentration of citizens. Thus I conclude that is why the war started here." Henry sighed. "Happiness is acreage per head."

"You make us to be cattle," said Lucy.

"God's law applies to life in all forms. Cramp any living thing and you create strife." Henry sighed. "More than that. War. To confine is to confound."

"When will you return from the north?"

"Soon, I pray. I have a note from General Washington which gives me free hand. He promised to me a thousand dollars, which must purchase all that I will require to acquit the task."

"What will you require?"

"Never having yet transported a hundred tons of metal through snow and over mountains where a road is uncut, I cannot say."

"A hundred tons," she repeated.

"More or less. Cannon are not fashioned of feathers."

"But beds are." Lucy pressed closer to him.

"The day you first set foot in my store," said Henry, "I shall long remember. I carved the date into the wood over my desk. I knew when I first beheld your face that I would take you to wife."

"You surely did."

"Then I learned of your father's Tory leaning."

"And of mine."

"So I vowed to convert you to a Whig and our cause of liberty. For you were too lovely not to be a part of all I believed in, or hoped to become."

"You are an angel of a man, dear Henry. A big ox of an angel, to be sure, but nonetheless angelic. Without this unholy war, how our life would bloom. I remember that day in your store. Never had I entered a shop so charming. So many, many books, of so many inclinations. I shall wager you cannot recall my purchase."

"But I can. A concordance, bound in calfskin."

"True, but I saw so much of excellence in all your stock. Sermons, Roman history, and even music. You had farm journals, telescopes, wallpaper, baskets and even flutes and fifes. And a lute of cherrywood."

"I miss the store," said Henry.

"As do I."

"I ponder when it will again open its doors."

"After the war, surely."

"Yes," said Henry. "And the sooner I get the iron to Boston, the shorter our war."

"Then it *is* war?"

"Yes, my Lucy. It is war. We cannot turn our tail now. And need you ask if the British will?"

"You'll be a top officer, Henry," Lucy said with certainty. "If our noble Virginian likes you, you'll rise up."

"What say you?"

"Listen, I beg. The general cannot appoint *all* Virginians to high place. Somewhere he'll have to dub a Massachusetts man to knighthood, and my guess 'twill be you, sweet mountain."

"Tomfoolery."

"Not so. This Washington is a social animal. Not a farmer, mind you, but a planter, an aristocrat. Our friends Hancock and Revere would sell a mother's soul to wear a general star, but Washington will never promote such."

"How do you know this, woman?"

"One's a tinsmith and one's a smuggler. But you, my great

Henry, are a scholar. You could be a governor, a head of state, a king! To be a mere general would be skittles."

"Lucy," laughed Henry, "you are a proper schemer."

"Am I not Lady Macbeth?"

"Indeed. Yet a lady who wed but a shopkeeper."

"And the nephew of the Reverend John Knox," Lucy insisted.

"That's all I have to boost me. Except for you."

"And the Virginian."

"Yes, and the Virginian. But if fortune favors me in his eye, it could be because I so highly regard our stately general. I see rare traits in this man, dear Lucy. I know he fervently asks his God for help. A cleaner man I have yet to meet. He puts up a front before the footlamps, our George. Yet as he exits, I judge that the player is honorable and worthy of his part."

For several minutes, they were both silent, listening to the tick of the great clock in the hall. Knox could think of no way to tell his wife how very much he cared for her. Words all seem so wee beside a war. He drew her closer, his left hand (the one that was missing the last two fingers) softly stroked her hair. Be a king? Does she not know, he thought, that I am consort to a queen? And what a patriot she has blossomed to. Had she been on Breed's Hill with Warren, I dare say my loving Lucy would have loaded muskets for our men. Nay, fired them; and eaten sulphur smoke with our best. Before this confronting is ended, we shall enlist many a woman to do just that. Many a mother, many a child, and every ton of brass and iron artillery that the Verdmonters nabbed at Ticonderoga. Every ball, every dustspeck of powder, every last chip of flint. We'll grind a fresh edge on the knives in every kitchen. And we shall haul rakes and hoes from toolsheds. Throw stones, if we must, until the last Redcoat lifts his arms in surrender or dies with his face breathing Yankee mud.

Horses.

"Henry, someone comes."

"Stay. I'll light a lamp."

"Soft now, as they could well be British."

"Not here in Worcester, wife. At least I see none." Henry Knox parted the curtains of their bedchamber, looking down to the riders below. "Seven men. Five on horse and a brace afoot. Continentals, from what I read from shadows."

In the lamplight, he threw on his robe. Turning to Lucy, he held a finger to his lips. "No use in waking Cousin. So if you stay upchamber, I shall go down and ask their purpose."

"Nay, I shall come with you."

He would not argue with Lucy. Once her mind took a set to a matter, he would waste breath in convincing her to skirt the excitement. Before he could lift the lamp, she was already ahead of him, hastening down the dark stairs. In her hurry, she had put on an overrobe belonging to Cousin Ann, a much larger woman. The sash whipped behind her as her bare feet slapped the stairwood.

"Mister Knox," a voice outside said. The words were followed by the rattle of the brass knocker against the door. Throwing the clanking bolt free of its loops, Henry Knox opened the door.

"Who comes?"

"And at this hour," said Lucy.

"Mister Knox, we got prisoners," said a gaunt soldier in a Yankee uniform. "We got two. One of these here birds claims to know you. Not very likely, I says. But this old codger here . . ."

"Codger, and a pig's eye! Cut me loose 'n' I'll learn you a trick, you dang simpleton! Henry, that you?"

Henry Knox smiled. Little need now to ask the identification of at least one of the pair, no other than Durable Hatch.

"Mister Hatch," said Henry.

"Claims to be bound for Boston," said the soldier.

"We caught 'em," said another soldier who was short and stout. "Crept up on 'em asleep in a barn. Luke Donner's place, a mile west of Worcester. Are they spies?"

"Cut me free, ya polecat, or I'll skin you alive and nail your worthless hide to the door of a privy!"

"Free this man, please," said Henry, "as he does indeed know me as I know him. Mister Hatch is a Verdmont man of good faith."

"A dang Verdmonter?" said the tall soldier. "Little wonder he smells so putrid. You know this'n as well?"

Two other men pushed the second prisoner forward until his face entered the circle of light from Henry's lamp. "This'n here is an injun. Damn redhide. Tell your name to Mister Knox."

The indian said nothing, as one of the soldiers kicked him; and still not a word, even when another Continental held a pistol to his ear, pulling back the hammer to a threatening click.

"I'll blow out his brain, if he had one. This'n don't talk, Mister Knox. Nary a word," said the soldier. "All he does is stink."

As the savage began to laugh, the soldier who held the pistol to the indian's ear reacted; his jaw dropped, his mouth popping open in the awe of hearing a man laugh as he is about to die. Everyone stared at him in disbelief. He is surely touched, Henry started to think.

"He's addled, sir. Weak in the old pate, I say," said the soldier. He lowered the pistol as if to admit he lacked the stomach to shoot a fool.

"Mister Hatch," said Henry Knox, "is this red man a companion of yours?"

"Yer dang toot he is. This here's Blue Goose."

"A murdering Mohawk," the fat soldier said. His voice was ugly.

"No he ain't! He's a Huron, ya fool idiot. You never seen no Iroquois wear mocs like his feet's got. Open your dumb eyes, ya hog head."

"Gentlemen," said Henry, suddenly feeling the cold of the November night, "perhaps we all err in good faith. As these are troubled times, perhaps you acted with prudence. But now I can assure all five of you that I do vouch for Mister Hatch and Blue Goose. They are my guests."

One of the soldiers finally cut the thongs that bound the old man's wrists, freeing him. He stepped forward with his bowlegged gait to present his right hand. Henry took it.

The old man partly turned to give a so-there nod to his former captors. His lean and spindled body was covered with buckskin from neck to ankle; his feet wore mocs. On his head was a beaver hat of rich fur. A small knife rode the belt at his left hip, balanced by an indian tomahawk on the right. He carried neither musket nor pistol. Pulling his knife, he cut the leather thongs that held his indian companion. And then presented a swift kick to the seat of the surprised soldier who had earlier booted Blue Goose.

"Thank you, gentlemen." Henry quickly waved to the five as they mounted their geldings. "I shall be responsible for the safety of these two men."

"Ya got a barn to sleep us two?" Durable asked.

"Nonsense," said Knox; "you and Blue Goose may share our quarters and welcome." He widened the open door.

Durable Hatch shook his head. "Me an' Blue Goose ain't exactly custom to houses."

Blue Goose, dressed also in buckskin, just stood at Durable's side, slightly behind him, smiling. Again and again he nodded his grinning head as if to agree with the conversation.

"You couldn't have come at a better time, Mister Hatch," said Knox. "That is, if your cause is our cause. Boston is nigh to dormant, sir, and occupied by the British. Most of the shops are closed. Businesses have failed, or moved elsewhere. I boarded up my store last May as Lucy and I decided best we flee to the safety of this fair town of Worcester."

"Doggone," said Durable. "I promised Blue Goose he'd set eye on Boston. We was aiming to come see your shop. We wanted to buy a certain article."

"Perhaps I can still serve you," said Henry, "as I fully intend to ask service of you. Now what was it that you wished to trade for?"

"A new fife," said Durable.

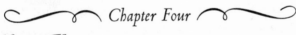

Chapter Four

Mister Knox,

This letter writ by my own hand and in
great haste will introduce you to its bearer;
by name, Cotton Mayfield Witty. His father
is my friend, a neighbor of Mount Vernon
who is at loss as to how young Cotton
should be educated, or rather disciplined. The
lad is but 16. It is my assessment he was oft
attended by too many servants, surrounded
by affluence, and given too few chores and
even fewer trouncings. He has partly failed in
his studies and yet proven to be apt in pursuit
of the violin. The boy also made publick his
fevers for a young slave girl owned by his
father. In addition to hauling tons of iron to
Boston from the northern stronghold of Fort
Ticonderoga, may I beg of you, friend
Henry, to take young Master Witty with
you in an effort to warp him to some
semblance of manhood. My good friend, his
worthy father, will ever be in your debt for
this undertaking, as will be your humble
servant and comrade in arms

— G. Washington.

From my headquarters at Cambridge,
Massachusetts on this 17 day November
1775, I also write Major-General Schuyler
who prepares to assist you in your endeavors.

Henry Knox looked up from the letter, seeing before him now a hatless youth of sixteen years astride a chestnut mare as though he had been weaned there.

"You are Master Cotton Witty?"

"Your servant, sir." The handsome face did not oblige to smile down at Knox. The boy's hair was the color of cornsilk, if not even yellower, tied neatly back by a tiny black bow. His uniform looked to be of white satin, cuffs well laced, and topped by a cape of pale blue, the precise color of the lad's eyes. The mare was of spirit, in season perhaps, and started to bolt. Yet the young Virginian held her in with a soft hand of the reins, talking her to quiet with his pleasant voice.

"Your horse?" asked Knox.

"She is, sir."

"A true beauty of an animal."

"She should be. Her cost was more than most men see in a lifetime." The young man's voice was polite, yet impatient to be off about superior business. "No less mount fit for a general's aide."

"Is that who you are, General Washington's aide?"

"Of course, sir. I am Lieutenant Cotton Mayfield Witty of the Army of Virginia."

He wheeled the mare in place, allowing her to prance a complete circle. And as he spoke, Henry noted, the boy possessed the infuriating habit of not looking down. Virginian arrogance. Norman and Saxon arrogance. How many peasants, thought Knox, could barely control a desire to knock a puffed-up aristocrat from the back of a costly-bred horse? Were the Wittys of this world the reason for so many poor families leaving Europe and coming to America? In

England, it was Lord this and Lord that. Would it occur here in America, the same smugness that cut like a riding crop? For another matter, General Washington's letter made no mention of the lad's rank, yet his words introduced himself as a lieutenant. Self-appointed, I daresay.

"Is there a reply, sir?" Witty looked above Knox's head.

"No, no reply."

"Then I shall return to my duties at headquarters."

"No," said Knox, "you shall not."

Witty looked down at Knox for the first time, and all the fine features of his sharply sculptured face showed Henry a genuine surprise. "I beg pardon, sir?"

"Master Witty, you are from this day forward assigned to my compliment, which for the nonce will be here in this town of Worcester, until you are ordered to present yourself elsewhere. General Washington did not inform you of your being newly assigned?"

"Trust he did not, sir." Witty's voice was cold.

"I see. Well, first you may dismount. Has your mare yet this day had water and feed?"

"No, sir, as it is still early morn and the general awakened me to reach you by message prior to your departure for New York."

"See to your mount, then."

"You have no squire to attend her?"

"Dismount, sir!"

Cotton Witty waited for nearly three beats of a heart before his leg swung easily across the chestnut's rump. Both feet lightly met the ground as one. He obeyed me, yet not too promptly, thought Henry. "Tend to your animal, young sir. And see that she's not put away wet or hungry, as we shall need every horse as well as every soldier before this war concludes. Then come to the house and report to me."

There was no response. The blue eyes of the young Virginian studied Knox as if to challenge the authority of a civilian. He eyed the clothing of the older and bigger man, noting that Knox wore no uniform. Finally, he spoke. "Very well, Mister Knox."

"To you, I am Colonel Knox. I hold the rank of an acting Lieutenant Colonel in this Continental Army, approved by Congress."

The boy was without words, as Knox, who was a taller and larger man, took one step closer, towering over the dismounted Witty. Looking down into the young blue eyes, Knox said, "Just so we do understand each other, Lieutenant Witty. When I order, you obey. This is not Virginia, you are nobody's son, and you are in the service of your country to marshal to the needs of your superior officers. We shall intend, all present, not to glorify our own persons but to win a war. Understand only that your cause and my cause in this instance are one and the same and no grievance shall divide us. Countermand my orders and I will have you flogged. And if you do treason in any respect, I will see that you warrant a courtmartial and you will hang." Henry smiled. "Be a stout lad and together we shall soldier well."

The big right hand of Henry Knox rested, not too lightly but in a gesture of kinship, on the lean shoulder of Cotton Mayfield Witty, one-time aide to General George Washington. Underneath his palm, Henry expected the young shoulder to slouch slightly, as an indication of obedience. It did not. The shoulder did not falter with physical weakness nor spiritual submission. The mare snorted. These two Virginians, thought Henry, mare and boy, are beings of strong spirit, to be bent perhaps but not broken. I wonder, thought Knox, as he saw Cotton Witty lead his chestnut toward the barn, if I now see George Washington when he was but sixteen.

"Lucy!"

"Come," she called from the kitchen as he stomped into the house.

"I have changed my mind," he said, sitting at the large table near the big brick hearth, watching her hands as she cracked eggs into a spider.

"You and William do not ride to New York?"

"Yes, we shall this day. Soon as he comes."

"What then?"

"My clothes."

"What about them?"

"I have decided to wear the uniform. Childish, I know. But I have so decided for divers reasons."

"Who was the courier?"

"A lad from Cambridge."

"Ah, from the noble George."

"Yes. All the letter states is that the boy is now here assigned."

"To do what? Watch over me in your absence? My, but it be flattery to have such a handsome youth as my attendant, and it will surely turn my head if not my heart."

Standing, he came up behind her, locking his big arms around her and holding her close. Neither of them spoke. Closing his eyes, he kissed her hair. "Lucy, a plan is forming in my mind."

"What sort of plan?"

"As brother William and I this day ride for the town of New York, I must send an advance party north to make preparations. We'll need draft animals a-plenty, horses and oxen, carts and sleds. And stoneboats perhaps. More than that, a company of teamsters who are able to handle their beasts, plus a willingness to forgo all comforts from Ticonderoga to Boston."

"It sounds like an adventure."

"Indeed it is, pet. And I shall view it as such. An adventure of such dimension that the brain boggles and my knee doth quake. Yet I am anxious to witness the northern wilderness, having both heard and read that it is a country of breathtaking delights. But I must know of it in advance."

"How shall you?"

"Providence has smiled our way, pet."

"How so?" Lucy poured eggs on a warm plate, added hot biscuits and jam, plus a large cool glass of buttermilk.

"In the form of our fragrant Mister Hatch."

"That . . . mountaineer?"

"Yes. He is exact to fit my need. Yet better, the red friend who travels in his company."

"The one who grins like a brainless fool."

"Agreed, he grins. Yet the reason is not apparent to me. I do believe, wife, that Blue Goose is neither brainless nor a fool. Per-

33

haps he smiles because he is one Huron who cannot speak our tongue, yet wishes to tell us that we are his friends."

"When the soldier put a pistol to his head, the poor savage laughed. I could not believe it."

"Nor could I. But he did so for a reason. From what I read, indians are literal folk. Straightforward, if he be a friend of Hatch. I have seen the old man before as he entered my store years back and purchased a fife, which he has no doubt lost. Hah! He does not read."

"How can you tell?"

"As the owner and proprietor of a bookstore, I can easily spot a reader by the manner he holds a book in hand. Our old friend Durable Hatch tried his best to browse among my texts as if convincing me he could read when I could see in a glance he does not discern A from Z."

"So say on."

"We began to chat. Hatch told me of his travels north to Canada where he has seen the great white bear. He also fought in the French war. He is a Verdmont man; which speaks much, as they are an independent lot and silent as the mountains in which they roam. I know little of Blue Goose except that he worships the old man, cantankerous though he be. Apparently they now travel as one, a grumble and a giggle."

"Well put," said his wife.

"As I said, we talked of Ticonderoga, which is between the upper lake and the lower. Durable Hatch knows these lakes and the cord of white water that connects them as a mother to an unborn child, even though the smaller feeds the larger. Mister Hatch is no fool, nor would he keep company with treachery. He left my store in search of a bawdyhouse, beg your pardon, and I saw him never again until last eve."

"He smells to high heaven," said Lucy.

"Likewise the indian, pet, but they have come to us here in Worcester most timely. Yet I must approach him with care, as I deem his bent is a visit to Boston and its rum, taverns, and disorderly women. He's head-on for a spree, my guess being that he's

34

spent weeks, even months, in the wilderness and he now seeks to show his young red friend a kick of heels in the town of Boston."

"A proper pair."

"So say you, and truly, but you have not heard all."

"There is more to the tale?"

"Durable is gifted in natural geography, and his friend Blue Goose is no doubt an excellent woodsman. Yet neither is literate. I may have to send them a message which will never be digested by the eyes of Mister Hatch, and he will be too proud to have it read to him, thus discarding it undigested. Therefore I have a third member for my advance."

"The handsome lad?"

"Yes, my dear. Our young Virginian is a son to a friend of General Washington and illy favored at home."

"An odd trio."

"To be sure. Yet well formed, as each will serve in an original capacity. I have no doubt we shall cross paths of the red heathen in the northern wilderness, and our smiling friend Blue Goose may aid us then. Durable, our geographer. Cotton Witty is to be our scribe and recorder of notes and ledgers, be they of military or topography."

"Eat, or you'll have cold biscuits."

"To fight a war is thus far a puzzlement to me, Lucy," Knox reflected. "Yet one by one, with patience, we must fit the pieces together. To look at our young Witty, at first glance, one would hardly pair him in a trace with Durable Hatch."

"Nor have you. Best you get *their* opinions ere you pat your back too heartily, sir."

"Sound advice. Ah, these biscuits are good!"

"Honey runs down your thumb."

Henry's mouth was full of breakfast. Thinking always hungers me, Knox thought. The brain needs as much fuel as the belly. Yes, she's right, my clever wife. Soon as I eat I must arrange for my unlikely threesome to set out for northern climes while William and I ride southwest to New York. The buttermilk was cool and filling and Knox poured it down his throat almost in a gulp. William's horse would be in earshot within the hour. Wanting more breakfast, yet realizing there was no time left in which to eat it, he raised his big body from the table.

"I shall be out in the barn," he said.

"Your uniform will be ready. I polished the buttons."

Giving her brow a peck of a kiss, Knox left by the kitchen door, passing a well where a dipper of cool water washed down the remaining sip of buttermilk. A cold swallow ached his throat to tell him that winter was on its way. Except where his boots tracked green footprints, the grass sparkled wet and gray with hoarfrost that was busily melting to dew.

Entering, at first he thought the big barn was empty, until a snort of Witty's mare turned his head. Cotton was wiping her dry. Bending low, the lad gently lifted up a front hoof to examine it. He cradled her hoof between his knees, unmindful that his white satin breeches might soil, and with delicate fingers checked the iron of her shoe to be sure it was well married to her hoof. She tossed her head. Quickly he rubbed his temple against the barrel of her chestnut flank to quiet her. His soft voice spoke to her in the fashion a man might whisper intimate caresses to a woman he loves. Henry could not force himself to speak. It seemed as though his own words would disturb the sanctity between horse and rider. He sighed. The war would not wait.

"Aha, there you are."

The boy took his time before turning to face Henry, as if the mare were far more important than a lieutenant colonel. Well, thought Knox, perhaps she is. Could there ever be a prettier sight than a chestnut with a white mane and tail?

"I am looking for two men."

"Two men, sir?"

"Yes, as they now occupy this barn as a sleeping chamber."

"Soldiers, sir?"

"Not in the sense that you mean. But it will be my duty, and yours, to enlist their talents to our cause."

Henry walked past the mare's tail, along the row of empty stalls, once occupied by horses now in the service of the Continental Army, animals that might one day haul the king's iron into position to batter the British. Even though the barn smelled as barns do, he detected a strange odor of sweat and deerhide, as though it came from a heap of straw. Hearing a hearty snore made Henry smile. To his ear, the snore was an angry one, as if it cursed the very hay in which it rested. Walking closer, Knox bent to sweep away the dried coverlet of hayshafts. Digging deeper, he at last uncovered Durable Hatch. Less than a musket length from his side, Blue Goose was already awake, a knife in hand, staring up at Henry with a mirthless smile.

"Mister Hatch, good morning."

There was no answer.

"I say, good morrow to you, sir," Henry repeated.

With a slight turn of his red face, Blue Goose whistled a two-noted birdcall toward the old ear. Henry recognized the whistle of a bobwhite quail. Durable's eyes cracked open, squinting up at Knox.

"Aye, I'm up."

"I must disrupt your rest, Mister Hatch, for I have business with you and with Blue Goose."

At the sound of his name, Blue Goose smiled, sheathing his knife and gaining his feet. A red hand brushed hayseed from a red face. But the other hand rested on the knife handle as if prepared to again strip the steel naked. I am thankful, thought Henry, that I come as a friend and not one who wishes to enact harm upon the person of the old man. Loyalty is an honorable trait. And here I stand, disloyal to Mother England. Lord, I lack equal character to this unwashed heathen. He is less the turncoat than I.

"Business? What business?" Durable forced his stiff old frame upward and into a sit.

With a grunt, Henry sat himself down in the soft hay, in order to be on the same level as his audience, eye to eye. For the favors I am about to ask, he thought, I should assume bended knee.

"Mister Hatch," he said, "I have need of a man I can trust. Aye, a man like yourself. Someone who knows the land, the lakes, and the flow of the territory 'twixt here and Fort Ticonderoga. All of us hereparts are foreign to that place, except for you and Blue Goose." Henry nodded in turn at both men.

"Come to a point, Henry."

"I shall. Certain supplies are to be portaged from that place to this in a week or so, properties that are best not spoke of until you are well en route and away from Tory ears that abide in this locale."

"Me an' Blue Goose is head for Boston."

"Boston's gone."

"What's that?" Durable hollered.

"I mean the Boston you saw a year or so ago is no longer. Houses are boarded up."

"Ya mean places like Nell's?"

"Nell's place of exchange was not exactly what I had in mind, but, yes, Nell's is boarded up, too."

"No doxies? No rum for a dry gullet?"

"Soldiers occupy the town, Mister Hatch. And believe it, sir, it is not to our liking, the quartering of Redcoats. But you see . . ."

"What about Britchie?"

"Ah . . . who?"

"Britchie's the plumpest lass at Nell's place, so don't tell me she'd up and take her leave of old Boston. You know Britchie."

"I cannot claim I know the lady."

"Most men do."

"Yes, I wager so. But what I advise you is that there's precious little merrymaking in Boston these days."

"They dassn't board up Nell's."

"Confound it, Mister Hatch, let me make my point."

"Make it, then."

"I am about to ask you and Blue Goose to . . . to delay your celebration in Boston and instead go on a mission northward, for me."

Durable spat. "North to where?"

"North to Fort Ticonderoga."

"Jesus, we just come from there. We got a bale of early pelt-money in our stockings. Figured we'd sweat out a hunk of winter down yonder. For once I'd like to wish Merry Christmas to a Christian face and not be up to my arse in snow while I do it. And pay call to Britchie."

Knox coughed. This was no soft nut to crack. The old man had his fill of the forest and wanted more civilized pursuits. How can I offer a pleasing alternative? he asked himself. I cannot. Can I lie to this man? It would be folly to tell him that doxies a-plenty await him at Fort Ti. Yet there might be a chance if I appeal to his sense of justice. God forgive me for what I am about to do.

"Look you, Mister Hatch, the Redcoats now occupy Boston, and they're a dastardly lot. They've even closed up Nell's place . . ."

"Them louses."

". . . And if we're ever to restore Boston town to its former prosperity it means driving the British Regulars into the sea. Then and only then can we rescue Nell and Britchie and the rest of the girlies from an English dungeon."

"You say a dungeon?"

"Well, what other can I conclude? To be perfectly honest with you, I have not set eye on Nell or Britchie in a dozen moons or longer. So I am afeared they are in irons, in some foul prison, shackled to some musty wall, eating food unfit for . . ."

"Them dirty Redcoat varmints."

"They'll stop at nothing," said Henry. "And as I view the matter, there's only one thing to do."

"What's it be?"

"Bring force from Fort Ti to Boston, chase the English out, and save the ladies, before . . . before . . ."

"Before what?"

"Ere it's too late." Henry faked a swallow.

"Too . . . late." Durable's face turned ashen.

"Little time to waste. So what say you, Durable?"

"I don't believe it," said Durable Hatch.

"All true, sir."

"You got proof of that?"

I am trapped, thought Henry. Leaning back into the hay, the entire bulk of his big body was about to slump on defeat, when the

39

crackle of a paper in his pocket caught his attention. Sitting up once more, he unfolded General Washington's letter concerning young Cotton Witty and handed it to Durable Hatch. I am risking the chance, he thought, that the old man will not admit his illiteracy.

"There," Knox pointed at the letter as Durable blinked his eyes. "If that isn't proof enough for any man. . . . And signed by Washington's own hand. Read it yourself. Even our commander-in-chief is in distress at the closing of Nell's place. So it is somewhat at General Washington's personal request that I send you and Blue Goose to Ticonderoga, and there's his signature and seal. See there, where it says G. Washington?"

"I see it."

"Well, are we to let our sweet trollies rot in prison, wasting away their beauty on dank walls, or are we men who will alter the situation?"

"I'd like to alter them British."

"Well said, Durable. We have no time to lose. None. Are you and Blue Goose prepared to leave this very day?"

"This very minute, sir!" There was more than just an edge of resolution in the crusty old voice.

"Spoken like the man I know you are. One more thing."

"Well, speak up."

"There is one that I wish to go with you."

"Me an' Blue Goose travel by our lonesomes," snorted Hatch.

"Of course, of course. But these are troubled times, my dear Hatch."

"George Washington wants him to tag with us?"

"I am sure of it."

Durable Hatch was upon his feet, suddenly standing as tall as his bowed legs would allow. Henry thought for a moment the old man was going to salute. Instead he made a strange sign to Blue Goose, who also regained his feet in one quick gesture, lightly as would a moth.

"We're ready, Henry."

"Lieutenant Witty, come you here!"

At the command of Henry's tone, and much to the surprise of Knox himself, the young Virginian came forward and stood near to attention. Eyes coolly arrogant, Cotton Witty looked at neither Durable nor at the Huron.

"Young man," said Knox, "I am sending you on a mission of grave importance."

"Dang right," said Durable with a nod.

Knox cleared his throat, blocking any further mention of Nell and her varied forms of entertainment. "You shall accompany these two men on a trip to the northwest wilderness."

"Where, sir?"

"To a fortification far distant, called Ticonderoga, near which place General Schuyler will await you with instructions on consequent measures to be taken. Is that clear, Master Witty?"

"It is, sir."

"Then I bid you greet your companions. Shake the hands of Blue Goose and my friend, Durable Hatch."

Witty's face was expressionless. After the second handshake, Henry noted that the lad's hand seemed to seek wiping itself on the leg of the white satin britches.

"You will take no weapons, as both these men are versed in woodlore. But you will draw two horses for these men, as it will save us time for the trio of you to horse as far as Claverack, which is to the south of the town of Albany. Clear?"

"Horses?" Durable looked at Blue Goose.

"Do you ride, sir?" Witty asked Hatch.

"Course I do. Him too. Any gentleman can sit a horse."

Cotton Witty smiled. "Good."

"Then go select two mounts," said Henry, "as sound as your own proud Virginian, and then report back to me. Be off." The young man left.

"Horses," said Durable again, and quietly. Blue Goose did naught but stand and smile.

"Our young friend," said Knox, "is not to learn the purpose of this mission. Tell him nothing of Nell. Do you agree?"

"He'll hear nary a word from me, Henry."

41

"Excellent. And once you're afoot, take the lad under your wing if you can."

Knox moved slowly to the rear. "My brother William awaits me, so I must change my attire and be off for New York. Remember, not a word about the reason for this mission to young Witty."

Durable Hatch tightened his lips as though compressing cider from an apple. "Well," said the old man, "if'n we ain't going to Boston, I don't guess I need a bath."

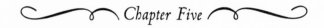 *Chapter Five*

Cotton Mayfield Witty of Virginia sat his mare knee to knee with William Knox, both men watching Henry fondly bid his Lucy a farewell. Henry's big hands held her small ones.

Cotton saw the flesh of her arms encircle her husband's neck, feeling no envy, yet aware of the exploding blush of wanting that suddenly possessed him. He thought of Kino's arms, round and black, and of her strong black legs. Father owns you, Kino. But I own you the more, in ways that he and Mother could never understand.

He thought of the girls who had come in coaches to attend the last ball at South Wind, of Anne Chandler and her dimpled face still sprinkled with freckles. And of Kate Dubois, the daughter of the Frenchman who had taught him to play the violin. Betsy Talbot had come, too. Dancing with him, she had whispered into his ear to leave the dance with her as they both had stolen away from an earlier dance, to kiss beneath the tree where the moss hung to touch the earth. But he had not left the dance with any of the three. Instead he walked alone, out among the blue shadows of their stables, tossing his silver snuffbox into the air and whistling the tune that he hoped Kino waited to hear.

He lingered, smelling the rich smell of expensive horses, hunters and racers and matched pairs for the carriages. In the distance, the rigadoon drifted from the mansion windows, blending with honeysuckle and jasmine. The orchestra stopped and he again whistled the tune to beckon Kino. It was "Sweet Mary." As he whistled, he waited for her, sitting on the top rail of a white fence and hanging his legs down to kick gently at the lavender heads of a thistle.

"Kino," he whispered.

He heard nothing. No answer. For years, they had played as child and child. How old was Kino? No more than thirteen, three years younger than he. And yet three centuries older. He could never forget *that one time,* when he had sat alone under a tree, their sycamore tree beyond the east meadow beside a brook. Alone in the dark and to no one he had whistled "Sweet Mary" and she had been near enough to hear, and come, and smile at him. No one spoke.

He had continued to look at her, welcoming the company; and then he began to slowly clap his hands to partner his own whistle. And then Kino began her dance, her bare feet kicking. He whistled more, and more she danced, her body moving to the song, moving inside the faded rag of muslin that served as her dress. He saw the dress was damp. Unknowingly, his whistle came faster. But she did not change her own cadence; as though his whistling and claps were unneeded, she danced to a beat within her body that perhaps her ears had never heard, a song or tribal chant from Africa that lay dormant in the blood of her body until this very moment. It was time for her. A wild flower blooming in the dark, and only for him; to pluck and smell and devour. He had slowed his whistle to conform to the soft rhymes and rhythms of her young body. At first she had smiled, but now the smile had left her.

Her body teased his blue eyes, which he could not force to abandon her. Up came the raw edge of the dress, above her knees, to where her thighs were full and swollen. Up and up until there was no dress. She had tossed it away; yet he had not seen it go,

43

being only aware of her coming nearer to him as he sat leaning his back to the sycamore's smooth trunk. Inside his belly he was shaking.

Father must never know of this. Nor Kino's people. As she danced closer, thoughts of his father or mother or all else left him. There was only Kino. How tiny she was. Yet there was no mistaking her womanhood.

Only that once had he had her. Yet she had torn the seed out of him. It was a charge beyond control, mindless, as he was possessed of a starving about which he had been unaware. It was almost hatred, as reason ripped the sense from his brain and the manhood from his loins. Then she had held a white water lily, wet and fresh and cool in her slender fingers, tucking the lily up under his chin, then slowly dragging the flower down his chest.

"Kino," he smiled aloud, sitting on the fence.

Why wouldn't she come? Where was she? What was she doing? The sudden answer hit him squarely; only a thought, yet the jealousy battered his brain with enough force to stir his balance and nearly unseat him from the white fence. Where else would she be? With a man!

"Kino!" he screamed.

He ran through the night heat, down behind the dark of the stables, along the rows of pines that led to the cabins below, and to a fire burning in an outside hearth. The Virginia moon was behind a cloud, and the shapes of men and women bore no similarity to the young woman he sought. Black faces looked at him, empty of expression or emotion, eyeing him as the intruder he was. He heard singing, but then the singing softened and stopped, dying in the night. No face spoke aloud or offered any answer. Did they know? Of course they knew. They know everything. Old Aunt Martha up in the pantry, big and fat and warm and wise, knew it all. She knew about his cousin and the riding instructor, and about the missing table silver, and why the Evan children from down country all had the red hair of a Browning.

"Kino," his mind screamed.

All that answered was the crackle of their fire, broken twigs for a broken race, the only light in their black lives, he thought. But where was Kino? Martha would know. Some of her children were half white. But no one said *white* about halfbloods. It was always yellow, as if all the fine gentry of Virginia had come to America from China. Is *my* baby alive inside Kino's belly? If so, I am sorry, Kino. And I will beg your forgiveness.

"Where is Kino?" He was out of breath.

"Nobody know," a black voice said slowly.

"Who are you?"

"Moses, Master Cotton. I be Moses."

"My mother needs Kino at the house," Cotton lied.

"She done gone, suh."

"Not run away." The vision of her being pursued by hounds sickened him.

"No, suh. Jus' sort gone. She come back. You sick, Master Cotton? You want me fetch water from de spring?"

"Who are *you?*" he demanded, squinting into the darkness.

"I Adam, suh. Kino's daddy." There was no anger in the voice.

Curse you, thought Cotton, for understanding so much.

He suddenly hated all of them. Because in the cover of the dark they were laughing at his making a damn fool of himself over a half-grown slave girl, little more than a child. Why don't you demand satisfaction from me, Adam, you black coward?

"Kino!"

Only the choir of bugs responded, all out there in the night, all knowing about Kino rolling in the dirt with some strong young black, all laughing. His hand reached down to grab a burning branch, to hold it high overhead for a torch. Dear Lord, I am an animal just like these fieldhands. And worse. Satan pity them if a black man ever shouted the name of a white woman in his passion. He'd be beaten to death, as when they set off in the swamp with the dogs and ran poor Daniel to death. Daniel had looked up at Isabelle Downes when she was mounting a carriage, looked up her petticoats and smiled at a white ankle. So they ran him to death, caught him and beat him to death, and then at last they let the dogs tear at him. And they threw his foot into the cabin of his woman, and she wailed half the night and way into morning.

His face was wet with rage, with humiliation. The faces he saw questioned him: Weren't his own kind loving enough?

Days had gone by. Then weeks, and then the Army of Virginia was formed. Still he had not found her. Then came the trouble and he had run away, asking his uncle if he could go north with the forces; and Washington, after conferring with his father, had agreed to take him along. So here he was, in a Massachusetts town called Worcester, watching a giant of a Bostonian bid his wife farewell.

Two big horses, each carrying a burly Knox, cantered off to the southwest, headed for the town of New York. Cotton Witty wheeled his horse. Mary, my mare. Five years old now. A princess when she stands between the two cows I selected as mounts for my two companions. God, what unwashed scum.

Curse you, General Washington, sir!

And to think I once called you Uncle George and broke horses for you, even the white stallion that your gang of grooms were afraid to rope.

Turning his head and his thoughts, Cotton Witty watched the old man and the Huron trying to mount their horses. Worst two plugs I could find, he snickered to himself. A mare and a gelding, neither at home under a saddle or under a man's weight. Suddenly the black mare whipped around her head, her lips curled, as her yellow teeth found the bony shoulder of Durable Hatch. Shaking her head, she shook the old trapper as a dog shakes a snake. Witty smiled. To add to the merriment, the gelding kicked the red man, sending him sprawling into a stack of newly-made kegs. The small barrels tumbled down upon the poor savage as though he'd shaken a tree of ripe pears.

"Dagbust your damn eyes!" The old man's shoulder was free of the mean mouth, but bleeding. His deerskin blouse was torn.

Witty paused to reap his full enjoyment of the scene before his heels gently moved his chestnut forward. Grabbing the black mare's bridle, he held fast while the old man clumsily hooked a thin leg over her back and into the saddle. Blue Goose was less fortunate. The gelding had turned on him, rearing and striking at him with both front hoofs.

Blue Goose laughed.

Is the savage insane? Cotton asked himself. Yet the red man did not loose the reins but held fast, despite his trying to hide his face and body among the fresh-cut kegs. He is afraid, thought Witty, yet not cowardly. It would be my guess that his red legs have yet to straddle his first horse. And what better mount to start on than the meanest geld I could find. Two of the most sorry mounts I could cut from a pathetic string of wild-eyed Yankee horses. If the soldiers of the Army of Massachusetts befit their steeds, then they muster a shabby cavalry.

Hatch's mare bolted forward, siding against the trunk of a large elm, perhaps in an effort to crush the leg of his rider or wipe him from the saddle. But the old man stayed astride despite the fact that his shoulder had been bitten and his leg bruised.

"Ya dang poxhead!" Hatch yelped.

Blue Goose still laughed. Urging his mare to where the black gelding held the confused indian at bay, Witty reached for the leather rein and managed to calm the confused animal, leading him around and around in a circle to allow Blue Goose to regain his feet and his composure. Stripping off his blue cape, Witty blindfolded the animal, which then stood stock-still until the indian approached his right flank.

"Other side," said Witty.

Blue Goose still smiled. A smile without mirth. Durable Hatch made a sign at the man, and Blue Goose responded by walking in a wide ring, avoiding the rear hoofs, to the left stirrup. With some difficulty the indian finally sat the saddle. Keeping the gelding blind, Witty handed the savage his reins, taking away the cape.

But now the gelding stood still as a stone, doing nothing to thwart the seat of his grinning rider. The savage is a fool, thought Cotton. A halfwit. Sweet Jesus, why am I going with these two?

And to what northern wilderness? Where in Hell's fire is Ticonderoga and what is it? A fort, that much I know, having heard talk for the past months of the fabled Ethan Allen, along with the other fellow whose name sounded like some sort of a monk. Benedict? Ah well, it was folly to try understanding the northern mind, as it seemed to Cotton Witty to be bereft of wit or charm. What graceless men. If their dancing is as awkward as their horsemanship, I do pity the toes of their ladies and the soft mouths of their unfortunate and unbroken foals.

Blue Goose laughed again as his horse tossed his head.

"Mister Hatch, is your friend a fool?"

"We're both fools," yelled the old man, "for I come east to Boston to ride fairer beasts than the one I now sit."

"Let us depart."

"Best we take the west road," hollered Durable, "as we come this way. West to the township called Springfield."

"I have a map," said Witty, "supplied me by Colonel Knox."

"So do I."

"Where is your map, sir?"

"Between my ears, so we won't need no paper. My guess is that the tomfool who drawed up yourn never been west of Cambridge or more than a hoot distant from his mother's knee. Whoa, ya son of a skunk."

"Your mount is a mare, sir. Which is to say, of the female species."

"Daughter of a devil then."

"If you would desist from sawing her rein, she might portage you more properly."

"Don't tell me how to sit a horse. I was forking hinnies before your first saddle was a bellyband."

So you know it all, mused Cotton. You and your stinking indian. Well, my dear old Hatch, we shall see who is a horseman and who is not ere this day is ended.

The black mare was trotting in a circle, bouncing the old man with every pace. Good, thought Witty, trot we shall. Turning his mare with just a caress of rein on the right of her neck and slight pressure by his knee, Cotton Witty headed west at a trot. Behind him rode the two, their bowels bumping to each hoofbeat. Posting easily, he gave the chestnut her head, allowing the smooth rhythm of his own thrusting body to dictate the gait of the horse. Often he would ride Mary free of both saddle and bridle; and once, to show Kate Dubois and Betsy Talbot and Elizabeth Rutherford his mastery of his mount, Witty had had them bind his hands behind him. Thus he showed the three girls, with neither saddle nor rein, how his legs guided his mare in circles of eight, in squares, at a walk or trot or canter. Then he rode off, still with his hands bound, to be alone and free with only his mare to love, feeling her strength and her spirit between his legs, trusting her as she trusted him.

Witty felt the morning sun burn his back as he rode to the west, toward Springfield. November in Massachusetts. He had yet to wade through a northern winter. Only once, he thought, have I felt snow come down from the sky and kiss my face with its white lace of softness. Magic from the heavens. The ground had been white, the way big old Martha would flour her cakeboard; then the white flour melted away, and again the Virginia earth was brown. Resting for winter, Moses had told him.

A rabbit darted across the wagon road.

His mare snorted. "Easy," Witty said. She hardly broke her stride, her long easy trot that ate up miles as though they were stolen sugar cubes. At his back, the other two riders were less prepared. The black mare reared, the gelding plunged; both the old trapper and his red friend were unseated, falling heavily into the dust of the wagon road. The gelding tangled in a trailside thicket, where Cotton retrieved the shaking animal, leading him to his limping rider. Without pause, Durable Hatch remounted. Blue Goose did likewise, smiling his smile. Again they rode west; Cotton in front, the two friends to the rear.

Mary trotted, ears forward, looking now for her next rabbit, permitting her rider to stroke her saddle with his knees, riding easily. Here was a team that moved together, while the other two horses and two riders fought. Often the pair of blacks would break gait into a canter, wasting strength, as their raw riders would tug to hold them in. The two blacks moved up and down and sideways, instead of forward, in a twisting battle of a pace that tired horse and horseman alike.

Without turning around, Cotton smiled.

Soon, he thought, the old white and the young red will be walking, leading their foam-flecked and spent animals, while his chestnut mare would still be fresh. He patted her neck. If only I could leave these two clowns alone with their puckerbrush ponies. The four of them deserve each other's company. Peasants upon peasants. Scurf astride scum. He heard the irregular hoofbeats behind him, harnessed with the heavy breathing of both blacks. At every planting of their hoofs, he could see the two arses of Hatch and Blue Goose punish their saddles, beating their horses with an exhausting awkwardness, whipping their reserve, wringing every drop of stamina from both animals, until all four of them would be nigh to dropping at roadside, unable to go farther.

"Cussed fool animal!" he heard Hatch yell.

The sun rose higher; and like fragments of a broken bottle, the sunlight fell down between the leaves of the tall maples on the south side of the wagon ruts. There were no farms, no people, no open meadow, no grass, and no pasture. Only trees. Thick forest on left and right. Hell! There is no war in the wilderness, Cotton told himself. The conflict is behind me in Boston, where other young men will win glory for themselves and for Virginia, while Cotton Mayfield Witty dodges trees with an addled savage and an unclean woodsman, who ride the way a scrubwoman sits her jackass. Has either of these two ever read a poem or heard a cello, or even taken the first bite of a cured ham, baked in honey the way Martha cooks it? I hunger. I long for so much, if only to converse with someone who knows a minuet from a muskrat, at least some civilized soul who wears stockings. Good, he looked down. My stockings are still white and I have an extra pair. But not a shop in Boston is to my liking. Shabby shops run by dismal proprietors whose shelves and counters teem with goods stitched by clumsy American hands. I shall wear no article made elsewhere but in London, or Paris, and ride no mount that is not dropped as a Virginian foal. Purebred and haughty as Mary. Not even Mistress Washington can walk as proudly as my mare.

"Mary," he said aloud, "you are indeed patrician. Perhaps I should have named you other. Seeing you as a filly still wet from the pain of your brood-mare mother, and dubbing you Patricia."

"What'd ya say?"

"Little of sense, old man. I was enjoying a bit of gossip with my jolly mount."

"Best ya not," the man grumbled from behind.

"I beg your pardon, sir."

"Best ya keep you lip shut. Else we all have a jolly conversation with a jolly arrow from a jolly Mohawk."

"There are no Mohawk in these parts. They are far to the west, as every idiot can attest," said Cotton.

"Yeah? Well, sonny, here's one old idiot that admits on a Good Book that he don't know where the Mohawk is holed up, and who has lived a passel of winters keeping shut about it. No sense calling out for trouble when there's a spate of it in all forms and on all sides."

"I scoff at you, sir."

"Scoff all ya hanker to. But yer pretty white uniform won't be too scoffy when ya wear an arrow, with feathers out one side of you and flint out the other."

"Tosh."

But yet without moving his head, Cotton Witty let his eyes swing left and right, searching the dark of the forest floor for any sight of a naked red body. There were indians in Virginia, back in the hills, giving up their land as the white colonists pushed inland and away from the great sea. Yet even in Virginia he had heard of the Mohawk.

They walked their horses, afoot and leading them at rein. It seemed restful to walk for a while, through the canyon that the wagon road cut, dividing the stand of massive pines. He smelled a cool green smell. Beneath their feet the path was brown with fallen needles. Soft underfoot. The pine needles rustled like the petticoats of women skipping down the great curved staircase at South Wind.

No one could descend a stair like Elizabeth Rutherford in a white dress, her sable hair floating behind her like the tail of a red fox at chase. I must not think of my boyhood at South Wind, he told himself. I am a man now, a soldier, a young warrior to free Virginia from England. So I shall draw my imaginary blade and with one slash of my cutlass cut the cord 'twixt mother and daughter. How shall I ever serve Virginia in these northern climes? I do wonder if General Washington asks likewise, so I shall presume. He does. I dare venture he'd not choose Massachusetts folk for company. Nor would I. Yet here I am at elbow with a red savage who giggles at his own lunacy and this old stranger-to-soap, this . . . Verdmonter.

Verdmont? Is there such a queer place? For if so it is newly heard by my ears. A land of simpletons, if I am any judge, if old Hatch is a remnant of their habitants. Hard to imagine an entire township of people like Durable Hatch.

I do wonder if they smell one another.

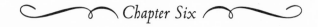

Chapter Six

I hurt, thought Blue Goose.

My legs are made for running through a forest, or to kneel in a canoe, and not to straddle a white man's animal that is half an evil spirit and half a black bear. I wonder if the backbone of Old Ax stabs as does the backbone of Blue Goose. My heart is also heavy that I saw nothing of the place called Boston; and now, before my eyes learn of all its wonders, I know that I will die of the backache.

Standing in the evening forest, his spine lightly leaning on the shaggy bark of a hickory tree, Blue Goose tried to eat the hot beans that Old Ax had prepared over the tiny fire. Hot beans and cold meat would be welcome to any stomach. And I also have, he thought, the white man's tea to wash my throat and to warm my belly. Old Ax eats his beans standing up and in the same manner as does Blue Goose. If my young back carries so much pain from riding the black animal called a horse, I must be aware of how the aged bones of Old Ax must pound and pound in agony.

The Huron shifted his gaze to the young Virginian, who sat easily on a bank of dark green moss beneath a stand of dogwood trees. I see that Child Face feels not the war drum of pain. I know why, because when Child Face rides upon his animal, he and the horse move as one body, like the birch canoe that glides in peace upon an early morning lake. It is not thus with the behind of Old Ax or Blue Goose. The rump of Blue Goose is not a canoe and the half-bear is not a gentle current. We are enemies, my horse and I, and there is much hatred and much war between his back and mine. Tomorrow I walk.

I do not like, thought Blue Goose, the blue eyes of Child Face, nor is he a friend of Old Ax. I see much. I saw that Old Ax is a friend of the big man, Half Hand. The two talk of Boston place where there used to be a Nell but now there is one no longer because of the British. Blue Goose spat. There is much evil in the British, as any Huron knows. Only the French to the north, in Canada, are friends of the Huron. Soldiers in red coats are enemies who bring smallpox that hide among the folds of what they pretend are friend-blankets to keep the Huron warm, the British officer told us. But instead, the Huron die of smallpox; and die in pain, speckled as the egg of the oriole. The heart of Child Face laughs to see the back of Old Ax in pain. I will not give the young heart joy, so I will not let him see that Blue Goose also suffers.

I care little for the black animal I sat upon and he thinks little of me. I hate the horse much, and I am glad that he is a male without his parts. Ha! Blue Goose would laugh if there were not so many tears of sorrow along my spine. I wonder if the horse now laughs at Blue Goose? I know that the young belly of the one who now

53

travels with us laughs at us, yet his face shows no happiness. Inside he laughs. The ear of Blue Goose listens to more than the white man's tongue. He laughs. So I will force my rump to sit.

Blue Goose sat.

I wonder, he thought, if Child Face can see the water pour from my eyes because of the hurt in my back. I do not like his face. But I will remember the thing he did when we slid from the backs of our animals. He prepared oats for the horses before he fed his own belly. He was hungry, as we had no high-sun meal. I wonder if there is good in Child Face, as my father told me there is goodness in all men, except the British. And I wonder if it is oats that makes the horse such a cruel animal. Old Ax is not cruel. He is kind, and yet he spoons oats into his belly when the sun comes up and he breaks the fast of night. I will eat no oats, for I do not want the spirits to make me into a horse. And if I owned a horse I would not ride it. Instead I would eat it.

I wish, thought Blue Goose, to be a horse for one day; to wear upon my feet the hard ring of iron so that I would kick the white faces who are cruel. Givers of smallpox. I would not kick Half Hand, for his face is open, like a round moon. Would I do so to Child Face? Perhaps. Yet his girl-horse does not kick him. There is friendship between the horse and the rider, a friendship like the one that lives between Old Ax and Blue Goose.

"Golly to be," the old man grunted.

"Are you in discomfort, sir?" asked Child Face.

"None yer dang business, sonny."

"From what you earlier announced, I presumed you were accomplished as a horseman. Are you not?"

"It's my lumbago. Acts up when the weather gets damp."

"But, sir, the weather has been dry."

"Don't tell me what the weather be. My lumbago tells me all I fix to know." Old Ax pointed his knife at Child Face, but not to kill, as its blade was heavy with beans. One bean fell off and into the pine needles, so Old Ax quickly fed his mouth.

A log shifted in the fire, causing sparks to fly up into the night like a tribe of tiny red bugs, higher and higher until each red spark died in darkness, somewhere in the forests of Massachusetts. A quiet place. Here there is no war, no thunder from all the cannon that spit death with a hot breath. To the north there is war, on the lower lake that Old Ax once called Champlain, so Blue Goose and his old friend paddle away from the ugly sounds to see the Boston place. And then Half Hand tells us in his big voice that men in Boston will also make war. Many soldiers and much guns. No place for Blue Goose. We could stay here among these quiet trees, a place where a man can hear a hawk scream from many arrows away. We need not hunt or fish, as one by one we can eat the three horses. Eat mine first.

We have no fife, thought Blue Goose.

I like to hear Old Ax blow on the fife, soft as the night wind, and make music as easily as he makes fire. When he plays the fife, Old Ax is a bird, full of song and spirit. There are holes on the barrel of the fife, and when Old Ax covers them with his fingers, the bird inside the fife changes his singing. Listening to music is a happy thing inside my ear. My heart sings to hear it. War is a sad sound, as though a storm comes in a black sky to kill all in its path. Or to cripple. I wonder if Half Hand lost his fingers in battle. Did he bare his own knife and cut them off in sorrow, grieving for a lost father or mother or child? No, as white men do not grieve. White eyes water little and white hearts do not crack. The Yengeese are strong as a giant rock is strong. And cold.

Old Ax speaks that the Yengeese who are sons of the British now hate their own fathers. And fight the one Great Father, the man called George in the England place, the one on whose head sits gold. Why does a man wish to put gold on his head where he cannot see it? Blue Goose has seen gold, shining like the sun, and I would like a gold bracelet to choke my arm. I wish to wear it, to show my gold to Sky and to barter with her father, Wolf Eyes. For his daughter I would give a gold bracelet, and more. Blankets, tobacco, meat, skins of mink fur and beaver, medicine, and rum. Even a gun, for I find that guns make too much noise for the ear of Blue Goose. Ugly noise.

"Old Ax," said Blue Goose.

"Aye?"

"We not trade for a fife."

As he spoke, Child Face looked at him, and Blue Goose was aware that these were his first words of the day. There had been little hunger in him for talk. Only sadness when they did not see the Boston.

"I startle that he can speak," said Child Face to the old man.

"He can speak. Mostly listens."

"Does he understand our discourse?"

Old Ax nodded. "He truly do."

"Then you play the fife, Mister Hatch?"

"Only try to."

"Pity we have no instrument."

"Pity it be." The old man sighed.

"Do you sing?"

"No! Can't say I honest do. You sing?"

"Very little."

For a moment there was no talk, no sound but the speaking of many a bug to another. Blue Goose closed his eyes. The song of a cricket sings sweeter than the voice of a man. Does the cricket who now reaches my ear cry out for a female, as my heart cries out for Sky? If so, it is the hope of Blue Goose that the woman cricket hears the scratch, though there are but two holes in his flute, for he sings one short song again and again.

"My mother and her sister sing," said Child Face, as if he wished now to listen. His heart is home, thought Blue Goose, where Old Ax called the Virginia place. A far place, more days away than Canada. Old Ax has not seen the Virginia but he said he might go while his old eyes yet see. It is my wish that the light in the eyes of my old friend does not burn out, as his ears already clog with too many winters. When he speaks, his tongue hollers, as if the ears of Blue Goose hear little.

"Will you sing?" asked the old man.

"Only if you demand it, sir."

"*Dee*mand? Looky, pup, I ain't no army officer."

"I'm a lieutenant."

56

"You?"

"Lieutenant Cotton Mayfield Witty, sir."

"Then service me a tune, unless your melody is as sour as your nature."

More quiet. Eyes closed, Blue Goose wondered if Child Face would sing. What is an evening fire with no music to brighten its burning? No soft drums to stir the heart as though it, too, were a drum. As a boy, he remembered the songs that Wolf Eyes sang, about the victories of the Huron when they made war, and how the Mohawk ran like dogs. He remembered how the warriors dragged home a captured Mohawk, his arms bound behind his back and over a branch. The women and children were allowed to beat him with sticks, and to hurl pebbles at his face. He did not die quickly, and Wolf Eyes had smiled much because the Mohawk lived long to swallow much hurt. Wolf Eyes sang. Then he had told all the Huron that his song was not as pretty to hear as the scream of a Mohawk in pain.

"Well? Sing yer song, boy."

"I will, sir."

"I'll not beg ya to favor us."

"Very well. I know a song called 'Brown Eye Susan.' "

"So do I. Can't remember all the verses. But it is a lively tune and fair. Sung it as a boy in Connecticut, as a lad in York, and as a man in Verdmont. So sing out."

"What about enemy ears, sir?"

Blue Goose could see the firelight on the face of Old Ax. The old man was thinking, not answering the question. Then he spoke. "Guess we be fer enough south to miss them Iroquois, or fer enough east. Dang it, we can't stop living to account a passel of savages. Hearing no music's like a death all its own. So sing, lad!"

The boy sang:

> Brown eye Susan,
> Brown and sparky eye.
> I hope I hug my Susan
> Once more before I die.

57

I long to take a wagon trip
Way to Dover town.
But I'll come back to see my
Susan eye o' brown.

I long to take a river trip
Up the steamy Nile.
But I'll come back to see my
Brown eye Susan smile.

I long to take an ocean trip
O'er the salty brew.
But I'll come back to see my
Pretty brown-eye Sue.

Old Ax joined in on the chorus after Child Face sang a verse. Somehow to the ear of Blue Goose, even though the music was the strange music of white mouths, the song was pleasing. Inside his deerskin moc, his foot danced.

Brown eye Susan
Brown and sparky eye
I hope I hug my Suuuu-saaaaan.
Once more . . . before . . . I die.

The song was good. I like your song, Child Face, better than I like the look in your eyes. But I forget my hurting back as the music heals my bones and the aching meat that rides them. Music is a good thing. Even white music works like mud on ivy poison to soak up the soreness. My heart is glad that Old Ax also knows the song. I do not know of Susan. She is perhaps a horse; and if so, Blue Goose will not come back to her. Better I would return to a pox.

"Ya see, boy? I know the lilt of it."

"Yes, you do."

"Good song to march to," said the old man.

"So they say. I wonder how many English lads have marched off to a battle singing that song, and yet never again returned to their Sue."

"Goodly count."

"Then it is a sad song," said Child Face.

"Aye, but by then it's served."

"I don't understand."

"By that, lad, I mean that a general who knows his onions gets his pups to sing on the road to war, and it somehow robs their pates of the reason. Or lack of it."

"Think you our reason robbed, now that we turn like curs against the shank of our sovereign?"

"Who knows," said the old man. "All I know is that the British took our trip to Boston and turned it rotten, turned it like cream in July. I don't guess I got too much Tory in me. How 'bout you?"

"Nor in me. How stands your red cousin?"

"Blue Goose be a Huron, friend of the Frenchies from up north. Don't cotton the British none. Not no Huron."

"I rather like England."

"You seen it?"

"Yes, with my father. He goes every brace of years, for matters of commerce. But he hasn't been in five years or more. When I was ten, I accompanied him on one excursion and we were departed for more than six months. I even saw Paris."

"Paris, France?"

"Yes, what other?"

"Skin me for a frog's leg."

"You have been there, too, of course."

"Me? Sure, sure, I seen all them places. Paris ain't as big as Boston, though. Or would you say it was growed more?"

Blue Goose studied the face of the boy from Virginia. He toys with Old Ax, thought the indian, as does a young panther with a water rat. He talks with Old Ax only as sport, as if the old man has the brain of a toad. Ah! Is not Old Ax doing the same? So they talk, for they have no work for their hands. The claws of the Child Face are soft and white, as his hands have not paddled a canoe for many lakes. He did not paddle the canoe when he went to see the England place. He rides and does not paddle, this boy. He works little. Old Ax said that the farmers in Virginia place do not bend their backs and their fingers do not brown with soil. He said that they have captured warriors of another tribe to plant corn and dry meat. Black warriors.

Old Ax said the black people make no war but are gentle like the white man's cow. The white people like gentle things but they are not gentle. Except for Old Ax.

"Blue Goose can drum a drum," said Old Ax.

"I well imagine he can," said the boy.

"Used to churn out merry and fair, with me on the fife and him thumping a tight hide. Of late, though, my breath runs up short and I have to stop. But years back I could fife and clog dance to once."

The boy's face shows no feeling, thought Blue Goose, and he does not yet know the worth of Old Ax. He cannot reach out to take what the old man gives. All he sees is a fallen leaf, and he will not look so close as to see that the leaf is red and yellow with the colors of early frost. Blue Goose laughs inside his own face and behind his eyes, in secret, laughs at Child Face, who cannot play a fife. Old Ax can. He is wise. On his face there are many winters and many skins of tough old bark, but inside he is sweet like the juice of the maple when the snows melt. Yet he shows only the bark and not the sap.

"Why stand here idle?" said Child Face.

"What speak you, boy?"

"Just my thoughts. Or rather the thoughts of another who expressed them with much spirit that day in Saint John's Church, back home in Virginia. I sat with Father. The pews were hard as walnuts, and outside the March air was gray and wet, yet the man who spoke kindled a fire in our breasts. A friend of Father's, Peyton Randolph by name, introduced this mountain man of the hills to the assembly, and a real hickabob he appeared to be until he began to speak fervently and with grace."

"Who be it?"

"His name was Patrick Henry."

"Don't know him."

"Nor did we. Yet I warrant many a tongue will repeat his sentiments before this conflict jells."

"He the bird who asked why we stand idle?"

"Yes. And we were strongly moved. It is now November, and when he addressed our gathering it was March last, yet I still recall his expressions as if he had carved words into the trunk of my soul."

"Speak them."

"If I can. He said that America grows; and as we do, our king thwarts our desires to stand afoot on our own." The voice of Child Face became sober as he spoke. "Are fleets and armies necessary to a work of love and reconciliation? Have we shown ourselves so unwilling to be reconciled that force must be called in to win back our love? Let us not deceive ourselves, sir. These are the implements of war and subjugation, the last arguments to which kings resort. We petition, we remonstrate, we supplicate, we prostrate ourselves before the throne."

"Heck we do," said Old Ax.

"Why stand here idle? What is it that gentlemen wish? What would they have? Is life so dear, or peace so sweet, as to be purchased at the price of chains and slavery? Forbid it, Almighty God. I know not what course others may take, but as for me, give me liberty . . . or give me death."

"Aye, strong words."

"Strong indeed, sir. Try as we may, our ears would not forget them nor ignore their cause. Yet all did not applaud. Some rose to their feet and yelps of 'Treason' echoed throughout the chamber. Temper stood toe to toe with temper on that day."

"How stood you?"

"I stand for liberty, sir. I am no Tory, albeit Father has friends who are, and he states that their politics are their business and none of ours. His heart is with Virginia, his birthplace, even though his father and mother lie buried in England's soil, in the town of Bristol. As of now his alliances go with his friend, George Washington; and more, Father cracked open his purse to help General

61

Washington outfit the Army of Virginia. And when asked by Washington if Boston should be retaken, at the expense of leaving our own Virginia less defended, it was my father who urged our forces to go north and help free our Boston comrades. A year ago, Father sent a wagonload of food to no particular souls. Just to Boston."

Old Ax did not answer. Instead he cleaned his knife in the black dirt, wiping the shiny steel of its blade on low leaves, drying it over the small cooking fire before returning it to the buckskin sheath on his hip. Old Ax will do as Half Hand asks, thought Blue Goose, and will not betray our hunt to Child Face. I wonder what he thinks, the boy. His face is troubled, as a sky darkens before a storm, and his body crouches like a great cat who eyes his prey. Blue Goose remembered the tawny catamount that he and Old Ax had seen. The cat's big body coiled like a rattlesnake atop a rock, not leaping, yet the cat's feet were much alive, dancing with the desire to spring on a small doe. I see the panther's body on the face of the Virginia boy. He may spring on Old Ax or upon Blue Goose. But when he does this thing, he will die, and once again Old Ax will clean his knife.

There are signs on the handle of the old man's knife, carved there in the old man's tongue, that say A. A. H. I am told by Old Ax that his mother named him Andrew Angus after his two grandfathers, to keep peace in the family, as the two who were earlier called Andrew and Angus both had hair of red and war in their natures. Both were Scots, from a Scotland place, and the two quarreled much. Also they fought, even before the birth of Old Ax, over how he should be called. And yet Old Ax tell that the two old Scots were good men. Blue Goose swallows little of this story, as only a fool would fight over a name. So now their grandson is called Durable by the white mouths, and Old Ax by me, so let the two old ones do battle in their earth holes where they now rest. My friend tells me that Half Hand is called Henry Knox, but the name I give to him is more clear to the eye, as the big man has one good hand and only half another.

He is blood of the other Henry?

62

Blue Goose does not understand the words of Henry from the Virginia place, the man who is a hickabob in the mind of Child Face, and who longs for death or liberty. Much white things I do not understand.

Why, when there is so much land and so much forest, do white guns battle over the Boston place so there is no longer a Nell? I wonder if Old Ax aches for a woman, as I ache for Sky. And now the heart of Blue Goose dances because now we again go north, closer to Canada, where soon I go to Wolf Eyes for his daughter. I will sing to Wolf Eyes about Sky so his ear hears her beauty. Our sons will not run from Mohawk arrows. Unless the arrows fly like the white man's bees, and then it is wise to run, as only a fool will choose blood instead of breath. I will buy Sky and together go deep into Canada forest. Her belly will be swollen for time upon time, with sons whose ears will never hear a gun and whose faces never feel the stinging spit from a Yengeese mouth.

Old Ax is Yengeese.

Blue Goose cannot hate Old Ax. True, I cannot call all men my brother; only Old Ax. Nor can I hate all men. Blue Goose remembers the talk with the fat Black Robe who called himself a Jesuit. Why are there so many names? The white belly hungers more for names than food. I am only Blue Goose, no more; but a white man must be a General or Lieutenant or Captain or Colonel or Governor. Or like the Black Robe, a Jesuit, who said that Blue Goose must become a Catholic or he sees not the face of God. Hah! I only have to look west at the sunset to know that God sees Blue Goose. When my body is naked among green leaves, I feel the wind touch my breast and I know that God touches me as a mother's hand can touch her child. No wind touches the Black Robes, as they wear too much dress and too big a black hat. The Jesuits are good men. I like them. They say their friends are the Huron, yet they do not sing to watch us tear flesh from a Mohawk brave. And this same Black Robe is silent when French officers flog the naked back of a soldier. I do not understand the Black Robe's heart as he says that we must love our enemies. That means that we should hate our own people and stripe their backs with a lash until blood runs down their spines

63

to soak their britches? This is the white man's law, speaks the Black Robe. But is it the law of God?

It is the fat Black Robe who does not see God, because he looks only in his little black book. God did not make the book. This I know. God lights a morning sky, and sings in the wind as a breeze kisses a leaf, and draws my nose as a bee to a flower. One breath, and my nose tastes honey. But the nose of the Black Robe smells only his book, which has no more smell than a dry rock. I pity the Jesuit, not hate him. He is a good man, for when the officers cut down the French soldier who took the whip, it was the fat Jesuit who ran to hold the bleeding boy in his arms, and the face of Black Robe wore tears. Yet as the soldier felt the lash, he did nothing.

Old Ax nods.

I also see the eyes of Child Face close as he rolls tighter inside his blankets. He sleeps. Nearby the horses may sleep standing up, as Old Ax said that this is their way. They also are heavy with the burden of distance. Beneath their knees Child Face tied a tether to hobble their wandering. Blue Goose cares little if the three half-bears walk away in the night.

I will add more wood to our fire so that Old Ax will sleep as warm as his beans.

 Chapter Seven

Lieutenant Witty smiled in his sleep. His dream had taken him home to South Wind to attend an afternoon tea.

"I say," he spoke to Barclay Hote, Allen Trent, and Loren Grayfield, "let us entertain the ladies with a bit of horsemanship. Are you sporting?"

All three were mildly eager, and curious to learn what scheme Cotton Witty had concocted.

"We shall all," Cotton explained, "ride with a blindfold, our hands securely bound behind, and at a gallop we shall urge our mounts, without bridle, to clear the pair of fences that shoulder the lane. From the veranda, the ladies will command a view of our activities and applaud our valor."

"A capital notion!"

"First one to spill from his saddle has to remove the tack from the mounts and return them to the meadow, leading them like a stableboy. Are you game?"

"We are."

Cotton Mayfield Witty had smiled, when in fact the incident about which he now dreamed, was about to happen. A week earlier he had practiced the stunt on Mary, his chestnut mare, until he became its master. First with his eyes closed, until he felt her sudden surge of speed three paces before the jump. Over and down, two more paces and then up for the second fence. Then with eyes open, he held his hands behind his back, leaning forward, his teeth locking into the stiff hair of her mane that (like her tail) was the color of pale straw. He would go first; and with his back to his fellow contestants, they would only see him lean forward. His body would mask his cheat. And his teeth would take their secret hold.

They bound his hands to the rear, tightly and with ample warnings that he would be the first to fall as he was the first to try. When they saw how manfully he dominated the feat, they too would have a go at it and his amusement would be complete.

Tonight, he would whistle for Kino.

From the corner of his right eye, he saw the girls and the ladies, all pink and white and yellow, up on the long veranda and looking his way. Father will disapprove of this, he thought, as hands cinched the white blindfold so snugly over his sight that it was near to cutting his nose. Between his legs, he felt Mary shift her weight. She snorted, as if to claim her readiness for the twin white fences that stood in her path.

"Give her a slap for you?"

"No need to, my friend," he answered Loren.

With a sharp backward flick of both his boots, his heels shot Mary forward. Beneath him he felt her easy canter. Then breaking her gait, she stretched into the three gallops, judging for herself the needed speed and height. One, two, three, he counted . . . leaning his upper body forward on her neck, smelling her smell, tasting her mane between his teeth. Up and over! His head bounced hard against her neck, but his teeth held. On his right and up the grassy hill was the great white mansion of South Wind, its long veranda adorned with ladies; so on the mare's neck he bent his head to the left, allowing no girl or woman to witness his deceit.

Two more gallops, then up for the second white fence, and safely down. There was a pleasant ripple of female voices, "ahs" of appreciation that could not deny his daring. Wheeling his mare to face the mansion steps, he sat erect, still bound and blind, bowing his head as respectfully as a knight of the lists would so favor his king or his queen. He smiled.

Flair, he told himself. You have it, Sir Cotton. His face felt the flush of their stares, and though blindfolded, he knew they were all looking at him in admiration. And none of the other young men would now lack the honor to equal his courage.

Allen Trent got his hands tied behind him. A kerchief masked his eyes. His mount was a gray gelding, Sword. Doing just as Cotton had done, he kicked the animal into a canter. Then, at the sudden sprint that marked the sharp break of his gait to a gallop, leaned forward. But too quickly to maintain balance. Up went Sword, off went Allen into the red dust of the road. His body hit hard, as he was deprived of the use of his hands and arms to help to soften his fall. When they reached him and cut him loose, a finger appeared to be broken and his mouth was puffed with blood. Cotton pretended to be concerned, even though he had always held the opinion that young Trent sat a horse the way a fat slave squatted on a kitchen stool.

Barclay Hote, his cousin, was next to try from astride a black mare, Midnight. She was a difficult animal to handle, but his cousin was an excellent horseman. Bound and blindfolded, Hote clucked and kicked the black mare to a canter. Leaning forward at the precise moment, he and his mount cleared the first fence, but the second was trouble. Midnight changed her course slightly, twisting to the left and away from the chatter on the veranda. Unprepared, the rider lurched forward, unable to maintain his seat. He, like Allen Trent, had his ride halted in red dust. Barclay was lifted up and cut loose, and once the blind was removed from his scarlet face one could tell by the contortions of expression that the lad was in no small amount of pain.

"Your turn," Cotton stared at Loren Grayfield.

Loren's face betrayed his doubt. His eyes snapped from one white fence to the other, both the height of a standing man's chin.

"It's a breakneck scheme," he said.

"Only for sorry riders," said Cotton, "and all of us will honor your try. However, try it not and every lady and gentleman at South Wind this day will mark you for a coward."

"Intelligence is not cowardice," said Loren in a voice that was somewhat less than stable.

"So if that is your wish," continued Cotton, ignoring his retort, "then a coward and a sowbelly is the title you shall ever bear, to match your wit."

"I'll try it."

Cotton Witty smiled. "Good lad." Inwardly he thought him a fool, for Loren Grayfield was a fine pistol shot, but far less a horseman. Up on the satin back of Nutcake, Loren appeared braver. His eyes measured the distance to the two white fences as they bound his wrists at his back. They covered his eyes. His back was rigid and correct as he sat Nutcake at a stand, and no tremble could be detected in his body or attitude.

"Your turn," said Cotton Witty in a low voice, "if you dare."

"Only the addled are daring," spoke Loren, his blindfolded face staring down at Witty with distrust. For a moment Cotton saw eyes burning down at him, eyes of a ghost or a god, and the mutton and wine inside his stomach turned sour with guilt. Don't go, he almost said. But suddenly it was too late for words to abate a folly.

67

"Hhaahh!"

Loren's command, coupled with a vicious kick with each boot into Nutcake's ribs, shot the young gelding forward. Cotton stood silently, hearing only the hoofs, seeing only the white ruffles of Loren's shirt flap with gathering speed. Up and over went horse and rider, up and over the second fence. Loren did not fall! But now his horse did not ease into a gentle canter. Its gait was an unreined gallop, wild-eyed and without direction. Nutcake's head tossed side to side, undecided as to which way to run, tail arched with fear. The burst of applause from South Wind's veranda faded into a moan of concern. It was obvious to all present that Nutcake was a runaway and carrying a blind and helplessly bound rider. Circling, the horse turned away from the meadow clearing, advancing through a thicket of thorns that no horse or rider would ever have chosen. In less than one breath, both Nutcake and his rider were torn and bleeding from the countless barbs and brambles that were so thickly entangled that even a fox before hounds might not have sought it as a retreat. The horse reared in agony, throwing both rider and half-torn saddle partly off to one flank, yet not to the ground. People poured from the porch, surging forward to stop the madness if they could, running in velvet and silk toward the plight of Loren Grayfield.

All ran, except for Cotton Mayfield Witty.

Cotton stood, a dead tree, feeling nothing. This was not revenge, as he had always considered Loren Grayfield and his family to be close friends as well as near neighbors. Closing his eyes, he tried to blindfold his perception. Yet his mind still saw the rearing horse thrash helplessly in the giant grove of thorns, whipping the bound body of young Grayfield into little more than a bloody rag. Up went Cotton's hands, to mask his ears from the horse that now screamed like a badly butchered pig, a woman's scream, a widow's scream that rose in pitch and pain and panic.

A gun fired!

One single shot was all he heard. The horse cried no more. All was quiet, no one spoke, and not even a lark piped a solitary note. Dead quiet. Then soft crying was heard. Their guests had included

Loren's mother and his sister, Marian. How could he now face these people after what he had done? But what had he done? Nothing. Well, little more than arrange an afternoon's sport to determine the superior rider. No person here would ever have to know that he had rigged the feat to favor his winning. He practiced, he cheated; and worse, he dared Loren Grayfield to his death, defying him with cowardice. I won, Cotton told himself. And yet Loren also took both jumps, clearing the two white fences and hearing the warm whispers of admiration from the ladies above the lawn. Without practice, Loren was the champion, in fact.

Cotton stood alone, holding his mare's mane in a tight fist.

His feet refused to move, and he could not force himself to run forward to where the swarm of guests tore their own finery in an effort to reach Loren Grayfield's body. Nutcake was dead, one of their handsomest horses, and he knew that Loren too would be. He still saw the eyes of Loren Grayfield looking at him, staring down through a blindfold, as though to mock him with shame. Thank you, the eyes said softly, for wasting my life on a chance, an empty and honorless dare that proved naught, unless it was to evidence your insatiable hunger to dominate or deride.

He saw them coming his way, some of them in torn lace and tatters of satin, bearing the lifeless Loren. At first he thought that they would approach him as an angry mob, to drop their dead friend at his feet, blaming him and shaming him with one final gesture. Never, he thought, did I wish for this. But instead, they all passed him by, as if he too were dead and as though their preference was not to know him. The last of them passed by, not looking his way, nor allowing him to share their grief over Loren Grayfield.

"You wretched whelp."

Turning quickly, he faced the tall man who wore a white wig and a dark blue suit of linen above stockings as pure white as the ruffles of his shirtfront. His father's cold gray eyes looked through him, and beyond, as if Thomas Witty had no son.

"It was . . . only a prank, Father. We all . . ."

"You are a pack of mindless curs. And the wages of your buffoonery this day are one dead lad and one dead horse, both of which died in a torment resulting from your whimsy. How can we ever again share the company of the Grayfield family and claim we are their neighbors? How can the parents of that fallen fool ever look upon you without absolute disgust?" He stepped one pace closer. "And tell me, please, how I can ever behold you, Cotton, and claim you as my son and heir?"

"I am sorry, sir."

"You disgrace us beyond measure. And I confess that my son is a cheat, a conniver, an arrogant mophead who would extend his follies so far as to risk the limbs and the lives of young men whom he should cherish as friends. These who share our table and our bread are folk who would stand at our shoulder through any and all calamity. Yea, even against our King. And then such a swine as you deems it his whim to discard such riches as carelessly as one might play a low card. A boy's life matters little, eh? Or the health of a fine animal? What you treasure is some insanity that will hoist you up as a hero. Poor lad, you have chosen to ride upon false shoulders and let your ears ring with petty praise."

"Father, please let me . . ."

"Stand silent and listen, for I shall not address you further than this day; as the presence of you, the very *sight* of you, young sir, spoils my stomach. For me to advise you that I have no son, that is a phrase which I cannot bear to issue lightly, yet it straddles my tongue as a foul taste that I have want to spit out. You have shattered the hearts of our friends. You dash to earth all hope I ever dared wish in silence as I prayed for your manhood. What am I to do with such a . . . such an excuse for an offspring?"

"Forgive me, Father. Please."

"Forgive you? Your mother and I have given you pardon for so many of your foul deeds that there is no forgiveness in the balance. We have no store to offer, none to give, as you have little to take. At every step, you heed us not, nor can any tutor educate you in learning or humanity. There is little hope for you, Cotton, and less promise."

"I will make amends, sir."

"You make naught but trouble, boy. You create heartbreak, disappointment, embarrassment, shame . . . and now death. Last evening your good mother and I discussed you until the wick burned low. She is at loss as to your future as a farmer or land-owner, even as a member of our colony. She finds little in you that willingly contributes to the affairs of South Wind nor to the politi-cal plight that soon may befall Virginia. It is thus with regret and with relief that I forbid you to further share our shelter. South Wind may once again be your home only if you prove worthy to being a master. Slaves do not run plantations, young sir, and you are no more than that very station. I find you a slave to plot, to scheme, to every shallow and backhand act and disposition that can ill the human spirit. Days ago, I discovered you rehearsing the double jumping of our lane fences, thinking little of it. Had I only suspected correctly that evil was afoot, some silly wrongdoing to nourish your passions was aborning, and had I only had the vision to then snuff it out ere some black misfortune was its fruit. Too late. I tarry too long in my apprehensions and distrust of your intents. But no more. This day ends it, sir, as this day forward finds you departed from South Wind. So may the Devil take you, Cot-ton, as I can behold you no longer. Farewell and begone."

"Where shall I go?"

"Away. Join the militia if they'll have you. But ask not for my blessing to warrant you a commission, for I think you no figure of an officer, nor would I curse Virginia with your service that de-mands your being responsible for the welfare of your fellow com-rades at arms. Speak no farewell to your mother, as she now detests you as do I. Yes, I say detest. That very inclination, after her years of cuddle and coddle in your behalf, until you grew to be a large baby, a giant child in conduct and in . . . Be off with you."

"Father, please . . ."

"Git!"

Walking away without his mare, Mary, he felt empty. Feeling also the eyes of his father piercing his back with loathing. I deserve my destiny, Cotton Witty thought. Nay, far worse. For my deserts would bind me to a mad mount and be whipped into a thorny thicket. I won a caper. And now I lose South Wind. Rightly so, for

71

on this day my pockets are now as empty as my soul. If only Mary had bolted, thrown me and broken my miserable neck. I should hang or stand to pistols. My body should fill Loren's coffin instead of his.

Walking north from the great white house which had ever been his home, he passed through their orchard. Slave after slave nodded to him in respect, bracing his back, forcing him to appear still to be the young master.

Their voices all sounded as one, and yet he sensed they already knew of his ousting. They know! Yet they fear I will one day return and be their master, and their black backs will be wet with work or red with lashing.

Kino!

Walking among them, he saw woman after woman, stooped with work, their bottoms aimed at him in mockery. I can, he thought, take one of their women now, and let them watch. Which one? I am mad. Have I not hurt enough for one day? Have I not caused a full measure of pain? I wonder where Kino is. Who knows her now? Damn them all! I hope to make every black who touches Kino suffer for it.

"Kino!" he yelled.

Now I care not if they know. My life is as exposed as the raw belly of a butchered calf, so I shall worry little as to their thoughts. Hah! They don't even think about themselves, say naught of us white folk; for if they did think would they not long for liberty? They hate us and we hate them. I wonder if even Kino hates me? Perhaps she did indeed, with her arms clinging to my neck and her legs entwined about my body. She is a drum. Dare I call myself a song? Nay to that, for I do myself excess honor. Not a song, but a savage chant. A white heathen and a black one. And if she bears me a son, I pity him, as he will be the cruelest savage ever to walk this earth.

Only once did I have Kino. And although never have I known sweeter pleasure, we loved in error. Now I pray she will not bear my child; for if she does, the babe will be born a lighter shade. The blacks will hate her for giving life to a white master's child, and may even drown her infant. Kino will be beaten by black hands? Nay, I pray. And grant me this one wish, Lord, above all other wishes that I could beg for on this dreadful day. Grant that Kino's belly be as empty as innocence, and I vow never to be a man with her again. Only a friend to her, as we were friends since I can remember, for fishing and for fun and forever.

Father and black Aunt Martha are friends. Master and cook, yet there is somehow a truce between them, proud as a banner. He respects her wisdom; and her kingdom, for never would Father enter her pantry unless he first asks her permission. I have seen it and heard it, their humble little ritual that has meaning for only the two of them. How can I ever complete my life and never again hug Aunt Martha? God, I am about to weep.

A horse!

Turning, he saw the horse leap over a stone wall, carrying a coatless rider, heading his way at a gallop. He recognized neither man nor mount. Then suddenly he did, as the horse thundered closer as if to run him down and then braced his forelegs to a rude stop, allowing his rider to swing easily to the ground in one graceful arc of a leg. Stuart Turnbull carried a riding crop and a scowl. Cotton stood fast, not wanting to flinch at the dramatic arrival of both horse and rider.

"Cotton Witty," said Turnbull, and the riding crop cut the air like a whistle, cracking across his neck with a sickening pain. "As you know, I am cousin to Loren Grayfield, and only now do I learn of his death and in what manner. And by your hand."

"It was an accident, Stuart."

"So is this!" The riding crop struck him again, stinging his ear to such extent that he feared he would vomit.

"Please . . . please . . ."

"Sir," said Turnbull, "you now feel the smart of my crop. You have my challenge. Swords or pistols, as I am proficient at either, and am now at your service."

"Pistols," he heard himself reply.

"Well chosen, for I do so prefer to crush your heart with a ball of lead, than merely to wound with a nick of steel. This evening at sundown, I so choose the spot as do you our weaponry, beneath the tree you call the grandfather willow at swamp's edge. Bring a second and so shall I. My cousin's pistols will suffice?"

"Very well . . . I do agree."

"Cotton Mayfield Witty . . . I will kill you."

Cotton Witty nodded.

Alone, and in the alders beyond their orchard, he waited for evening. Having lunched well, his inwards demanded no supper, nothing but a yellow apple. But in his mouth and down his gullet, even the apple had a sour taste that lingered long after the last scrap of golden skin had been worked away from between his teeth.

Bug after bug told him that it was now time.

Leaning against the trunk of an alder, he unfastened the buttons of his britches in order to empty his bladder. As if in rage, his yellow urine hissed into the earth. Empty at last. Never, he told himself, enter a field of daring with a full bladder, as oft the spirit is less puny than the flesh. Once he had wet his clothing when astride a fierce stallion that bore the Rutherford mark. I hope, he thought, that my spine this night will not be as yellow as my water. Can I be as brave as Loren Grayfield? Or was Loren a fool who died a fool, attempting the foolhardy feat? What had Loren proved, except that he could proudly die?

Cotton longed to see Kino.

Keeping well in the shadows and among the trees, he walked close enough to the slave cabins to smell the fatback from their cooking fires, and hear their laughter. Tired people with tired voices. God, he thought, what hell to be a negro. Yet there was an urge in his loins. To bid farewell to Kino suddenly seemed paramount in his mind. Hell is a place for dead men who have no women and no horses.

"Kino," he whispered.

No one would hear, yet I call as one spirit to another, he thought. In my rage I make addled statements, such as my imagination that I bear hatred for all blacks who witness my follies. I cannot hate Kino. Nor could I feel anything but polite affection for

74

old Aunt Martha, big and black, warm and wise, rolling her sugar and butter and flour as if she herself was a sumptuous pastry. To dislike her would be to hate the earth or the sky, or South Wind.

Aunt Martha, *you* are South Wind. And you love our land as do I, yet you would not bring it shame as I have done, and there is more honor on your frosty cakeboard than in my entire soul, old woman.

Could I hate Moses? Always there with cold water for someone else's parch, be the dry throat black or white. Caring as much for the horses and all the other beasts, even the hogs, as for himself. Could my hand ever whistle the whip to cut the back of a man like Moses? No, nor could Father's. No slave was ever flogged on South Wind, save one, and that was Raddick, who deserved it much. Raddick was as unruly as he was black. I wonder why he finally hanged himself?

The thought of the tree under which Raddick ended his life made Cotton Witty think of another tree; and perhaps another death, his own, by the hand of Stuart Turnbull, whose grandmother had been a Grayfield, or so they said. It was also whispered that the Grayfields and the Rutherfords looked like peas that a thumb could pop from one pod, and only Aunt Martha in the pantry knew why. As she perhaps knew about Kino and Cotton Mayfield Witty. She shared secrets with the wind. About the Washingtons, she knew more about Uncle George than the other Martha, widow of old Custis.

Trees, he thought.

Each family here in Virginia is one tree in our great orchard of a colony. Above ground, the trees do not touch and seem to remain aloof, each from its neighborings. Yet beneath, in the dark bedchambers of earth, so many roots meet in unlighted halls, to touch and share and spawn fruit. We are white only above the soil and in day's light; and yet below, we are blacker than our servants. Deeds darker than hide. Kino is a white lily compared to me. In this oncoming darkness, how the roots of my soul, little Kino, stretch out to meet yours. Our roots are white, Kino, both yours and mine, for much that we share is pure.

75

"Tree," he said softly, "I come."

Under the grandfather willow (as children, he and Kino had named it so) he saw the two men, but they did not see him. He saw Stuart Turnbull, taller than he had ever stood, pacing to and fro. Near him, his second held a pistol box of mahogany that shone in the quiet moonlight like a tiny coffin. Stuart's second was William Britt, not as tall or as lean as Turnbull, but yet of similar build. The pair stood waiting, thin and resolute as whips, one for killing and one to witness. Have you no second, sir? That is how they will question me, and so I will tell them that no man in Virginia would stand at the hip of Cotton Mayfield Witty, so it would be a waste of air to ask. I am alone, unhorsed and unlanded, and in my solitude I will face my God.

Can I pray?

How long it has been since I submitted to my prayers. Years; ever since boyhood, when I discovered that South Wind was indeed a kind of earthy Heaven and I was its young and golden god, waiting to ascend my father's throne of high place and there sit in judgment on worthy matters. So here stand I this night, a fearful urchin who lurks in a buggy swamp, too afraid to show myself to my assassins. Thus they are, for Turnbull and Britt come this sundown not to do me honor but to do me in. Duel? Or execution? More likely the latter, as it is they who sit the golden throne of circumstance, to judge me and carry out the sentence.

Not to show would be disgrace.

Tarry a bit, dear Cotton, and ponder a whit. To be forthright, I confess that I am not much; but dead and draped in a black shroud, I am even less. Better I retain what little I have, a scrap of hope for tomorrow *versus* a cold corpse for tonight. Wait there, lads, and enjoy your discourse on my puny cowardice, for you'll have no joy in my prostrate person, one who lies kicking at your feet with a ball buried in his bosom. I am ill prepared for dust.

Behind my back!

The noise spun him about, his body flushing wet with the terror that he had been discovered. By another Turnbull or Grayfield or Britt? Who then?

He saw Kino.

Black as the night, shiny as silver moonlight through the lace of swamp leaves, soft and strong. He smelled her sweet smell. Looking at her was so much more than a brittle breath of love. He felt hunger, thirst, pain. She smiled and ran, and suddenly he was chasing her through the night. He panted as he ran, knowing now her direction, the tree where they so often met. And so he raced through the trees, hounding his soft young rabbit that teased to be overtaken.

He swung her easily over his shoulder, toting her as a child carries a beloved doll. It was only a short stroll to the stable, where he saddled Mary. A dog barked. Mounted, he pulled Kino up behind him. With her warm belly against his back, legs close, her arms around him . . . they galloped Mary into the Virginia night.

"My two loves," he whispered to the stars.

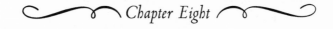

Chapter Eight

Dang, thought Durable.

Dang it and damn it all to Hell. Here I lie, in a Massachusetts forest, heading not toward the lamps of old Boston but rather away and in a sorry direction.

It is not quite morn. I sleep in one pose, as to roll gives me naught but agony. Old bones, too old for another war. Twenty year ago I fought with the Rangers and at the hip of Major Robert Rogers. Lived heathen, loved heathen, fought heathen, and little doubt we turned savage ourselves. The times that we ate a raw rabbit for fear of a cooking fire and a Huron arrow. Or worse, death from a Saint Francis knife. They were the worst, as not a one of their hands did not drip red with Yankee blood. That's what Robert said. He preferenced to meet Old Satan in the greenwood than a half-growed Saint Effy. Damn the French! And curse the British for souring all the fun in Boston town.

Lordy Moses, my back's broke. Or dang near to be.

I ain't forked a horse in a generation. More, by the goshy. It was before we fit against the Frenchies, long ago than that, and even then I was none too pleasured with the riding. Poor old back. I do ponder how the young spine of Blue Goose fares. Worse than mine? A horse is an illness, if I be the judge; and by damn I am, as it is my own ribs that rip. Old age. I heard some fella recite poetry about the crimson joys of November years. Huh! I trade 'em all for a green spring morning to chase a young maiden through daisies. Long gone. That dang fool of a poet never slept in a November frost. My blanket's wet. Snow will come soon. How I hope I can see the melt of one more April.

Go south, you old varmint.

Heard tell that it ain't so cold in New Jersey as north in Verdmont. And far to southward, say as far as Virginny, the snow don't hardly fall. Imagine a winter with no snow, Durable thought. No traps and no tracking. Be like a bed with no blankets.

Blue Goose giggled.

Turning to look his way, Durable Hatch saw that the Huron still slept. Oh, he winced, my old back! I wonder what's so funny that tickles his red ribs into a merry. Some simple joke, I wager, or perhaps the daughter of Wolf Eyes comes naked as birth to his lodge to slide beneath his blankets. Little wonder he smiles with so comforty a dream. We sat once, he and I, at a low fire when he spoke of her face and her eyes and hair, and of the strength of her hands. He spoke her name. What was it? A big name, as spread as the earth, and yet a mellow one. Now I do recall it. Her name is Sky.

Was it Wolf Eyes who named her so? Well done, like his own, as his eyes are burning lanterns of the night.

Wonder if I can rise up. Can I?

We rode a piece yesterday. Many a mile, but that there young fawn from Virginia never knowed it. Trotted all day. His young arse sits a horse like a granny sets a rocker, rocking to and fro, easy as knitting. What was it Henry Knox said? This here lad is an aide to General Washington, or was, until he got leathered to me and Blue. He dislikes the pair of us, as his manner reveals, both eyes and chin. What I find ornery in the lad is not how he looks at me, but how he don't. Well, I shall endure it, as a spate of townfolk eye woodfolk as if they smelled something foul. Probable do.

Huh! I had my summer bath.

"Blue Goose," said Durable.

The Huron opened his eyes.

"Awake, are ye?" Durable asked.

The indian nodded one nod. His face showed discomfort as he sat up, pointing to the sleeping Cotton Witty. And then the red face spat, not in the direction of the dozing Virginian, but Durable Hatch understood. We agree. We accord on that yellow-haired scamp; yet if these two lads of mine can sweat one more day across the spine of a horse, so can one Andrew Angus Hatch. The young rascal who can outride or outwalk me ain't yet dropped from his dam.

"Good morny, Lieutenant."

"Child Face sleeps as a rock."

"Sure do. Best we rouse him up and poke him to reason, as we be a long pull to old Fort Ti, and this here weather don't fix to warm much."

Blue Goose shivered. Yet he pulled the buckskin shirt off his back until, half-naked, he could wash his upper body in the cold water that ran away from the freshet. Durable watched the Huron wash. Liquid ice, he thought. No wonder some say that abundant washing can kill a body. Kills me just to eye it.

Despite his back pain, the old man creaked erect. Once on his feet, he pulled his knife to cut a sheet of bark from a birch (white outside and rich tan within) to fold into a boiling pot for tea. With the toe of a moc, he kicked the fire to let the gray ashes know that it was now morning and there was cooking work to do.

"Wake up, fire."

Adding dry wood in small and brittle twigs leaner than mouse bones, he nursed the embers, blowing to redden them into labor. Filling the bark pot with cold water from the freshet, he hooked the pot over the young flames. Empty, the bark pot would burn; but abrim with water, it would only bubble a breakfast. Soon the cold spring water would be hot tea for an old belly.

His hand felt inside his pouch.

"The last," he said to Blue Goose. This is near the last, he thought, of our English tea. Could of got more in Boston. But I'm cussed grateful we didn't trade for more of that Massachusetts turnip-leafs them folks west of Worcester tried to pass off on us for tea. Some folks'll fool their own selves into saying a mule is a hinny. Well, she ain't. And all the tomfool greenleaf in New England won't steep as much as a swallow of tea by claiming it will. Liars! Folks lie theirselves; to their own ears. Just on account they fix to fight the British don't make tea outa turnips. They don't know a tea leaf from a rat turd.

"You remember Britchie?"

Blue Goose smiled and nodded.

"No, you don't, ya ignorant redskin, as you ain't set foot into Nell's. I just related about her."

The Huron laughed.

"Well, there I sit. Cozy as a pig in straw, sitting at Nell's a brace o' years back, when all a sudden our dear Britchie dumps me a hot cup of something from a teapot. Tea, she says! Tea, my toe. I can piss a better drink than that, I says. So then Britchie yells out to Nell and the gals and the fine gentlemen nearby quartered that I, Durable Hatch, ain't a patriot."

"What then?" said Blue Goose.

"Well, I says to all, gladly I'll be the whoppinest Whig in town as long as I don't have to pour that there sewer-swill down my gullet. There ain't a nary wrong with British tea, I yells out, as I gets up on the table to do it. The trouble rests with the critters that peddle it."

Blue Goose nodded.

"You don't savvy one whit of this, so I don't guess I should waste good breath on the rest of this story. So that's when Nell lets loose on me and hits me with a broom to knock me off her new parlor table. Bash to the floor goes I, and there stands Nell and all them others. Nell points to the teapot, in which there is only Lord knows what, except tea, and she shouts out that no Britisher peddled that."

"Uh," said the Huron.

"No, I says to Nell, as that there American drink you call tea weren't peddled. It was piddled."

Blue Goose smiled, wider and wider.

"So out the door I get throwed, by Nell and Britchie and Glenda and all them rest, out on the cold cobble of Boston with naught but my humor to keep my feet warm."

"You like Nell?"

"Like her? No, you stooped son of a treefrog, I don't like her. Well, not that I hate her, mind ya, but it all ain't that bad. The straight of it is that the one I rightly cotton to is sweet little Britchie. If she ain't the darlingest little packet of spice this side of Hades, I'll eat my horse."

"And I eat mine," said Blue Goose.

Witty was awake now, his eyes open, looking first at the old man and then at the indian. "If you are companions, why do you converse as enemies?"

"None yer business."

"Very well, as you say. Then I shall resume my sleep, in hopes that the pair of you will desist and not disturb my slumber. Goodnight."

"Rise up, pup."

"You address me?"

"I do. Or else I undress ye and duck yer blessed whelp head in that there freshet. What's your aim? To sleep the morn away? We got travels, boy."

"At night?"

Durable snorted, stretching his body to as close to upright as the pains in his back would allow. One more day in that miserable saddle, he thought, will sure afflict me misery, but I won't uncle under for no damn calf from the southlands. Why's he up here?

Ought to keep hisself to home and hassle over Virginia and let us good northern folk tend to what be ours. Trouble is, nothing is mine. Or all of it, the entire wilderness, the whole and the wondrous all of it. No, I don't guess it belongs to me. I belong to the wilderness.

Cotton Witty sat up.

"You perform as if it is morn," he said.

"It certain is. Maybe it ain't morning to you and Virginny folk. One thing sure, before men agree on a thing, best they first decide on what the thing is. So I say best we accord on morning."

"Aristotle said that," said Cotton.

"He from down your way?"

"No. He was a Greek. My tutor instructed me in matters of history and philosophy. He said that Aristotle's first rule of logic is to define terms. He was truly a philosopher."

"Thought you said he was a Greek."

The boy smiled. "What cooks for breakfast?"

"Tea and a hot twist of sweet dough, for them that works his keep, so go rustle some dry wood for the fire. If'n there's one thing more cussed than a Verdmont winter it be a Massachusetts morn. I'm froze up stiffer than Christmas."

"Why does not your indian fetch wood?"

"He did it last night to cook supper."

"Then why not you, old man?"

"I be cook."

Cotton Witty grunted in disgust.

"I s'pose," bellowed Durable, "you think you can serve it up a mite better. Well, do ya?"

"A horse could have prepared a better table than last night's supping, if you favor my opinion."

"Who wants yer dang opinion?"

"You did."

"Did like Hell."

"Do we have bacon, sir?"

"Bacon? I don't aim to tote hogfat for days through a wilderness.

Roast that stuff and all you get left is drips of grease. Dry cow meat is best. It's lighter to pack and it be sweeter than deer."

"Then we eat beef?"

"No meat, not for sunup. Too heavy for your inwards, and besides it likes to clog a man's juices."

"You don't have any juices, you old dried-up goat," the boy said under his breath.

"What'd you say?"

"Nothing. Except to ask if you ever eat goat."

"Sheep or goat is all the same to me. But I'll not plug up my fluids in early morn with the likes of meat. Only frog."

"Frog?"

"Frog," smiled Blue Goose. "Good meat."

"A curious conceit."

"You fixing to tote wood or no?"

Cotton sighed. "Yes."

"Make sure it be dry."

"Of course. Credit it me at least with a trace or two of reason."

"Well, fetch it, then."

"I shall."

Durable watched the lad rise from his blankets to stretch his body. He appeared not to be stiff. Oh to be a boy again instead of a dry old stick, brittle and broke as a dead branch. Lordy, I'm probable dead and don't yet know it, lacking the brains to lie down. Soft, old man. Your friend Blue is also young, and yet his back flinches from horse bouncing as do my ancient bones.

"Done," he said to Cotton Witty, who came with an armful of dry wood.

"Delighted you approve, old man."

Hatch squinted at the wood, holding a twig in his hand, then shaking his head. "You brung spruce. Soft wood. Hard's better to cook over, as any tomfool knows, except you."

"Aristotle was right."

"Huh?"

"Nothing of matter. I was just recalling what he said about the definitions of terms, in logic. So when ere I again fetch you wood we shall first agree on the tree, its location, and whether or not it was formerly nested by robin or wren."

"You argue aplenty, boy."

"Discourse is not always argument. Perhaps it is in Verdmont, or whatever your place, yet not so in Virginia."

"Well, best you mark you ain't in Virginia."

"No, I ain't."

"Wishing you were?" asked Hatch, as he added the spruce twigs to the gray of the fire. Bending, he blew the dust away to uncover the tiny gems of orange heat that were still asleep. "Wake up," he hollered into the coals.

"No," said Witty, "no longer."

"Run off, did ye?"

"Not of your affair."

"Right you be. It ain't."

"Then why ask?"

"Curious. When I was your age . . ."

"Why must old men commence their remarks to younger ones by using that infernal phrase . . ."

"Habit, I reckon."

"Besides, old sir, when you were my age, darkness was upon the face of the deep."

"Whose face?"

"Of no matter."

"Well, when I was a pup, I run off. That's how I got north to Verdmont. I helped build the first church in the settle of Westminster. So you see I heard my share of Scripture."

One by one, the tiny twigs burst into flame, burned and bent gray with heat, twisting in their dying agony, begging for more wood to take their place. Durable yawned as he continued to feed the fire more spruce. The young whelp should of brung hard wood, he thought. He don't know much; and what little he has squirreled away in his blond pate, he thinks is his alone. Like the Genesis he quotes.

"Huh!" he grunted.

Blue Goose also let out a solitary snort.

"Enlightening discourse," the young Virginian commented as he washed his face in the cold water of the freshet.

Days yet, thought Hatch. How many, he wondered, until we see Fort Ti? Maybe five, six or seven in snow. No ice yet, but it will come any morning, soon enough for my old arches to crack over. Winter comes. And I growl, to spit at the word as winter stalks me like my old white enemy. Not theirs yet, not the enemy of youngsters like Blue and Cotton, but the foe of folks like me. One cold old man in a pit to confound another, hand to hand, white battling white.

Blue Goose will leave me soon. Who needs him? Huh! Let the lovesick loon go chase his Sky. Pity the day when I hanker to have some young reddy to wetnurse Andrew Angus Hatch. Curse the day. So best I let Blue go his way and I'll go mine.

A horse nickered.

Looking up from staring into the fire, Hatch saw the boy attending the three horses, the young hand rubbing down each leg as if to reassure each animal of its own soundness. Then he fed the two mares and the gelding the last of the oats, measuring the feed into three just helpings. Today, thought the old man, will be our last on horse. If I just can hold on to the back of that cussed beast for just one more day, tonight we will turn them loose at Jan De Groot's farm. Tonight the three of us'll be close to Claverack and a hot Dutch supper. Our three mounts will be near dead, as will I, but we shall be up and over the mountains.

One by one, the young Virginian led the animals to the freshet. After finishing the oats, the horses drank deeply. But for each horse, the boy cut the water short, denying the beasts their fill. "Easy, little girl," Witty said to the black mare, "or you may rew⁻⁻ your gut with bellyache. We'll drink again at midday, all of us, so no need to make a cow of yourself."

A moment later, Hatch watched the chestnut touch her mouth to the boy's cheek, seeing also the face of the lad as his eyes closed with the soft caress. He feels. Perhaps there is something of worth in him, albeit I see little but pride, and a spate of dislike for both me and Blue. The boy kissed the soft nose of his chestnut mare. How rich. Even from over here at the fire, I share the closeness of boy and horse.

Durable unwrapped the scrap of linen that he earlier had removed from his pack. Inside were strips of dried flour and yeast, plus some sugar and salt. Butter would taste good on the dough once toasted, but there was no butter, not this day. Stripping bare two pine boughs no longer than his arm, Durable rolled the dough to and fro between his hands, adding a few drops of warm water as needed, until he had two snakes of workable tack. Both then entwined the pair of sticks and were held over the fire to swell with heat until they were brown. Tearing each hot strip of dough twist into thirds, he handed steaming portions to the two younger men.

"What is this?" asked Witty.

"Hot twist o' sweet dough."

"We have no butter?"

"Nary a chew."

"Our provisions are *your* selections, Mister Hatch."

"They truly be."

"Meager enough, so I say."

"Worse where there's none."

"I do wonder."

Blue Goose chewed his hot toasted dough with a careful mouth. He nodded one nod of approval at Hatch. His cheeks swelled like a chipmunk with a mouth full of hickory nuts.

"Will he also eat the stick?" Cotton muttered.

"Food is not an every day thing to red folks. Lots of 'em starve come winter."

"You live among the heathen?"

"More'n once."

"I see."

"No, ya don't see. What I'm tried to tell ya is that an indian is grateful for his food because it is oft dangable hard to come by."

"It would be hard to be grateful for *your* cookery."

"Sonny . . . I don't never pretense to be no whizbang with a skillet or a pot. But by damn, I sure can pick provision as good as you sort horses. And to hand you the straight of it, this here toasty'll set my belly a whole durn sweeter than your black animal will set my arse."

"Agreed," the boy laughed.

"Water's bubble. You want tea?"

"Of what brand?"

"Look, we only got what's here, so why waste a breath on asking?"

Durable searched his packroll for a tin cup which he easily found, then poured the boiling water over the small black grits that were the last of his tea leaves.

"We got sugar," he added with a note of pride.

"How sumptuous."

"Well, you want a pinch of sweet in your tea or no?"

"Yes, if you can spare it."

"What's real good to swallow," said Durable, "is good English tea with sugar and a squeeze of apple. Now there's tea for ya."

Cotton Mayfield Witty put the tin cup to his lips, taking a modest sip of what Hatch had brewed, then making a wry face.

"What's the trouble?" asked Durable.

"I taste naught but hot water. There is little or no tea taste in the whole cup, if you want my opinion."

"I don't. I guess we've used them tea leafs a couple three times before."

"They hardly discolored the water. It remains near as clear as when it came up from the spring. It may be hot and sweet, but no one other than an idiot could nominate this beverage as even a distant cousin of *tea*."

"Ya know, ya young pup, who you bring back to my mind? A woman I lived with one time for near a week. She didn't like this and she didn't like that. That female couldn't cotton to a thing. Did I say cotton? Well, whosomever give *you* the name of Cotton must of been deaf, dumb and blinded. Ain't nothin' ever fancy enough for ya?"

"To be honest, Mister Hatch," the boy let out a long breath, "most things are too good for me to deserve. And I shall now partake your tea with renewed thirst and down your toasted dough with vigor."

"Best you do. Else I cook for me an' Blue Goose to let you hustle yer own vittle."

"The twist is good, Mister Hatch."

"Bet yer bum it is."

"To be truthful, I was earlier prepared to dislike it, but I cannot. The wood smoke gives it flavor, even without butter to christen it, and it cures like a ham."

"Want more?"

"Only my share."

Durable stripped the second skewer of spruce, portioning into thirds the toasted dough. He watched the face of Blue Goose as the Huron tossed the hot bread from one hand to hand. Blue Goose smiled, as always, delighted with any form of food. Except that he would not eat raw mushrooms. Here was where the belly of Blue Goose drew a line. Mushrooms first had to be boiled in a birch pot or speared and roasted slowly on a stick. Only then would he eat them.

"You like mushrooms?" the old man asked Cotton.

"I know them not. Are they food?"

"I'll tell! Best there is."

"What is a mushroom?"

"Earth fruit."

"They don't grow on trees?"

"Shucks, no, they don't. We maybe catch a batch for supper, if they ain't been kilt by frost. Cold weather is good as long as it don't freeze 'em to pith. We got apples, too."

"What kind?"

"Jilliflower."

"Good."

"Glad you like something . . . besides horse."

"I do."

"What else?"

The boy ate in silence. He remembers something back home, Durable told himself; of some one thing, or some sweet young gal, I

88

reckon. Same as Blue Goose dreams about Sky. Dangerous. My ears are deaf a-plenty as be, without I keep company in Mohawk lands with a brace of lovesick swains to poke alert.

"Eat up," said Durable Hatch. "We got a passel of miles to swallow 'twixt here and Claverack."

"Easier to swallow," said Witty, "than your tea."

"Grateless pup, ya!"

Blue Goose nodded. He did not smile.

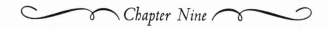

Chapter Nine

"Haaahhh! Git up!"

Above his head, General Washington listened to the husky voice of the coachman, urging the four black horses through the misty evening along the road from Cambridge to Roxbury.

I should have foreseen, the general thought, *that a carriage owned by John Hancock would have little bounce. A springless coach possessed by a springless man. And I greatly fear that the forthcoming events this eve will prove as bumpy as the route I now ride. Yet it was decent of the man to send the carriage for me. Not without purpose, I wager, as it be my surmise that John Hancock of Boston makes few moves that hold no design, and so he now doth shuttle me as a pawn on his board of checks.*

Closing his eyes, General Washington again saw the note delivered to his hand as of yesterday:

General Washington,   Ye would do us honor to be our guest to dine on the morrow with my wife Dorothy and our nephew

Libertus who welcomes an opportunity for further discourse regarding progress of our mutual coucerns: Our thirteen cousins. My personal coach will arrive as your convey-ance. Unless we do receive your regrets, we shall then expect you. My coachman, Thomas Owen, knows well the road so please trust your safety to his worthy care and protection.

Your humble servant,   J. Hancock

George Washington slapped his knee, thinking of the note. Your humble servant, John Hancock. About as humble as the king of all peacocks. I yet see the smile drain from his face (like the dye that fades in washing from an inexpensive garment) when I was ap-pointed that day as Commander-in-Chief of the Continental Army. Our beloved John received a stout blow that afternoon, one he will not soon overcome. He wanted command. John could taste it like cider, tart and heady, adding even more of a lilt to his already confident swagger. And that is, no doubt, how our dear Hancock sees his dear Virginian. Well, best he learns in these times that there are more feeholds in our world than just Massachusetts.

A groom, our dear John. Married on August last and with much fanfare, so the story goes, to Miss Dorothy Quincy. I doubt she was a pauper, as John's head for business is well respected. He surely did not become so weighted with wealth by forming shabby alli-ances. Henry Knox tells me she is a lady of both wit and grace. Well, Henry should know, as his Lucy is all of both. A bit chubby, perhaps, but as we would say in the southlands, ask not a lean nag to gallop beneath a robust rider.

Oh, for a jolly woman!

How many weeks go by in my life with neither song nor dance? Too many. Pressing matters do geld a man, until a general can near become a high-voiced lad in some Roman choir. So let John pursue his Dorothy and Henry Knox his sweet Lucy. I shall bless them with joy.

When our proud John wed his Dorothy, I wonder if such ceremony was held in the commercial streets of Boston, say at the Merchants Club. I wager Miss Quincy had a pretty penny in her purse. And what a social affair. Pity the Boston *Gazette* failed to account the union on a page entitled Business Transactions.

George Washington laughed.

Thomas Owen, he thought, up there riding the driver's bench, will no doubt think me daft, as I laugh to myself alone in a coach behind closed curtains. Damn! Why didn't I choose a more fitting entrance than as luggage in a borrowed rig? I come like a packet delivered by some freckled messenger, at the bid of the rich and regal John Hancock of Boston, to be dumped at his doorstep like a lump of lard. To hell with you, Sir John. Oh, how the fevers of curiosity doth humble us all. So here I travel through the night to learn what I can of our country's politics, and to see for myself the wondrous beauty of Dame Dorothy. Or so I inform myself. But the real reason is to chat again with Libertus. My nephew, John calls him. Hard to imagine Samuel Adams as nephew to even Elizabeth herself. But I warm to the confrontation with this Adams, if John will allow any mouth to speak other than his own expansive organ.

At least I can comfort in the thought that James Otis will not be present, awash in his cups, and spewing with speeches longer than a new deacon's prayer. Otis, you bored me. I weary of all the nouns you modify with countless adjectives, and verbs with endless and needless adverbage until I could shriek for brevity. Or even levity. As to humor, you are as witless as John Adams, that is if any man could dare approach such a sour sovereignty. Solid as a Massachusetts rock, that John Adams, and nearly as amusing.

Parting the curtains, Washington squinted out into the rainy night. Naught but blackness to see. I wonder where I am and where I go.

Where do we all go, we thirteen "cousins"? Away from King George, yes, but to what distant shoal? A rudderless frigate, all guns and no helm. Firepower bereft of brainpower. Will we finish off each other to go down in a swale of petty bickerings, sinking slowly into some murky slime that has neither sovereign nor creed? Well, we have Samuel Adams to direct public thought, and me to lead an army . . . and, be it said, we have Hancock to mold a government, because that is what he deftly does. Yes, I do confess it. Arrogant he be, yet our blessed Hancock is a man of towering talent, this Bostonian who holds the reins that stretch all the way to Philadelphia.

And should we win this war, it might well be Hancock who may crown himself King John of America. Such happenstance would startle me little, as already he doth possess half of Boston, and takes vows with a lady whose kith pretends the other half. Well done, John. You are indeed agile enough to be a Virginian planter, for how else are tiny tracts quilted to a coverlet, except by merger or marriage? The links of land couple more surely, methinks, than the entwining of nuptial limbs.

Hell is being unwed in Massachusetts; or even being wed, as I see the womenfolk of these parts to be colder than clams. Their men are surely a soggy lot. Never do they seem to favor frolic, nor doth my ear ever hear a naughty jest about some friendly maid who serves rum in a local tavern. And not one of them, not even Henry Knox, steps forward to whisper the name of a lonely widow who might welcome into her warm bed a general's cold sword. Is there not one pretty miss who wonders about me when the candle blows out? If so, then her secret is well kept. Massachusetts, I am informed, is an indian name, which I must now conclude means monastery.

The coach stopped.

"We are here, General."

A thick hand opened the door of the carriage, allowing Washington to abandon the coach. Before him was a large white house on a quiet village street of similar dwellings, around which was a white fence of pickets. The gate was open. When he rang the pull bell, the door flew open almost without pause, attended by a coffee-black servant, who relieved him of both tricorne and cape.

"Ah, our General!"

"Good evening, John."

John Hancock, in faultless suit of dark red velvet, sprang up from a stuffed chair of brocade and drew him into a spacious but inviting parlor. Portraits hung on every wall. The fireplace was lit, plus numerous sconces that glowed with a warm candlelight. Much of the room was decorated in buff and gold, and its quiet good taste did not escape Virginian eyes. As he questioned Hancock, Washington's eyes tried to avoid the gaze of a woman on the sofa, who possessed a startling good looks.

"Do come in and toast your toes." John Hancock presented Washington to the former Dorothy Quincy, his wife.

"I am honored, General." Her voice was soft.

"Madame, were this a war of beauty instead of battles, I am outranked."

"Well spoke. John, I would guess that General Washington would welcome a glass to chase off the chill of a November mist," she said.

"Indeed I would."

There was a rich tinkle as an expensive stopper was removed and then replaced in the neck of a crystal decanter. The noise was followed almost at once by another, the second sounding even more brittle than the contact of glass against glass. A man cleared his throat. Turning, the Virginian saw a small person dressed in a shabby suit of neither brown nor gray, which was most decidedly old. The scrawny throat cleared again as if preparing to make an unimportant remark that no ear would hear or remember.

"Samuel," said Washington.

"I greet you, General Washington."

"And I greet you, sir. Once again."

As their hands met, he felt the feeble fingers trying to match his strength, then grow limp with the resignation of a handshake that seemed to be aware of its own insignificance. The face of Samuel Adams twitched as though apologizing for attending a meeting, which included dinner, with John Hancock and George Washington.

"You two have met before, of course," said Hancock.

"Indeed we have," said Washington, "at which time our Mister Adams charged me to conclude with dispatch the conflict that it has taken his fiery pen years to ignite."

He sipped, allowing the brandy to rush his gullet and burn his insides. Not as tart as Virginian cherry, he thought, but more than welcome on a damp evening. Again he tried not to let his eyes rest on the creamy cheek of Dorothy Hancock. Her arms were bare, soft, and graceful as the necks of swans. He smiled her way; she caught the gesture and tossed it back. Again he heard Sam Adams clear his throat, a disturbing noise to interrupt pleasant fantasies, discordant in sound and image, as a cur dog might trample an impeccable bed of lilies.

"What news?" said Sam.

"That was the very question," said Washington, "I brought for the pair of you. Forgive me, Madame Hancock, for I did mean the three of you."

"Thank you, General," she said above the subtle rustle of her pale blue taffeta gown, "that you do so gallantly include me in your thoughts."

"Well?" asked Adams.

Little sir, thought Washington, you are indeed blessed with all the diplomacy of a hornet, and how I would appreciate your allowing me to seat myself in this fine New England chamber and at least know a modicum of comfort prior to your interrogations.

"News," said Washington, "comes slowly to Cambridge, as there we only hear the news that Boston creates."

"Surely you train a spyglass on General Howe," said Hancock, leaning against the mantle and striking a perfect pose of gentry. The swallow of brandy that he allowed himself would hardly, thought Washington, have wet the tongue of a chickadee.

"I do, yes. As he doth send many a spy to share the maneuvers of the Continental Army. We caught one only yesterday."

"Who?" demanded Hancock.

"He called himself Peter Grimley."

"Called, you say?"

94

"Yes, in past tense. He hanged."

Samuel Adams made his throaty noise again, a dry sound, raw and reedy as a cough among brambles. As Adams crossed the room, Washington observed his walk to be as brittle as his talk. No, he thought, please make not the mistake of standing beside the handsome Hancock in his velvet. You'll look a stable boy, or worse. Sam, you must share with me the name of your tailor. Were you thrown naked into a bundle bound for the poorhouse and bid to robe in the dark. And look you, to boot, even a hole in your stocking. Yet you are a great old Sam.

The dining room was as perfectly appointed as the room in which they had earlier consumed the brandy. The room was slightly oval, as was the fruitwood table, and each wall was lined with extra chairs, although the long table at which they now dined sat but four. Hancock and his wife occupied the ends, while at the sides, Washington and Adams looked at each other. Beef was served, rare and running with its own juice, onions in cream, turnips, squash and cheese. Washington ate well. Then came a most elegant cake, cut and served by Dorothy, who offered him a generous portion.

"I taste apple," he said to his hostess.

"Indeed you do," she said, "as I oversaw its baking this very afternoon. Do you approve?"

"Most heartily."

"Are we here," snapped Adams, "to discuss cakes or cannon?"

"Cake, I dare say," said Washington quickly, "as it is well known by all in attendance that we have no cannon."

"We have sore need of it," said Hancock.

"Agreed."

"Well?" said Adams. "How do you propose to obtain such artillery?"

"I have a plan," Hancock offered, "and more. We have in Boston as fine a British barrel-molder as I have yet to see. Were I in charge of our army, iron would have been molten long ago, poured and formed and dunked to temper."

"Correct me," Washington patted his mouth with white linen,

"but it's my understanding that you have in fact *been* in charge here in Boston of all the local Cadets, and lead them on horse in many a parade."

"So I have."

"And paid for uniforms, I hear."

"Yes, that also."

"During those proud years of parading on the King's birthday, how many barrels for artillery did your metalsmiths temper for our troubled times?"

"We needed none at that time," said Hancock.

"A conclusion that has no doubt been a comforting delight to General Howe, whose warships now occupy your harbor."

"True enough." Hancock's voice was unruffled, but Washington noted how his hands began to twist his napkin.

"Times change," croaked Adams. "None of us foresaw this damnable war."

"Strange you say that to me, Samuel," said Washington, "when your quill has labored so long to foment a war upon our doorstep. Did you bite into too big a dumpling for even you to swallow?"

"As you know, General, we did not have the Continental Congress until only recent," said Hancock. "But now we are all united with a similar purpose. Few of us had what one might call a military résumé, other than a parade or two. That's why the Congress stitched the braid on your shoulders."

"And the blame," said Washington. "Very well, I accept both the glitter and the guilt. We need cannon. So we shall procure them."

"How?" demanded Adams.

Washington sighed, thinking that the fewer who knew of Henry Knox the more apt the mission to Ticonderoga was to succeed. Should I tell all I know? Surely our dear John would not. Of the two, Sam is more open and aboveboard. Like a game of whist, it is difficult to detect what cards John holds, and how he will elect to play them. Has he given up on riding his charger at the head of our army, *his* army, like a warrior king? I do truly think nay. Yet the talk is that our friend Hancock conducts well the affairs of Congress, and doth preside in able fashion, hearing from all quarters equally. So in Congress, he listens. But he sits not the presidential bench now, for on this night he commands his own turf, being more confident near home in Roxbury than in Philadelphia. So here he struts a bit. Corner me, eh? Is that what you willfully depose, dear John?

"Tell us," said Samuel Adams. He pointed a finger at Washington, a digit so gray and meatless that not even a hungry cat would stoop to chew upon it. "You have a trick or two, eh?"

"Yes, Samuel, a trick or two." Washington nodded.

"We demand to be privy to your tactics," said Hancock. "It's my right. I put up a fat purse to wage this war. It's my right to know how my money is spent."

"And I agree, John. So I will answer your posing with a question of my own. How much do you think adequate artillery would cost?"

"Explain you must," said Hancock, "what you mean by adequate."

"I mean, sir, enough to force Billy Howe to hoist sail and forsake Boston's harbor for more welcoming waters."

"You mean such as New York?"

"Perhaps. We have General Schuyler in New York, and the defense of that colony in both city and wilderness will be his responsibility," said Washington.

"Enough," squawked Adams. His little hand hit the fruitwood table with a resounding boom. "The British sit our harbor like so many complacent ducks, and Boston festers with their presence."

"Truly it does," said Dorothy Hancock.

"Act, I say," said Adams. "Attack!"

"Not without artillery," said Washington.

"Tell us, General Washington," said Dorothy in softer tones than either her husband or their ragged guest would employ, "where the cannon you expect is at this very hour, and whom you assign to transport it to overlook Boston?"

97

God, thought Washington, she asks the most piercing queries. She doth truly corner me, as though I were a helpless mouse, and forward she comes on the soft paws of a panther.

"Madame, I salute your directness."

"And I, dear General, your ability to dodge and duck and out-maneuver my husband's desire to learn the whereabouts of all this cannon you tell us is en route."

"So I do."

"Or is it yet en route?"

"In a matter of days, yes."

"En route from where?" asked Hancock.

"Very well, gentlemen and Lady Hancock, you have me in a snare. The wilderness of north New York confounds me much, even as I stare at maps, but General Schuyler has under his command in this wilderness some cannon that he can readily spare us. Even more, I learn from Schuyler that he plans to send this to us here at Boston, employing great haste and worthy teamsters. That is the precise statement I was about to make, my friends, when I asked you how much it would cost."

Hancock scowled. "Why in all that is unholy do we have to buy our own cannon from Schuyler?"

"Exactly, dear Hancock. But as you well know, mortars and cohorns and howitzers poured of iron and brass do not fly, and New York is afar off."

"There at the town of New York?"

"North of there." Washington felt no need to say, two hundred and fifty miles north. "So we must outfit sleds and wagons, plus horses and oxen to haul such, remembering that teamsters do not work without wages."

"How much?" asked Adams.

"A thousand dollars."

"That's dear money," croaked Adams.

"I agree, Samuel. But it happens to be *your* town, *dear* Boston, and not mine. So I pray you, is one thousand too dear a price to save her?" Washington asked.

Adams swallowed.

" 'Tis a huge purse for mere teamsters," said Hancock.

"If you please," said Washington quietly, "think you your feelings if I were using all thousand of your precious dollars to free Virginia?"

They were silent for a moment.

"Bully of a shot, General." Dorothy Hancock's voice was even and cool. "We entreat you to forgive us our urgent manner, knowing that we do indeed treasure your appearance on these heights, and will support your advances upon General Howe."

"Madame, I accept your allegiance. Never, not in two wars, have I had so charming a comrade at arms."

"Our pleasure, General."

"Three years ago," said Hancock, "in seventeen seventy-two, I was captain of our Cadets. Yet credit me with enough sanity to appreciate that I knew I was no general. The day you were made Commander-in-Chief, my dear George, was a bitter day for me. I confess my own eye saw the apple and I did study to reach for it."

"Admirable of you to make such admission, John."

"What I wish to make clear is this, that you, General Washington, are in command. Not to sit in Cambridge and delay, but to *act,* overtly to drive Billy Howe and his Lobsterbacks not only away from Massachusetts but all the way home to merry England. I want General Howe to cower beneath the throne of King George like a whipped pup and return no more to plague our persons, our property, our very liberties with his unwanted presence."

"Is that all?" Washington asked.

"No. One thing further do I add. If you fail to so do, then your rank may soon perch upon more able shoulders, until we discover a soldier to perform the purgative, to puke out the British from Boston. Clear?"

"Very clear," said Washington.

With his hands to his chest, Hancock touched the fine white lace of his shirtfront, as if to preen. I should say something, thought Washington, but all I have to say is that a very large and trustworthy Presbyterian soon leaves New York and goes north to Ticonderoga. One hundred tons of iron and brass, through a roadless winter, and each day I wait weakens our force. Each morning and each hour.

"Cannon will come."

"How many pieces?"

"Enough firepower," said Washington, "to bombard."

"Have we your word?"

"Gentlemen, I am unfit to swear an oath before you and under God Almighty as to the count of our cannon. But you heard me say we now have this artillery at our disposal, as plans are now being carried out to transport the iron from that place to this. I know more, but military prudence forbids me to expose a man, about whom I think highly, to unnecessary pitfalls, as tongues wag oft with little purpose."

"Who is this man of yours?" asked Hancock.

"Tell us," cracked the voice of Samuel Adams.

"Very well, I will share with you his name. But press me no further, as to the count of cannon, the length or bore or weight of ball, for I will keep these secrets to myself. Ask not, I pray, as to the whereabouts of this artillery, for I will not share the location with you. Best you know little."

"Then who is this man?"

"Henry Knox."

Returning to Cambridge later that evening, and once again alone in the carriage, George Washington closed his eyes and prayed for the Knox expedition to make haste. Henry, I want that iron, my lad. More than I long for Virginia and that is a most strong comparison. Bring it, Henry. Drag it, haul it, lug it and tug it, but get it here. Beat those oxen until they die in yoke.

God keep you, Henry, for hardly could I dare ask Hercules what I beg of you.

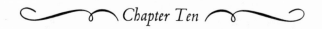

Chapter Ten

With his left ear close to the warm forge of her great flank, Jan De Groot bent to lift up the left front leg of his brown Belgian mare. As though it were a babe, he cradled her big hoof gently between his knees.

"Easy, old girl," he spoke to her in Dutch.

By touching her hoof he could tell that, inside the dirt and gravel that his thumbnails carefully chipped away, her hoof was soft and wet and springy as it should be. The iron of the shoe still married well to the rim of her hoof, he noted, telling him that the shoe would not need to be reset or the hoof cut. "Old girl, your hoof grows more slowly now, or is it my imagination? Yet I can tell when you are to winter in foal, as it seems to my eye that because new little bones grow inside your great barrel, your hoof grows little. And when the spring grass comes to warm us like a great green blanket, a new colt will run at your side and suckle your sweet milk. Or will you drop a filly?" He set her hoof softly down. "Katty, my big old workinghorse of a girl, you are some mare. But I teamed you with Hans, my big brown gelding, and you did not pull . . . until I loosed you for a pair of days at the end of summer with Van Gloon's stallion. Then you pulled. You are pregnant and full of promise, and come spring you will bloom with life, but the foal you now carry goes to Van Gloon."

He kissed her soft face.

"A long day today," he sighed. Reaching his hand over the oak barrier that divided the stalls of his team, he patted Hans with a broad hand.

"Hans, you and Katty did more than a day's work. All three of us did, for we uprooted a row of stump, and now we shall have more meadowland for the new calves. Our farm grows, Katty, just like the foal within you."

Hans snorted, his ears forward.

Looking quickly between the slats of the barn, Jan De Groot saw the men approaching riding on horses that held their heads low. Spent horses, he thought. In less than a breath, his musket was in hand, and the hammer snapped back with a defiant click. Dusk, he told himself, is no time for marksmanship; yet they do not come as wolves, creeping in shadows. They ride toward the house, at a walk, as if they know the place.

"Hello, the De Groots!"

A trick? Dammit, I know that voice from somewhere. A note or two sounded like Mark Dornburgher from way downriver. Couldn't be. Dornburgher was burned out by Mohawk. Squinting his left eye, his right followed the line of his musket barrel until the bead of the front sight became a black spot that almost masked the entire chest of the lead rider. The dark bead showed well against the white of his clothes. De Groot's finger tightened on the trigger.

"Who comes?"

"Jan! Jan De Groot!"

Now he knew the voice. Smiling, and relaxing his beefy body, Jan carefully eased the cocked hammer, returning it to a closed position.

"You old varmint," he called out in English.

"What say?" came the old voice.

De Groot again chuckled. Deaf as an errant child, our Mister Hatch, who comes to Claverack only once a year yet never passes us by without a merry holler. Who are the other two? Ah, one I recognize, as he is the indian who came with him before, and before that. But who is the third man on the chestnut horse? His clothes are white, a lily flanked by two potato sacks; he sits his mount far easier than the others. And very young, little more than a child, if I am the guesser.

"Welcome, you old goat!"

"Ya dang Dutchie!"

"Where do you come from? Not the north."

The three horses stopped, heads sagging. In one glance, Jan De Groot picked the chestnut mare, ridden by the boy in white, as the best of the three. I have never, he thought, seen so beautiful an animal, a chestnut with a creamy mane and tail. And so delicate. Not like Katty and Hans, who were more oxen than horses.

"We come west," said Hatch, "over the ridges by them big ponds and down to here." Slowly, as though his old body was being pulled apart, he dismounted from his black mare. As his crooked old legs touched the ground, his face contorted as if he rode his own agony. The old man grunted.

"Always," said Jan, taking a step forward and holding his long musket in the crook of his arm, pointing downward, "you come to see us, with news."

The big blond Dutchman and the old trapper locked hands. Again, the old face twisted as Jan shook his grip, his arm, his entire frame.

"You are ill?"

"Dog right I am," the old man yelled. "Ill in the pate to hook a leg across the spine o' this here infernal and ride the son of a bee over hill and dale where there ain't much as a stoat path. How's yer Katrinka?"

"Well and good, thank you. Katrinka! Come see who is here! Winnie! Come look, all of you."

Jan De Groot observed the other two men dismount, contrasting the stiffness of the red man with the almost dancing grace of the boy in white. A rider, the young one, and no stranger to his beast. But the other two have fought their horses for many a mile, a fool could see that.

"You recall Blue Goose," said Hatch.

"Yes, and a welcome to you all."

"This here," said Hatch, "is a soldier boy from Virginia who travels at our side. Sonny, shake the hand of our friend, Jan De Groot."

"Howdo, young man."

"Lieutenant Cotton Mayfield Witty, sir."

As the boy spoke, he extended his hand to the farmer, and yet De Groot felt the eyes look through him as if searching for more fitting company. At his back, Jan heard laughter. Turning, he saw his wife and their five children tumble from their log house in an effort to be first to greet their company. The young Virginian hand, he thought, has done little work.

"Katrinka," said Jan. "You know Mister Hatch and Blue Goose, and this young man has come all the way north from Virginia to serve his country." He felt proud introducing his strong and handsome wife, and their five kinder, who favored her good looks. Skin like peaches and hair as yellow as sunlight. "And our children," he said, "Winnifred, Cloot, Anna, Henry, and Gerta, our baby, who is not yet five."

"Alike as peas," said Hatch.

Jan saw the old man scowl, wondering if it was the pain of travel or too many people. Woodsmen, he had observed, prefer their own company to a flock of others, especially a herd so outspoken as the De Groots. Back in Zeeland, in the old country, children were rarely allowed to share the guests of adults. But here, in America, customs were different. Callers were so few they became as precious as gems. Blue Goose smiled at tiny Gerta, and as she held out her arms to him, lifted her quickly into the air, high above his head. Then quickly his face made a frightening frown. As he set her down again, she ran screaming for her mother's knee, unsure whether Blue Goose was a friend or foe. Again the Huron smiled.

Winnifred, noted Jan De Groot, is a woman now, or very near, as I mark how her eyes seem to not quite meet the eyes of the young blond soldier. Yet he sees *all* of her, with her clothes on and even without them, as hunger lights up his face. Is it my imagination, or do her breasts swell? Winnie will be as ample in bosom as her mother, though she is yet to turn sixteen. Years ago, I remember how I was but a clumsy oaf of a lad who stared at Katrinka Vanderhoff, who is now my wife. I ached for her, as this young lieutenant now aches for my Winnie. Pity he owns no land here in our valley, or the milky peaks he now desires would be his pillows and his land would affix to ours.

"How old are you, Cloot?" the young soldier asked.

"Seven, sir."

"Here then," he lifted the boy high and set him lightly on Mary's saddle, "how well you sit a Virginian mare." The lad smiled like a cut pumpkin. "But I shall lift you down again, as my sweet Mary is fatigued from our journey, as we all are."

"Lift up Winnie, too," little Cloot said, "and let her try your beauty of a mare, please, sir."

How well they speak English, thought Jan, thanks to the new schoolmaster in Claverack, who insists on teaching English as often as Dutch. Perhaps he is right, Jan thought; the Frenchies have been driven north, and those who come now are mostly speakers of the British tongue. Never, he almost spat to himself, did I dream the day would come that I swell my chest in pride that my offspring talk in English. Ah, times change. But take care now, Jan De Groot, before you become a grandfather this night.

"Our horses," said Cotton Witty, "are undone, sir. For two days past we were in Worcester, west of Boston."

"Fast traveling," said Jan. "And tomorrow you ride farther?"

Not on those nags, he told himself. Boston to Claverack in three days is enough to turn a horse to cold meat. And as well a rider. There is not another furlong between the three if I am a judge of exhaustion.

"Handsome horse," said little Cloot in his high voice, and it made everyone smile, he sounded so old as he said it.

"Thank you," said Lieutenant Witty, directing his thanks to Cloot; yet as he bowed, his eyes touched Winnifred.

Hah! thought Jan. Never has this Virginian seen the golden skin of a Zeelander girl. Well, look all you please, starving lad; but you will not have my Winnie though your head spins as the blades of a windmill and your young heart pounds like the mill within, beating your soul to grist.

"Supper already cooks," said Katrinka, "so you will stay, eh? Yes?"

Ah, thought Jan, her English is not as flowing as when our kinder speak. A new tongue belongs to freckles. I speak it like a lame cow.

"I hear supper?" asked Hatch.

"A good supper and a warm hearth. Our house is yours, Durable Hatch," said Jan, "our bed and board. Not a better barn between here and Canada. Nor one as sturdy."

"Barn?" asked Witty.

De Groot felt his own face cool to sober. "Why yes, our barn has welcomed more than a score of passersby. Plus the three of you. Alas, if our house were large . . . but with seven in a loft, little room is left for even a snore."

Winnifred De Groot looked at her feet.

Take care, Jan warned himself.

"I will tend our mounts," said the lieutenant, "if someone will be so kind as to . . ." His voice stopped, and he looked about as if he had want to ask Winnifred directly.

Foolish tad, thought De Groot. Our clearing offers but a pair of buildings, one house and one barn; and yet he is vacant of mind as to ask which is which. Yet he hides not behind the face of a fool's mask.

"Over here," said Winnie, pointing at their barn, causing Jan to observe how her manner was as open as a tulip.

"Winnifred," said her mother quickly in Dutch. "Come. Ten mouths empty a pot. I have work for you by the hearth."

Good for you, Katrinka. Jan De Groot smiled as he saw Lieutenant Witty lead the three animals to their barn. The horses, with their noses almost touching the ground, would barely get that far. Riding them tomorrow would stagger all three. The boy was concerned for them, and well he should be. They must be rubbed dry and not put away wet. He suspected the boy would do this. He is a stranger to me, yet his care for his animals earns him the right to be nearly a neighbor. I wonder how far Virginia is from Claverack. Too far for him to court our Winnie, and yet I am in awe of how a war can shrink a wilderness. My kinder speak British. And if that is not enough to chide a Zeelander like myself, now my ripe daughter sets her eyes on a Virginian. He felt little Anna, age ten, at his hip. Touching her hair, he looked down into the bellflower of her face, framed neatly in a white cap. When will you, my darling Anna, grow up and scamper off to share your blankets? My mind gallops like a runaway nag, trying to catch up with a racing world. Too much happens. I don't understand it all. Am I growing old? Why must I be a philosopher when God made me only a farmer?

Lifting up Anna to ride his bull of a shoulder, he walked toward the house. I wonder, he thought, what my mother and father imagined when I told them that I, along with two other young boys, intended to board a ship to New York, never to again be a Zeelander. I still see their faces, God rest them now, wondering how any sane soul could leave Holland even for Heaven. Well, for them it was a rightful and upward journey, as I am nigh convinced how sure they both were that God is Dutch.

Mama, Papa, how I long to see your faces and show you our visitor, the indian. And the old Scot who walks the wilderness without a gun, and who now shares his company with a young soldier from Virginia who could pose as the son of a king. An odd trio.

War comes again to our valley. How do I know this? As the elder Van Gloon remarked to us all, when we see a bear and a deer walk side by side as though they were popped from like loins, a war walks with them. As he approached the door of his cabin, Jan De Groot held his daughter more closely.

Supper was bubbling and fragrant.

Blue Goose would not sit at the table, even though there was enough room. The harvest table was long, and when Cloot and Henry sat on small cider kegs, and with Anna and Winnie sharing a workbench, there were seats for all. But the Huron would not join them. Instead he sat cross-legged on the dirt floor of the cabin, stared into the fire, and quietly dipped his fingers into the wooden bowl of corn mush that Katrinka had served him. He speaks little, thought Jan, if at all. Yet his appreciation smiled at us, even though he knows he is a red man and not a Dutchie like me or a Scot like old Hatch, or a Virginian.

107

"Where are you from?" asked Cloot.

"Virginia." The boy's voice sounded to Jan De Groot's ear to be as far away as his homeland.

"Are you a soldier?"

"Time only knows."

"I do not understand you."

"Cloot, the lad is weary," said Jan in Dutch to his son, stilling him. I must teach my children that it is rude to plague a guest with so many questions. Much of hospitality is silence; which, for a tired traveler, is as welcome as a meal and a bed.

"I enjoy his questions," said the soldier.

"You understand Dutch?" Jan felt his own eyes widen with surprise.

"My tutor spoke some German and many words in French."

"And you learned, eh?"

"Very little, I confess to you. Least of all in geography. Ere I go to sleep, where in this world are we?"

"Claverack."

"Near what places?" asked the lieutenant. "Are we yet in the colony of Massachusetts?"

"No! This is New York. Before it was New Amsterdam, and then the British decided to bull their way in as they always do."

"Jan!" said his wife.

"Well, it's true. And you are British, yes?"

"I am a Virginian, sir."

"What does your father do?"

"He is a planter."

"Like me."

"Yes, Herr De Groot, like you." There was a smile on the boy's face, a smile that Jan did not think sprouted up from the ribs, but more from the toe of his boot.

"Not like me. But you have a horse; that much I already know about the Witty farm."

"We have two," said Henry.

"How many do you have?" asked Cloot.

"I have one," said Witty. "My mare."

"And your father?"

"He has perhaps a dozen."

A dozen! What a tract of land Farmer Witty must own, thought Jan De Groot, to demand the work of six teams. My head spins, in an effort to cipher the feeholding of this boy's father. Now if my one team can clear fifty acres, a dozen horses . . . no, no, six teams will work six times that. Three hundred acres! Perhaps even more, with orchards and gardens and meadowland.

"Cattle?" The word broke out of Jan's mouth like a runaway cow.

"Yes. Some beef and some milk."

"Oxen?"

"Three yokes. And a team of mules. Chickens, goats, pigs. We had some sheep, but they were sorely grieved with an unknown disorder and died, save one."

"I am sorry," said Cloot.

"Winnifred, perhaps the lieutenant still hungers. We cannot have passersby leave the home of Jan De Groot with a whining paunch. Step to. More cider? What is a crisp November without cider to sweeten our thoughts of winter, eh? Another potato. And more for you, Mister Durable Hatch."

"What say?" Durable's eyes sagged.

"I say to you, Mister Hatch, your cup is empty and do you crave another swallow of cider to wash down a long day's travel?"

"I was durn nigh to asleep. Yes, I will."

"Winnie, our good friend Mynheer Hatch will drink more of De Groot's delicious cider. And so will Lieutenant Witty, will he not?"

"He will," said the lad.

"Good, good."

"You are a warm host, Herr De Groot," said the young soldier.

"Travelers are welcome at this table, if they come here in peace. Isn't that so, Katrinka?"

"Yes, if you do not question them all to such a weariness that they never again stop by."

"Katrinka!" My wife, thought Jan, becomes as outspoken as a drowning pig. No wife in America holds her tongue. Before, yes;

before all the womenfolk learned the new ways, they were silent and obedient. But now, here is one more thing in America I find difficult to digest. Wives speak up. Huh, say I, and the next thing we know our children will want to have their say . . . and have that other thing they talk so much about in Philadelphia, according to the whisperings in Claverack.

"Sweet cider," said their Winnifred, "is it not?"

Ah, that's the girl, Winnie. Lean over as you fill the cup of Lieutenant Witty, whose papa owns three hundred acres and a dozen horses or more. Fill his cup slowly, Winnie. Ache, young sir. Long for my Winnifred as I long to own many horses and much land. Shame on you, De Groot! Do you not claim enough here in Claverack that your lips wet for the wanting of all of Virginia? For shame, De Groot. You have enough riches.

"Sir, we need your favor." The young soldier set his cup down with a gentle clank on the boards of the harvest table.

"Yes?"

"We must leave our horses with you. They cannot tote us further and another day's travel such as this will surely undo the three of them. I care little for our brace of blacks, Herr De Groot, but the mare . . ."

"She is your pet, eh?"

"Far more. She is all I have."

Katrinka smiled. "Was there ever a soldier boy who did not carry some wee wisp of home to his war? And yours carries you, Lieutenant."

"She does and well, Frau De Groot, but no longer. I cannot take the risk of mounting her for even one more rod."

"You want fresh horses?"

"No, dog bust it, we don't." The crusty voice of Durable Hatch seemed to interrupt the softer and younger words from Virginia, as again he spoke. "Here on, we go afoot."

"Walk, sir?" Witty spoke as if in accusation. And De Groot wondered at this disagreement. Where do they go and what is their mission? Should I ask, or have I already questioned them a-plenty?

Be still, farmer. Your father once told you that a busy mouth oft plugs an ear.

"Yes, ya tadpole. How else? It's overland, but there ain't no trail, and I'm plum sick of trailing. Can't tell who meets up with who, or what with what. All them dogfool Mohawk in bed with the British, watching every cowpath 'twixt here and Hades, so reckon we watch them old boys instead."

"But we are English," said the boy to Hatch.

"Maybe you be, but I can attest that Blue Goose ain't, and it don't take a hawk's eye to see it. And I be a Scot. And you hail from Virginia or so you tell it; so I won't be too sure, if I be you, them Mohawk cotton to your wondrous ways. My guess be that you mix with redskins like an owl with crows."

"General Knox informed us that we would be supplied with animals enough for the task."

"He did, eh? Well, ain't that all spice and petals? Guess if you aim to ride, come the morrow, best you borrow an animal from our friend De Groot."

Jan laughed. It would be a strain to the eye of imagination to envision the proud Lieutenant Cotton Mayfield Witty astride the broad back of Hans or Katty, at the canter of a turtle. I think that old Durable Hatch would savor such a scene, as I do smell an odor between these two men. They travel together as smoothly as a limp and a sprint. Mind your affairs, De Groot, and tend to the furrows of your own farm. Yet I find all three of these visitors of interest. I would like to know why the Huron hunts with the old man and why they pick a high-chin Virginian to lead them. Or does he follow? How does a lad become worthy of being a lieutenant?

Later, as Katrinka slept beside him, Jan De Groot wondered about what Van Gloon had said concerning another Virginian, the fellow who was now the top general. Would this commander now appoint all Virginia boys like Witty to be his officers? And, as Van Gloon worried, if a war was won, would the wig of this General Washington wish for a crown?

And if the Continental Army were whipped and beaten, would

the British Redcoats come through our valley? Worse yet, would their savage allies come with painted faces, the Mohawk? Or the French with all their Huron friends from the north? My dreams hear red shrieks.

His big arm gently hugged his sleeping wife.

 Chapter Eleven

He saw Winnifred in the barn.

It was still dark, not black but gray; night trying to be morning. The animals were awake. A pig grunted as he rubbed his pink padded hip against a post to combat the itch of a tick. In its hole, the fence post thudded to and fro, in beat with the scratching.

Awake now, Cotton inhaled the strong barn smell, filling his lungs with it, a heavy smell of horses, even though the two draft animals were hardly fit to clear a top rail in pursuit of a fox or hare. Mary snorted. He welcomed the sound she made. He saw Winnie dump a measure of oats to all five of the horses. And to Mary his mare.

"Good morning, Winnifred." As he spoke her name, he admired his own judgment in not calling her Mistress De Groot, as using her first name would better serve to establish himself as an army officer and Winnie as an adoring child. Calling her Winnie would be too informal. Jumping to his feet, he smiled at her.

"Good morning, Lieutenant Witty."

"You are early up. Do all the others sleep?"

"No one sleeps late on my father's farm."

"Thinking of you, it is nigh impossible for a man to sleep a wink."

For a moment, for one half-breath, her hands stopped in their labor, and he noticed how her fingers seemed to tighten on a fistful of oats. As her hand relaxed, a few sprinkles of the white grain fell like flakes of snow. Yet her hand was steady.

"You thought of me?" Her voice softened.

"So very much." It was true. Hour after hour, he had listened to his sleeping companions, the hoarse breathing of Blue Goose and the sour mutterings of Durable Hatch, as he had rolled back and forth in the straw, hoping that this girl ached with a like agony, wishing that she would steal softly down from the loft, lightly on tiptoe as to not disturb her snoring papa, and come to him in the barn. And now, she had come.

"Best we not awaken Mister Hatch and his red friend." He walked toward her, holding his finger before his lips as if to beg their mutual silence. With a quick sideward nod of his head, he indicated two gray mounds beneath twin piles of yellow straw.

"Do they sleep?"

"Yes," he said.

"But not you."

"No. I was born on a horse. I do not tire my mare or myself as do they."

"Your mare is a beauty, sir."

"Indeed she is, Winnie. But please do not call me sir."

"What shall I call you?"

"My name is Cotton Mayfield Witty." Suddenly he wanted to hear her say his name, softly.

"Cotton," she said.

"You have a comely face."

"Thank you, Cotton. I know that I am no beauty, but my mother tells me that my face is strong. I am a good worker."

"So I see. Here, let me help."

"If you wish."

Together they walked toward the rear of the barn, the bucket between them. It happened quickly. Their hands slid upward on the half-ring handle, and touched, turning their faces toward each other. Katrinka De Groot was only partly right. Her daughter

113

Winnifred did have a strong face, but also a lovely and open face. It was yet too dark to see her eyes now as he wanted to see them.

In the depths of the barn, Winnie turned to her right and he followed her, their hands still sharing the weight of the grain bucket. Now they were near the tackroom, its wall holding large frames of leather that could contain the bullish thrusts and charges of a big team of Belgian workhorses. Returning the bucket to an open oat bin, Winnie closed the wooden lid, doing so without making a noise that would disturb the two sleepers.

"Cotton," she said. "I like your name. To say it, I mean. It sounds sweet and pure."

"Winnifred De Groot is a very Dutch name."

"Yes, very Dutch. My father is a real Hollander, born and raised in Zeeland, where many a good farmer is raised. Your papa is also a farmer?"

Cotton nodded. "In a way."

"I am glad of it. We are Protestant. Are you?"

"Indeed. Of the Anglican faith."

"And are you English?"

"English, but not Tory."

She smiled. Light sifted through the window to cream her face with dawn. Standing a step nearer, he took her face in his hands, moving closer to her. She looked at first his left eye, then his right, left right, left right, as though undecided. Up on her toes, she touched her nose to the tip of his. Her act surprised him. Nothing, he thought, is as rewarding as when a girl makes a gesture on her own, without being prompted or instructed . . . or begged. Here was a girl who would create many such gestures that would inspire a variety of pleasure for each.

"Have you ever taken a man?"

Inside he trembled, shocked at the boldness of his own question. He wanted to jolt her a bit. Yet the expression of her face was one of purity and trust. I believe, Winnifred De Groot, that the only males you know are your brothers and your big papa. Slowly, and oh so childlike, he felt her face move in his hands, as she shook her head from side to side in answer to his question. No, she was saying, never. Her eyes were wide with fascination. Perhaps, he thought, she is flattered that I considered her aged enough to love.

"You will be my man," she said.

"I want to be. Right now."

"It is time for me," she said. "I am fifteen, but I now see life as my mother sees, and my brothers and sisters are children to me as they are to her."

A bow of plain string was at her neck. He untied it, then feeling his heart pound as she easily pulled her blouse up and over her head. Her skin was neither white nor yellow, but rather in hue like her face, a rich golden cream. Before he could even swallow, her rough brown dress fell to her feet along with the white of her undergarment. She came to him, and in one sudden rush, all her womanhood pressed against him. Touching her, everywhere and anywhere, he fought the mindless insanity of utter joy.

Her mouth found his mouth. Hunger discovering thirst. His hands were too shaken to undo his uniform. Hers were not. Weakly the pair fell to the straw floor, laughing and kissing.

"God damn you, soldier boy!"

On the dry hard-packed mud of the barn floor, the big boots of Jan De Groot pounded like a Percheron as he ran toward what he saw as his child and her attacker. His fist was a hammer.

"I fix you . . . good!"

"Nothing happened, sir."

"Nothing?" The hardwood handle of the hayfork caught Cotton Witty just below his left ear, sending Witty naked and sprawling into a pile of stacked field tools.

"Damn you, boy. I kill you!"

"Please don't, Papa. It is my doing, not yours. And not his."

"Your doing?" Jan De Groot held the tines of the big fork above his red face.

"I am a woman now."

"Yes, *now* . . . because of that no-good."

"Before he came to our farm, I was a woman. Yet his seed is not in me. I will bear no fruit."

115

"You lie to me?" Jan De Groot seemed almost to plead.

"Winnifred tells you true, sir. Like you, I am a farmer, and I know a man must first own land before he sows it with his seed. We have lain together, sir, but she is yet a maid."

Here I stand, thought Cotton. Like an unrobed fool, and yet I feel not foolish. I feel full of wonder. And with a bit of good fortune, coupled with some fast thinking and clever words, I may flee this stable ere its owner amputates my enthusiasm.

"Why do you smile?" asked Jan.

"Because I am happy," Cotton answered him.

"And I, too," said the girl.

"One day," said the Dutchman, "you will sire a daughter and see her grow to near a woman. Then you understand Jan De Groot. Clothe yourself. And you, daughter, cover your shame."

Turning, he threw down the hayfork, walking toward the open door of his barn with fast strides. As he passed by the mound of straw, it suddenly sat up and rubbed its eyes, becoming no other than Andrew Angus Hatch. Like a cow, Durable started to get to his feet, hindquarters first, presenting his unprotected rump to a father much too irate to resist such a tempting target. Jan's big boot sent Hatch hurtling headlong into the hay. As the Dutchman departed, the old man rubbed a place other than his eyes; and punched Blue Goose.

"What'd ya do that fer?" he hollered at the surprised Huron.

Alone in the tackroom, Cotton and Winnie heard the exchange, and laughed to such an extent that they held onto each other for support. And then, arms about each other, the laughter softened to love.

"I can't stop my face," she said.

"Does it smile by itself?"

She nodded. "As I am so merry."

"No happier than I. What's my name?"

"Cotton . . . Mayfield . . . Witty."

"Please, only my first."

"Cotton," she said softly.

"You turn my name to a prayer."

116

"And my heart turns to a dance."

"Dream of me, Winnie. My old Aunt Martha told me as a child that if I dream enough it is more apt to come true."

"Do you believe that story?"

"Yes, as I wish to believe," he said.

Winnifred's face asked a question. Will I ever see you again? She is, Witty thought, too proud and too Dutch to ask me. We both are too young for vows, and a barn is not a kirk, and there is a war. They dressed slowly and embraced.

"I am a soldier, Winnie."

"Yes, an officer."

"Self-made, or very near to it, as Commanding General Washington is friend and neighbor to my father. You know, this is the first time that I ever looked into a mirror to see the real me. A confession of sorts. I am stripped strangely naked in more than one respect. Ah, now when I robe my person once again in uniform, shall I again play officer? Or will I become a soldier?"

Standing naked before him, her body glowed warm in the first light, a creamy lantern of loveliness. He stood still, as if in a strange stock, while her hands redressed him into the white uniform that only moments ago she had so desperately torn from his body in her hunger to have him.

"You stare at my heart."

"Touch me."

He did. Manhood never stops, he thought. It only hides for a while, like a spent animal who ducks into a hidden lair.

She knew! Her fingers undid a button she had just fastened, and she laughed to enjoy her own comedy. Somewhere, beyond their world of two, another world called as he heard the husky rattle of Durable's voice.

"Witty!" The old man coughed.

And then he heard the grunt of Blue Goose, as if to tell the old man that he was asleep and cared not for the whereabouts of anyone, including the horses.

"War is calling," said Cotton.

"I could weep. War is calling, as if some unholy god awaits to bloody our lives and burn our crops. I want to live where *all* people are Dutch like my father."

"And no British?"

"No," she said.

"And no French."

No, she shook her head. "And neither Mohawk nor Huron. Only we Dutch, as we farm instead of fight. I will wed a strong Zeelander, as did my mother, and raise children with hair more yellow than corn and stouter than flax."

"At fifteen, you are a firm-minded girl."

"I am a firm-minded woman." She slowly stepped her pale feet into her white undergarments, pulling them up over her buttery body. Then her rough brown dress of wool.

"Dutch sleep Dutch," she said.

"Why do you tell me all this?"

"A robin will not mate with a sparrow," she said, "for if they did, our sky would have no more of either."

"Farewell to you, Miss Sparrow." He kissed her very gently. "I'll come back," he said.

"Perhaps, sweet Robin."

"In a way, it is a pity that your good pa will never know how pure we are together." He softly touched her face with his fingertips. "You are a candy girl."

"You err in your judgments, Lieutenant, as I know fully that I am neither candy nor a girl."

"My meaning was liken to confessing that you make me a candy boy. Manhood is yet a mystery to me, yet one that will soon unfold, I wager." He sighed.

"Come to the house with me," she said, "so that we De Groots can fill you before you pack north."

"You are kindly disposed to three strangers. I wonder for what reason."

"For good cause, as my father holds no truck with the British. Nor with their Iroquois friends, the red Mohawk."

"Our good Mister Hatch and his Huron friend hold a like sentiment."

Now they heard the grumblings of Hatch as the old man mentioned his interest in a hot breakfast to a Huron. Ignoring the sounds of the voices, Cotton and Winnie continued to look into each other's eyes, not touching. Her face seemed to say how much she wished to hold him once again. He tried to speak, but no words would be coaxed forth. Yet in less than one beat of his heart, her body filled his arms, and he felt her mouth all over his face. Tiny kisses, here and there, on his eyes and cheeks and chin. He wanted her to whisper his name. Why do I wish such a small wish? Yet I do and oh so very strongly as though I long for little else. Except for my home to be mine. Can I picture Winnifred De Groot on the veranda of South Wind or twirling about to the lyric of our ballroom? Or astride a mare such as Mary? Ah, my heart has so much to treasure and yet I do not love wisely. Will I ever be more than an ungainly boarhog who thrashes among stacks of brittle crockery, only to smash and deface whatever item I touch?

"Love me not," he said, his lips against her ear and feeling the caress of her yellow hair against his brow, "as I am not yet worthy of love. I must go," he said.

"You will return our way." Her voice was as confident as her body, content in her power to attract him. Inhaling, he felt himself suck her strength deep into his own lungs as though her nearness was some hardy provision to store away, to sustain his mission with some uncanny nourishment. Strength, he thought. Not beauty, but the reality of strength that I admire in her, as does she with me. God, am I finally blessed with a modicum of manhood? Perhaps one day I shall be more than mere butter and honey, as Winnifred already is.

"You are some woman," he said. "You make me desire to prove my own soldiery. You gild my war with a reason."

"Stay alive," she said softly, "and do not die. Of all the persons I know, *you* were created to feast."

Her fingers bit his flesh harder than the jaws of dogs.

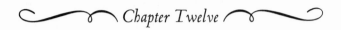

Chapter Twelve

Durable scratched himself.

"Which way?" asked Cotton Witty.

"I got to cogitate," the old man answered, squinting at the fork of the trail. About them on all sides, the trunks of oak and ash and maple offered no help as to the route they should follow.

"Are we lost?" the boy asked, wiping sweat from his face.

"No, ya cussed whelp, we ain't lost. I stood this place before, years back. Only it'll cost me a breath or two before I recollect which leg of this here fork we follow. Run north, the both of 'em. But best we don't drift too close to Albany. Blue! You smell anything?"

The old man and the young one both looked at the Huron who had dropped to his knees in order to touch his nose to the earth. Brushing away a scatter of brown leaves, his nose bent low to the black forest soil in order to listen to whatever his nose could whisper to him.

"Two," he grunted, "three. No more."

Cotton sighed. "What does he tell us?"

"Two days," said Blue Goose. "Horse drop water on here place."

"Fascinating," said Cotton. "But tell me why we can't head toward Albany? At least it is a town."

"Too many Dutchies," snapped the old man.

"De Groot is Dutch."

"Reckon he is. Nobody's perfect."

"You trust him, do you not?"

"Aye, lad, but not all the Dutchies do I favor. This is their country, not ours. Weren't my hanker to call Fort Orange by its new name."

"What new name?"

"Albany, ya puny-pated cluck. So if it be all the same to you and Blue, best we give 'er a go around, just to be on the safe side."

"Is there a safe side?"

"If'n we keep comfortable to the east, there be no need to ford water. On our left there's the River Hudson, which is flowed into Albany by the Mohawk River from the west. Cross too early, going north, and we got the Mohawk to wade through or boat over. So I say we keep east and fork right."

"Two days," said Blue Goose.

"How many horses?" asked the old man.

Blue Goose shrugged his shoulders. He was naked from the belt up, his chest covered only by the diagonal cut of his bowstring. Five arrows rode his back, as well as his buckskin blouse, which he had rolled into the folds of his red blanket. Again his shoulders bobbed to say he could not count the horses.

"Horses go," his arm pointed north and up the left fork of the trail.

"We go right," said Durable Hatch.

"I'm hungry," said Witty.

"Had a breakfast, you done did, same as us rest," snorted the old man.

"Yes, but it is now noonday." Witty looked south at the sun. "And it is most warm."

Durable could read both heat and hunger on the boy's face. Still growing, he thought. And not yet learned to deny himself as little as a meal. Well, he waltzed his chestnut mare for three days while me and Blue near to tore open and busted. Now the worm turns, and we'll see ere sundown what the pup is cut from, mush or mutton. Today we go afoot and we'll cross the kill to Kinderhook before we camp. Then we'll tally who keeps up and who lags to the arse end of our party.

"Two meal a day," he snapped at Cotton, "on account I ain't

fixing to pack no provisions to high-hog it. Enough to fire and feed us. Morning and night and that be the sweet of it."

The boy's eyes narrowed as he leaned against a tree. He hates my insides, he does, thought the old man. Well, let him hate, as it'll keep him mean enough to keep up to me and Blue. If he hates me enough, he may yet be the soldier that befits his rank. Saying nothing, the old man started north on the right fork at a dogtrot that was neither a walk nor a run. Just an easy wolf-gait that chewed up miles. Legs, he told his old body, keep on a go, as a man can't die less he first lays down.

"Must we run?" Witty panted from several paces to the rear. The old man did not answer nor did the Huron. Trot, trot, trot all day.

At times they would keep to the trail; but for other stretches, Durable would branch away to follow little but wilderness, keeping the sun on his back. Due north. Blue Goose said nothing, as the dogtrot pace was to his liking. He goes north and closer to his beloved Sky, who is the daughter of Wolf Eyes, the old man chuckled to himself, and so his light heart sews a wing to his moc. His feet are feathers, he once told me, whenever he travels to the northward. Closer to her, the poor lovesick calf, and closer to nodding his neck into the noose of wedlock. How well do I remember his face only a week past as us two was bound for Boston. His heart sinks like lead whenever his back is to Canada. He will go north this time, to Fort Ti and beyond, and continue his northward flight like the mallards of spring. This is our last trip together, me and Blue; our last trip, and I'll not ask him to turn south again. No, not ever. There is a chant in the lad's heart that sings only for Sky, and with each footstep the drums beat louder, and faster, to make his blood outrace even his feet. Lucky young kit.

On and on they trotted, moving a bit quicker than a very fast walk, yet never breaking into a run. He and Blue Goose had passed through much of the northern wilderness and outrun many an enemy at this speed. All day, the old man told himself with each kick of his leg; all day, all day, until even the sun is weary enough to stretch out upon the western horizon and doze from exhaustion into the darksome.

"All day," he whispered aloud.

Blue Goose had heard, and understood; his Huron face smiled at the old man as the two of them trotted side-by-side through the bush. All morning the leaves had been wet and dark, but slowly the heat of a November midday began to bake them to a lighter brown, some yellow, some red. Dry now, the leaves began to whisper and crackle beneath their feet.

"Bad," the Huron told him.

So he swung to the east ridge and into the darker shadows of pines, where the forest floor would cushion their footfalls with a brown blanket of needles and help them to share their secret with no other ears.

Blue Goose nodded.

Durable understood the gesture. I am so deaf now, he thought, I don't realize when my mocs rattle leaves louder than a weasel in a cider barrel. Best I remember that all ears in this wilderness are not plugged with the wad of age. Their mocs were silent now, as the Huron and the trapper glided like smoke between the thick trunks of evergreen, making little or no sound. They heard little but the chirp of wrens and the breathing of Cotton Mayfield Witty, who followed several paces behind.

"Stop," pleaded the Virginian.

Durable Hatch ignored the request. Damn that young cur and his infernal horses. Let his legs ache as my back still aches from the pounding I took astride that cussed animal. Devil take him. *His* turn to follow, by dang, and follow he will; as it sure ain't my intending to ease up on him. Trot, you young buck. Trot until you puke up your breakfast all over the Dutch woods, and neither Blue Goose nor me'll as much as wipe your chin. So work them kiddy legs off, on account you don't keep stride with me and Blue, you are one lost babe.

"Can't we rest?" the lad asked again, between gasps for air as though he were wading nostril-deep through a swale of his own exhaustion.

Blue Goose made the boy a gesture that they would all rest come sundown but Witty understood little the indian signs. He sure has got a spate of learning to do, thought Durable Hatch. Well, I don't guess he spent this day without getting taught at least one lesson, and that be that an old Verdmonter like me ain't so dogblame easy to keep up to. Run, you corn-haired cuss. Trot until you wear holes in them fancy riding boots, and then maybe you will learn what footwear is tuned for a dance in the wilderness and what ain't.

A hawk screamed.

Hatch pulled his pace to an easy walk. The backpack was drawing the straps into the meat of his shoulders and a stop would serve to shift weight. No affording a blister. Ahead was the canoe, and then they would glide on the waters of the upper lake, but the canoe was still days away. I must not kill myself, Durable thought, in order to tucker out a boy.

"We rest here," he said, sliding the pack from his shoulders and, flopping his body down on a green bed of moss, he lay still as stone.

"Oh . . . thank God." The voice belonged to Cotton Mayfield Witty, a Virginian in a white satin uniform that was now dark with sweat. He crumpled to a heap on the forest floor and did not even bother to remove his pack. His eyes are glassy, Hatch noticed, and he pants like an August dog.

As the old man's eyes moved from Lieutenant Witty to Blue Goose, he saw the shoulders and chest of the Huron were wet, gleaming with the shine of haste. Huh, the trapper snorted to himself, how odd it be that I no longer sweat. Nary a bead. Too old, too dried up to fluid. Too old to cry nor care, I be. Why in the name of Old Harry am I bound for Ti? Henry Knox must think me a tomfool to swallow his yarn about Nell and Britchie and all them others. Admit to yourself, old soul. I don't guess I was blinded by his trumpy tale of the British playing turnkey with them Boston gals and tossing 'em into a jailhouse, or worse. Reckon I was just sitting out a watch, hoping that somebody would up and ask me to do for the cause. I'm too gray for the militia, they said. Hell with them! Who wants to wear one of them fooly uniforms and parade

124

up and down, left foot, right foot, with the rest of them chickens. God bless you, Mister Knox, and I shall learn soon enough your real intent.

"Soon we will see Half Hand," the old man said to Blue Goose, and the Huron answered with an understanding nod of his head.

"Big man. Eight fingers plenty."

From high in the pines, Durable heard the scream of a hawk, and then another, the echo scream coming from a new direction. His hand touched the tomahawk at his hip. While they ran, earlier, he had thrust the wee ax deep into its loop, but now he loosened the choke of the strap, his fingers moving little. Rolling his eyes to look at the Huron, his breathing eased a bit to see no scowl of alarm on the red face. You are my ears and my eyes, Blue, and your face whispers to me that the scream was a hawk, and not an Iroquois.

Beneath the brown-gray deerskin shirt that covered his upper body, Durable felt the pounding inside his chest, and his awareness of it seemed to increase its tempo. Moving his fingers from his ax, he covered his heart as though his hand were a quilt, asking the throbs beneath to be still. Am I afraid? Yes, only a jackass in times such as these would not be. Every soul you meet talking war, war, war. So be it. Better perhaps than the Britishers telling us all to bow down, and resting a boot on the back of a Yankee neck to humble a man before his King. Well, all them fancy Redcoats is in for eye open, so say I.

Again the hawk screamed. High above his head, Durable Hatch saw the sudden twitch of a limb, the great fawn-colored wings and the red fan underside of the tail, as the hawk soared away to hunt, becoming a tiny speck upon the blue of day.

"Hawk," the old man said to no one.

"Sky," said Blue Goose.

Durable heard the groan from the mouth of Cotton Mayfield Witty, causing the old man to roll his head to confront its maker. He read the lad's expression to himself, remembering how he (as a boy) had first heard conversation between two indians, which filled his youthful ear with little more than moans and grunts. Long time back, he thought, before the French War as much as by a generation. Was it 1730? Or 1735? No matter. I don't guess I even as much as know my own age; and best I do not, as to learn the straight of it would surely ax-nip me as a felling tree.

"Aye." He turned to Cotton who sprawled on the ground, back pressed to the earth, arms and legs stretched out as though his body were being pulled toward all four points of the compass. "Aye, I don't wonder ya question our talk," he said to the Virginian. "Sky. Now that there is the name of a comely Huron lass far to the north of us. Sky is Blue's sweetheart. You must of got one for your own self, a stout young strapper like you, to pine away for your return to Virginny."

"To be sure," said Cotton. "Sweethearts and trueloves I have by the score, each sitting in candlelight by a mansion window to await my heroic return. And if, perchance, General Washington and I arrive on the same day, more's the pity that his homecoming will be so overlooked in favor of mine."

"Heard tell you know General Washington."

"Well enough. Ah, or perhaps too well, as his wife is close friend to my mother. As an aide, I served our commanding general well, and there now dawns in my mind the real reason I am in Coventry."

"Coventry?"

"An expression, dear Hatch, meaning in disgrace. True, I am of shallow experience and strut about with my arrogant nature, yet I honestly can claim my service to George Washington was with diligence. Even so, the general thinks I need seasoning. Methinks he trusts me not."

"You know this to be true?"

Cotton nodded. "And more. General Washington does trust in Benedict Arnold and in General Schuyler as he does in Schuyler's second-in-command."

"Brigadier Montgomery," said Durable.

"You are acquainted?"

"Some. I soldiered with Amherst when he took Fort Ti, years back in the French War, and so did Richard Montgomery. Good soldier, even if he is an Irisher lad, but I don't cogitate he's a lad by now. Must be forty or nigh on, and all mustard."

"Do you also know Benedict Arnold?"

"Seen the man a pair of times."

"What is his nature?" asked Cotton.

"Worse'n mine."

"Not possible."

"Give him this. Arnold's men would follow him to Hades, on account from all I hear. But Ben Arnold would set the first foot into the fire. Best we got, and that even takes in Ethan."

"You refer to Colonel Allen, do you not?"

"Right enough do. He's a Verdmont man, like me."

"There could naught be two of *you,* Mister Hatch."

"Nor a pair of him. Ethan took Ti and not a shot fired. Well, maybe a single. So I say the man's got pepper in his bowels. Him and Benedict don't get on so good, as the story goes, and a pair of aches they be to our friend Montgomery."

"What think you of Colonel Knox?"

"Half Hand," grunted the Huron.

"Is that how he calls big Henry?" asked Cotton.

"That be how. From them fingers he's missing."

"As he calls you Old Ax."

"He do."

Cotton was quiet, looking at the old man and then at the red man, to and fro. He wonders, thought Hatch, and he will probable ask.

"No doubt he has a name for me," said Witty.

"Best we move on, lads. Ticonderoga ain't in our pockets, not by a day or a durn sight, so let's travel. I figure we be east to Kinderhook."

"What is Kinderhook, sir?"

"Settlement. Chock full of Dutchies, if'n you borrow my whiff of the place, and a good spot to stay away from as I don't favor them no more than they do me. Dang foreigners."

The old man got to his feet, turning his back to Witty to prevent the boy from reading the twist on his face. Poor old back, he said silently, shifting the shoulder strap of his burden. He wants to ask, he does, and that's for a sure and certain. Wants to know how Blue Goose regards him. I hope to Heaven he never truly finds out as Blue would knife him as quick as he would a supper squirrel. Reckon I don't guess I want to visit Virginny if all them folk are kin to this here whelp. Henry Knox, I do this for you, as I hunch you'd cook me a good turn were I to ask it. Give him this, Henry spoke up quicker'n scat to that pack of louts who marched us to that house in Worcester. Size gives a man a purchase, true enough, but young Henry has more than a bag of bulk.

"On yer feet, puppy."

"Go to Hell."

There weren't much ornery in his voice, Durable thought. Just that he be all a-tucker from what my old Pap used to call the high-noon dropsy. Once you stop, it ain't easy to whip up yer mules and start again.

"Boy, much as me and Blue Goose can fast from your company, we ain't about to leave you rot here. I could threat to go on without you, but I wouldn't mean it, as by morn of the morrow you'd be probable dead. And that handsome hair of yours would hang at a dangle from the bloody belt of a lean young Iroquois who just might want to take a piece of you home, a piece too personal to mention, to show his dear old ma." Durable spat.

"Strong words, sir. And of conviction."

"No matter. What I speak is barely worth a listen, say little to writ down. But as we left Worcester as a threesome, by dang we ought to crack Ti with nobody amiss. You agree?"

Cotton sat up. "Sir, I agree. It's just that I dislike being ordered about as though I am a slave or a blackamoor."

The old man leaned down to almost whisper in the young ear. "Son," he said, "good manners ain't my strong point."

"No, but your odor is."

"Looky, I'm fed up on your prattle. Me an' Blue Goose is head north. So git up . . . or git lost."

The old man stood watching the Virginian labor to his feet,

straighten the wrinkles from his uniform of white satin, and hunch up his pack. Blue Goose wore his burden on his rump, high up, to prevent its bouncing as he trotted. The Huron took the lead, followed by Cotton and then by Hatch. Not a trot, not yet. Ease into a gait, thought Durable, and let me loosen the bowstrings of my legs. I don't guess it'll be ever when I set my next horse. No, never again will I fork such an infernal critter, even if the entire Iroquois nation is one breath to the rear with red paint beneath their eyes.

Feels good, he thought, just to walk instead of trot. Sure enough, Blue Goose knows. One thing about that lad is that he don't never need telling. His heart can see and hear and understand about as much, or more, than any white man's I ever knew. If'n I ever sired a son, and God only knows if I have or no, I don't guess he could want to be growed up no prouder a man than Blue. Ain't a better feeling in the wide world than just for a man to know he's got one true friend to his credit, and I got Blue Goose. Reckon he'd die to rescue my twopence hide, so best I keep the young scamp from killing his own self in doing it.

Soon he will have Sky.

One thing certain, I'd like to go up north to Canada to his wedding and maybe chase myself a Huron woman who'll be probable twice as old and half to pretty. More'n I warrant. Who'd want a loony old coot like me? No more teeth than a hen. Old age starts with pity. Damn if I'll lay down much as a wink for it. One way's to show this pair of pups that keeping abreast of Durable Hatch is an all-day chore. Press on, you young hellions, else I'll leave the brace of you to rearward and go on ahead all by my lonesome. And the two of you can catch up come spring. Hah! What a jolly picture that, Blue and Cotton to the rear, and me away out front, leaving them two in the wash of my dust.

Dream, old man, Hatch told himself.

For three more days the men traveled north, passing Fort Orange that was more newly named Albany, and northward. To reach the town of Saratoga, they rafted over the Hudson River, traded for a bit of sugar, corn, spiced beef, a swallow of rum to heat the belly of each man, plus a real bonus of a find in the form of a small tin of genuine English tea. Leaving before noon, the three recrossed the Hudson to reach Glens Falls by late evening, where they slept in what little remained of a recently burned barn. They lit no fire, as the stone and ground beneath them was still warm enough to, as Durable phrased it, "shoo the hoar."

Looking west, a few miles farther north, they saw the lights of Fort George which held the southernmost tip of the upper lake.

"Beds," said Cotton.

Durable snorted. "Beds, and maybe British."

"*We* hold Fort George!" insisted Witty.

"Maybe so and maybe no. Fewer the folk who know where I be and which I go, the easier I rest come darksome. Besides, think you upon my cookery for two more days."

"My gut turns ill with such thought, old sir."

"I say we leave be. Boy, it ain't no cinch to keep you alive, and ofttimes I wonder why I even effort it. But it just might be a whole healthier if'n we don't share our directions with any devil we happen to stumble on. Take note, did you, of how little I told of our comings and goings with Jan De Groot? Not that I detrust the man, you mind, but ain't too many souls ever get sent to the Holy Hereafter on account of what they *don't* say."

"They are Americans." The lad nodded at the fort.

"Truly be. But all Americans ain't friendly to us three, no more than all of us three is even friends to each other."

They approached the hidden canoe.

But before uncovering it or nearing even within an arrow shot of its cove, they waited, watching the screen of blue-gray juniper boughs they had earlier bent over their craft. Year after year, Durable told them, he used the same boughs to mask his canoe, as it would be folly to cut branches as a thatch, for the leaves of needles would soon turn brown to betray the hidden property. Still, he waited, until he was sure no others also waited with bow or musket.

Blue Goose, as they waited, went off to hunt, complaining that the hungry panther in his belly howled for food. Without further talk, he left, leaving Cotton and Hatch in a thicket of hemlock.

"He has a name for me," said Witty.

"For sure and for certain, and I don't guess you could wait even one more breath until you hear it for yourself. That true?"

"I admit curiosity. Is he your slave?"

"Blue Goose?" The old man slapped his knee softly, feeling his face crack into a grin. "Even though I did buy him, in a sense, to save his young arse from burning. Naw, he ain't no slave."

"What is he?"

"Well . . . he's just Blue."

"No more."

"Somebody to weight the rear end of the canoe, to hunt with, and to yell at. That's the straight of it and there ain't be but a mite more."

"He calls you Old Ax."

"Yes, that's how he sees me, an old man who carries no musket but only a knife and a hatchet. He sees the missing fingers on Henry Knox and the big man becomes Half Hand, as he sees a woman bright and blue whose name just happens to be Sky."

"What is his name for *me*, Mister Hatch?"

"Won't be cozy for you to hear. And before I tell ya, best you know that Blue Goose ain't a mean soul, as I don't guess I ever see the first mean thing he's ever done to anybody. Nope, not one thing. He's a merry sort."

"He laughs at odd times," said Cotton; "I recall, even when a horse is bent on kicking his brains in."

"Blue laughs when he thinks he may die, so's his spirit will travel happy for all eternal. Part of his religion."

"How does he call **me**?"

"He named you . . . Child Face."

Cotton Mayfield Witty was silent. For a moment, Hatch was thinking the boy might weep, Lord forbid. No mistaking his hurt. I wonder, he thought, what so lodges in this lad's mind. Some hatred, I will wager, the old man was thinking. For both me and Blue.

The boy's hands became fists.

Chapter Thirteen

"My count is fifty-nine," said Henry Knox.

Extending his right hand, he patted the icy iron of a cannon barrel, allowing for a breath the bitter sting of cold to invade his fingers and run up his arm. The cannon's color was a smoky black; but perhaps, thought Knox, its black may have once been cleaner than a September stove.

"That is also my tally," nodded Major General Schuyler, resting a shiny boot on the high south wall of Fort Ticonderoga as he looked eastward over the still blue of Lake Champlain. His arm pointed toward the Verdmont territory and beyond, southeast toward the town of Boston. "And my guess is, Colonel Knox, that it be nearly three hundred snowy miles from Ti to where General Washington camps at Cambridge."

"Aye," said the big man, "and there he waits, thrashing to and fro in a dimly lit cage of a bedchamber, wearing a crimson blanket about his shoulders to ward off a chill."

"I trust him," said General Schuyler, helping his nose to a pinch of snuff from an oval snuffbox that Knox presumed was gold.

"As must we all, sir." Knox sighed, looking downward to one of the fifty-nine big guns that he soon would lug to Boston. "He once called this ordnance the King's iron."

"The King's iron it is," said the general, "or was, before Allen and Arnold came across that very lake, May last, to convert these pieces to our cause."

"Never have I seen Verdmont," said Henry, his gaze seeming almost to follow where General Schuyler had earlier pointed. "But

132

from all I hear, 'tis a wilderness of unsurpassed beauty, and its people wilder yet." An aristocrat like you, Knox remarked to himself about Schuyler, would be ill at ease in their dirt-floor cabins. "And one I know is wilder than any beast."

Schuyler looked at Knox. "Think you as do I," asked Schuyler, "of that certain Verdmont individual who bears the name of Hatch?"

"Indeed," laughed Knox. "A pithy old porcupine to be sure, sir, with a tongue more colorful than his aroma. My dear Lucy was in awe of Mister Hatch and his personal . . . prodigity, if one can mint such a word."

"A preposterous person warrants a fit term."

"I would near to imagine," said Knox, "that Durable Hatch just might be Verdmont's counterpart to our Samuel Adams. I am fond of both parties."

"Indeed, so," said Schuyler. "Almost a week ago, your friend Hatch was spied at a trot, hurrying down the portage path with a Huron indian in tow, and another lad from Virginia. A most ungainly trio. Although I did not arrive until a day or two afterward, I learned from Captain Woodson that little or no time did they fritter away. My special order to this garrison preceded their arrival, thus allowing immediate preparation to transport artillery of your choosing back to General Washington."

"How did you find Cotton Witty, our young Virginian?"

Schuyler's eyes narrowed a bit. "More than exhausted, according to my report from Woodson, and then more than arrogant after only a few hours' rest. On his own hook, he approached the trappers and traders and teamsters that are ever present at any fort, to solicit their advice on the uphill shuttle, this fort to Lake George, and their assistance in the construction of sleds. He lacks neither cheek nor initiative. He addressed Sergeant Alworth, a tough old soldier we have hereabouts, in a most undiplomatic manner, so I heard."

"The reaction?"

"Alworth spat a brown stream of tobacco on the lad's boot, then turning about he left the boy to instruct empty air. Yet later on that same day, I observed no other than our sergeant himself conferring with the lieutenant on proper sled assembly. The lad was listening to learn all he could. So I deem that his ardor for our patriot cause outweighs his overbearing expression in the eyes of Sergeant Alworth, who, I understand, is a better-than-average assessor of manhood."

"And of boyhood. For at earlier times, we all were boys, were we not?" asked Knox.

"Indeed. If I may be so bold, Colonel Knox, despite your impressive girth, you cannot much be more than a boy. May I inquire?"

"I am twenty-five, General. Strange though it be, I was asked my age more or less a fortnight ago, by George Washington."

"As for me, November last, I turned forty-two. And if our young Witty is too green to wage war, then I wither much too brown. I fought in the French War, twenty years ago, and methinks one war is aplenty to each man's life. Hah! Especially for a *gentleman* like myself."

"Are you married, General?" asked Knox, enjoying the joke.

"Yes, and only this past September, so it is high time I root the earth in order to help to people Albany. And you to be off on your return to Boston."

Turning, walking with Schuyler toward the great gray fortress of Fort Ticonderoga, Henry Knox admired the massive walls of masonry. Angry mouths of cannon protruded from crenellations in the gray stone. The walls, he noted, need repair. Not since Amherst gave this fortification its last battering, Henry guessed, had much been done to maintain the stronghold of Fort Ticonderoga. A box within a star was its design, the former composed of a three-sided rectangle formed by two-story barracks, the latter, a perimeter of walls much higher in places than a man could fall from and not be bodily broken on the scattering of small rocks below.

"It is my impossible wish," said Henry, "to have been witness to Fort Ticonderoga when first built by the French engineers."

"In seventeen fifty-five," said General Schuyler, "if I recall."

"Three flags have flown from her staff."

"And many more, perhaps, when you and I are dust."

"Ticonderoga fascinates me. Always has. It is my understanding that General Amherst, a Britisher, gave it the name."

"Yes," said General Schuyler, "I so believe, as the French originally called it Fort Carillon."

"A fort of bells."

"Montcalm was here then, in seventeen fifty-eight, and with only three thousand lads, he waited for the approach of the British up Lake George under General Abercromby. Come, up these stairs and we'll look westward. You have a sight in store."

Climbing the stairs, through an attic trapdoor to stand at last atop the slanting roof of gray slate, some of the tiles even a shade of light lavender, the two officers looked west.

"There." General Schuyler pointed. "Of course it is overgrown by a generation of fresh timber, but you can see the scar that General Montcalm cut through the forest."

"Like a great snake, a gray shadow beneath the snow."

"There ran the French lines. A breastwork of felled trees atop a ditch. Now that it's December and the foliage leaves our trees as bare as a hag's broom, we can see Montcalm's plan, as he honed his boys to greet fifteen thousand Redcoats."

"And mostly Highlanders."

"Correct, my lad. You are a scholar of history?"

"I like reading. I study military tactics when I can, and if I rightly remember, 'twas the Black Watch that came as far as that great ditch and not a bayonet farther."

"Once," said Philip Schuyler, the sleeve of his faultlessly tailored cream-trimmed blue uniform waving to indicate the extent of Montcalm's trench, "I talked to an indian who called himself Fawn Charbon. As a boy, a mere lad, he had hidden himself out there to see the battle here, 'twixt Montcalm and Abercromby, describing the slaughter of the Black Watch most vividly."

"An articulate savage?"

"Quite so. Fawn was a scout for Benedict Arnold and also the son of a French Jesuit who came here even before this fort was built. The man spoke both English and French fluently, as well as his native Mohawk that was no doubt taught him by his mother. Fawn became of high use to Arnold and his many negotiations."

"I would enjoy meeting these men," said Henry.

"So you would. Ben is both delight and damnation to me. In fact, I would enjoy meeting with him myself, as I am rarely privy, nor is anyone, to his current whereabouts . . . except that he now attacks Canada. Could I but locate Ben, I would demote and decorate him all in a gesture, if 'twere all possible. My wife Catherine thinks him charming, *sometimes* as do we all, and also a bit of a strutter. But I tell you one thing about Benedict."

"Permit me a guess," said Knox. "He is an able soldier."

Schuyler seemed to force a patrician nod. "He is."

"All who know Ben confess it."

"He," smiled General Schuyler, "most of all."

"We are fortunate he's ours," said Knox, "and not theirs."

Schuyler nodded. "And there has been only one other warrior of his stature, in my opinion."

"Who?"

"Major Robert Rogers. In my mind, the two stand as twin guards at the Gates of Mars."

"To be sure, sir," Schuyler added, "General Washington must have a high regard for you, or he would not have nominated for approval anyone so youthful to be the Commanding Officer of Continental Artillery. Yet he also favors Horatio Gates, perhaps as much as Ben Arnold pukes at the mention of that fellow's name."

Henry Knox looked at General Schuyler. I do wonder, he thought, what you are thinking now so quietly to yourself. That our gallant George plays one officer off against another, in order to relieve his own person as the common target, and to remain the top dog on the hill. Schuyler is too shrewd to say so; and too gentlemanly, as such a remark would compromise us both.

"To learn so much of the infighting of command," Knox confessed, "I'm nigh content to remain a civilian, as I now am, and may continue to be. And if my superiors address me only as acting colonel, then *act* I shall, and fill the stage with my playing. For the next three hundred miles of my life, I shall be the officer in charge of oxen, as we shall be whacking a goad to the backside of many a beast from here to Cambridge."

"Surely you will. Now, let us abandon this roof for more secure a roost. Note how the snow runs off from the sunlit slate. Enjoy the dry footing while you may, sir, as ye shall wade many a drift this December."

"Your lakes are not yet frozen."

"No. The ice comes earlier to Lake George, it being smaller, of a higher elevation, and fed by cold springs. You'll greet ice aplenty. Best you skid the cannon up the hill, using the indian portage, to the upper lake and load the boats. Then, once you reach Fort George to the south, decide on wagons or sleds, wheels or runners, as conditions may dictate."

They entered General Schuyler's personal quarters, on the second floor of the south barracks. The room was small, with walls of oak, and a modest cherrywood bed. Schuyler motioned Henry to a substantial rocker while he sat on the bench beneath the south window.

"Another winter," sighed Philip Schuyler. "And up here it is a long and gray beard that hangs from the chin of a hermit. I miss Catherine, though best she stays snug in Albany. She would chastise me to overhear me claim that no woman is hardy enough for a northern outpost. You should lie awake on a cold night and hear the ice expand to such extent that it sounds as though the entire length of Lake Champlain cracks like a bullwhip. Oft as loud as a clap of thunder. Luckily, I winter mostly in Albany as this northern nub of desolation I find as lacking in charm as in comfort."

As he spoke, a gust of wind rattled the black-wooded shutter outside General Schuyler's window, causing both men to turn. A cold sound, thought Henry, and soon my men and I will truly take the stab of winter. Please, let not the upper lake freeze, or else it will delay us further to wait for the ice to thicken.

"Would you care for a tot of rum? I recently brought it north from Albany, although, personally, I prefer the cruder joys of gin."

"Sir, I admit to being not much of a user of spirits, being raised a Presbyterian. And to be honest, the taste of rum is too sweet for my notion. And gin spins my reason."

"Cider then?" Schuyler's voice sounded condescending.

"Please."

"Apple crop was stout this year. On even the most puny of trees, limbs bent over, heavily laden with fruit. We have barrels and barrels of apples here, yellow and red, so outfit your provision boats with a goodly supply. Men get the rash on just jerky and biscuit. Mix in some fruit, as well as a ladle of honey each day, if you wish them a bounty of a breakfast."

"I shall, sir."

"No need to tell you to eat. Pardon my rudeness, young sir, but you are a rather bulky chap, and near to the biggest man my eyes have ever seen."

"I am glad to learn I excel at something," smiled Knox, "if only with my mastery of knife and fork."

Schuyler laughed. "I only taunt men I enjoy, my lad, so take no offense. You are more than tolerable company, according to what our General Washington pens to me, and I feel at ease trading you jab for jab."

"Thank you, sir."

Henry Knox sipped the cool cider from the pewter tankard handed him by General Schuyler. Tart, thought Knox, much in manner of its giver. It commences to be clear in my mind why Washington holds this major general in a right regard. The cider is more than sweet, claiming also a stubborn core of flavor somewhat too subtle to discern at first swallow. Philip Schuyler speaks with a lamb's voice, unharshly; yet my ear gulps a hardness. His face carries more than his forty-two furrows. I wonder how old we shall be, in spirit, when this conflict ends with England. Well, first chores first.

"Our preparation goes well," he said. "Thirty and more artillery pieces have already been broken down and packed for the uphill portage to Lake George."

"A short distance" — Schuyler nodded — "thank the Almighty for that."

"Earlier," said Knox, "I rode uptrail to inspect the completion of our rafts and scows. Our men work well, and the crafts they assemble are stout and . . . seaworthy, if you will allow an unfit phrase. I worked myself, as I use an ax at home. Alas, I am a mite clumsy with my hewing, and according to the warnings of my wife, I may lop off even more of my fingers."

Lightly the right hand of Henry Knox curved about the barrel of the tankard. "My hand is still sticky from the pitch of today's work. Even if I choose to, my fingers could not release the pewter."

"Hold fast, Henry. Fast to your cider as we all hold fast to our liberties. My, but a swallow of rum doth turn my lips a bit lofty."

"Fancy language can amuse, sir."

" 'Tis true." Schuyler's hand hit his knee as if to wake it for merrymaking. "The notes I receive from Ethan Allen of Verdmont are surely treasures of a kind."

"How so?" asked Knox.

"Well, I can easily detect when Ethan's enormous chin has sagged into his cup of ale, as the more sottish he becomes, the more posies do sprout from his sentences, as daisies from a dung pile. Did you read, perchance, his letter he wrote to the Massachusetts Council, his pen no doubt dipped not in butternut but into the depths of his bounteous bowl. Did you see that report?"

"No, sir, I did not."

"My, how the Garden of Eden looms dull compared to the floral blooming of Ethan's sentences, signing off with your most humble and obedient servant."

"An intemperate accounting?" asked Knox.

"Suffice it to say, sir, that a day or two later, he wrote a less poetical version that carried more facts and cooled his emotions. He owns half of Verdmont, along with his pack of brothers, or so the story goes. And now he speaks of annexing Canada."

"Canada, sir?"

"Precise. Imagine! And not a one of his ragtag followers doubted it for even a breath. My mind pictures that he may hold deeds on the farmlands of many of his disciples, to borrow from Scripture, so best they concur with even his wildest fantasy. Next, as the Governor of Canada, he'll appoint Hatch."

"I'll not permit it," Knox laughed. "Yet to be honest with ourselves, dear General, much of the hauling depends on the redoubtable Andrew Angus Hatch, and yes, the Huron who attends him."

"Quite so." General Schuyler looked out his south window, the only window, twisting his head to the left as though to study the portion of Verdmont that he could see to the east. He turned to face Henry Knox. "When will you and Hatch depart for Cambridge?"

"Sir, my estimate is soon, within days. Five at the outside. Washington is waiting for cannon and, by Heaven, he will get his iron. Earlier than he imagines. I suppose this sounds like a brag, a hollow echo of egomania on my part, but I am determined to surprise General Washington with stronger firepower than he expects."

"Colonel, I checked your selections, just to satisfy my own mind that you choose wisely."

"And do I?" I know that I have, Henry thought, but a second opinion would do no harm.

"You do. Brass and iron in, from what I observe, equal measure. Included in your sixty tons you balance your artillery with surprising versatility, considering that your military background is limited in the area of heavy gunnery. How did you acquire such astute sophistication?"

"Books," said Henry.

" 'Tis said you own a bookstore."

"We do. My lady enjoys helping select our stock. For she, as well as I, is a reader. Our tastes vary somewhat. She enjoys a novel, while I sop up my pages to learn things."

"What writer taught you gunning?"

"A man named Holliday; and Muller, who also is versed in military engineering. I read the works of Pleydell and Coehorn. So, with what little I learn, I match with Yankee reason, on what mortars and cannon and howitzers can support a troop assault on

Sir Billy down in Boston. Sir William Howe, I mean. We'll take coehorns, ball, flint, powder . . . anything we can use, but no more than my judgment tells me we can transport. About half of what's here in Fort Ticonderoga."

"Sixty tons," said General Schuyler, "through three hundred miles of snow."

"We can do it, sir. Believe in us."

Schuyler nodded. "I do."

Chapter Fourteen

"Half Hand."

The bedchamber was totally without light. Knox opened his eyes. Again he heard a fist pounding wood.

"Half Hand, open door."

Who, wondered Henry Knox, comes to a barrack door at midnight, with something about a hand? Rolling his big body from the bunk, his bare feet took the shock of meeting the icy plank of the floor. As his room was wee, hardly a step was necessary to throw the black latch in order to see who caused the disturbance, or why.

"Blue Goose?"

"Half Hand sleep."

Henry Knox's brain fought to stay awake. A gust of December wind hit his chest, and the Huron filled the doorway. Behind him it was snowing. The top of Blue Goose's head was white with flakes, making his face run wet with their melting.

"Come." Knox struck the one stubby candle that Fort Ticonderoga provided. As the flicker of candlelight grew bolder, Henry was suddenly aware that he and Blue Goose shared the bedchamber with a third party. The Huron allowed a deer to slip from his shoulder, its hooves hitting the floorboard with a hollow thud. It was a young buck, a spikehorn, not yet forked into a four-pointer. The tawny fur was snowy and wet to the exploring touch of Henry's hand. Knox sat on the bed's edge, aching for sleep, wondering why Blue Goose had brought a slain buck to awaken him.

"Thank you."

"Him good eat. Young buck. Old buck make teeth hurt, tough, like Old Ax." The Huron gave a nod.

"Do you expect me to eat it now, horns and all, or may I save it for breakfast?"

"Gift, for Half Hand." Smiling, the Huron rubbed his belly in small circles.

"I thank you, Blue Goose."

"Half Hand hungry?"

Ah, his brain brightened, I understand the hand business. Blue Goose has noticed my two missing fingers, and sees my left hand as only half of its nature, so he names me as he sees. A gift? Somehow there must be a higher purpose to this visit that now escapes me. Blue Goose suddenly twitched, and Henry could see that the man was wet and chilly. Pulling a quilt from his bed, Henry draped it around the warrior's soaking shoulders. Doing so, his hands felt the indian shake. Looking up at Henry's face, Blue Goose forced a smile. "Cold."

"Yes. Why do you hunt this night?"

"For gift."

"Again, thank you. You want someone's ax?" Henry felt his own eyelids sag. Why, he asked himself, do I converse over the borrowing of hewing tools at this hour?

"Old Ax," smiled Blue Goose. "Hatch."

"I understand," said Henry Knox, wondering if he really did. Blue Goose names men with his eyes. I want to go back to sleep. Now. Heavily, Knox sank his bulk once more to the bunk and stared questioningly at his nocturnal guest. Seeing the man shiver, Knox remembered the rum that an earlier occupant had forsaken in his bedchamber. Reaching to the hickory nightstand, his fingers fumbled for the neck of the rum bottle: then he dumped a measure of liquor into a tin cup. Handing the cup to Blue Goose, he watched the indian cautiously swallow a first gulp, and make a wry face.

"Burn," said Blue Goose, making a sign at his throat. Yet he continued to drink in careful sips until the cup was drained dry and an empty clank sounded its return to the hickory stand.

"It will make your belly warmer, like hot medicine."

"Medicine melt ice."

"How long did you hunt?"

"All night. Walk long time so bring meat here." He pointed to the animal. "Heavy."

"I well imagine."

Blue Goose nodded his head. "Cold."

"Tomorrow we'll have a feast, Blue Goose, for you and for me and Mister Hatch. A roasting party, and we shall all eat the venison. As for now, you must be as weary as I, and even more, so best we both get some sleep."

Blue Goose did not rise to go. Saying nothing, he folded his arms across his chest, staring at Knox. "No sleep. Talk."

Knox sighed. "Talk about what?"

"I give deer. You give."

"Fair enough. What may I offer you?"

"Blue Goose take Child Face."

Knox scowled. "What?"

"Child Face."

"Is that a doll, a toy?"

Blue Goose shook his head, scowling. "No." It was now the Huron's turn to sigh. "I want."

"Yes?"

"Child Face."

"Who is Child Face?"

"Boy in white clothes. Virginia place boy."

"Lieutenant Witty?"

"You give."

"Blue Goose . . . people do not give people to people. It just isn't our law."

"Good law, good trade."

"Why do you want Witty?" Knox felt his stomach begin to cringe; as though he were already fearful of the savage's reply.

"Go north, take Child Face to Canada place, give boy. Wolf Eyes give Sky to Blue Goose."

"How can you give the sky to people? Or trade it? The sky belongs to all men."

"No, to Blue Goose!" A fist shot upward. The Huron beat his own chest, one solitary thump. His face seemed frozen with hatred, and from deep in his throat came a growl that Henry imagined could only have been made by a bear or panther. Sky? Does he mean he wants to go to Heaven? Oh, if I could only think with my poor mind that is groggy for want of sleep. I must, Henry told himself, settle this business or throw this red lunatic out of my chamber. An idea came to him, for interpretation.

"Where is Mister Hatch?"

"Sleep."

"Well, best we wake him."

Blue Goose shook his head. "No, old man sleep in ball, like squirrel. All sleep. Sentry sleep. Blue Goose talk, Half Hand talk."

"About what?"

"Child Face."

"Oh, we are back to that."

"Want. You give."

"Now look here, Blue Goose. I thank you for the deer you bring, but if it means that I must give you a person, I must now ask you to pack up your meat and go."

"Go to Canada."

"Very well. Go to Hell for all I care. Why not just go to bed and come the morrow we shall confer, the three of us, with Hatch."

"Old Ax."

"Right enough, with Old Ax."

"Talk now."

Knox raised his voice as his arm raised to indicate the door. "I don't intend to sit here all night to debate who gets a deer and who gets a sky."

"Blue Goose get Sky."

"Fine, fine. Good enough. Blue Goose gets the sky and Half Hand gets his pillow."

"Sky," the indian said softly.

An odd chance made Henry ask the question, for the thought entered his mind that the two of them were perhaps considering divers meaning. "Who is Sky?"

"Woman."

"Of course," said Henry, aware that his eyebrows suddenly lifted on their own accord, a signal that he finally understood. Blue Goose smiled at him as a patient philosopher might humor an idiot.

"Daughter of Wolf Eyes, in Canada."

"Yes, yes, now I understand. But what in the name of midnight mercy does Lieutenant Witty have to do with your transaction of the heart?"

"Child Face."

Knox took a deep breath. "Very well, what does Child Face contribute . . . give . . . to all this matter?"

"Give."

"No, I shall not give you Child Face, or anyone."

"Blue Goose kill." The Huron's voice was void of hatred now, merely even and resolute.

"If you do, I shall see you hang."

"Bad. Mean eyes."

"What are you saying?"

"Mouth on Child Face talk. Eyes in Child Face not see Blue Goose, not see Old Ax, not see God."

"You must explain."

"Child Face hurt Old Ax? Blue Goose stop. Blue Goose go Canada place and Child Face hurt Old Ax." He growled to punctuate the declaration.

"I see."

"Blue Goose take. No hurt."

"Yes, I see your concern. You are afraid . . ."

"Blue Goose afraid? Ha!"

"Hold on. You are concerned that if you go north to Canada to be with Miss Sky, then Lieutenant Witty will harm your friend."

"Arm?"

"Yes, you know . . . hurt Old Ax."

"Hatch."

"Yes," Henry held up his head with a hand, resting his elbow to his knee.

"Him no hurt Old Ax."

"No, he will not hurt Old Ax. Understand, if you will, that I view Hatch as my friend. I am his; and as a member of my command, he will warrant my protection."

"Half Hand got two eyes. No more."

Knox nodded. "Only two eyes, but I have ways to have others watch out for Mister Hatch, so . . ."

"Durable."

"Please, please . . . to look out for Durable Old-Ax Hatch and guarantee that no harm, no hurt, befalls him. Do you understand?"

Blue Goose nodded. "Do you?"

Even in the pale yellow of candlelight, Henry could tell that the face of Blue Goose was now painted with concern. In this crass world, Henry thought, how rare to discover a human being's concern for his brother. Blue Goose, heathen though you may be, methinks it is not oft I find such Christian charity. I think him a child, as his English words are few; yet, how well does my own tongue speak Huron?

"Gun."

"You want a gun? A musket?" Henry knew how quickly he would scotch this particular request.

"No want. Child Face got."

"Lieutenant Witty has a gun?"

"Cotton."

"Yes, for Lord's sake, spare me. Any name we wish to use is suitable. He had no gun when the three of you left my home in Worcester. Did he?"

"No gun. Huh! Gun now."

"A musket?"

146

Blue Goose shook his head. "Pistol."

"And you think he plans to hurt Old Face. No, what I meant to say, as the hour slips my tongue . . . he wants to hurt Old Ax?"

"Hatch."

Henry sighed, nodding his head. "Will he hurt Hatch this night, as we now sit here?"

Blue Goose shook his head. "No, not hurt Old Ax now. Blue Goose go Canada place." He nodded. "Hurt bad kill Old Ax."

"I think not."

"Soon." He raised three red fingers, slowly, as though they were stiff with cold. "Old Ax and Blue Goose and Child Face," he said slowly, "all ride horse. Two three days, then Old Ax and Blue Goose trot. Child Face cry with mean eyes. Belly cry, like old woman."

"What do you want me to do, Blue Goose?"

"Half Hand kill Child Face."

"No! Don't be daft. I do not kill people."

"You soldier."

"Yes, but it is our law. Because you dislike a man is a shabby reason to undo him."

"Good man live. Bad man die. Good law."

"It is," nodded Henry Knox, "indeed."

"Half Hand got God?"

How do I answer him? What do I tell this red man who looks at me with a blank face and whose breast is torn atwain by divers allegiances? Here a friend and there a sweetheart. Can one discuss religion at midnight with a savage? Well, why not. Many was the time, as schoolboys, we stayed up half a night asking ourselves if there was a God in Heaven. Blue Goose is a member of the Creation, and if I am to respect my own faith, then best I honor the work of His hands.

"Do I have a God? I pray that I do. And you?"

"God . . . got Blue Goose."

Henry Knox nodded gravely. Jesus asked us to love God the Father, and also our neighbors as brothers, and these teachings the

Huron manifests in practice. These, spake the Carpenter, so that two Commandments of the Ten would be fervently followed. Looking at Blue Goose, he spoke softly.

"Upon this rock . . ."

Blue Goose appeared to be puzzled.

"Something to do with my Presbyterian faith; and to be more precise, just a dialog between two men. Workingmen, as one was a carpenter and the other a fisher."

"Fish good, like deer meat."

"Quite. However, the two of us do not solve the question of Lieutenant Witty's newly acquired weaponry. Nor the purpose of its ownership. Cotton has a gun?"

Blue Goose nodded.

"Best I make you this promise. At sunup of the morrow, which I feel is nigh upon us, I will apprehend Lieutenant Cotton Mayfield Witty, question him; and be it necessary, confiscate . . . take away, his pistol."

"No gun?"

"No gun."

"No kill Hatch."

"Your friend will be safe in my care, upon my honor and word."

"Swear it."

Henry was startled by the remark. When, I wonder, shall I ever cease being surprised by this man?

"Gladly would I, but alas, we have no Holy Bible."

"Hatch say Good Book."

"Yes, that's correct."

"Swear on blood." Reaching for the sheath at his hip, the Huron quickly drew a small skinning knife, its silvery blade shiny in the hissing waxlight. And before Henry Knox could think to resist, or react, he suddenly felt a searing burn across the palm of his right hand. Openmouthed, silently in pain, he saw Blue Goose then cut his own left hand. In a trice, their fingers interlocked, knuckles up, and Knox felt the warm ooze of fresh blood betwixt their hands. The act happened too fast for Henry to utter a sound of protest, or

148

to cry out. His hand throbbed. It felt as if he had been scorched with molten metal.

Holding the big paw of Henry Knox with his left hand, the cold knife in his other, Blue Goose said one word:

"Swear."

"I so swear, upon my honor to country and to God, that I shall faithfully perform my duty, that being, to preserve and protect the life of one Andrew Angus Hatch, who is my soldier, my scout, and my friend."

Blue Goose grunted.

His heathen Amen, no doubt, Henry Knox told himself. And, I daresay, his prayers are heard and heeded as well as any white man's. Slowly he felt the lean fingers release their interlocking hold upon his own. I want to look at my hand, he thought, and bandage it. Yet my eyes cannot seem to abandon the Huron as he wipes my blood, and his, from his wet blade. At last the man sheathed his knife. And then the lean hand moved up and out until it rested on Henry's large chest.

"Half Hand . . . not half heart."

"Are you my friend, Blue Goose?"

The indian nodded one time.

"Even though you know me little, you feel confident enough to call me . . . a friend?"

"Blue Goose know."

Henry smiled. "I believe you do. You are a man of heart, of courage, of admirable loyalty. So if you call me friend, I will be. Somehow I sense that this northern wilderness of Ticonderoga holds many discoveries for me, and in my diary of this trip, you shall surely be one."

Blue Goose gave a snort.

"When do you go to Canada?"

"Soon."

"Have you told Mister Hatch that you go?"

"No."

"Yet he knows?"

Blue Goose nodded.

"Tell me about your Sky."

The young Huron said nothing. Standing, he lifted his arms slowly above his head, looking upward, as though he were about to utter benediction. Instead he said only, "Sky."

"Beautiful and far away, like the sky above us."

"Much."

"Yes, I understand you, as I feel likewise for my Lucy, my wife. Though never shall I be poet enough to describe my affections for her as eloquently as you pantomime for your Sky."

"You got wife. Soon I got."

Henry smiled. "Go to Canada."

"Sleep, then go."

"Before you go, Blue Goose, I would consider it an honor if you would accept a gift, a wedding gift for you and Sky."

Knox fumbled for the pack beneath his bunk. At last he extracted a small packet, carefully wrapped in purple velvet and tied with ribbon. Pulling a tail of the yellow bow, Henry opened the parcel and showed a small silver spoon to the Huron.

"It's a silver spoon, which I got of a smith in New York. 'Twas for a dear cousin. However, it is just one more ounce atop sixty tons that I heave homeward. Take it, as it is for a baby. A baby spoon."

"Silver."

"So it is."

"Sky happy . . . smile like day."

"Good, I am glad of it."

As gingerly as a man with a slashed palm can work, Henry Knox redid the wrapping about the tiny silver spoon, handing the restored parcel to Blue Goose.

"Carry in mouth. No drop."

I am much too weary, thought Knox, to explain to a Huron that spoons do enter mouths, yet are not necessarily transported by same. Well, if planted betwixt tooth and cheek, at least he will not misplace it.

"Blue Goose, go to bed. And thank you."

"Sleep now."

"Excellent, and I shall see you at dawn."

"You like deer?"

"Very much. Tomorrow we eat. Now we sleep."

With his strong arms, the big Bostonian almost lifted the Huron to his feet, half carrying him outside. The air, raw and mean, tried to fight its way into his bedchamber, but once again Henry Knox engaged the bolt, feeling the rusty grit of tired metal against his hand. He wrapped a clean linen handkerchief about his clotted palm, his big body fell into its bunk, and his eyes closed with no effort. Opening them, he blew out the candle.

Lucy, I miss you.

Sky of Canada is indeed a fortunate woman, for I perceive her warrior to be a man of character and worth. Well, presently she shall become Mrs. Goose or whatever it is that Huron ladies become. I must tell this to Lucy. Better yet, perhaps I best put a bung in the bottle. And then, upon the end of this war, I will undertake to write a book. Why not? Cannot a vendor of so many volumes pretend to be an author of one? Good jest. That, too, I shall record.

Let's see, how shall I entitle my work?

"Experiences En Route Through The Northern Wilderness from the Fort of Ticonderoga to the Heights Overlooking Boston Common."

Too long? Perchance too brief. Best I employ some of what General Washington nomenclatured my Presbyterian bluntness. Lucy will bear a title, as she instigates well matters of this nature.

"Adventures While Transporting Military Equipment For General George Washington, That Being Fifty-nine Pieces of Iron and Brass Artillery for the Continental Army."

Hard to say it all in a phrase. Small wonder I have read titles of prose works that seem, at first glance, to be greater in length than the material within. Henry, you knave. Here you lie, wide awake on a snowy December night and miles from home, yet all you think upon is an entitlement for a book that will, most likely, acquaint its episodes with neither ink nor paper. Tomorrow, I must write Lucy a letter so that she knows that William and I are here safe.

Dearest Lucy, I miss you very much. Indeed I do, dear wife. Your fond husband, Henry.

Puny, my pen. Yet, in times such as these, lucky I'll be to write a longer letter. Perhaps I'll dash a report to Washington, or ask General Schuyler to include mine with his. He posts a rider for messages at least once a week. I do wonder if writing reports can win a war. Certainly wage one. Never yet have I seen General Washington without his traveling desk, papers in and papers out, this to read and that to answer. Where is he this night? And lo, he must ask of my own whereabouts.

Washington is a haughty Virginian to be sure. Best I not waste my fluids thinking of General George, as now I have a younger Virginian to contend. Or to contain. Happy to say, I see our lad on the hustle, building this and packing that. If this mission fails, surely it shall not be the fault of Cotton Witty. What is his reason? Does he move at a gallop because his superiors are about to witness his industry? Possible. So be honest with thyself, Henry Knox. Do you not parade an inch taller or a degree more erect when the eye of Washington reviews? Confess it, Henry. Indeed I do. Well, my next parade is south by east, and a precious long one. I must not falter in this undertaking. Before sleep joins me, I suppose I should pray, and yet it seems unfit to beg the Almighty to help me position artillery that can explode some British lad to bits. Dear Lord, help me to splatter the entrails of some young Redcoat so he'll ne'er again see his sweet mom. Indeed, a sorry calling.

Why can't I sleep?

Damn, I must not employ temper, else I shall never drop off. Lucy chides me on this. How I desire, dear Lucy, that you were here to laugh at me, and better, to get me to laugh at myself. Sweet mountain. How I would enjoy hearing her voice whisper to my ear in the darkness, and that very brace of words.

Strange how Washington crowds his company with his fellows of Virginia, and yet he pawns young Witty to my command. Where did I put that letter concerning this boy? Small matter. What is now paramount is the boy and his gun, plus his intent; and my duty to frustrate such ambitions. Perhaps our friend Blue Goose is more concerned than the condition warrants.

My hand smarts. Damn savage! Well, one good thing to recommend the Bible. It doesn't cut your hand.

Goodnight, my Lucy.

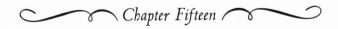

Chapter Fifteen

"She be an old gray whale."

Cotton Mayfield Witty watched the old man loading a gray cannon that appeared to be twice the length of a man's body, onto a gondola. The boat was cut from fresh pine and recently pitched, causing it to shine brightly in the December morning sun.

A dozen men lifted the cold barrel of the big gun, their faces twisted with strain. One man let loose his hold of the iron, shoving his hand quickly into his mouth in order to thaw the painful sting of frost that his bare fingertips could no longer endure. As the enormous gray barrel settled into its deck cradle, the entire raft sloshed deep into the icy water of Lake George, wetting the feet of soldiers and teamsters.

"Dang," said Durable Hatch.

Cotton saw Henry Knox remove his own gloves, handing them to the soldier whose hand seemed close to being frozen. "Here," said Knox, "take these for now. Mark me, I want them returned to my keeping at noon meal." Knox smiled. "I would disdain eating barehanded."

The soldier laughed.

I wonder, thought Cotton Witty, where Blue Goose has gone. For three days now, or perhaps four, I see no sign of that giggling gander. Perchance he hunts. The men said that he killed a spike-horn in the forest with only one arrow, delivering the deer's carcass to Colonel Knox; as if his fat Scottish arse begs for sustenance. He could endure the winter long on his own suet, the hoghead.

"Aye, the Gray Whale," he heard a man say.

"Gray Whale's a fit name for her." A second teamster pointed at the cannon. "My guess is she be eleven foot long or even twelve."

"She's our biggest," said Knox, "and General Washington shall open his eyes and wide when he sees this piece. She's a beauty, so lash her fast, my lads."

"I ain't yer lad," said Durable.

"Indeed you are not, Mister Hatch, and I ask your pardon." Knox bowed slightly.

Hatch snuffed.

The smelly old boar, thought Cotton. And yet I thank Providence that my own nose is now too stuffed to gather in a whiff of my own person, as I have washed little for over a week. What was it the old man said during our trip north? A skunk don't sniff his own hole. Hatch's clothes must be older than he; and were he to bathe, he would probably need to pry off his raiment with a fullering iron.

"All to one," came the informal command of a Yankee voice close by.

Cotton rammed his pole beneath the brass of another cannon, rolling it off the sled. With a soft puff of a sound, the gun spun into the snow. Working with two other men, also equipped with cant poles, Cotton levered the brass toward the floating edge of a gondola. As the snow was loose from the stamping of many feet, and the lakeshore earth beneath solidly frozen, the point of his pole slipped on the hard ground. Its scratch could be heard as the iron tip left its unseen scar.

He felt the pistol.

Days ago he had traded away one of his most treasured belongings, a tiny silver snuffbox, to a northern trader. The man's name was Timothy Middle and he was an Adirondack resident, not from Verdmont across the lake, nor had Cotton even once seen Middle in the company of Hatch. Was it a week ago? Cotton had seen the man cleaning a small pistol until the fruitwood of its deep red handle sparkled like a freshly shucked buckeye. I want that pistol, Cotton had said silently. Coming closer, he sat near the woodsman, tossing his silver snuffbox in the air. Let him first admire my treasure, he had thought, ere he marks how I do covet his.

Thus it happened.

"What ye got there, laddie?"

"Good day, and you may address me as Lieutenant. Just a silver snuffbox," he had said with a most noble British accent. "A gift from the King of England to my grandpapa. Upon his late passing, he to me. Care to look?"

He had handed the man the silver.

"Me oh my," Middle had said, his eyes open wide as his thick fingers took it as though it were a human heart, "ain't this a jewel to behold. And from the King, ye say. It surely be a fair thing."

"You favor it?"

"Aye," said the woodsman. "It's so prettysome."

"My prize chattel, that. 'Twould demand a rich ransom to warrant it, as there is no other like it on the face of the earth."

"Oh, I dare believe." He handed the box to Cotton.

"Priceless, and yet my own circumstances force me to . . . to trade it in, once I reach Albany. Not that I am in debt, mind you, but I must purchase a pistol to replace the very weapon that some worthless scoundrel succeeded in stealing from my bedchamber only this very day."

"A pistol stole, ye say?"

"Yes, and my! How much it resembled the very pistol that now rests in your hand. What is your name?"

"Middle, sir." The man was surely startled.

"Not assigned to this garrison, are you?"

"No, sir. I live north of here, with my woman, north toward Crown Point. My name is Timothy Middle, sir, and I am full known by the soldiers here as honest and . . ."

"Sir!"

Cotton's stern word forced Timothy Middle to remove his beaver hat with an unsteady hand. The man's head was bald, his gray hair less than a spiderweb.

"Are you a thief, Mister Middle?"

Timothy shook his head slowly, as if he were too deep in shock to utter a sound. Then he spoke in a hoarse whisper. "Not me, sir."

Cotton's hand touched the lace at his own throat. "I am Lieutenant Cotton Mayfield Witty, and I serve directly under General Washington himself . . . and were I to report this incident directly to Major General Schuyler, I am confident that satisfaction would be demanded, and received."

Middle's mouth hung open. The man was hardly a tower of wit, that was plain to observe; and a bit on his knee with those, Cotton told himself, of superior rank and station.

"Very well, I believe you to be, Mister Middle, an honest gentleman and in good standing with those in command here at Fort Ticonderoga. I shall seek no writ against you."

"Thank you, sir." Middle spoke in the voice of a man more than just modestly confused. He was empty of face.

"Instead," said Witty, "I shall even bend so far to prove my good faith by offering you a bit more. You would enjoy to own this silver box for your snuff, would you not?"

"Own it, sir. *Me?*"

"Of course. Unless there is a statute hereabouts to prevent a citizen the stewardship of possessing an item so finely crafted that it would boost him to the envy of his fellows." Cotton pretended to return the snuffbox to his waistcoat pocket.

"No, there is no such law, to my knowing."

"Here then," he tossed the box to Middle, "treat your eyes to another closer look."

Middle's hand was a bit slow, being busy with his pistol, to catch the snuffbox. It clattered to the flagstone, ringing like a tiny silver bell, as though to protest and evade the company of so crude a paw. The clumsy oaf, thought Witty. Father was correct. Never deny an opponent a chance to display himself as awkward.

"Dear, dear, dear," said Middle.

"Well," snapped the Virginian, "does the craftsmanship by the most gifted of English artisans deserve the approval of your discerning eye?"

Middle only nodded, as though speaking in the presence of such an icon would be near to blasphemy.

"Luckily for you, my dear Middle, you catch me at rather a negotiable mood. My ears have listened well to the advantages of fair trade, and I hear that Fort Ti is one of the hubs of colonial commerce. Pity you have no trinket on your person that you would offer me in return."

I am waiting, you simpleton. I do all but ram the silver up your nose as a pinch of snuff. So if you trot for a trade, what more may I do to promote same? Have I not already tossed you astride your mount and slapped its rump?

The man's face brightened. "A pistol?"

"You wish to trade me, sir, a pistol of iron and wood for a box of silver? Ah, my good Timothy, you are indeed a crafty one." Cotton shook his finger at the man as one might warn an errant child. The man smiled. Rare was the day, the boy told himself, that any one would label such a dolt as clever.

"I do, sir. Please look ye at the gun," said Middle, handing it to Witty, who delayed for a breath before accepting it.

How I wish, thought Cotton, that Father could see me execute this primitive transition, and he would indeed welcome me home to South Wind in order to assist his bargaining at the waterfront exchange. In his hand, he could see that the pistol was small, light, and thoroughly balanced, the metal married well to the polished wood. He knew that he must own this weapon. Where would he ever find another of such delicate sculpture and molding? Not to add its modest size making it easy to conceal.

"Fortune smiles upon you this day, Middle."

"How so, sir?"

"Ah, it becomes apparent that you, sirrah, long for a silver snuffbox. And I suddenly hold a pistol that so nigh resembles a weapon recently converted from me that I could almost testify that the two are one."

"Shall we trade?"

157

"Done."

"And done," said Timothy Middle. As he spat his palm, he offered his worn hand and the grip was taken and returned by Witty, who did likewise. Father should see me now, he said silently, as so oft he implored me indulge in the worldly arts of tradesmanship, that of being able to bargain amongst the most common lowly dealers as well as in the climate of gentlemen. I market well.

All this Witty remembered as he now leaned the cant pole against a nearby spruce, in order to be sure that this greatcoat, the supply sergeant at Fort Ticonderoga had issued to him upon arrival was securely fastened to hide the small weapon from all eyes. Believing my own story of theft, he laughed aside, I dare not leave my piece behind in my bedchamber. Without it, I would lose an opportunity were I suddenly alone with our Mister Hatch. The old boarhog.

Earlier in the day, he had overheard a soldier ask Durable Hatch the whereabouts of his Huron. Blue Goose, he then learned, had gone north to Canada. Hatch had snarled about a "lovesick swan," insisting that he preferred to hunt alone, and that Blue Goose held him back from running his trapline in a shorter span. Upon hearing Hatch, the boy found the professions of the old man somewhat difficult to swallow. Goodbye and good riddance seemed to rupture what he believed to be Hatch's creed. On the other hand, there was never an accounting for old age and its reverses of temper. Hatch was, to be sure, old. Yet, Witty reflected, I must take care to not underestimate the man whose endurance is tougher than hoofmeat.

Moving closer to the team of black and white oxen that had just hauled the sled up the portage from Fort Ticonderoga to Lake George, the upper water, Cotton Witty felt the heat of the massive animals that stood stock-still in the snow, like twin hearths. Touching the nearest ox, as he now did, warmed his hands. Gloves and mitts were rare. The limited pairs available were often shared by all hands. But this day was cold. He saw Henry Knox looking south, toward the head of the lake, to a Fort George over thirty miles away that they could not see. He asks the blue of the lake, Cotton thought, if it will whiten to ice ere we launched our many bateaux and rafts and gondolas with a southmost heading. He shivered. Virginia could be chilly on winter mornings, yes, but never as cold as this Ticonderoga.

A white Hell.

When will we eat?

My inwards echo with emptiness and my hunger prays loudly in an abandoned kirk. Never in my entire life have I labored so long and so hard. Work is for slaves. Best they tar me and brand me a bondservant, for all I have become. "Like you," he said softly to the ox, who turned slowly to look at him with a giant gem of a brown eye. Who was that woman in the book that Homer wrote about the ancient Greeks attacking a city called Troy? Was she not Hera, the ox-eyed queen? Strange, but as I read Homer's verse, it was my understanding that the poem described a ruler who was large of eye, like a frog; some gawking empress void of beauty. Now, thanks to this great furnace of a fellow whose flank could heat Purgatory, I examine the eye of the ox. You are comely, old boy. And so were you, Queen Hera, and I shall long remember your oxen eyes.

He thought of home that night.

Is there, he wondered, an illness so intense it could equal one who longs to return homeward to a home forbidden? Sorrow enough to be away, yet to live so far and never to return until Father passes away is sadder still; God knows I am not bereft of compassion as to wish for such a happenstance. Could my mother carry on without Father? Yes, she probably could. Mother is no weakling. How fortunate I am to sprout from such stalwart loins, to have been born a Witty and to be also the grandson of Charles Mayfield.

How dear Grandfather would have sputtered his protests at seeing me play tag in shadows with Kino, our bodies wet with summer heat and aglow with laughter. Oh, how that old gentleman would have sermonized on the subject of racial mixture. Did he actually think, season upon season, that the blacks of his own slave children softened to brown because of the Virginia weather?

Hell, no, Grandfather Mayfield . . . or rather Sir Charles, as so many addressed him. A tall man in a white suit. Even disrobed, my granddad was white still, as if his cloak of whiteness could never be stripped from his bearing.

Reaching under his corn-stuffed pillow, his hand felt the new acquired gun. Drawing it out from its haven, he held it in the small beam of winter moonlight that brightened his small quarters. Even in the dark, the red cherrywood seemed to almost burn; as anxious as he, perhaps, to be about its business. The wood was smooth and the metal cold to his touch.

"Mister Hatch," he whispered to the weapon, "this pistol I now hold in my hand shall be your undoing. So sleep well, old hillbilly, for soon you will share the sleep of ancient kings, to occupy the final fiefdom to which we all inherit."

Hush! I must still my intentions, else other ears may pass outside my window, or door, and mark me for the plotter I am. The pistol was of excellent workmanship; it rested so lightly, and yet with such resolution in his fingers. My hands are stiff with work and winter. How many cannon did we cart that uphill route this day? Did our skid make six trips or seven? I try to keep count, to hold fast to a wisp of my reason. Were men ever created by the Almighty to what we did this day? I think not, or my fingers would be the front hoof of an ox, and I should not ever again fondle a fiddle. How I long for my violin, my mare, my snuffbox of silver, and . . . The faces crowded around him.

Why do I hurt to hold so much?

And what is manhood? Is it not the wanting to fulfill a passion, or is the desire a mere dream of boyhood? Ah, and manhood the fulfillment. Boys want and men take. In Cambridge, I was introduced by Washington to John Hancock, and I stood at arms to hear one aristocrat converse to another. General Schuyler, from what I see, would surely form a trio, as he is not shy to profess his whims. Bring me this and fetch me that, like another Washington.

Apparently only aristocrats get to be generals. Then why not Hancock? And why not my father? Bolder still, I ask, why not Cotton Mayfield Witty?

I shall surely surprise a spate of men in this Continental Army before this war burns out. Even myself perchance, as well as Father and Uncle George and that great pumpkin of Massachusetts who is Henry Knox. Now I see a wee more of the map of war! I see George, Henry, John . . . all Americans, to be sure, and yet each bears the name of an English king, as does General Richard Montgomery. And even the mild brother, William Knox, has a sovereign song. William of Hastings. Daresay I have yet to hear one living soul ever say . . . King Cotton, or King Witty. Ah, but Grandfather's namesake held the scepter . . . King Charles. Oh dear. Cotton, my lad, a pity you shall not be destined for royalty or rulership.

And yet General Witty is not out of grasp.

Sir Cotton and Lady Kino. Hah! What a jest, and how the heads would turn, were I to drive up that long circular drive at the Washington manor; and at my velvet side, a black pearl in white satin. Kino is far more to me, I imagine, than Aunt Martha is to Uncle George.

"Rank!" he said aloud, with sudden inspiration.

My only chance to dominate South Wind and be master of what is rightfully due me, is to earn my return in braid; upon my shoulder as a crown sits a regal pate. My rank as an officer in General Washington's Continental Army will prove me gentleman enough to return to South Wind. Perhaps not as a general, but a captain or major or . . . dare I dream a colonel's eagle on my tunic? With rank comes reason. It's my only recourse, so best I not play the game with unsure steps.

Step one. Kill old Andrew Angus Hatch. I shall then be the one officer able to retrace the trail 'twixt Ticonderoga and Cambridge. Henry Knox knows it not, nor does his brother William, as the pair of them rode from Boston to New York and then due north. I alone know the route! I know what not even Colonel Knox is privy to; and so, gentlemen, on to Boston Town. I, Lieutenant Cotton Mayfield Witty, shall lead you and break the trail. 'Twill be I who rides ahead. I'll need Mary, and I shall recover her from De Groot's barn on the trip southward, and perhaps uncover the lissome loins of Mistress Winnie.

Now, the scene changes. Days later, or perchance weeks, who is to canter a chestnut mare to the quarters of General Washington? It will be me, gentlemen, for I shall be first to bring the glad tidings of great joy. Forward from my day as a herald in Cambridge, our gracious Uncle George will remember 'twas I who brought him the news; and even more, the cannon of Ticonderoga.

And only Hatch prevents it all.

Mister Hatch with his woodsy ways, Mister Hatch marking out the trail to be followed while Cotton Mayfield Witty grunts out his guts on the guns that wallow in snow. Think it again, Mister Hatch, for I was not weaned to wag tail to your cur, but for a far fairer fortune that you would have me dealt. Thus creeps my chance! With old Hatch out of my path, I shall advance the column.

"And a little child shall lead them," he said aloud.

Patience, dear boy. Here inside Fort Ti we are much too tight to the courts of martial justice; which in times such as these could, I so imagine, be severe and swift. No, I shall not be so frisky to dispatch our old trapper too early as to return me in irons to this garrison and its gallows. Knox would hang me, or have me shot or flogged to raw meat, and likewise would General Schuyler.

Mister Hatch, your death awaits you to the south, old troll, so beg not for my lead this night or next. Yet soon.

'Twill be I who knows, upon Durable's death, the trail to south and east. And I who calls out "De Groot" as we cut southeast to bypass Claverack. Better yet, I shall let Winnie see me at Colonel Knox's side, advising the advance, my fingertip indicating pond and parcel upon his many maps and charts.

Cotton Mayfield Witty smiled, punching his musty pillow.

Pity that I never took my revenge on Blue Goose. But what better way to even the score with that red savage than to do in the friend he so worships like some odorous oracle. A dungpile deity, his Hatch.

Envy doth surely sicken a soul. I am jealous, no doubt, of their bond of friendship; for never have I known such a luxury. True, I had Kino and Mary, but truly they were slave and mare. I chain one and bridle the other. How could we assess these unions as covenants to stand unsupported on equal footing? Alas, we cannot. Father once said that best we scrub clean the mirror of our minds and mood, lest we becloud to ourselves what we really are. Never shall I be the man I wish to be until I can back off to judge Cotton Mayfield Witty as he doth honestly be. Beware, sweet lad, that you not allow pride and ambition such a liberal tether that you see only gold braid shining upon your shoulder and close your sight to a dead old man in the snow.

Cleverness is, I dare imagine, a gift that can confound as well as comfort. See how cleverly I won the jump; bound and blindfolded go I, up and over the bars, while other young men in my company bust their buttocks in the dirt of a lane. My cleverness wins the day and loses my South Wind home.

Would I kill to regain South Wind? Yes! A question to answer in less than one breath; as one's kingdom seems, I observe among birds and beasts, to be the righteous rewards of slaughter. How well I remember Billy, our male goat, and how he stomped and killed every other male who challenged the mastery of his meadow. Like a stallion among his mares. Need I ever ask if Father himself would be a slayer to defend South Wind? Indeed he would; and before even the blink of an eye, a usurper would lie upon our land beneath a cloud of pistol smoke. And a six-foot trench in our soil would be the only South Wind feehold that any invader deserves.

Right or wrongdoing are the twin customs that seem to have well skirted my deliberations, as I donate little of my attentions to propriety. No coddled whelp is fit to be master of South Wind. Our manor is a state of grace, and warrants no less a gracious lord; someone like Father, who can chastise a slave with as much charm as he can so flatter a party guest. Few men prosper more than he, and yet he is a tribune to the keystones of character. Alas, he is as worthy as I am worthless. So it renders down to which matters the more; my manor, or the manner in which I attain its title.

As we left Virginia to ride north, I was but a boy in a white uniform. But work now smudges my whites to brown, and yet the tatters of my lace holds now a better soldier, so let the container not outdo the contained. A new uniform might be had for the asking. However, best my devotions tend to the inner warrior.

By damn, I will show all of them a Virginian, and not some dandy in a dress. With lace at my throat and my white stockings I must cut a caper in the eyes of those in Ticonderoga men who behold me, as they wear clothes less smooth than a saddle blanket. Silks and satins befit a Virginia summer far more than a Ticonderoga winter. If the weather turns more crisp than today, surely I shall expire, and my bones will snap like twigs. My industry shall well serve to mask my intentions to undo Mister Hatch. Unless the trek fells him first.

A pity, this killing business. Yet the old man stands in my path. A way of near to three hundred miles; and along that route, Hatch must meet our Maker.

Durable will die.

 *Chapter Sixteen*

"How many of you carry firearms?"

Durable Hatch did not raise his hand. The question had been asked of the men by Henry Knox, and far fewer than a quarter of the company indicated that they bore weapons. Mostly pistols, Hatch observed.

"We shall take only six muskets," said Knox, "for the purpose of killing game, as two hunters accompany us to Albany. There we shall pick up two other huntsmen."

Hatch snorted his disgust. Little chance, he was thinking, that a deer will tarry within a day's walk of us; there was a chatter to this party that seemed never to hush. If the deer are deaf 'twixt here and Holy, perhaps then we will harm his hide. Hatch spat a ball of chewed-out tobacco; it made a brown hole in the snow of the lake-shore, and steamed. Dang, it's cold! Thanks to Moses we turn south and not to Canada. I wonder if Blue Goose found the daughter of Wolf Eyes. Yep, he probable did.

"Our heavy guns first," said Knox, hands to his mouth to yell into the frosty morning. "And by the time, God willing, that all our craft reach the head of the lake where stands Fort George, I shall have dickered for sleds and oxen, along with teamsters a-plenty to man them overland. If there be a thaw, wagons await us. I now shall ask you one last question. Will this artillery reach General Washington?"

"YES!" the men roared their answer.

"Good." Knox stepped his two hundred and fifty pounds into what would be the lead boat, and Durable noticed freeboard diminish by the inches. Knox stood in the stern, tiller in hand, as four oarsmen pushed off. Hatch lifted an arm to Henry, a gesture of farewell and good fortune; and Knox waved back with his weak hand, leaving his right fist firmly on the tiller. What a ham of a man, thought Durable. Big in all ways, from what I judge of him, and a thinker. There will be supplies along the route, at least until Claverack. So he tells me.

"God keep you, William."

"And you, Henry," William Knox hollered back to his brother. "We meet at Fort George."

A gust of north wind filled the sails of the two-masted boat, thrusting it southward and causing Henry Knox to sit suddenly on the stern thwart. The men on shore laughed; and looking astern for one last time, Henry laughed with them.

"We lack not for ballast," Knox allowed. Then the boat sailed out of earshot.

"Mister Hatch."

Durable turned to Captain Woodson, a short man in a blue

uniform. A long muffler was around the man's throat, which he pulled down with the crook of a finger to let his commands steam from his mouth.

"Aye," said Hatch.

"You have no musket?"

"Never did have."

"A pistol then?" asked Woodson.

"No need, as I probable blow off the tip of my toe soon's I stuck it in my belt."

"Have you no weapon at all?"

"Yup."

"I see none."

"Got a knife to one hip and a hatchet on yonder, so's I cogitate two's a-plenty."

"Regulations say that civilians traveling in . . ."

"You an' yer regulations can stick up." Hatch made a gesture at the young officer that was not meant to be seen by ladies, children, or clergy.

"You are coming with us, are you not?"

Hatch cackled. "Hell I am! You and all the rest of them dangfaddle canoes is to go with *me.*"

"With you?"

"You heard me straight, Captain. On account if'n I don't go in front of you rest, ya probable all march straight to Kentucky and think it's Quebec."

"Were that true, Mister Hatch, you would now be already southward bound and aboard with Colonel Knox. Instead you stand in Ticonderoga snow."

"Son," said Hatch, "once we set south from Fort George . . ." Why bother? Don't he know 'twas me that Henry sent north to git stuff ready? The young pup. And it'll be I who puts Henry down again in Boston, if we ever git there. I never see such a ragtag troop. Cannon all broke down to bits so they'll not never know what piece goes with what. Sixty ton. A-plenty of iron and brass.

"Please take your place in your boat, Mister Hatch."

The young cud said please. World's coming to its end. Well, I don't guess I'll load myself in that fool contraption until I git good and dang ready. I'm so froze up, if'n a snowflake hits me, it'll slice me to twain.

"Where is your friend?" asked Woodson.

"North." Hatch nodded his head toward Canada.

"I don't refer to Blue Goose."

"He's the only friend I got."

"Small wonder," said Captain Woodson.

"Ya damn . . ."

"Where is Witty?" The wind took his voice.

"Who?" yelled Hatch.

"The lad from Virginia who came with you."

"Him?"

"He is to occupy your boat. And to remain, sir, in your custody until we all reform our column at Fort George. Colonel Knox's orders."

"I wet-nursed that miserable scamp clear up from nigh Boston, and I'll be figged if'n I tote him back," said Hatch.

Durable quickly knew he was talking to no one, as Captain Woodson had turned away in order to fill boat after boat with oarsmen. What a tomfool army this here is going to be. Look beat before they even git a bite of battle. And that Woodson's a captain? I'd soon pin a star to a mule and call her an Ass General.

Funny it be, how I miss old Blue. Here I stand in the snow, and I probable look like a dead potato to these fellows. Noise is all they make. Say one thing for Blue Goose, he weren't wordy.

"Witty!"

Hatch turned about. Captain Woodson was talking to the young Virginian, and pointing. What ya point at me for, ya lamehead?

"Mister Hatch!"

"What ye want?"

"You and Witty will go in this scow," said Woodson. "Can you work an oar?"

"I was rearranging the water in this lake before you was watering yer own cradle, ya wet-eared whelp!" (I never set foot in nothing but a canoe, but I ain't about to tell it to him.)

Fair with me, thought Durable. But I'll get into this here boat only on account's my own two feet is close to froze and Hudson's Bay can't get no colder than Ticonderoga on this day. We'll have luck to beat the ice to Fort George or close to. Somebody said it was thirty-five mile from Ti to Fort George. That's close right. Thirty-five in *July*. I don't guess I ever tripped it this near to Christmas.

"I'm freezing," Cotton Witty said. He and Hatch shared one of the seats, sitting hip to hip.

"Who ain't?" said Hatch.

"Turn yourselves about," shouted Woodson.

"What say?"

"Mister Hatch, face yourself backwards with knees to the stern."

"What'd he say?" Durable asked Cotton.

"He suggests we sit backwards," the boy said.

"With our backs to where we're going? What kind of a dang fool geegaw are we in?"

Cotton turned around, but Hatch refused to do so. He sat as he had at first, looking forward up Lake George. The dark dot in the distance was the broad back of Henry Knox. Damn that Huron! He probable took our canoe.

More men joined Hatch and Witty. Oars were brought, and yet the old man refused to ride backwards. A canoe, thought Hatch, is a fair craft compared to this gawk of a boat. At least in a canoe, a man looks forward to what he paddles to, and not backass. Well, I won't turn around. He heard grumbling.

"Mister Hatch," said a man who faced him on another bench, "as our knees knock, best you spin yourself and face the tillerman. We're to set sail, if wind catches us."

"Then set."

Oars were fitted to the oarlocks; and several of Woodson's crew pushed the scow from land. Hatch still faced his original direction, ignoring Cotton Witty. The two men that Hatch faced looked at him darkly.

"Mulehead," one man muttered.

All worked the oars, including Hatch from his reversed position, and the craft moved heavily through the deep blue water of Lake

George. Once beyond the cove, wind filled their sails, and the oars were shipped. Both sails were billowing full, which made rowing unnecessary; in a trice, the men aboard had changed their position and now all in the boat faced southward to the head of Lake George.

"Ya see?" Hatch told Witty.

The north wind blew strongly at their backs, causing the old man and Witty to sit together snugly for warmth. There was no room to stand up and move about. Hatch squinted ahead. The lead boat, bearing Colonel Henry Knox, had pulled far ahead — it was the only craft not encumbered by mortars or cannon.

"Mister Hatch?" asked Witty.

"Yup."

"When will we get to Fort George?"

Just like a tomfool kid, thought Hatch. We barely took leave of Fort Ti when this here pup starts to study on Fort George. "Thirty-five mile from now."

"By tonight perhaps."

"I don't guess so."

"Why?"

"Wind'll change. I know this lake as well as a face in pond water. She's changeable, like a woman."

"Men are changeable as well."

"Not so much," snorted Hatch.

"Are you an expert on women as well as geography?"

"All I got to say, sonny, is that a woman's geography is a whole toot more worth a study than all the froze-up geography this column fixes to cross over 'twixt here and yonder."

Cotton Witty smiled. "I agree, sir."

"Do ya now."

"Indeed." Cotton Witty shivered.

"Homesick, are ya?"

"I suppose so."

"Don't get this frosty down in Virginny, I hear."

"You heard accurately, sir."

The boy's legs were bent up high, and his arms folded across the tops of his knees. Leaning slightly forward, he rested his chin on his palm and closed his eyes.

He dreams of home, thought Hatch. "Tired, are ye?"

"I truly am."

"You worked well at Ti."

"We all did, sir."

"True enough. Rough and righteous work it be, to lug all that iron and brass up that hill from that lake to this'n. Wager all them oxen was pleasured to see the last of us."

"I wish I had one now."

"An ox? And fer what?"

"A day or two back, I warmed my hands on the flank of one big fellow."

"Hotter'n hearth."

"They truly are. My hands have not been as warm in over a week."

"All that August hay burning up inside 'em."

"Yes, I suppose."

"Your pa got oxen down to home?"

Cotton nodded. "I pay them little mind, however."

"Plow good, I well suspect."

"Yes," the boy answered, "but so do mules."

"Ox don't kick so often."

"Only at sundown," said Cotton. "Seems as though if an ox bears a grudge, he cradles it inside himself, to let it grow and build up. Then at day's end, he just releases his passions on whoever is un-witting enough to be within the swing of his horn."

"Sounds righteous."

"I wonder why."

"An ox gets tired, same as humans," said Durable. "Like me, I be ornery all day."

"And you snore ornery all night."

"I don't snore."

"Some night you must lie awake to listen."

Durable nearly laughed. This lad has a swipe of humor in his breast. And yet his eyes never sparkle the way the eyes of Blue

Goose do. Well, best I not think of the Huron. If the dang fool wants wed, ain't a soul to jaw him out of it, no less me. Let the young goose find his wings. I got me another gosling to watch out for. So be it.

"What think ye of Colonel Knox?" he asked Cotton.

"Personally, or professionally?"

"Take your pick."

"Why should I betray my opinions to you, Mister Hatch, as you could well share what I tell you in confidence."

"Sonny, if ya think me a tattler . . ."

"I do not."

Hatch said nothing. The lad be as lonely as I be. What do I say to myself? I ain't lonely. Doggone, if I didn't git along before I got teamed up with Blue, so I don't guess Andrew Angus Hatch cramps for company. To be sure, it's a fair thing to git to Boston and like places, but I can easy do without.

"As I see Colonel Knox," said Cotton, "he is able, intelligent, and, most of all, congenial."

"What's congenial?"

"Friendly, easy to be around, as are you, Mister Hatch."

"S'pose I am." Durable winked.

"Also I see our great Knox as a man able to convince other men to do his bidding. Witness, if you please, how he ordered about the bathless brutes of Ticonderoga, all of whom seem willing enough to take orders from this Boston shopkeeper."

"Your shopkeeper," said Durable, "is a giant of a gent."

"Yes, in size. My father is not a tall man and yet he is respected by neighbor and servant."

"You got slaves?"

"Many."

"Them poor black devils. If these colonies had a heart, you know what?"

"We should turnkey their irons, set them free, and boat them back to the thickets of Africa."

"And rightly," nodded Hatch.

"The blacks are property, sir, and it is unlawful for one man to

171

usurp the property of another. Covet not thy neighbor's ass."

"Seems to reason, you folks did a mite more covet than according to Scripture."

"All men do."

"Not me."

"Your traps do, Mister Hatch. Which, to my mind, marks you as much a taker as the next man."

"Sheep ain't goats."

"I beg your meaning, sir."

"One ain't the other. Just adds up wrong to my notion, for one man to claim he owns a fellow."

"Did you not own Blue Goose?"

He asks a question he already knows the answer to, Hatch told himself, but he is bent on playing games. "Reckon I did in a sense."

"And he ran away."

"Not without pay."

"I don't understand."

"Blue bought hisself back from me."

"With money?"

"Paid me his hundred pounds, that which he earned from time to . . ."

"A hundred pounds?"

"I wanted more, but old Blue bargained down his price, so I softened on the deal. You know me." Durable winked and tapped the buckskin over his heart.

"Yes, I know you, Mister Hatch."

"No ya don't. Nobody do. And I just as sooner keep it that-away."

"You and Blue Goose are friends."

"We was."

"No longer?"

"He's to Canada by now."

"His home?"

Durable nodded. "Tell me about your home."

"We call it South Wind. Our manor looks to the sun, south-ward, as do we this day."

His voice softens, thought Hatch, as he remembers his home. Dang if I recollect mine. My history is a blur, like what's up ahead. Eyes weaker than memory with ears to match.

"Our house is white, and white fences line our lanes and meadows. Flowers grow well in South Wind soil, as they seem to be, like us, well situated to its recipe. When we give a party, Mother will festoon every room with roses, freshly cut. Our front veranda is garnished by honeysuckle and jasmine. Mint and wintergreen abound. Many a cool beverage is served at South Wind that contains a sprig of mint to cheer a guest with its greenery."

"You're a poet," said Durable.

"Am I?"

Hatch nodded once, looking at the boy. "Never forget your home, or folks. Cling to their memory like woodbine to an oak, like a locket about your neck that bears a wisp of your sweetheart's hair."

"I have no sweetheart." The boy's voice was bitter.

"So here you be," said Durable.

"In the Continental Army, not knowing whether I serve Virginia or only endeavor to serve myself."

"No matter. You ever hear of Ethan Allen?"

"Yes, as he and Benedict Arnold took Fort Ti."

"Merry right. Them mortars," Durable nodded to the two brass pieces of artillery, seven hundred pounds lashed to the center of the scow's deck between the two masts, "they would still be in British hands if not for Ethan."

"So we hear, but . . ."

"Leave me finish. You think Ethan Allen done it all for the Continental Congress, or whatever it's called? Heck no. Him and his brothers stake out half of Verdmont. I know for a fact. Call themselves the Onion River Land Company, they do. You can't tell me naught of Ethan and Ira Allen and the rest that I don't already know. Bunch o' landgrabbers if you want my notion. Ethan is fixing to be a whole lot more to Verdmont than just one more Whig."

"Such as what?"

"Ethan maybe hankers a crown."

"Fie to that. One king, an ocean away, will suffice us all. And for many of us, I daresay, might be one monarch too many."

"Aye," said Durable. "So says Durable Hatch. Reason be I tell you the tale is on account we all serve ourselfs as well as Congress. The town of Boston is chock full of profits and purses, and I hear tell."

"You heard tell of what?"

"There's a spate of folk who calls themselfs Whig, and patriot, and mean-mouth all the Tories. But I know a thing or two about the horses some Verdmont folk sold to General Schuyler, and some piety Yorkers as well. Patriot go hang. The price smelled a durn sight more of profit."

"I well imagine."

"So do your darndest for your own cause. Just so's no one else is too wise to your aim, or creeps up behind you and sights along your barrel to see what you're to cut down on."

"You convince me, Mister Hatch."

"To do what?"

"To do what I must so as to earn back my home in Virginia. One act, a single deed, and my road is downhill. The trail of my ambition runs across the lawn, climbs the steps, and ends at the front door of South Wind."

Hatch nodded. In comrade fashion, he placed an arm on the shoulder of Cotton Witty to give him a friendly shake of encouragement. The boy smiled at him.

Except for the eyes.

Chapter Seventeen

Cotton Mayfield Witty heard a sharp impact, hard and cold, a new noise to his ears. Objects cracking one against another.

"What is that?" he asked Durable Hatch. Or was the old man too deaf to have noticed? Hatch's face had hardened in the last day or two until his expression had become a portrait of northern winter. But now the old face brightened.

"That," said Durable, "be sport."

"Sport? In this frozen Hell, what sport could possibly be enjoyed, other than expiring from cold?"

"You'll see," said the old man, snuffling a drop of winter back into his crimson nose. He wiped his upper lip with a woollen mitten of blue yarn that was frosted with clean white snow. "Come on, lad, and we'll have ourselfs a look-see."

For two days they had been camped at Fort George, several miles north of Glens Falls, waiting for Knox. Henry had retraced his journey northward to look for his brother, William Knox, whose giant scow had foundered and sunk. Or so the message to Henry had read, a message that Knox had shared with several of the men. Snow had come, and sleds were ready with oxen and horses and teamsters carrying long goads and whips. All was ready for the overland trip southward, except for the substantial presences of the brothers Knox.

"Downhill, boy," hollered Hatch on the run. "There's a pond that's froze early and I ain't even yet seed water that'll run uphill. Maybe it do in Virginny, as from what I see of down there, they got it all strange."

Ahead of him, Witty could hear the heavy wheezing of the trapper's breathing, and he watched the feathers of vapor that Hatch expelled into the morning air. Wine or woman? What else could attract the old coot?

Again he heard a *clunk,* closer now. Hatch stopped his sprint to lean his shoulder on the gray shaggy bark of a hickory. Cotton overtook him, leaning likewise on the hickory's yonder side. Following Hatch's blue mitten, he saw five, no, six men on the smooth ice of a small pond. The ice was young and clear as the finest window in South Wind. Two of the men held brooms, the handles of which were short and with bristles as yellow as cornstalk. More than a dozen rocks the size of a pumpkin speckled a circle drawn up the ice. What appeared to be a woman in a short plaid skirt, with diamond stockings from the knee down, swept the ice in the stone's path with a short broom. Never had Cotton seen such vigorous sweeping. The rock resembled a large teakettle.

"Is this insanity?" asked Cotton.

"Same thing as, but 'tis a game to a Scot."

"And what game?"

"*Curling,*" said Hatch, as though the one word that passed from his lips demanded to be voiced in reverence. "Come on, lad. You're in for a sport of a time."

Bounding through the snow, Hatch yelled to the six persons on the ice. As the two neared the players, Cotton noticed that more than one filled a skirt of bright plaid. Nearly all did. Yet some of the women wore beards. When they hollered to a stone as it slowed its slide to rest in the ring along with other rocks, their voices were of men — men talking to the stone. And indeed there was not a woman among them.

"What is that?" asked Cotton.

"A stone."

"Why did I ask?" Wider than high, the stone was belted with a twine from which four straps rose to the wooden handle on top.

"Aye, a stone is its name, laddie, for a rock it be. Granite turns the sweetest curl, so say I. Some favor marble."

"Curling?"

Hatch ventured out on the pond, where four players stood about the ring. The other two were a long throw away, coming on the run along the ice.

"You got but six," panted Durable to the players, "so the lad and I, if you're willing, will fill the sides."

Fill the sides? Aha! thought Cotton Witty. He wants me to join one trio; and himself, their opposition. Curling? Some old Verdmont pastime, I wager, to replace the deadly sin of bowling.

"Welcome." A bearded man in a skirt held out his hand. Hatch took it. The man's whiskers were red as fire, his face wet with sweat, and ice sparkled his beard and hair. On his head he wore a woollen hat; in design, like what a Frenchman in Virginia had called a beret.

"You like me hat?" the man asked Cotton.

"A beret, sir?"

The man scowled. "Nay, young sir, not that but a *tam*. A tam-o-shanter it be." He turned to Durable. "Do I know ye?"

"My name's Hatch."

"Mine is Cam Ferguson."

"I am Cotton Witty, sir."

"Are ye now?" The redbearded Ferguson was bareheaded, and Cotton pulled off his mitt to feel the almost painful crunch of Cam Ferguson's handclasp.

"Curlers, are ye?"

"He ain't," said Durable, "but he's a will to learn."

"Every man's a curler in his heart."

"And every woman," laughed a shorter man with a red cherry of a nose, who offered his hand. "I am Donald MacHugh, and if our team is to trounce Ferguson's four, let's be aboot it."

"Aye," said Hatch. "Who curls?"

"Why not you, Mister Hatch?"

At his feet, Cotton counted the stones. Fifteen or sixteen, as near as could be tallied up. Eight with tufts of red yarn on their handles. Eight with blue.

177

"How much do they weigh?" he asked.

"Forty-two pound, and oft a grunt more," said Ferguson. "We'll start afresh, lad, and you can lead off."

"Lead off?"

"Throw the first rock. Go with Hatch and he will lead for the other rink."

"How many ends?" asked Durable.

"Twelve," said Ferguson, and then to Cotton he said, "Meaning all sixteen stone come to and go fro six time. Twelve ends."

"Stay here, lad," said Durable as the two captains walked down to a second circle down the ice. "He's my skip, and he'll point his broom to call the shot he begs me make. Ya want red or blue? We'll take blue."

"Red," said Witty, with a resigned shrug.

"Done, lad," said Hatch, "and I'll throw the first." He spat on his right hand. His left held a broom, which he chose to ignore. "Now, then, watch me, lad. Watch careful. I aim to spin the stone so it nigh curls her path like a fishhook."

"I am fascinated," said Cotton. And truly he was.

"Aye, for it be the sport of all sports, a Scotsman's curl. See how my right foot nests in this wee pocket that was cut in the ice? 'Tis called a hack. Hold now. I see the call of my skip down yonder, and a rock in front of the house he wants."

"House?"

"The circle, that's the house."

Pulling the blue-tufted stone behind him, for a backswing, Hatch suddenly thrust it forward, gliding smoothly on his left foot. His right foot trailed behind him as he balanced his gliding body with the broom. He released the stone to go its way. The two men who trotted on either side of the moving rock held brooms, but did not sweep. Then the stone began to slow and curl to the right.

"Sweep!" yelled MacHugh.

As if suddenly commanded to act by God, the two sweepers attacked the path of the moving stone, their brooms whacking the ice with determination. "Why do they sweep?" asked Cotton. The ice looked clear and clean.

178

"Sweep, ya lazy lunks. Sweep for a biter," yelled Hatch, trying to run down the ice so his broom could add to their industry. Donald MacHugh, who had stood in the center of the circle to mark the call, ran forward to be a third sweeper, or a fourth.

"Your rock will stop short, Mister Hatch," said Cotton.

"Sweep, ya blasters," hollered Hatch.

Much to Cotton's surprise, even though the stone had slowed, the slap of three brooms before seemed to pull the heavy rock closer to the circle's near edge, as if to nibble the circumference.

"Up," yelled the red-haired Donald MacHugh, lifting his own broom in the air. The other two sweepers also stopped, yet stayed with the stone as if to nurse its retard. "Not deep. I just want a biter." The stone stopped.

"Did we get a piece of it?" yelled Hatch.

"A wee short," MacHugh answered, "but I rather be out front than deep for a first rock."

"Your turn," Durable told Cotton.

How do I do it? That was the question Witty wished to ask, but as he had seen the delivering of the blue stone by Durable, he selected a red rock. As he waited in the hack, Cam Ferguson, at the other end of the sheet of ice, tapped Hatch's stone.

"Take 'er oot!" he hollered, placing his broom a yard to the left. I understand, Cotton told himself; the gap accounts for the curling finish.

"Does it matter which way I spin it?"

"Aye," said Hatch. "You skip calls for an in-turn, so spin your stone like a clock. Not hard. Two spins is a-plenty 'twixt here and there to curl a rock. Now then, don't look at your own rock, but keep an eye on your skip's broom."

"Like a pistol shot from one's hip?"

"True enough, lad. Easy on the comeback, now forward and slide, keep your right arm stiff as a poker and let it swing."

As he released the handle, Cotton gave it a slight twist. The rock shot forward on the ice, turning clockwise as Hatch had hinted, heading for the broom of the one named Ferguson. As it slowed, surely enough it curled closer and closer to Hatch's blue rock. Yet

179

not so far to the right as to bump it. The two sweepers did not sweep.

"You're wide," muttered Durable. "Or he gave you a bit too much ice to make the shot."

"Let 'er curl," yelled Ferguson, his red whiskers touching the ice as he had lowered his body prone to receive his first rock. Cotton saw his stone glide by Hatch's and curl sharply behind it as the red rock neared the center of the circle. "Sit," Ferguson said to the stone, "sit right there." As the rock came to rest, Ferguson and his two sweepers held their brooms high in the air. "Bonnie rock, lad."

"Bump it up," yelled MacHugh.

"What does he ask you to do?"

"Promote," said Hatch, already in the hack. Carefully he wiped off the concave bottom of a blue stone with the blue mitten on his left hand. His delivery hand was bare. "Donald asks me knock my first rock up into your bit of luck."

"A demanding shot."

"Maybe for some," snorted Hatch, releasing his second stone. "Dang it, I'm narrow as a Boston Baptist. Sweep! Sweep!" His suggestion was echoed by an order from Donald MacHugh, and the sweepers vigorously whacked the ice before the stone. "All the way!" hollered Hatch.

"Sweep hard! Sweep hard!" yelled MacHugh, "and we'll get a piece of her."

Hatch was down, his belly on the ice, yelling encouragement to the two sweepers, who swept as though required to clean Hell for the Devil. "Narrow," said Hatch, as his second rock chipped his first to one side. But then the old man smiled, as Cotton's excellent shot was now exposed for a take-out. "Hah! The blanket's off the babe."

"Guard," yelled Cam Ferguson, his broom tapping the ice before the house. "Play short and we'll cover the kist."

"We'll bring her home," said the second sweeper, "so don't hurl too heavy a rock. You lay it, lad, and we'll hatch it."

Cotton then delivered it easily. They swept hard, polishing the ice to such a gleam that his rock almost sailed into the desired position. Taking a final kick, however, the stone curled sharply as it died, leaving the shot-rock partly in view.

"Now we sweep," said Hatch, "while our seconds and thirds throw two rocks each."

"Do you and I sweep as a team?"

"No, ya loon. We be on enemy rinks."

"I see."

The next curler tried to make the take-out shot, but his aim was wide and his weight too fast to allow the stone to curl on target. The other second was short. Stone after stone, the house grew rife with granite, until both skips walked to the starting end, each to curl two rocks. Donald MacHugh threw a blue, Cam Ferguson a red; then Donald his second, which was the final rock for the blues. Three blue stones nestled close to what one of the skips had called "the button," the exact center of the circular house.

"Good we got last rock," said Ferguson, his right foot in the hack, aiming at the broom of his third at the far end. Cotton held a broom and was more than ready to sweep.

"What's your plan, sir? To blast our red stone hard against the trio of blues, or to nestle in among them?"

"Aye," said Cam, "the latter. Curling's a light touch."

At the back of Cam Ferguson stood Donald MacHugh, hands behind him, his broom horizontally resting across his spine in the crook of his arms; his pipe lofting up wisps of satisfied smoke. His three blue rocks were all "counters," as a red rock lay only fourth closest to the button.

"I'd fancy to break up your threesome, Donald."

"A devout wish, Campbell, so blast away."

"Aye, ye'd like that? Well, not me, MacHugh, as this rock's a shy birdie that floats on a breeze to her homing."

"Hah! Then shoot, Mister Ferguson, or do ye count a hoose o' just fifteen stone?"

"It'll count but one, Donald, and it be this sweet little lassie that is about to bid farewell to my lovin' and gifted hand."

"Much ye say, and little ye curl."

"Little, ye say? I'll show ya wee little."

"Then show us, Campbell."

"Aye, I will. To rest this bonnie pebble of red into a nest of blues as though your rink, MacHugh, did naught but gather a chamber to lay me head."

Smoke spurted from MacHugh's pipe, and his nose looked redder than ever. "Deliver, ye Campbell Ferguson, and then we'll walk doon together to count up all my bluebells. That is, if your brain can add up to three."

"Hah!"

Back came the last red rock, its handle lightly held in the bare fingers of Cam Ferguson. Then he paused to look back once more at Donald MacHugh. "Wager?"

"Aye, any stake your musty purse could cough up."

"I'll bet," hollered Durable Hatch, "I'll bet the siller in my poke."

So these men are Scots, mused Lieutenant Cotton Mayfield Witty of Virginia. Father once said that the Scottish were an argumentative tribe, as unwashed as they are uncivil, and what better proof than this present company of curlers. Yet beneath the curse of one curler to another I do detect a comradeship. Upon each other's ears, how they crack, as do their curling stones; but there's a brotherhood among them to overcome their oaths.

Finally the wager between Donald MacHugh and Campbell Ferguson was complete, with a side bet executed by one Douglas Houston versus one Andrew Angus Hatch.

Once again, the red rock pulled back and then shot forward. "Sweep!" yelled Cam. "Sweep the Satan off 'er. Damn, I'm too light. Sweep it! All the way! Backing to boot I had, and like a boob I throw light."

"Like a boob," said Donald.

Never, thought Cotton Witty, have my hands ever held a broom. Certainly, not to sweep the many floors of South Wind; yet here I am, my back bent and at a trot, polishing ice in order that a hunk of Verdmont granite slides a foot farther on a Yorker's pond. One must be half insane to be a curler, and totally daft for a sweeper.

They were met halfway by Ferguson's vice-skip, who added a

third broom. Try as he would, Cotton could not raise the clatter with the corn of his broom like his two Scottish rinkmates. How old Aunt Martha would lift her eyebrows to witness such frenzy by males for a household duty. One look would warn her of the collapse of all our reasons.

"Sweep!" yelped Cam Ferguson, running down the ice after his stone. "Beat the mule! All the way, hard, hard!"

At his back, Cotton heard the mutterings of Mister Hatch, though he was unable to perceive his precise words through the slap-slap-slap of the three brooms. Though the red-tufted stone slid slower and slower, it somehow seemed to continue its float, closer and closer to the desired house.

"Now! Now!" he heard. Footsteps were coming, hobnail boots on the ice. Men yelled and hollered and swore at a rock. If the rock heard, it seemed to care little for the eight opinions, most of which were Scottish and voiced without reluctance. The stone stopped, but not before it came in to the button and wicked on two of the blues. A hole had been pounded into the ice at the exact center of the house, as if punched by a nail. To compass the circle, thought Witty. I am amazed such worldly facets of figuring geometrics are known among these aging Highland savages.

"Aye," breathed a breathless Scot.

"It's shot."

"Pig's ass it be."

All eight men crowded around the button to eye-measure for themselves to determine who won the end. Eight men, and a goodly share of sixteen curling stones, all on one area of new ice. There was a sudden noise.

CRACK!

"The ice," yelled Cam Ferguson.

"God no, not until we count the end."

CRACK-CRACK!

"Save the stones."

"Quick, the rocks are . . ."

All eight men jumped at once, which seemed to much for the thin ice to support. There were cries of help, brooms flew high, and

183

water rushed over the feet, up the body and over the face of Cotton Witty. Back home in Virginia he had been a swimmer; only in summer, and once on a dare in late April. But this was Adirondack water, in December, which stopped his heart, his breath, his mind . . . all in one rushing, merciless moment. He felt beaten by the icy whip of death, as his clothes filled with cold, his body on fire. Inside his chest, his heart swelled as though intent on a burst of its own.

"Help!"

The voice was weak, sputtering below water and trembling with cold. Yet he knew it was Durable Hatch. Turning his head, Cotton saw the old man's face go under, but not before he saw the wide eyes and the mouth frozen open into a toothless scream. Why? Why does my hand surge forward, and why do my fingers close on the dirty deerhide of his collar? He reaches for me. Let him drown. Suddenly the old arms were around his neck, forcing both of them to sink deeper into the black cold. Death sucked at his boots from somewhere in the dark depths of the pond. Even underwater, he could hear the choking cry of Durable Hatch, utter a watersoaked wail that only a drowning man can utter.

Save him? Why should I?

How easily I could push his white head deeper, holding him under with his face betwixt my knees. Second by second, I would feel the desperate twists of his body grow weaker, until the last kick, at which time I would loosen my legs and their headhold, allowing his old body to sink slowly into the black below. Hold him under! Now! Will I ever get a chance like this again?

Just free yourself of him, Cotton told himself, and let him drown as you save yourself. Air! God, let me breathe, for I cannot. Escape his grasp or he will drown you, now, this very moment. My boots fill and weigh a ton. Other men at his side were kicking, fighting the suck of black water that tugged on them, pulling them down. Always down. I am lead, he thought. A froze stone of death that cannot swim through the fire of this ice. Up, please God, raise me up to the light of air above me, beyond me and above the reach of my hand. Release me, Hatch, you old fool. Turn me free or we shall both drown. South Wind? Kino? Father? Help me, God. Please!

Somehow his boots touched something solid, deep in the water. Sinking more to bend his knees, he then called upon the drive of young muscle, as the thrust of his thighs sent him upward. His face, and the old man's, broke the surface. Air!

"Hang on!" he somehow said to Hatch.

Not now. Hatch was still useful. No, not yet. I must wait for the time for him to die. Turning the old man around, he kicked toward the edge of ice, his fingers closing on it with a numb grasp.

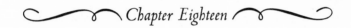 *Chapter Eighteen*

"Mister Hatch?"

"Ho!"

"It is I, Henry Knox."

"How come *you* be up and about so bung-busted early?"

"I could not sleep, sir."

To the east, the gray New Year's Day morning seemed to spy on the black of a January night. Both men looked at the ice of the river, still white in moonlight, and Henry Knox wondered if they were both about to ask one another the identical question.

"Last night was cold a-plenty," said Knox. "But the question remains, is the ice of the river thick enough to hold oxen pulling iron?"

"We'll know," snorted Hatch, "when the iron falls through and pulls them poor unfortunate beasts down to a death."

Knox shuddered. "A cold thought, Durable."

"Aye, a death I cannot abide. No death's easy. But to die with iron pulling you under the cold water is no death for me."

"Nor me. I learn that you near wound up in a like manner."
Knox placed a big hand on the old man's bony shoulder.

"Who said?"

"Alarm not. Am I not myself of Scots blood, sir? So I too appreciate the ritual of curling."

Hatch coughed. "Damn near died of it."

"As your sporting occurred during my sojourn north to rescue my brother William from his own dunking, I hold no grudge. This excursion is not to be without breathers of adventure, else we be not human."

"Come close to be my last breather."

"And 'twas young Witty that fished you out, according to the report I received, not directly, from Campbell Ferguson and Donald Mac-Somebody."

"MacHugh."

"Yes. They tell you all took a bitter bath, stones and kilts and all."

"Worst of all, we lost the rocks."

Knox laughed. "Methinks the thickness of ice was a problem, there as it be here."

"Well, if cold's a measure . . ."

"Quite so. I am so chilly I'll never thaw out. But I prayed for cold, to thicken the Mohawk. Where are we, Mister Hatch? Whereabouts on the river, I mean."

"Half Moon, or near to."

"My map shows no such place as Half Moon."

"Ain't much of a place. Soon we cross this here Mohawk River, we'll be only a half-score miles north of Orange."

"You mean Albany. That much I know."

"If I'd a meant Albany I'd a spoke it straight out," snarled Hatch.

Knox sighed, taking a long look at the silent stretch of ice that lay between Half Moon and Boston. "Well, if we're to issue General Washington his iron, cross we must. Even if we swim it," he said to Hatch.

"Not me."

"One baptismal sufficed?"

"I don't swim so good."

"Do you swim at all?" asked Knox.

"Nary a stroke. The lad spooned me out like a turnip in porridge. Yet I admit . . ." Hatch paused.

"What do you admit, sir?"

Hatch shook his own head, as if to rid his mind of a thought in order to swap it with a fresher opinion. "I sure had a hanker."

"To do what?"

"Tickle that whelp with leather, that there Cotton Witty."

"Would you now?"

"Not stoutly. Just a smart lick or two."

"Fond of him, are you?"

"Me? I ain't *fond* of nobody." Durable spat.

"I understand, sir."

"So do I. Not all. At times I cogitate that I don't begin to understand one doggone blessed blooming thing. And I'm a damn fool to trust that corn-hair cub, and so are you."

Henry remembered his midnight talk with Blue Goose about a pistol. I have so much on my mind. Sixty tons of iron. "Well, if we get only trouble from our young Virginian, he shall go the remainder of the trek in irons. That's a vow."

"No need to bracelet the boy."

"If necessary, I surely shall."

"Ain't right. He's a whelp. Young and a tomfool, like all kids, so I don't hold with making him spit out all his spunk. I done that once, long ago."

"Did what?"

"I gelded a proud young colt and hoped he'd be a filly. Fool I be. So now I say don't cut him. Let our lad open up his lungs and beller a bit. He worked a-plenty at Ti."

"Did he?" Knox already knew that Cotton Witty had performed well. To hear it substantiated would be further comfort. "Did he, now?"

"Aye, he righteous did. He'd tally up this and set up that. Kept all them records, just like you told him to mind, a regular quartermaster. Lug and tug, too, same as us rest."

"You like him."

"Didn't say so, did I?"

"No, good sir, you did not."

"Then, sir, leave it that I just don't hate him so much."

"Aristocrats are a rare breed, Mister Hatch."

Hatch looked strangely at Henry, and the big man wondered what the old trapper was about to say. Removing his beaver hat, the old hand chased the bite of what Knox imagined could well have been a louse. "Don't do it, Henry."

"Do what?"

"Ya can't question yer salt this far along the trail. Either the iron gits to General Washington or it rusts here on the Mohawk. Or in it. Maybe it be important to travel it all to Boston. Maybe it ain't. All I know is one thing."

"Sir?"

"It matters to me."

"So," said Knox, "let's be about our business."

Black water, thought Henry Knox. Not a cozy image of what is now only inches beneath my boots. Considering my bulk, I should rightly float like a gob of tallow. Well, perhaps we will see ere this day ends. We shall cross, by damn. If I have to smash the ice and swim over with a cannon in my teeth, like a water dog retrieving a tossed stick. And what moves my heart is that many a soldier would swim at my side.

Two hours later, the day had come, cloudy and colder and with flurries of snow in the air. Knox mounted his husky seventeen-hand gelding, feeling more than the wind on his back. Scores of teamsters, and soldiers, watched him guide the brown horse down to the icy edge. Without constant urging from the heels of Henry's boots, and soft words of encouragement, the animal would not have set hoof upon the ice. Step by step, Knox advanced. The steel shoes of this mount sound hollow and lonely, he thought, looking at the ice beneath them. God, if those men knew how afraid I am. But they shall never know. Shall I pray?

God get me there; Amen, and now let me think of Lucy, for

some night soon I shall lie abed with her, touching her, telling only my wife about this moment. My hands are soaking wet inside my gloves. Between the grip of his thighs, he felt the gelding tremble.

"Steady, old bean. We are halfway across," said Knox, "so let's show our companions our courage, shall we? Let us be a worthy model, old boy. So press on, we must. But, I pray you, do walk as lightly as you dare."

His horse stopped.

Knox slammed his boots back and into his hind legs; not with cruelty, yet with the dedication of destiny. The big animal grunted, then snorted. Tossing his head, he lifted his right foreleg, and with his hoof he rapped the white ice three times. The sound produced hit the ear of Henry Knox somewhat like to a spike into timber.

"Come on," Knox kicked again.

This time the big beast responded, and Knox's right hand patted the horse on the neck as a reward. No turning back, he thought. Not for ice, nor snow, nor biting wind. Naught shall stay us from reaching our Virginian, and soon cannon and Cambridge shall be one, Lord willing. God Almighty is no doubt more willing than my mount, whose hoof hesitates before each step. But we will cross, old fellow, you and I, as there is too much English in you and too much Scottish Presbyterian in me to allow either one of us to falter.

"We're not quitters, are we?"

As he spoke, softly, the horse seemed to understand, quickening his walk for a step or two, as if anxious to reach the white bank that was still more than the throw of a stone before them. If, thought Knox, I continue my chatter, the horse will heed me and I can thus help to relieve his mind from all the apprehensions that, I must confess, now plague mine.

"Good boy, good animal. Back at Glens Falls the farmer who lent you to me neglected to tell me your name. Well, as we brave this ice as one, best we be properly introduced. I am Henry Knox; and right now, your rider is as frightened as he is fat. A pair of big animals, you and I. So we shall show them, the ones ashore who watch our backs from behind us, those whose boots and hooves stand in snow, yet over solid earth. In spite of themselves and their own sweet reason, they shall champion the twain of us. Shout our names, by George."

Knox coughed, as a sudden cold wind whipped against his throat, fluttering the eyelids of his horse.

"You must have a name, boy. Alas, you cannot relate it to me. That's it, a few more paces. As I am an acting lieutenant colonel, it be only fair that I outrank you, don't you agree? Thus I shall bestow upon you the name of Major, as you carry us both proudly. Major, it is."

Closer, within a stone's throw now, the white bank rose up steeply from its shoreline, yet a more welcome sight Henry Knox could not recall having seen. Closer, closer, until the horse stopped, his legs locked. No amount of kicks could press him forward.

"Let's go, Major."

Behind him, Henry could hear the swell of male voices, the mutterings and comments of why the horse had stopped dead, refusing to move. God, I am hot. Knox removed his gloves, noticing the steam rise as his perspiring hands met the cold air. Then, as his hand patted Major's neck, his fingers felt the lather that had almost instantly frosted the animal's brown coat.

"You are foamy," said Knox. "Why?"

As the ice gave way beneath Major's hoofs, Henry Knox heard a cracking noise; not loud, but more of a soft shatter of the sheet that was muffled by the sudden rush of water. Wet cold closed over Henry's face. He had not been aware of falling, so suddenly had both horse and rider dropped. Beside him, Major kicked the black water. Knox felt as a man might feel who had just slipped and fallen into a great mill of thrashing gears and grindwheels. Then as Henry Knox reached upward, a hard object whipped into his face. And then again. Without thought, his hands went to it. Feeling it at last in the grip of his good hand, Knox identified it as a saddle stirrup. His fist clutched it; and as it did so, his ears heard the sound of iron on rock. Somehow, the gelding's hind hooves were kicking a rock, propelling both horse and rider upward.

The lunge of Major's body nearly tore the stirrup from Henry's right hand. He prayed he could hang on. Kick, boy, kick! Even though you kick me, his brain was yelling, drive those beefy hindquarters of yours into riverbed rock. Ice around them was smashing and splintering, as a sharp edge slashed his face. He felt the sting of it. He tasted blood.

Like two angry crabs, horse and rider scrambled through the smashing ice. And though the rip of the current hauled at them, they broke and cracked their way forward, toward the steep bank, in one last effort to reach shore.

Knox knew he had made it when he heard the roar of his men from the opposite bank. Snorting, the gelding stood hock-deep in the snow, shaking his shiny body to be free from the wet of winter. Henry Knox tried to stand on his own; yet his scarlet hand seemed not to relinquish its grip on the stirrup.

"Dear Lord," Henry said aloud, "can a human being be this cold and not be dead?"

The cheering did not stop. Puffs of smoke sprouted from the mass of men. A breath later, the puffs were followed by the sounds of the muskets.

Henry smiled, forcing his arm up to wave.

Across the river, on the Half Moon side, one of the soldiers was playing a fife. Durable Hatch! How unlikely a musician, he thought, and yet the old man forever surprises me with his divers talents.

"Come on, Major. Prance for our lads over yonder."

Amazingly, as though the brown gelding understood the words of Henry Knox, the big animal bounded to and fro through the snow. Knox waxed his hat, causing a cheer once more from his soldiers and teamsters.

"By damn, Major . . . by damn!"

Knox felt his eyes water, as he waved to the far shore. He could see Hatch, directing some of the lads to bring axes and sledges, cracking the ice to flood the surface so it would quickly thicken in the cold. It would freeze soon, the surface water. Other men were dipping buckets into airholes, lifting them up abrim, to dump water atop the ice. That is it, Knox cheered to himself. We'll help the

Almighty to widen his winter and fatten the ice by our own doing.

"Major" — he stroked the wet neck — "we crossed the Mohawk."

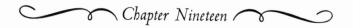 Chapter Nineteen

Cotton Mayfield Witty threw his arms around her neck, his body against her, to be as close to her as he could become.

"God . . . God . . . ," he said; not in blasphemy, but rather in a release of fervent gratitude too powerful to confine. Oh, he thought, I am so very happy for this moment. The velvet of her lips sought his face, nibbling his ear, causing Cotton to grin. Breathing in, he smelled her great warm smell, blending with the flavorful fragrance of Jan De Groot's barn.

"Mary . . . Mary, my own."

Closing his eyes, he rested his face against the warmth of her neck, his fingers locked into her silky mane that was as sorrel as his own corny hair. Holding the long strands in his lean fingers, as though to strum the strings of a golden harp, he kissed each lock as though every caress would bring him nearer to South Wind. She snorted, tossing her head.

"And I missed you, too, fair and gentle lady. You are all, Mary. The only remembrance of home. I have only you."

His eyes filled, and he wiped them on the rough sleeve of his blue greatcoat. His white uniform reeked of sweat and fatigue. Yet now he smelled Mary, his mare. Forgive me, Mary. You should be home in Virginia, rolling on a green South Wind meadow, or cantering fast and free.

Pulling back his head, Cotton Mayfield Witty looked at her. "Mary, were I to tell you about Fort Ticonderoga and the snow and ice and brass and iron, and the scores of winter miles 'twixt there and this, surely your ears would twitch in disbelief. Are you hungry? Has old Herr De Groot fed you oats? Well he should, as we fight his war for him, dear mare."

Slowly he moved beneath, lifting up each of her hooves, to assure himself that she was sound. Her hooves were cold and dry, and each ring of iron still married well. Although worn, her shoes need not be reset. Not until Cambridge; and then, fresh ones.

"I promise you, sweet Mary, no farrower shall ever pound cold iron to your foot. Never, my lady. Always shall the steel be hammered hot to your hoof."

Nickering, she gently tossed her head, as though she understood his lengthy discourse on the proper footwear for a palfrey. Once more her soft muzzle found Witty's cheek, and he let the nose search his face and neck and hair, closing his eyes in the comforting contentment, inhaling her nearness, while his heart pounded for home.

"Cotton?"

Without turning, he knew who spoke his name. As no other, not even Kino, had a voice such as hers. Still, he did not turn around. Not yet.

"Please . . . say it again," he asked.

"Cotton Mayfield Witty."

Eyes still closed, he wanted to take heart. But the warmth of touching Mary, and hearing someone (who perhaps cared a fig whether he lived or died) speak his name was almost as much joy as he could bear. Mary and Winnie, all on this one day. Now I have a horse to love and a pretty maid to laugh with, and how I long to be man enough to deserve at least one of the two.

"You tremble, Cotton." He felt her light hand touch the shoulder of his heavy overcoat. And thus, without turning to face her, he let the sobs and cold and days of lashing exhausted oxen through waist-deep snow melt from his eyes.

"You are safe," she whispered.

Her voice seemed strong, and he knew he was yet too brittle to tell her about the trek south fom Ticonderoga, over one hundred miles. A wade through winter that no man and no beast was created to endure; and yet, endure it they did, often straining on the thongs and leather traces and chains along with the steaming animals, to yank a cannon a yard closer to Boston. One frozen yard, buried in snow, unknown and forgotten and useless, up north in some roadless and untracked wilderness.

"Winnie . . . ," he wept.

"Your hands. They are purple and they crack and peel. Before, your hands were . . ."

As virginal as I, he thought. "Unworked," he said.

"You have no servants now. No hands but your own."

"No. I have nothing, Winnie. I am so cold. So near death that if your good papa comes again with his pitchfork to discover us in his barn, there is little left for him to destroy."

"He will not undo you."

"You know this?"

"Hold me," she told him. "Or shall I hold you?"

Turning around, he was rewarded by her strong face and flaxen braids from beneath a white and starchy cap. And as he spun, her belly pressed forward against his; she was plump and firm and ripe.

"I am going to cry," he said.

"Cry then."

Cotton wept, releasing it all to her, his entire body freeing so many secrets from out of his bosom and into hers. Not to have her, but to hold her. Isn't that what the minister said, the big barrel-chested clergyman who performed the ceremony when Rodney Carstair wed Jessica Harding? To have and to hold? Perhaps the holding was as sweet, or sweeter.

"You are changed, I think," Winnie said, "and grown."

"I am foul with lack of soap and water. My mouth reeks, as I have no tincture to sweeten my breath. All I bring you is a soldier's stench and the constitution of a corpse."

"You are thinner."

"Winter thin, my father would say."

"And I am more roly-poly?"

"Not more."

194

"And not less," she laughed.

"No, certainly not less. If the Garden of Eden held an autumn harvest, to glean the red ripeness of all once green and growing, it would be you, my Winnie."

She hugged him. "My poetic pup."

"Are not the courting swains here poetic?"

"Not the Dutch. We are painters, perchance, yet not poets nor performers of the dance. Can you see my papa step to a minuet?"

"Were I not so cold and dirty and homesick, I would laugh."

"Then come home. For we are a home and a family, even though we are only a farm."

Only a farm, he thought. Could I ever confess that South Wind was only a plantation? Farm is a better word. Plantation drapes itself too proudly. Soil in a satin purse. But a farm is sweet, like earth, like Winnifred De Groot. Indeed, this is home. Not mine, but justly theirs; and if they share it with me this day, I will honor them.

"Why," he asked her, "are farmers always so clean? Reason tells me that the contrary should be true, and yet you are as akin to angelic as anyone with whom I acquaint. If I be lyrical, it feeds from thy purity."

"And you, Lieutenant, are weary of eye and bone."

"You can tell?"

"Indeed I can. Your eyes are ghostly, as though you see things again that you once saw, to haunt your memory and rob you of your sleep."

"You are wise, for one so young. Yet, as the phrase passes my lips, I color that even now, I am less a man and less a soldier than you are a woman."

"To confess it fattens you."

He smiled. How charming, he thought, her slight misuse of a simple word in our own tongue. Yet I dare admit she speaks perfect English; were it compared to my mastery of Dutch. "So it fattens me, eh? Then fat I shall be. Honestly, I find posing before you, as I once did, trying to be more than what I was . . . I now find such a boyish practice distasteful."

"Do you? I am glad."

"And I, too. All I want to be, in your eyes and in your fair company, is just myself. No uniform and no rank. Only me."

"No uniform," she giggled.

"You," he touched the tip of her nose very lightly with his fingers, "are one imp of a girl."

"As you," she said, "are to me. At night, I go to my loft, and before sleep comes, I ache for you. Until sleep comes, as it always will to farm folk; and then I dream of your beautiful boy's body. You are lean and tight, like a length of rope pulled from both ends. So tightly are you stretched that I almost feel my hand could pluck you, as a finger touches a lute string, and your body would hum."

"A musical note?"

"Yes, and quite high in voice. My second cousin, Torge Hengle, plays a lute. . . . He says that the tighter a string stretches . . ."

"The higher the note."

Winnie nodded her white cap. "Yes. And I want to know why your string is so stretched and your scream so high."

"Why must you hear my scream?"

"So that your lute strand may sing, and not snap."

Not being able to answer, he could only swallow and hold her closer. How much she knows, he told himself, and yet how much can I confess to her?

"What hands?" she asked him.

"Hands?"

"Yes, whose hands are twisting pegs to pull you apart, Cotton Mayfield Witty?"

"Your fingers could tune me and not tear me."

"So they could. And tonight, perhaps I shall strum you."

"Tonight I must return to soldiering. Hah! What a jest. Instead of an army, we men are oxen. We lug and tug and strain, to transport . . ." He stopped talking.

"You mistrust me?"

"No, not you. Only it be wiser for us all if each man guards his gossip, and I know you will understand. More than that, agree."

"I do agree."

"Already I speak too much, an affliction of youth, according to my father."

"Where is Hatch and the indian?"

"Blue Goose went north. He is to soon marry."

"And the old man?"

"Who cares where he is."

"Do his hands pull you tighter?"

"From both ends," he said.

"You like him, you hate him."

"I did not come here to talk of Hatch."

"Why do you come?"

"To tend to my mare." He hugged her, tickling her ribs with his fingertips. He felt his entire body smile, and hers.

"Truly," she said, laughing. "Yet were your beloved beast elsewhere, still you would come to me. As I come to you."

"Would you?"

She nodded, her eyes widening, brightening with the excitement of her thought. "Cotton! Let me tell you."

"Tell me what?"

"I rode your mare!"

"No. She only . . ."

"But I did. A single time, and yet I rode her for miles, with only a bridle and no saddle. Some of the English girls at school say that it is not ladylike to ride astride. They ride sidesaddle."

"I . . . can't believe you rode Mary."

"Come. We'll ask Papa."

"He'll bury a musket ball in my head."

"No, he will not. Come."

The house was solidly built, like everything De Groot, from their mansions to their maids, and stood stout and sturdy, in Dutch defiance. As they entered, the mouth of Jan De Groot popped open, in absolute amazement.

"You!"

De Groot's wife smiled. Conversation had taken place, Cotton guessed, 'twixt a mother and her daughter that a sire's ears had not been invited to share. Yet it seemed that fatherly temper had cooled a bit, even though it was still too early to convince Jan De Groot that his daughter's belly did not sprout a young Virginian.

"Welcome, young sir!" said Katrinka, causing Jan to cast a cautioning glance at his wife.

"He comes back," said Winnie.

"Hello, hello, hello," yelled the four younger children, Cloot, Anna, Henry, and Gerta, who jumped on Cotton, eight little hands reaching for him. Jan De Groot cleared his throat, but said nothing. Alike as peas, Durable Hatch had described the De Groot kinder, as indeed they were.

Less than half an hour later, Lieutenant Witty found himself naked, and in a giant washtub filled with hot soapy water. In that same water, his clothing was later laundered and hung before a hearth where orange heat would quickly dry it to a stitch. The water was hotter than bearable, but his body drank it in by every pore.

Then they fed him; bringing apples, mutton, corn, and beans, topped off with cinnamon cakes and cider. Later, he drank a mug of hot tea. At the first sip, his throat told him that it was British tea, as no other afforded such flavor.

"Friends," he said, "I am warm."

Upon hearing his announcement, all five of the young De Groots shouted, with upraised hands, as though thawing a Virginian officer from the icy grip of winter was some worthy aim, fought for, and finally won. Katrinka De Groot smiled at him, though Jan did little else but glower. And even the tiny white puffs from the farmer's long clay pipe seemed short of patience. His powerful hands pretended to busy themselves with whittling a rung for a chair. Yet whenever Cotton Witty moved, the two Dutch eyes raced to him, as if to warn the young soldier to keep a distance from his daughter.

Keeping still of hand and body, thought Cotton, is nigh to impossible; as here I sit before an orange fire, robed in the oversized shirt of a Dutch plowman which is sewn from such a scratchy substance that a tunic of tacks would offer my chest more comfort. Does this man actually wear such a garment? Yet, Witty reflected, even men of property strolled about Cambridge robed in the texture of a tinker, which, at South Wind, we would employ only as bedding beneath our hounds. As if a well-bred animal in Virginia would lower himself, ha ha, to lie upon such humble spinning.

What can the trouble be with these northern folk, that they are so drably driven? Somehow, methinks, they equate discomfort to a state of grace. Can one *suffer* a soul up to Heaven? Their faces. seem as uninviting as their furniture, sawn from hard maple, bereft of any hospitality. And yet, here sit I, scrubbed and fed and well tended by De Groots. Ah, but these are not Massachusetts folk. Nor would I dare to point a finger and call them New Yorkers. Does not Herr De Groot refer to his feehold as New Amsterdam? Or was it Rotterdam? Well, one dam for this God-forsaken turf is exchangeable for another. And for a flag, they could hoist a harshly-weaved homespun where a stiff-back woman sits a straight-back chair, rampant upon a homely hymnbook of moral discomforts. The north country is a bed of rocks. Oh, to be home . . . home . . .

"Cotton sleeps," he heard a child whisper. Who? As it mattered little, he allowed his eyes to close, his head to bob forward into the prayer of a nap. Chin to his chest, Cotton Mayfield Witty was aware of less and less and less.

Up bobbed his head. Asleep? For how long? The fire is now a stranger in shape. His nose smelled fresh baking. Smiling, he looked at Winnie as though she herself were a sweet confection.

"This afternoon," said Winnie, "before you return to your duty, we all have a gift for you."

"How could you all give me more?"

"We wish to give you back a day that you missed, if we can."

"What day is that?"

"Christmas."

Chapter Twenty

"He is dead, sir."

Pulling off his glove, General Washington wrapped his fingers about the wrist of the young soldier who was leaning against the leafless tree. He felt no pulse, no heartbeat. A white face. The eyes were closed. Frail hands still clenched the cold iron of the musket.

"Who is he, Sergeant?"

"Name of Clapp, sir, from the near town of Concord, where his pa is a blacksmith. He's frozen, sir. Froze to his death on sentry duty this night."

"You are Sergeant Stillwell, are you not?"

"Yes, sir, that I be. But so freezing up my own self, sir, if you don't mind me saying out, I am near to finished from the cold of this January."

"As I am, Sergeant," said Washington. "If you will bid your scribe supply me with the name of the boy's father, I shall see that he and his wife receive a letter on their son's loyalty and service."

"Gladly, sir. They'll enjoy that."

"Enjoy?"

"Not that way, sir. Cold stops my tongue as well as my reason, sir."

"And mine, Sergeant. How loathsome to lose a lad to such folly as this. No more than a child, yet there he stands, waiting in the snow for his relief to spell him. I say, is it midnight?"

"Near the stroke, sir, is my guess." Stillwell rubbed his nose with a brown rag of a mitten, and snuffed in a breath of the night.

"How stand they now? By what tours?"

"Four on and eight off, General."

"Change it, effective at once. Stand their watches two on and four off. We cannot cast off a lad's life as though it were an empty bottle. What's the boy's Christian name?"

The sergeant paused, rubbing his whiskered chin as he forced his mind to remember. "Allen, sir. He is Allen Clapp."

"He was Allen Clapp. And all he be now, by the standards of war, is a blot of ink in our record books. How do we ledger a life?"

Sergeant Stillwell shook his head, unable to answer. And I, thought Washington, am less able.

"There's so little that any quill can write to replace a fallen son," he said to the sergeant. "Each time that duty demands my composing such a sorry missive, my wit is as blank as my paper. . . . Well, then, carry on, Sergeant, and a good evening to you."

After he returned Sergeant Stillwell's stiff salute, Washington turned away, his boots kicking the powdery snow with each heavy step. Are my toes still alive? Or do they now expire here in Cambridge of Massachusetts, as did the young colt of a Concord smith? One more letter to scratch out this night, until I blow out my candle. Come the morrow, I shall address it when the sergeant provides the information. And if he do not, then I presume that Clapp the smith, Concord town, will suffice.

He sniffed.

A lone curl of woodsmoke entered his nose, a wisp of warmth against winter. From where? Looking about him in the dark, he saw the rows of ragged cabins that quartered rows of ragged men. Snoring soldiers that dream of sweethearts and mothers and wives that they may ne'er see again. Squad upon squad of Allen Clapps, scratching in cold bunks that crawl with vermin, perchance awake and remembering sweet Virginia. Which cabin once cradled Soldier Clapp? Which empty bunk? His quilts are cold now; blankets not to be toasted by a bedded boy. How I have longed for a son of my own, or a daughter. Ah, and how the blacksmith and his wife, folk I shall never meet, will long for their lad.

201

God grant them a large family, with offspring so plentiful that they be 'twixt dozen and score. Could it lessen their loss? Washington shook his head.

How many winters, he asked, looking upward to the black of a midnight sky that was dusted with stars, how many winters to a war? Three? Five? And how many Allens?

From the corner of his eye, he spied another sentry, alone and stamping his feet. Then, as General Washington watched, the soldier leaned back against a walnut tree. Inside his cape, and beneath the white lace of his blouse, the general's heart seemed to suspend itself, recalling the pose of the frozen soldier. Walking as stoutly as his numbing feet would take him, he moved smartly toward the sentry's post; coughing as he did so. It would hardly be appropriate, he told himself, for the commanding general to be mistaken for a Redcoat spy, only to be felled in the snowdrifts of Cambridge. So again he cleared the nothing in his throat.

"Who goes?" The sentry's voice was young, and southern, hitting his cold ear as welcome as a balcony breeze.

"Only a Virginian, like yourself."

"Not much like Virginia, this place."

"No." Washington walked closer in the darkness, so that a tree trunk interposed between his face and the silver wafer of a moon. "So little like Virginia. Are you ill for home?"

"Yes, are you?"

Washington nodded, moving still closer. "Indeed, so ill that I must ask it of others as I did of you, as the posing is a poultice to ease my own emptiness."

He saw the lad shiver inside his greatcoat, then stamp his left foot as though his toes were freezing. The sentry looked not at Washington, but straight ahead, as though to twist his neck would surely crack it. "You speak like a gentleman, sir. Are you an officer?"

Washington paused. How shall I honestly answer him? "Nay, not yet an officer, but I feel in my bones that soon I must willy-nilly become one."

"I feel naught in my bones. Are you a rover?"

"A roving sentry? No, I am only an old soldier who cannot sleep, whose billet is as clammy as yours, and whose heart also recalls Virginia."

The boy was silent.

"Let's walk together," said the general. "Alas, I cannot sleep no more than you can desert your post, so perhaps a to-and-fro may give a perky poke to all twenty of our toes."

Side by side, they walked through the snow. Washington kept the moon on his right shoulder, the lad to his left, so that his own face would be a secret of shadows. Beneath their boots, the dry snow whistled.

"Listen," said Washington, "how our footfalls fiddle in the night."

" 'Tis a music, eh?"

Washington nodded his head. "Is this your first frosty experience in snow; I mean, to any extent?"

"Well I have seen a bit of it, but not every winter. These are my first mounds of the stuff. Hard to believe that all it be is only frozen raindrops."

"They say no two are alike," said Washington.

"So they say."

"Liken to soldiers, I suppose."

"Yes. Yet I mean to be a preacher, not a soldier, one day, sir."

"So your wish is to become a minister, eh?"

"It is, sir, if I prove worthy."

"Worthy at war?"

"Well, if I must be a worthy fellow. Only then can I step the stairs before a congregation . . ."

"To pound your pulpit, and to fright all of all us who doze in hard hickory pews with the flames and fires of Hell. Sir, I repent!"

They both laughed. And the boy suddenly stopped his walk, looking at General Washington. His face twisted slightly into a quizzical expression.

"Golly be, but I haven't laughed in days."

"Nor have I, son."

"There seems so little mirth in Massachusetts."

"Well spoke. You are indeed glib enough to be a cleric, and more, I wager that you shall achieve your aspirations and become a minister of merit." He clapped the boy on the shoulder.

"I thank you, sir."

"Why do you *sir* me?"

"My parents raised me thus, to have manners to my betters."

"You are a well-bred boy, and you do credit to yourself and your seniors. But enough of this deportment of a social nature. I should like to know your intent as a preacher, and what shall be your first sermon."

"To preach against slavery."

"Am I to presume that you and your farmer father own no blacks?"

"We own none. My father and I think different about more than one issue, but we are agreed to work our farm with our own backs and hands."

"I see nothing wrong with working one's own land."

"And I see evil a-plenty to whip a slave to do it."

"Do you?"

"So do I, and we Hanovers shall never."

"That is your name, Hanover?"

"Yes. My Christian name is Clovis."

"Perhaps one day," said Washington, "folk of these many colonies will refer to your commentaries as the writings of that able abolitioner, the Reverend Clovis Hanover."

"You fun me, sir."

"Nay, I bait you not. If we are to have a nation, Reverend Hanover, she shall embrace in her bounty more than only one opinion."

"I wager we disagree on slavery."

"A vexing point. Yet hear me out. To build into beauty, whether it be a quilt by your mother's needle, an artist's portrait, or a musical composition for the viola, I say to mold whatever it be from divers fabric."

"I don't follow you, sir."

"What has all this to do with slavery, eh? Ugliness to my ear and

204

eye, is a melody of one note, a quilt of one color, and a woman's body constructed of straight lines."

"Say on, sir."

"The mind of man is perchance like a blooming garden, rife with such a spate of ideas and conceptions and inspirations that no farmer's plot, yours or mine, could beg to compare. Now, planted in those fields are a variety of color and taste and fragrance in flowers and fruit and vetch, in the furrows of your wit, which render your intelligence unique and your brain is a work of God's infinite beauty."

"Are you a writer, sir, of books?"

Washington smiled. "Oh, were I only this night, instead of just a soldier. And were you already the Reverend Hanover, you in pulpit and I with pen, perhaps we could better the world a bit. Agree?"

"Perhaps we could," the boy sniffed.

Turning, they walked back to the lad's original post, following their earlier footsteps. Again, the general's ear danced to the music beneath their feet. "Well, my boy, as I see the world, we need more than one opinion. And right now, I daresay that neither you nor I would long so for dear Virginny, were we both in accord with our sovereign, King George of England."

"Agreed."

"Have you heard of the Continental Congress?"

"Yes, we all have, sir. Virginia sent men to stand for us there and speak our minds, and I hear all the settlements did likewise."

"Indeed they did. And so if ever we forge these united colonies into some semblance of a country, our government will voice many persuasions."

"Politicians are not to be trusted, says my pa."

"Nor are kings," said Washington, "nor generals, nor preachers of Gospel, nor practitioners of medicine, or attorneys at law. Nor are farmers."

The boy laughed. "I see your meaning."

"Do you?"

"Yes, as you chaff me; and yet you are telling me that we had best hang together."

"Or," said Washington, "we may hang one by one."

"Do you think King George would rope us all, sir?"

Suddenly the lace at George Washington's throat seemed to pull more snugly to his neck. Without thinking, his hand reached up to slightly loosen his muffler. "Surely, my lad, if we lose this war, His Majesty's soldiers will hang some of us."

"Do you think they'd hang John Hancock, sir?"

The question forced General Washington to smile with a cold face, and the smile hung there on his cheeks as he answered. "My good Reverend Hanover, there are few things in life that are a surety, but I would almost bond you this promise . . ."

"What promise?"

"That no mere *king* would dare to hang John Hancock!"

"Do you know Mister Hancock, sir?"

Ah, do I? A bit too well, and his charming Dorothy not near well enough. Yet do John and I know one another? Have either of us had the patience to try?

"No, I know him not. Only that friend Hancock is a man of Massachusetts, which bespeaks much concerning the climate of his colony and the weather of his wit."

"Indeed it does, sir."

"I bid you good night, Reverend Hanover. Keep your feet on the move, and do not sleep at your post, as slumber is an early symptom of death by freezing. Dry your socks by the hearth."

"I did once, sir, and they were thefted."

"Then steal a dry pair from someone else. Did you know a soldier by name of Clapp?"

"No, sir. Do you?"

Washington shook his head. "Pity, I do not."

"Why do you ask, sir?"

"No reason. I must go, as I still have a letter to compose and reports to account for. Remember one more thing, Hanover, and tell the lads."

"Sir?"

"All these Redcoats have only *orders* to fight a war, but you and I have a *reason* to fight it."

The house was dark and cold. Once upstairs in his bedchamber, he noticed that the embers in his hearth had died a gray death. A shroud of ashes covered the coals. Sitting heavily on the bed's edge, he struggled to pull off his boots. Then his socks. Barefoot, he crossed the cold floorboards to unhook his sword and hang it upon its customary peg of pine. Bending over the fireplace, his hand searched slightly above the white dust for any trace of living heat.

"Damn!"

Without disrobing, he stretched his long hard body upon his bed, making sure his feet were buried beneath the goose feathers. Hands under his head, he searched the ceiling for a hundred unanswerable questions. Did I ask Knox to bring back flints for our muskets? According to Arnold, the flint unearthed at Ticonderoga tested to be of prime quality. Well, I wager that Benedict must know, as I deem him to be more flint than flesh.

Come the morrow, I shall whittle a fresh feather and write to blacksmith Clapp and wife, concerning the loss of their Allen, if I can find the phrases. Shall I one day write a like letter to the Hanovers of Virginia? No, I pray. Also, come dawn, I must read whatever I can about the Hessians. If rumor be true, we may all be their unwilling students, but then 'twill be too late. Billy Howe, I am going to best you, old boy. And down yonder in Boston this very night lies General William Howe, at a wonder how he shall outflank George Washington and his ragged wretches.

I wonder if General Howe sleeps, and is his bedchamber as uninviting as mine? No woman to warm me. No hand to hold . . .

The general slept.

Chapter Twenty-One

Smoke, said his nose.

Even though a morning fog seemed to connect the wet black trunks of the forest trees, there was more than clouds to smell. One fire? Many fires? Had he come to a camp of Huron, or enemy?

Blue Goose stood silently in the Canada snow, asking questions of his nose. Listening, his ears told him nothing. No gunfire from white hands and no victory song from red throats. He wanted to cough, but his will denied it. Tall Face, his father, had once told him that in an enemy wood, one foolish tongue can command the attention of one hundred wise ears. Thus he did not cough. Nor did he move. Beyond the thick stand of trees that Old Ax called hickory and walnut and maple, all of which were now leafless, beyond his vision lay the odor of death.

Be still, his legs shouted.

An owl screamed, far away, as if to say that dawn had come too early and his belly still ached for a rabbit or a mouse. As my own belly hurts with hunger, thought Blue Goose, for I have not eaten in two suns. If only the owl would strike a rabbit, or better, a snowshoe hare, which bears more meat; then I could run to the kill and steal it before the silent wings of the great owl carry the food into the high branches. The rich winter-bread of the white snowshoe hare would fill the throat of Blue Goose and let his complaining stomach smile once more. Again the owl cried out, as hungrily as before.

"Smoke," he whispered to himself.

Yet not the smell of feasting; rather the smoke of sadness crept into his nostrils; warning him to be silent, and yet to tell him to beware of what lay beyond the trees. As he moved his moc over the soft powder of dry snow, a twig cracked beneath his weight, causing Blue Goose to curse his lack of caution. Have I shared fire with the Yengeese for so many nights that Blue Goose himself becomes a white fool? Old Ax is not a fool; yet his ears are dying, which allow his lungs to holler much. I see little wisdom in noise. Would a fox bark at wolves? And now Old Ax ages to yap at all who will hear, friend or enemy, Mohawk or Huron.

Loud voices are the songs of fools, he thought. Why do the white men never learn this? It is a truth, a law, a thought to honor with my own caution. And see how easily my moc snaps a twig as if to yell out to French or British or Mohawk ears that the spine of Blue Goose will crack as willingly. Come, my enemy, and break the bones of Blue Goose, who now steps on snow with a white foot.

Without moving, he stood for many breaths, until the fog had lifted; and he heard little. But inside his nose, the smoke that rode the fog as slowly as an empty canoe warned him of many pits in his path. Each breath he drew into his nostrils became arrows that buried in his brain, asking that he listen to their chant of dying, written in smoke. Only when the unseen sun was higher, yet still behind a heavy gray sky, did the Huron ask his foot to walk once more. This time, his foot walked through the trees as the fog earlier had walked, with the silent mocs that encase red feet. My cold toes are now wise, he thought, and once again I am Blue Goose the Huron, instead of Blue Goose who hunts with Old Ax.

Suddenly, remembering Hatch, his heart smiled.

And in the same laughter, the smile of Child Face attacked his joy, to haunt his happiness. Why did I not draw my knife and open the white throat of the boy from the Virginia place? The blade of Blue Goose may be sharp, but my wit is dull; for I now stand in Canada while my old trapper may now lie beneath Ticonderoga.

Creeping forward through the trees and toward the stronger smell of smoke, Blue Goose let his mind spit on the pistol of Child Face. Why did I not steal the pistol? And if caught, Blue Goose would only giggle and say "pretty," so that those who heard the word would be turned into fools and duped. Was there ever a white mouth that did not whisper "thief" at a red hand? I think perhaps the white men pray about God so hard and sing so loudly on their sun day because they have no God. At least none in the heavens. On the ground and among themselves they have many gods, for they worship horses, whiskey, guns, loud women, land and houses . . . and *names*. How a white man would fret to learn that one name is as good as another. Or one flag, he thought, as he silently crept through the wet woods.

Is not a man a fool to pray to a horse? Blue Goose would sooner send his prayers to a skunk. Also sooner would I ride one. Little do I promise, yet I swear this one vow; never will Blue Goose again straddle a horse. Better to eat one! For such a large animal would skin down to much meat for many fires and fill more than one empty paunch. Old Ax has eaten horse and he tells that horse cooks faster and swallows better than a dog. They laughed at us then, that evening at the Ticonderoga place, when we tell of a dog supper. A white mouth that cannot chew dog meat is a mouth that lies when saying its belly has born the blade of hunger. To sleep without supper is hunger to a white belly. Hunger to a Huron is to not eat for a winter. My grandmother, Leaf, remembered the winter that mothers strangled their own babes to end their pain. That is hunger. It bites deeper than one supper.

There was little fog ahead now, only smoke, and as his mocs entered the forest clearing, he saw the Huron camp. Smoke of burned-out lodges pricked his eyes. Animals' hides burned quietly in huge mounds that had once been family shelters. Gagging, wanting to vomit, he stopped; the stench of dead flesh retching his throat. No longer were they fires, only burning humps of hides that smoldered in the midday mist. No crying. Here he saw a hand, blue and still with winter death. Touching it, he felt its cold creep into his own fingers and up his arm, making him release it as though it were aflame.

Using a blackened pole, he pried away a layer of ashen animal skins that were still smoking, and a few orange sparks tumbled toward him. Beneath lay a dead Huron woman, holding a burned child. The hair on both was burned away. Both dead, yet their bodies still roasted beneath a corner of the shelter skins. He dropped the pole.

Walking from one blackened pile to another, he searched for life, finding none. There were about three all-fingers, thirty lodges, and all had been burned. Finding more bodies, he looked for arrows; but there were no arrows. Not the Mohawk. No scalps had been lifted. Hair had been removed by flame and not by hatchet or blade. Who? Certainly not the French, as the white trappers of Canada slept and ate and hunted with the Huron; and were bringers of meat, even in snow.

Why? Why had enemies come north in winter, to raid the Huron? And leave no feathers, no lances, and take no hair? Who then?

Beneath the next pile of smoking robes and burned moss and bark he found what could be his answer. Face down, hands still holding a musket, lay a dead soldier, his uniform burned away so that the black of his roasted skin was exposed. White britches and a stocking covered part of his leg. Above that, tiny tatters of a red tunic blew in the wind.

British!

English fight in red coats. He had seen the French mostly in blue and white, and the farmers and trappers in deerskin. Never in red. He spat on the dead Redcoat. So the English were in Canada. But why only one? Was this not the village of Wolf Eyes? The Chief of the Huron would have slain and eaten more than one Redcoat; and had, when the French fought them many winters back. Wolf Eyes had fought with General Montcalm; and more, Wolf Eyes had wept when learning of Montcalm's death at Quebec.

At the side of the fallen Redcoat were two other bodies, both Huron. But it took only a glance to tell that the English died well fed. The two Huron were little more than bone and hide, and Blue Goose knew then that hunger had attacked the village of Wolf Eyes before the British came to torch it. Had the Huron been too crippled by starvation to resist? Yes, as the Huron took only the life of one Redcoat.

211

Under a charred blanket, he discovered another burned child, eyes frozen in death, mouth open with yesterday's scream. Part of the blanket was of use, so Blue Goose wrapped it about his shoulders, shivering as he exposed the dead child's body to its final winter. Without thinking, his moc kicked the dead soldier who had fought in a red coat. Again and again he kicked the man, until his breath could no longer suck in the gray gasps of smoke from the dying fires without causing him to bend double and spew out only air. His toes ached.

"Sky," he said.

There was no answer. So from one burning mound of baking death to another, he ran, calling her name and not caring who heard, expecting an arrow in his back, and caring little if the flint found what little remained of his heart. Flint, or a musket ball.

"Sky," he cried again. Beneath a pile of gray ashes he found more bodies, and her face suddenly looked at him, almost as if to speak his name.

He closed her eyes with his hand. Her face and body were cold. Her spirit had flown upward, to dance among summer clouds. Blue Goose knew as his hand felt the sharp bones of her cheek that there had been no food. Not even dog.

Each rock that he used had to be forced from the frozen earth with a lance, and often with a heavier staff. Yet stone by stone, he finally collected enough to build a cairn over her, having first lifted her frail form up from the ash, carrying her a short way. As he walked, he sang to her, to comfort and guide her spirit on its way. Then he wept over the place where she died, and his hands clutched the warm ashes, which he rubbed over his face to hide his grief. Hot embers he held in his hands, rubbing the coals into his hair, and holding a red cinder against his own tongue, so that he would never again speak her name without remembering her pain and her hunger, and her death.

He heard it!

A low moan, from somewhere behind his back, from underneath one of the fallen lodges still smoldering little wisps of white smoke that hid quickly, melting into the winter air. Again, his ears heard it!

"Help me."

There was no mistake now. All were not dead. One lived, and perhaps more. Where?

Loping from one smudge heap to another, Blue Goose paused only to listen; but the sound had stopped. Again and again he kicked at loose sheets of scorched hide, searching for the source of the sound. But now there was no longer a voice. And so he stopped, wondering how he could have imagined such a wail, and asking himself if not he too were dying. Ashes from his head sifted down his brow, the grit torturing his eyes. Then he felt the touch. A hand closed on his ankle as if to claim him to join this tribe of the dead. Looking down quickly, he saw the dying hand grip his lower leg, its fingers biting weakly into his deerhide legging.

"NO! No, dead hand!" he whispered hoarsely in his Huron tongue.

The hand had his leg, loosely and with hardly any force, but Blue Goose could not urge his frozen body to break loose from the grip that the dead hand had trapped to his ankle.

"Here . . ."

Had the hand spoken?

Blue Goose prayed as never before, his arm reaching to the heavens, his body trembling. Dare he look down at the dead hand? And then once more he heard the groan. Dead warriors, he told himself, do not moan or cry out to live ones. The hand lives. And it is Blue Goose who comes to it, and not the hand to me, for it is Blue Goose who walks.

"Gray Hand," he spoke to it, giving the hand a name.

"I . . . am . . ." came a weakened whisper.

"Who then?" asked Blue Goose.

"Wolf . . ."

"Wolf Eyes?"

No answer, but the fingers that quickly tightened on his lower leg seemed to tell him that the hand belonged to the Huron chief.

Drawing in a great chestful of air, he released it slowly, allowing himself a breath in which to summon his reason.

"I am Blue Goose, son of Tall Face. And my grandmother was Leaf, who could look into the fire and read wisdom for all the Huron to hear."

Kneeling, he pulled away the smoking strips of bark and animal hides; and layer by layer, the old man's face slowly became uncovered. The face of Wolf Eyes met that of Blue Goose. There was no mistake. Those eyes, even though in a face covered with ashes, could belong to no other warrior but the father of Sky.

"Wolf Eyes," said Blue Goose, feeling respect soften his voice.

Placing a lean hand gently beneath the old man's neck, he slowly raised Wolf Eyes to a sitting position. Portions of the chief's face and neck were burned, and the stench of old age and defeat in battle filled the nose of the younger man. Could this be the same Wolf Eyes who had stood at the side of General Montcalm? No, for I am no longer the Blue Goose who, as a young brave, was captured by the Mohawk. The lash of years has cut deep into the face of Wolf Eyes, leaving the lines that tell the story of many Canada winters. His face is now the web of a spider, a dried apple that bears no juice and no seed.

"Who burned here?" asked Blue Goose.

"They . . . they . . ."

The old chin shook as if not knowing how, or what, to answer. And to think, Blue Goose recalled, that this old man was the chief whose eyes I could not meet, so great was my fear of him.

"Can you stand?"

"They . . ."

"Place your arm about my neck and I will raise you to your feet. Up, now up! Stand on your feet, old man. And if you do not stand I will lift you."

The old man looked from one dying fire to another, bewildered, saying nothing. He dies, thought Blue Goose; and I pray he soon does, as gray life is sadder than death.

"Sky is dead." Blue Goose pointed where he had piled the rocks into a cairn. The old man slowly raised his arm to also point at the mound of stones, saying nothing.

As the snowflake hit his nose, Blue Goose looked up to see another and more. The sky seemed suddenly to fill with snowflakes, and he recalled that Leaf had told him they were little white ponies of winter. Snow, he said silently; asking more and more white ponies to come down and cover all the ugly death that his eyes had this day seen. Cover it over, he pleaded of the sky, until the disgrace of the Huron and of Wolf Eyes buries beneath a new winter. Let this camp now feed the hungry gray fox; and come the summer, melt to green to nourish the ant and the crow.

"Let the death," he said to Wolf Eyes, "blend into the land and be not again seen by the eyes of men."

"Our . . . shame," said Wolf Eyes.

Blue Goose nodded, holding the old man erect as best he could on little but his own hunger. "We are starved and burned and God turns his face from the Huron. We are no longer His children, and the flap on the door of His lodge closes in the face of Wolf Eyes and Blue Goose. There is no seed in the belly of Sky and no buds on Huron trees."

"Only the wind."

Blue Goose nodded.

"Walk my legs . . ." Wolf Eyes pointed to the rocks that covered his dead daughter.

Slowly, moving first one stiff leg and then the next, the old man moved with the help of the younger Huron to the grave of his child. Looking down, his old head shook from side to side. Then stooping low, his hand clutched a few fallen leaves, releasing them over her cairn. The leaves fell, scattering like a flock of brown sparrows, taken by the wind.

"Rest," he told Sky.

"Come," said Blue Goose, holding him.

"Come . . . to where?"

"We will leave this place of sorrow."

"And go *where?*"

"North, away from white guns."

"North?" asked Wolf Eyes.

"Yes, to the land of the great white bear. For some other Huron may be there, hunting the seal with a spear and catching the fat salmon. And we will sleep beneath the thick fur of the elk."

"Home."

Blue Goose sighed. "This forest is my home, but today the ashes tell us it is now their home. Canada was a word that could sing my heart and my mocs would dance, even in snow. But the dance is ended, the drums no longer beat. Canada is burned and buried here, yet Canada is a big place where geese will again fly north. Remember the geese? How each spring they would divide the sky, so high up that they were no more than a line of honking dots . . . a line one day that had no beginning and no end."

He pointed at the sky.

"I am . . . old."

Sitting the old man down on a fallen log, he left him, returning in only breaths with an armful of sassafras. As the old man had no teeth, Blue Goose chewed the green bark into a yellowy mush, stuffing the wet cud of pulp and spittle into the toothless old mouth.

"Eat," he said. "Chew and swallow."

Blue Goose repeated the chewing to feed the old man until the sassafras was nearly all consumed. Some he swallowed for his own belly, but it did little to fill the yawning hole of his hunger. He had cut only the past summer's growth, still green, not yet fully hardened by winter into mature wood. His throat balked, yet he forced himself to swallow the bark.

"Meat . . ." The old voice creaked out its dream.

"We have no meat, old man. We have no tribe, no village, no home. You have no daughter and I have no Sky."

"French?"

"Ah, the French Army is no more, and no longer will French cannon roar at the Mohawk. Our red enemies to the south and their white brothers, the Yengeese, devour the French as hawks eat moles. Once we hunted here, like hawks, but now the Huron are moles that must hide beneath the crust of winter."

Wolf Eyes covered his face with his old hands.

"You hide?"

The old chief slowly nodded, causing Blue Goose to move closer to embrace the shivering body, holding the old man against his chest as a mother would hold a child.

"Gone . . . gone . . ."

"Yes," nodded Blue Goose, "as leaves are first green, then brown. So live and so die the Huron. The body of Wolf Eyes is gray, yet his spirit will always be as red as the blade of his knife when it was warm with Mohawk blood."

"Die now . . . near to Sky."

"This day?" Blue Goose asked.

"Now."

"Bow or knife?"

"Knife . . . my knife." His wrinkled hands fumbled into the folds of his blanket, searching for an antler handle among the stiff layers of deerhide. Using both hands, the old man lifted the knife from its stocking, handing its handle to Blue Goose. Its blade was dull with rust.

"You hold," said Wolf Eyes.

"Yes, I will hold. And pray."

"Pray . . . for early salmon."

Blue Goose nodded, his fist tightening on the antler, not quite prepared for the sudden rush of the old chest against the tarnished blade. Wolf Eyes did not scream; but the old eyes widened, as if he saw beyond a distant mountain and his face waved to other Huron who had already gone and were all waiting for him to join their hunting party.

With his young face looking upward into the falling flakes of snow, Blue Goose sang for Wolf Eyes a warrior's song.

Chapter Twenty-Two

Cotton Mayfield Witty stamped his foot, feeling nothing in his toes. Again and again he forced his leg to jack upward, hammering his boot into the Berkshire snow.

"Come on, lad. Heave to."

The voice was as cold as his foot, yet he responded to the call for help out of habit. How many days since he had last visited the De Groots?

"Steady the ox on your side, boy."

"I will, but I am not your boy. I am a soldier like yourself."

"Aye, that you are. And I wager a better soldier than I be."

Four oxen worked their cannon, one yoke leading the second. Lead yoke and pull yoke, as they were called by the big teamster with the great brown beard and the big godly hat. Some religious sect, another had spoken of the man, referring to his black boots. A red face, a brown beard, and all else as black as Aunt Martha's stove in the South Wind kitchen.

"Goad him, son. Prick his rib."

"The beast is near to dead," said Cotton, noticing the staggering black and white animal, whose breathing no longer pulled in and out as evenly as the breathing of the other three animals.

"So are we all, near dead, if we tarry in these horrid hills. Spring won't even find us. So prod the poor thing."

The head of the ox hung from its bow, hauling little, and Cotton saw specks of shiny red blood freckle the snow beneath his snout. Foam sudsed from the great mouth, yellow and sickly, and now reddening with each heave of the body.

"Grieved, is he?"

"Yes, and poorly," said Cotton.

"Then he'll be our supper."

Nausea rose in his stomach, causing Cotton to stumble his footing, holding the small gray trunk of a tree for support. *If only,* he wished with his eyes briefly closed, *I could now retch up my entire life and this whole bloody trek, and begin anew.*

"He's ill," Cotton yelled to the bearded man in black.

"Ho!" The man halted the four animals, wading around through the fresh snow, ahead of the lead yoke to behold the floundering ox. The big head sagged lower and its lungs pumped unevenly. Removing the large black hat, the bearded man pressed his ear behind the shoulder of the beast, listening to a heartbeat with his mouth open. The man's own breath steamed out with each feathery puff, almost matching the panting of the weaving ox.

"We should rest him," said the man, placing the black wide-brimmed hat again upon his own head and straightening up.

"Can we?" asked Cotton.

"We can and we cannot. Must and must not."

"Why can't we?"

"On account we're the lead cannon, my lad." He leaned heavily against a tree. All that could be heard in the quiet forest was the axes of the six men ahead of them who cut their trail. To the rear, below them, more men and cannon were closing upon them, shouting and encouraging themselves and their oxen to lug the iron and tug the brass for one more lunge against the snow.

"It is all uphill," sighed Cotton.

"So it seem, sonny. Life is uphill and this is but one journey of living."

"Nay, of dying."

"You be too young a colt for such talk. And I say to you it be a grave mistake." The man smiled at his own joke.

"Sir, all I make is mistakes. An error at home, and an error by leaving it, and an error in bringing my mare."

"Your mare?"

"Yes, back of us somewhere. I could have left her with a Dutch family, yet I hoped to bring her with me all the way to Boston."

The big man sighed, filling his mouth with a fresh chew of tobacco. "All the way to Boston," he said awkwardly, his teeth busy with matter, chomping down like a cider press.

"It will be fortunate if we ever get this Gray Whale as far as the rise we now climb," said Cotton, his hand on the big cannon's barrel.

"How much think you she balances?"

"Our great lady is, according to the records I made for Mister Knox, five thousand and more pounds."

"An eleven-footer, our great Gray Whale. I measured her."

"How shall we ever?" Cotton sighed. "You know, I am near to the point of caring naught if we do . . . tote her to Boston, I mean."

"Likewise with me. But we dassn't bow out, lad. Best we just take her a heave at a once."

For a second time, the big man listened with his ear to the sickening ox. The great black and white hide was shiny with sweat as it stood steaming in the snow. The other three Holsteins looked little sounder.

"He is sorely troubled, our big boy."

"Will he die?" asked Cotton.

The big beard nodded, flopping against the black coat. "As I am a Shaker, he surely will. For I do know oxen. More than I ever knowed, or wish to, about artillery."

"A Shaker?"

"I be a Shaking Quaker, an offshoot of the sons of the noble William Penn. We are a plain sect, and as we shake when we pray, we carry the name and proudly. We believe a Christian should tremble before God. Do you?"

"Sir, I tremble before winter. And as the same is a facet of nature, and of God's hand, then I must also be a Shaker like yourself."

"Well spoke. You have book-learning, eh?"

"A bit. More than I need to whip oxen and iron over a topless mount en route to Hades."

"Tempt not Satan."

No, thought Cotton; nor will I disagree on theology to a Shaker with a barrel for a chest, a forest for a face, who wears no mittens and packs a brace of purple hammers for hands.

"Where is your mare?" the man asked.

"Behind us, as is most of our ragged column."

"Who rides her?"

"Henry Knox."

"Knox?"

"Yes, he needed a second and third animal to tote him about the business of nursing us all on toward Boston. I lent him my Mary, as he is not an unkind man."

"So I hear. How else do you find him?"

"He knows our task. At first I hated him. Yet I now confess his ability, and more than ever, his willingness to learn from others on subjects foreign to himself. As I learn teamstering from you and geography from Old Ax."

The big man frowned his question. "Who?"

"I refer to Andrew Angus Hatch, that piney philosopher and curler and pathfinder we all so regard with due esteem."

"You dislike Hatch?"

"Nay, I find him amusing. A delight to the eye and a blessing to the ear, especially to the hard of hearing, as he shouts every learned word. But I disapprove of curling. Like the curse of bowling, it is ungodly sport and wastes work-light in a blasphemous manner."

"Amen." The Shaker nodded.

Aha, thought Witty, I size this big fellow rightly, as a believer in work. Surely not a pursuer of frills nor a gamesman. And I was wise not to voice my dislike of Hatch. Truth to tell, I do not despise old Durable. He stands, however, in my path to South Wind.

"Let us move," said the big man, "and eastward."

"What about the ox?"

"He'll die."

"When?" Cotton stroked the big animal's ear.

"Inside a mile."

221

"Why don't we rest him?"

"To spell him will kill us all, lad. One by one, we all will be fallen if we not press on. Winter chases like a starved wolf."

With a prod, the four oxen strained forward, causing the dry wood of the bows to creak in their eyelets. Cotton wondered if the cotter pins would snap, but they held. The long Gray Whale followed the steamy oxen on her sleigh, resting on her side in her wooden cradle. Walking ahead with a snow paddle, Cotton broke as much of a trail for the lead yoke as he could and still keep up. A steep spot summoned men from the rear, bringing pike poles to pry the runners of the heavy sleigh up and over a troublesome rock and a fallen log. The men shouted and sweated and swore. A man's hand was crushed against a tree, a hand that was quickly padded and bound up in splint and bandages. Blood still dripped from the wounded hand, marking a tiny red trail. As the crippled soldier was sent to the rear of the column, Cotton Mayfield Witty partly wished his own hand had been so crushed as to pardon him from further duty. An hour passed, and another, as the young Virginian encouraged the oxen to strain forward through the deep snow, whacking them stoutly with a birch rod when they refused. Up and down the line of animals and iron and men, a line that seemed to twist in its own agony, the bellowing of beaten oxen was heard over the curses of impatient Continentals. Men threw their own shoulders against the rears of sleighs, grunting along with their beasts and burdens.

"Heyyyyy . . . *up!* Hyup! Hyup!"

The urging cry crept up and down the line, yelled by men who had stripped off their greatcoats, such was the heat of their labor. Behind them a man's leg was caught beneath the iron runner of a stoneboat; and the bone snapped, cracking the air like a whip. He was splinted and sent westward, downhill to Claverack.

The ox died.

The big fellow just fell down dead, as the Shaker had predicted early on. Like the furnace of a forge, the heat of the dead carcass turned the snow into watery slush. From the snout, the ox ceased his bleeding and finally lay still. The ox was stripped of skin and meat and even bones for soup. Naught was wasted. Scraps of hoof-meat were fed to a stray hound that had, for some reason known only to the dog, followed the column of teamsters from the settlement of Kinderhook.

"I will puke for sure," said Cotton.

The Virginian stood where the ox had died, which now was no more than a puddle of red slush. Some of the red ran downhill, back toward the rear of the column. As they waited, a fresh ox was led up to them and yoked to a tired workmate. The big bow looped under his neck, and up through the twin eyelets in the oaken mainbeam, and the two cotter keys were knocked to their place, so the bow would not fall.

As the day wore on, Cotton had ceased to stamp his feet into the snow. His toes no longer hurt. Indeed, he felt nothing, as though he waded forward on two dull and lifeless stumps. They stopped to eat, cooking over fires that sent tiny red sparks flying up into the bare branches of a black forest. Men were as dead with labor as the animals. Only their tiny orange cookfires seemed to hold even a whisper of life.

No one talked.

Somewhere in the night, a soldier tried to play "Yankee Doodle" on a fife; but the wind whipped in and stole the melody, washing it away and into the night. Truly a Berkshire winter could rob a man of his music, in a whim, and rinse away all remembering of lighter and warmer times.

There was no tea, no chocolate, and many of them boiled water to drink; sometimes soaking a raw potato or onion or turnip in the water as a hope to turn such a shabby tincture into porridge. Somewhere there were tents, too far to the rear to even climb down to and unpack, and they slept under the snow, curled up together in little litters of life. They inhaled their own stink. There was no distinction 'twixt soldier or civilian teamster; or even 'twixt ox, or horse, or dog. Whatever was alive was welcome to contribute body warmth to the wriggling and wormlike cluster of winter warriors. Bodies of all shapes and kingdoms huddled and entwined in an effort to knit a shawl against the January cold.

"Hey! You dying?"

Several times in the night, the rough voice had awakened Cotton, accompanied by an elbow jab in his ribs. He answered the query with a trembling chin.

"Why do you wake me?"

"Yer crying, boy. In your sleep. Hush up."

It was impossible to find comfort. Some soldier always seemed to kick out, or toss in slumber; and more than once, Witty's face had been nudged or kicked inadvertently by a fellow sleeper. Once he discovered a hand searching his pockets for purposes of enrichment. He bit the man's thumb in the dark and the hand did not return. Cotton's own hand rested on the handle of his pistol, the one he had traded his snuffbox for, leaning against the stone battlements of Fort Ticonderoga. Many miles back, he thought, and a near-lifetime ago. The lead I once intended for Durable Hatch may now preserve for myself, to terminate my own torment. Or for Mary.

Up from his sour stomach bubbled half-digested ox meat. Earlier, the darkness had hidden his revulsion, as he forced himself to partake it. Tomorrow, will our troops eat my mare?

Please, please, he thought, let me go to sleep. And do not awaken me, please God, unless I open my eyes and I am with Mary, back home at South Wind. I shall sneak softly into the great warmth of our kitchen and stuff my mouth with honey-biscuits until my bowels rupture. Or until Aunt Martha catches me and pretends to be annoyed, chasing me around pans of fresh dough, until I allow myself to be captured, taken and tickled by her big black fingers until I scream with giggling. Aunt Martha, herself an oven of a woman, warm and wise, knowing how much more I belong to her than she belongs to all of us, to South Wind.

I wonder. If dear Fate ever rewards me with my becoming South Wind's lord and master, will I ever grant Kino her freedom? Why, when it was so simple for us to be children, is it so distant a thing to grow up, and be a white man and a black woman? What would Kino do if she knew how very cold I am, so hungry, and so very alone? Mary and Kino and Winnie De Groot, and which shall spice my dreams this night? Oh, if my mind could only tire as my body is tired. Perhaps I should move my feet as I feel nothing now. Would only my mind darken to be as numb. Sleep, young sir, and dream sweet memories of South Wind and the fragrance of our kitchen. If only my mother and father could now behold their golden boy. Mother, a warm towel for my feet, if you please, before I rot on this ground. Your son is a fallen apple.

Off through the night, up on a ridge, a coydog howled, causing Cotton Mayfield Witty to shiver inside his greatcoat. Underneath the closely knit stand of hemlock, there was little snow, only a mat of short brown needles under his body. And out of the wind. Two other men slept there also, and his nose told him of how badly the three of them needed soap and water. But we are alive. I live, Father. Your son survives a winter that your most wild imagination could not endure.

He heard a tiny chirp.

Opening his eyes, he discovered a moving among the delicate green lace, just above his head. Within the stretch of his arm was the outline of a small bird, a round head and puffy little body, a short bill. A chickadee, he decided. In the daylight, the bird would have a dark head, a body of black and blue and white. Snow birds, Hatch had called them.

"Hello . . . hello, little bird," he whispered.

The bird should be asleep, thought Cotton, as should I. But here we are, daytime folk in a nightmare of a night, and perhaps he also longs to be farther south. "Do you?" he asked. Dropping to still a lower branch, the chickadee seemed to decide that Cotton was safe company. Lighting now on the boy's stomach, the bird found a sheltering little haven 'twixt thigh and bough, and became very still. I want to move, thought Cotton, and yet I cannot send my little friend away; not into a Berkshire wind and a Massachusetts winter.

"Wake up, ya young buck."

He heard heavy voices herald the morning; and it was lighter now, even under the hemlock bush. Looking for the chickadee, he saw nothing. Then he rolled over, fighting the stiffness of his wooden arms and legs. The shock came when he tried to stand.

Over he fell, face down, rough brambles scratching and tearing at his cheek. The shock of knowing his feet were useless hit him as he lay there, snow melting to water around his face and neck.

"God, my feet are dead!"

No one seemed to hear. He shouted, trying to kick with legs that had become granite, feeling no cold, no agony. Again he tried to stand on feet that felt nothing. His face ran with sudden sweat.

"What's wrong?" the bearded Shaker asked him.

"My feet are . . ."

"Stumpy?"

"They're dead."

"You know what you got?"

Cotton Witty looked up at the Shaker, wanting to ask. The question froze in his throat. He sat in the snow while the great purple hands of the big man undid his boots. The man was gentle, yet there was no need now for tenderness. The thick fingers pulled off the gray woollen stockings that the De Groots had given him, and the shock of seeing his own foot made his head spin. It was a sight of horror. He wanted to close his eyes, and did, yet he could still see his crippled feet and toes.

"You got blackfoot."

Witty's limbs were weak and shallow and shaking. From about the calves of his legs to the tips of his toes there was no Cotton Mayfield Witty. Watching, he saw the big purple hands touch his blue feet. He felt nothing. Somewhere below, coming up the hill behind him, he heard a familiar voice, as if the one who approached was a character in one of Cotton's dreams. He looked up and saw Hatch.

Bending low, the old man put his nose close to Cotton's inky toes and smelled. One whiff, and the old gray face looked up and into the eyes of the young Virginian. "Boil some snow," Durable snorted.

In a trice, the Shaker returned with a pewter pan of steaming water. With a grunt he set it down between Cotton's naked feet. "You'll cook him," the man warned Hatch.

"Maybe yes and maybe no."

Each man held a foot, dunking them in turn into the hot water, which Cotton could not feel. He wanted to scream with pain, but there was no pain, only the agony of knowing that there was no feeling in his feet, and no life.

"Fetch me some hoof tongs," said Durable.

The big Shaker held the stricken boy, sitting behind him in the snow, his massive arms and legs holding him so that he would not squirm while Durable Hatch worked the tongs as they were never intended to be used, on a horse or on a human foot.

One by one, he tore off Cotton's toes.

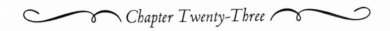

Chapter Twenty-Three

"Will I ever again walk?"

"Yup, you'll walk," said Hatch.

"How can I without toes?"

"Because ya have to. So you limp a mite, but you'll be walking, or maybe lean on a cane. You just won't do much dancing."

"I am crippled." Cotton's fists were doubled as he looked at Hatch, as the two of them sat the same fallen log.

"So you be. But you ain't the only crip that gets hatched out from under a war. Toes are easy to lose, next to fingers, or eyes."

Witty tried not to look down at the layers of bandages and rags that had been wrapped around the swollen stumps of his feet by Hatch, and yet he stared at the tatters of dirty muslin that, two days ago, had been boots and feet and toes.

Hatch spat. "I dang near to puked at the smell of your rot. So I done it. And if I'd a waited, the poison would a took your whole hoof, left and right, and ate its way up to your crotch. I don't guess a buck your age cottons much to lose that."

The old man gave him a knowing wink.

"No woman wants a cripple," said Cotton, "of any kind."

"And no army wants a griper like you. For two days, all you do is piss and moan about your dangfool toes. Well, we all be sad you lost 'em, boy. But the dag-busted world ain't about to stop its frolic on account some young colt don't kick up his heels quite so high. Half the men you see is froze and the other half is starved."

"Except for our fat Mister Knox," said Cotton.

"Henry had more to start with than most."

"He surely did."

"And so did you. From what I hear tell and mostly from you, all them Wittys down Virginny had life pretty dang easy. Softer'n a jack's ass. Summer all year long, with a crew of shiny folk to bend over. I seen your hands back then, when you and me an' Blue started out, and they looked to me like you ain't much as dug up a turnip."

Cotton was silent for a moment. Then looking at Durable Hatch, he said, "It's over."

"Over and done with, eh?"

"There's naught left for me."

"Be worse if'n you let it hobble your reason as well as your ramble. Them blue hoofs o' yourn will heal up. And best your brain does likewise, or you'll do little else but whimper the rest of your life."

"Is that so?" Cotton snapped.

"As I figure it, yes indeedy."

"Pig water."

"Looky now, lad . . . 'twixt today and the tail end of this here war, there's gonna be a spate of crippling, our boys and them Redcoat boys. War ain't so doggone heavenly."

"Here I sit. Unable to fight, or help the cause of Virginia."

"You already helped it, says I."

"Very little, sir. Damn you, did you really have to . . . ?" Looking down at the rags around his feet, Cotton Witty could not finish the question.

Hatch nodded his beaver hat. "I had to. And best you busy yourself and thank the Almighty."

"For blackfoot?"

"That I done what I did when I done it. Tell me, do ya feel the needles yet?"

"They hurt now. They hurt like the very Devil."

"Good and rightly. Stomp them stumps of yourn until you scream from the needles, and don't let your dumb hoofs sleep no more. Hear?"

"Why do you care?"

"What makes ya believe I do?"

"Such a simpleton are you, Mister Hatch, that you tend an enemy, one who would bind you with your own bowels to any one of these trees and allow you to await April."

"Laddie, you don't hate old Hatch."

"Why do you say this?"

"Because I be an old man who has a few decades put away in my pack. When ya live long as me, even a fool is bound to learn one thing or another."

"So what have you learned?"

"Love is one side of the tree and hate is the other. Ya know what you love? Your home in Virginny, and that cussed female horse, on account she's all you still got of the place."

Cotton nodded quietly. "You are correct."

"And the reason ya don't favor old Hatch too much is because . . ."

"Yes?"

"Because this war didn't turn out the way you figured, eh? Young Witty, who sits a comely horse and points a sword to order us common folk about. That about sum it up?"

Cotton felt his face redden. "I confess it."

"Hah! You're growing up, boy. Makes ya think that Virginny is more'n a couple of grunts away, and all uphill."

"Cannon to Boston," said Cotton softly.

"Exactly be."

Pulling off a mitten, and reaching a hand into the hip pocket of his heavy greatcoat, Cotton pulled out an apple. "It is a bit bruised, for I was saving it to share with Mary."

Hatch passed the boy his hunting knife, and watched him cut the red apple in two equal parts. "And now you have to half that there apple with yer old friend Hatch? Instead of yer mare? Say, that be some honor."

Witty wiped the blade clean, returning it handle foremost to the hand of its owner. "Must you make sport of everything?"

"Habit," said Hatch, his mouth and chin shining with apple juice.

"Durable, how you do master the art of expression."

"Yeah, a regular Samuel Adams be I."

"The King's iron," sighed Cotton, "is still in western Massachusetts. And here we sit, resting on a log. I hear two more oxen fell yesterday."

"Yup, two more. Knox'll bring fresh."

"How do you know?"

"It be Henry's disposing. Henry Knox'll fetch us beef enough to bull that there brass up and over, even if he loads it to here from . . . China."

"A determined man."

"Able of body and mind," said Hatch. "Now there's a lad who ought to be a general, like Schuyler and them all."

"Perhaps he will be one."

"My guess be. That is if'n the powers can study the straight of matters, and let politics be lone."

"You disdain politics as much as you seem to disdain everything else, do you?"

Hatch coughed. Deep in the old lungs there was heard a rattle and spewing that Cotton Mayfield Witty found alarming. God, he thought, do I concern myself over the health of my target? Or has old Durable amputated more than ten members? Did he also geld me? Cut off my enthusiasm? Stop coughing, you old woodsman, as it concerns me. For I have become a weakling. Or is caring for another a frailty? Hatch cares, and he totes the will of raw tripe.

"Dang this cough," said Durable.

"Best you mash the cherries, old man."

"Don't call me an old man, ya young whelp, or I'll cuff you into the winter like a she-bear do her cub."

"I am not your cub."

"Who says you ain't. Don't think it's my idea, as I don't warm to your company a whole bit, but I got orders to wet-nurse you 'twixt here and home."

"Home? Since when is Boston your home or mine?"

"It'll be both, seeing as we got the iron to guardian from this place to that."

"To *guardian?*"

"You heard me."

"Well, good sir, you don't have Cotton Mayfield Witty to guardian from here to our destination. In fact, you need not match me even one more easterly step."

"Ya can't make it on yer own gumption."

"Who says I cannot knows me not."

"I know ya."

Pausing to think, Cotton almost smiled at the old woodsman. "Indeed you do, Durable Hatch. You spotted my Virginia pride, threw a saddle across its back, and now you shall have me lash my own manner to bear me homeward. But I am neither pup nor puppet to you, Hatch."

"You are nothing to me, boy."

Am I to weep? Please, goodly God, let me not to cry before this old rascal. Yet already I feel the hot water in my eyes. "My father . . ."

"What about him?"

"He told me at our last confronting . . ."

For once, Hatch nearly whispered. "Tell me."

"Father said I was nothing to him and no longer his son, or Mother's. I did little to credit the name of Witty or Mayfield. And worse, by my folly a boy died and a horse destroyed, and with them my belonging to South Wind."

"You want to weep? Then weep."

"I am too grown to cry. I just want to talk about home, that's all," choked Cotton.

"Then talk, boy. Don't cost to talk."

And so Cotton Mayfield Witty talked, and Andrew Angus Hatch did listen.

"I wish we had another apple," said Cotton, at last.

"An' you'd eat it all yourself."

"But I'd make you watch me do it."

Hatch gave a grin. "Yup, you probable would. And then leave old Hatch freeze in the winter while you escort Henry Knox to Cambridge and let General Washington pin a tintag to your shirt."

"You . . . surprise me."

"Told ya I learned a thing or two."

"You read me like a book."

"I don't read. Always wanted to but never took me the time to learn. Seeing as you owned up honest, I don't guess it'd hurt me none."

"I . . . could teach you to read."

"Ya could?"

"Certainly. It can't be too difficult a trick, as I have met many who know reading and writing, and they are still near to being simpletons, compared to you."

Hatch smiled. "Which means either you got a lot brighter, or I did." The old man smiled again as Cotton felt himself grin.

"You are wise as my father is wise, and yet in quite a different way. Father does not read the wilderness like you and Blue Goose. Yet how I did marvel at how the brace of you studied as little as a bent fern and concluded what transpired. And how Blue Goose counted horses with his nose to the earth."

"Ain't he a dandy, old Blue."

"Was he your closest friend?"

"Yup, for late years. Winter and spring. I liked that red lad by the way he looked at life. The older a man gets, the more he respects youth. Long about every May, I stare at the ground and near to pray over a wee green sprout. Like I give thanks to the Benefactor that I can still see and smell what's coming up young and green. Youth fascinates me, be it a colt or a chick or a cantanky cub like you. Sounds like I'm a bit seedy under the scalp, but to look at you is like when I peek into an April nest and see a clutch of freckled eggs. Then comes May or June, and the doggone bird-lets bust out, and eager to taste it all."

"I understand, sir."

"Not yet ya don't. Not until you're hoary gray as me, all cramped and crooked. Old age sure be ugly. Maybe that's why us folk want something young around us. In all us crackly old brown leaves, there needs be a green sprig. But I pay the price."

"I don't catch your meaning."

"What I mean is, us old folks put up with you snots. I listen to Blue Goose whine for his Sky woman, in Canada. And I listen to you bellyache about this and that, and each time I hear myself give out an answer about as understanding as a cockleburr, and meaner than I truly be, inside."

"Now I understand."

"Good. Methinks time's come for you and me to meet each other halfway. Brown needs green for spirit."

"And green needs brown, to guardian." Cotton tried not to smile, and failed.

"Word of warning. I aim to call you Lieutenant Witty from this day on, 'twixt here and Boston. You earned it. But you got to *keep* earning. If a horse comes to a whoa, so does the wagon. I expect you to act like an officer, and serve like one. See to the men and see to the animals, as a real officer performs his office. Be a Lieutenant Witty, toes or no."

"But I can hardly walk."

"Hold fast. I got that into account. Hear?"

"I hear."

"And if you whimper that your hoofs hurt, or that your toes ain't around anymore to help ya count twenty, I'm going to boot your backside to Boston. You listening?"

"Sir, I listen."

"If you roll back downhill, and become that mean-mouth whelp again, or pity yourself, you don't get called Lieutenant."

"What do I get called?" Cotton smiled.

"Child Face."

233

"I wonder," said Cotton.

"Ya wonder what?"

"Oh, I was just wondering if Blue Goose were with us, if he would . . ."

"Still call ya Child Face."

"Would he?"

"He probable would."

"I would ask him to call me another name."

"Like what?"

"No Toes."

Gently, but with spirit, Hatch leaned forward and cuffed Cotton's head. It was surprising the old man could move with such quickness.

"Durable, I must tell you one more thing."

"About the pistol? I been waitin'. Figured it. And I see'd it on yer person. I been cogitating on you and all your dreams of home, and that I just might be a pesky pebble in your mare's shoe."

"You . . . *knew?*"

"Sure I knew."

"I had planned to kill you."

Durable Hatch stood up; his right hand rested lightly on the head of the small ax that rode his hip. "And I planned to stop ya."

"You planned to kill me?" asked Cotton.

"Like I'd swat a bug." Durable spat.

Cotton swallowed. "Truce?"

Hatch squinted, looking a bit uncertain. "Maybe."

"I will even give you my weapon to keep."

"Naw. Things are different 'twixt us now. You agree?"

"Yes, they are. I agree."

"Goody."

"I want to be your friend, as Blue Goose was."

"And I want to be yours." The old hand reached forward, and Cotton took it. Hatch's grip was hard and firm. "You'll do fine, lad."

"I thank you, Old Ax."

The old face twisted in a wide grin, and then came a laugh that held both its sides. "Hey! I plum forgot about yer present."

"A present for me?"

"Sure and certain. Sit right there and don't run off."

"As if I could. You got a mean old mouth."

"I got a mean old ax, too, and don't you never forget," the old man yelled as he scampered off through the snow. "Be right back."

He's some fellow, Cotton thought. Small wonder that Knox trusts him. What a fascinating chain of command. General Washington trusts Henry Knox trusts Durable Hatch, who now trusts Lieutenant Witty. How can I be so happy when I am also so cold and hungry and . . . he looked at the two wads of rags that covered the ends of his legs. His feet were still far too swollen to wear boots. Hatch had said his feet would soon heal and shrink, and be white again. Well, if Hatch said so, it must be true as Gospel. He looked up.

"Here she be!" yelled Hatch, leading Mary. "I fixed it with Knox. She's all yours, saddle and bridle and kick."

"But he needs to ride her, up and down the line."

"Not no more. I got your Mary a replacement."

"A replacement?" Struggling to his feet, he hugged the soft face of his mare. "How did you manage that?"

"Stole it," Hatch winked.

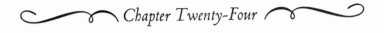 Chapter Twenty-Four

"Lieutenant Witty!"

Hearing his name so sharply spoken, Cotton neckreined Mary about. Urging her through the heavy snow, watching the great white plumes of her breathing, he joined the company of Henry Knox, who was also on horse. The same gelding, Cotton noticed, that Knox had dared to ride across the early ice of the Mohawk River.

"Sir!" Cotton saluted smartly.

"Good morrow, Lieutenant."

"And to you, Colonel Knox."

"Nay to that, lad, as I receive no word from General Washington that my commission was ever approved by Congress. I *act* as a lieutenant colonel and that sums it. However, I must thank you for the promotion in grade."

Cotton Witty laughed. "And welcome, sir."

"You still sit a saddle as though the two of you are one," said Knox, shifting his great bag of weight on Major.

The young man read honest appreciation on Knox's broad and open face. This, I do well, he thought. "Yes," he said aloud to Knox, "as my mare and I are more brother and sister than mount and master."

"I rode her thrice. A fine lady."

"Thank you, sir."

"Good to see you in boots again, lad. Soon you'll be right as rain." And then Knox frowned. "We have trouble."

"Of what nature?"

"Rebellion."

"Who?"

"The fifth team back. Stuck fast, and becoming surly. I am sending you on ahead to the town of Westfield. With you goes my sanction to employ two more yoke of oxen."

"Sir, there lies a town 'twixt here and Westfield."

"Of what name?"

"Blandford, sir. We saw it only from a distance, but we avoided the place."

"Good fellow. You recall your trip with Mister Hatch, do you not?"

"I do, sir. It was Hatch who seemed apprehensive about Blandford. And by the way, I enjoyed the jam you sent me, delivered by Mister Hatch. He ate some, too. More than half."

"Well, as his age be a problem, I dare not send Mister Hatch on ahead. He refuses to ride horseback, so the duty falls to your shoulder. So make haste and don't be lost in the snow."

"I shall return, sir."

"Of course you will, else I'd not advance you. Mister Hatch convinces me of your mastery of our route." Knox smiled. "Not quite equal to his own. So be off, and take a pistol." The look on the face of Knox said that he waited for Cotton's reply.

"I have one, sir."

"It pleases me, Cotton, to hear you confess it."

"Mister Knox, quite honestly it also pleases *me,* albeit hard to say good about a man who . . ."

"Amputated your toes."

Cotton swallowed, forcing himself to laugh. "Sir, I was born to ride a horse. And now I have less footage to catch in a stirrup."

"Aye, and well spoke. So hie yourself on to Blandford, claim you there be such a community, and conduct our affairs of commerce. Fetch us two yoke and a willing teamster. Stay the night and return the morrow."

Cotton paused. "Sir?"

"Yes, what is it?"

"Do you pack a pistol? If there's an uprising . . ."

"I am grateful, young sir, for your concern of my wellbeing. And God speed you."

Back along the column of straining men and beaten oxen, Witty rode Mary, until he found boxes and barrels in the snow, and a man in charge. From this quartermaster, a large white-haired man whose name was Isadore Mercer, he was given a fresh yellow apple, dried beef chips, a raw carrot and a potato. Upon being informed of Witty's journey on ahead, the big man added two sticky cinnamon buns and a square of maple fudge.

"Jaw it slow," Mercer warned him. "And a fistful of snow on

your bare hand'll slow your animal down so's she'll pace herself and not wind out."

As Mercer spoke, Cotton again wondered why Durable had, on their earlier trip to Ti, so carefully pointed out the Blandford settlement from atop a distant ridge.

Mercer nodded his great head, almost a bull scratching his ear against a fencepost, thought Cotton. "Foller them waterfalls, one to the other. You'll hear 'em if you listen, so they'll take ya due. Keep the sun on your right ear."

"I will."

"And tell the man who comes back alongside that we're at the ponds."

"Which ponds? There are many."

"The waters west of the high spruce, and the third ridge in. Understand?"

"Yes, thank you."

Turning, Witty left the quartermaster among his barrels in the snow.

An hour later, Witty and Mary were alone. First he rode her; and then where the snow was over his knee, he stumbled ahead of her. Dismounted, the going was slower. But he would not risk straining her heart, or her vision. The white snow sparkling in the sunlight was blinding enough to his own sight; so as he led her, his muffler was over her eyes. Even though she saw little from beneath the wool, Mary followed willingly, trusting him, close enough on his heel to slack the rein.

Later, stopping to get out of a quick wind, they sought a brief shelter in a dense stand of spruce, surprising a covey of ruffed grouse. The drum of their wings startled both boy and horse. In a breath they were gone, a dozen of them having exploded up from his feet. As a lone feather dropped, Cotton's hand captured it. The shaft of the feather was speckled brown; the tip was white, edged with black. For luck, he stuck the partridge feather in the band of his hat.

"And called it macaroni," he sang aloud, and laughed.

Mary nickered, tossing her head, rattling the bit rings of her bridle.

"Very well, I shall sing to you no more of Yankee Doodle. Since when, my dearest Mary, did you convert to a Tory?"

They moved on, quietly, rewarded when they heard the distant rumble of what could only have been a waterfall. Hatch had not brought him this way. Neither of them, nor Blue Goose, had seen a waterfall. Oh, a few rapids through rocky chasms, but no drop of significance. As they waded closer through the snow, the swollen sound filled his ears, seeming to come from every tree, every bush, and from under each drift of snow. Such was the omnipresence of its roar.

Bursting through a wall of spruce, he suddenly saw the falls; above him, a great white tower of water from a source somewhere high in the heaven, way above the trees. The spire of water came from over a rock ledge, through a narrow spout, then hurtled down in long and graceful shafts of bubbling silver, driving into the pool beneath. Some of the lances of liquid met rock, only to be instantly splintered to a fine mist. Every growth about was wet with fog, and each icy twig was beaded with wee drops of water. Touching a whip with his mitten, he saw the covey of drops flush downward to a snowy shelter.

They both drank from the pool, feeling the mist bathe their faces and backs. Cotton looked up at the falls until his neck ached.

"Mary, what guess you? I would estimate the waterfall to be over two hundred feet. There is a pond up there, but best we not climb up now to see it."

Again they drank, tasting a final icy sip of irony water that was tinted a subtle hue of reddish brown. Except where the water was fast, all rocks and fallen timber were frosted with glittering ice. Both banks were edged in white lace.

"We have seen it," said Cotton to his mare. "For we have discovered, you and I, what no man or horse has ever found. This must be the Palace of the Fairy Queen."

One last look at the sugary palace with its two-hundred-foot courtyard fountain, and off went horse and rider, richer than before they had seen such a sight. Due east, he told himself. Sun on my right ear, come midmorn. Now, I should say. Some of their passage had less snow and was downhill, which speeded their progress toward Blandford. There he heard another roar.

"The second falls," he said to Mary. "Well, old man Mercer was correct."

Following the noise, he found it; less high than the first waterfall. Down came the cascade. Crystal spines and quills of ice protruded from every bush and rock; and directly underneath the waterfall, the ice had formed a huge mound of white sculpture the size of the manor at South Wind.

"See that, Mary? Another castle for us to remember."

Over his right shoulder, he watched the sun weakly work its way westward, lower and lower, until the shadow cast by each leafless treetrunk grew longer to the northeast. Inside his greatcoat, he shivered. The day was growing colder as well as rapidly darker. Dismounting, he fed another handful of oats to Mary and fed himself a sticky bun, his mouth struggling to thaw its hardness. As he swallowed, a great cloud of snow slipped from entrapment high in pines overhead, falling with a muffled report that made him jump. His sticky hand tightened on Mary's rein.

Am I a coward?

His face was instantly awash. What was it that old Durable had said about the Mohawk? He didn't know where the Mohawk had holed up, Hatch had hollered, and lived a few extra winters admitting it. Right now, his trembling stomach almost warned him, at this very moment, red eyes could be spying on Mary and me. An arrow could already be fitted to a bowstring and thin coppery hands could be drawing . . .

Stop!

I must not allow my sanity to erode in such a manner. If an arrow comes, then come it shall. And to think I sang aloud. Would a Mohawk warrior sing aloud in enemy forest? Nay, nor would a Huron. Do I learn so little from Hatch?

"Let's go, Mary," he whispered, easily swinging his right leg up and into the saddle; like a bird to its nest, his right foot pierced the stirrup without his looking down.

The mare picked her way through the thick evergreen. Behind them, the sky held little sunset; only a faint crimson snake on the westerly ridge. How far back is my column? And how far ahead, he asked himself, is the Blandford settlement? Silently his hand patted Mary's neck. Darker and darker grew the day, until there was no more daylight. Only evening and nightfall. Hatch had warned him of this once, but perhaps he had not listened about night attacking a winter afternoon. Had he and Mary tarried too long to admire the waterfalls? At least, he told himself, I shall freeze to my death remembering nature's art and beauty. Dear God, I would be home. Please hear me, Lord, and take us back. My toes are gone, and I'll not ask for their restoration. But I know South Wind is still back home in Virginia. And if we die, take both Mary and me as one, and let Heaven be as fair as a Virginian May.

How fair the name, Virginia, and it skips like a merry little tune. A minuet, to which I shall not dance again. Do I allow myself to slip into the pit of pity? Hatch would not approve. But old Hatch is not here to see me weep; and were he, I would dry my eyes and try to be a man. Alone and lost and cold, I am not a man yet. Just a frightened cub. Is this what manhood is about, constantly performing deeds that wet the hands and unstring the knee? Smash legs and rip away part of one's feet? Beat oxen until they drop and then render them into stew?

Mary tossed her head, nostrils dilated as if to learn what news the winter wind could bring. Cotton sniffed. Smoke! Yes, it was woodsmoke. Only a wisp of it, here and gone.

"Whoa, dear girl. Stand fast."

Standing on her saddle, he pulled his body upward into the lower branch of a great pine. Shaking the tree, he covered himself and the mare with a mist of powdery snow. Upward he climbed, stopping only to bare his hands to sure his hold on the limbs. His fingers now felt the sticky pitch, safe and sure, as he climbed higher.

His heart leaped! Seeing the yellow specks of windows nearly caused him to fall. Was it Blandford? From his high perch in the pine, Cotton Witty's descent was closer to a sliding jump than a downward climb. Snow was on the brown of Mary's saddle, which he sat on with little care, as his neck was now wet with melting and his hands smeared with pitch as he pulled on his mittens.

"Come on, Mary."

She needed no urging, as if the enthusiasm in his voice told her that a barn was ahead, a stable already warm with the heat of other horses. Even cows would be acceptable. Water and hay and a respite from winter mountains. So she bounded through the snow, up and over it when drifts were before her. The mare's ear pointed forward, listening and smelling for further signs that the day's trek was coming to an end, where oats and sleep would be welcome.

"Easy, girl," laughed Cotton Witty, as woodsmoke again found his nose. The mare must have smelled it, too. Someone is *cooking!*

Bursting down from the pines, they were suddenly in pasture; a meadowland covered with snow, yet a clearing that was an upland part of the community whose lights now beckoned from below. Now only the throw of several stones distant. Almost within musket range. The bright windows made him yell.

"Hello, down there!"

It was all he could do to hang on; Mary seemed mad with impatience. Ahead, the posts of a fence bristled up through the white face of the meadow. Up and up, high into the winter night she bounded, almost disappearing into deeper snow on the yonder downhill side, deposited there against the fence by an upsweep of wind. For several seconds, the deep snow swallowed her body and his legs. Kicking, her head strained forward, up and out. Witty tried to rein her in, but Mary had never been an animal to be closely held. A meadow, green or white, apparently seemed a place where speed was called for. It took several more lunges on her part to free herself and her rider from the deep snow. Ahead, the yellow windows of homes and hearths brightened. Drawing closer to the first cabin, Cotton was slightly alarmed to see shutters bang shut, suddenly snuffing out (to his vision) the welcoming orange of the firelight from inside.

"Hello!" he shouted; in happiness, and as a precaution to skirt any suspicion in the minds of Blandford's citizens that he and Mary were hostile callers. He yelled a hello twice more, his own voice sounding crisp and cold in the darkness. Should I, he asked himself in caution, repeat here the name of Andrew Angus Hatch?

As he rode Mary close to the cabin, he saw a few lights from neighboring dwellings. Blandford, he remembered from last autumn, was a settlement of modest size. Hard to judge how many families. On the further side of the first house, a goodsized barn loomed out of the darkness. A calf bawled, making him smile.

A door opened. A musket barrel issued from it. Musket and hands and a bearded face. As the man turned sideways in the open door, matted in a yellow frame, the firelight at his back gilded the edges of his beard to a fire. The red beard almost appeared to be roasting.

"Who ye be?"

"Lieutenant Cotton Mayfield Witty, sir, of the Continental Army of our united colonies, en route with Colonel Knox of Massachusetts."

"What do ye want?"

"Shelter for now, please, for me and my mare, and to hire oxen for the morrow."

"Ye be no Massachusetts man," said the musket aimer. Behind him, a woman tried to keep children from pouring out of the door.

"No, good sir, as I am bred and born a Virginian. Have you heard of General Washington?"

"Who?"

"Washington, sir. May I approach, please? The only weapon I carry on my person is a small pistol in my belt beneath my greatcoat. But with mitts on my hands I offer no threat, sir."

"Ye don't favor no general to my eye." The man's musket continued to level at Witty's heart. His big white hands looked more than sturdy enough to pull the trigger. As he spoke, his thumb cocked back the hammer with a sharp click!

"My name is Cotton Mayfield Witty, sir," he said like a fool, as if the respected houses of Mayfield or Witty would strike with any weight upon a Blandford ear.

"Shoot him, Ferris!" It was the woman's voice, brassy and brittle, and as Massachusetts a voice as Cotton's own hearing had thus far experienced. A voice, he told himself, that has known little other than work or worship. God, he prayed, let me please not die in Massachusetts. Not in this forbidding feehold where hearts are hickory and where foreign faces stare at you like stones.

Ferris yelled at him, breath smoking from his mouth. "Ride off! Else I cut down on ye, hear?"

"I hear. Yes, I'll go."

As he rode away, Ferris fired. Lead whined over Witty's head, and its whistle close to his ear almost made him throw up. At the next cabin, the man who opened the door also had a beard, a greeting that made Cotton Mayfield Witty pause before stating his identity and business. But this man smiled, lowered his musket, and told Cotton to bed down his horse around back in their barn. And to help the mare to hay. Putting on a coat, the man joined Cotton in the barn, watching him as he eased the cinch and pulled off Mary's warm saddle.

"Who lives in that first cabin, sir?" asked Witty, his voice still a bit unsteady.

"His name's Jack. Ferris Jack. Pay no mind to him. He's daft, and his woman, too. And half them young he spawned. He shot more'n his share. Keep clear o' him, boy."

"I will, sir. I will keep my distance."

"Best ya do. If ye don't want no hole in your coat."

Chapter Twenty-Five

Barbara and Glenn Holding suppered Cotton well. Later they provided him with an extra quilt before sending him to sleep in their stable.

"Warmer out there than in here," said Holding, pointing to his barn, "so we hope ye don't bother too much. Here, have a nip of fruit brandy." He handed Cotton a gray earthenware jug the size of a melon.

"Fetch it abed with ye," Barbara said. "Glenn drips good spirits and right from our own orchard."

"Honey's the secret," said Holding. His lean finger tapped the jug. "A ladle or two adds sweet to it. Taste her again."

Inside his belly, Cotton Witty felt the rage of the brandy. The smooth sweetness of peach warmed his throat. No burning, only a warmth which was as welcome as wool to a body craving for heat as his belly earlier had echoed for food.

Barbara nodded. "Our own peach tree," she said with pride in her voice, as though such a fruit tree was their one indulgence.

"My, that's tart," said Cotton.

"Thanky. Bring the jug to your bedside."

"Help ye to slumber," said Barbara. Like her husband, Mrs. Holding was a lean soul, hands red and shiny from work. A strong face, not without beauty. The Holdings were, Cotton concluded, folk who could laugh along with labor.

"Your supper, my lady, was most filling and fine. And its partaker will require little bedtime spirits to put him to rest." He suppressed a yawn. "I owe you both a debt."

"Fair enough, and come morn," said Holding, "we shall yoke our oxen and be for hire. My young cousin, John Holding, will add his yoke to mine to go west at sunup. Just ye and my cousin if he be willing. He has no wife. Leastwise, not yet."

Out in the stable, Cotton arranged his bed of straw close to where Mary would stand the night. As his host had promised, the stable was warm from cattle heat with a clean fragrance of milk cow. Feeling full and festive, he tipped the jug again, allowing the peach brandy to flood his throat. Warm, oh how warm! Cotton made sure to pull off both boots. Yanking down his stockings, he scratched his legs in relief from their contact with the itchy cling of all-day wool. Ah, he thought, how pleasant 'twould be to don white stockings again, and satin britches, and clean white ruffles under my chin. Lace at my wrists, and a lace handkerchief to blot a shred of falling snuff. How perfectly dear Father had mastered the grace and flourish of such a gesture.

My feet hurt.

Thank the Heaven they do. He eased the belt of his breeches, pulling Barbara's great quilt of pink and white squares over himself. As his head sank into the pillow, he felt the yielding muslin puff up, rising to caress each of his ears. The good fortune of feathers beneath a tired pate is so humble a comfort; and yet how seldom did I ever, when abed at South Wind, ever appreciate so homey a haven for my head. A pillow!

As Cotton closed his eyes, brandy washed over his brain, causing his wit to spin, and the dim rafters overhead to twirl as if they were no more than twigs in a tempest. His eyes opened quickly, to force the whirling to abate, as it slowly did. Yet with each droop of his lids, the spin would again begin, throwing his senses wildly about and dunking his reason in a peachy pool. A hiccough startled him awake, but only for a wink, his eyes once more sagging away from the woes of vision and the responsibility of consciousness. His mind rode Mary over forbidding fences and straight up frozen waterfalls aglitter with embroidered icicles. His hand reached out, broke off a frozen spike; and between the bite of his teeth, the icicle was flavored with orange and lemon and spice. Ice that tasted like brandy, he wanted to suddenly shout to all the sleeping ears in Christendom, and of a comb of honey.

Looking over at Mary, he saw only her shadow in the darkness. He had been given neither candle nor lantern. Fire and hay were unsuitable bedfellows. There were no windows in the stable, but a thin crack did allow him a slit for curiosity. Outside, he saw as he rolled over to peek, was bright with moonlight frosting the snow. Tomorrow I return westward, he thought, back into those cussed Berkshires, to ledges and loads and lifting, to the bellowing of blistered men whose bowels rupture with the budging of brass. To bulls with no balls and to men with no music. So here I lie, Cotton Mayfield Witty, from two established families of Virginia, I shall have you know, and who will now bestow upon his one craw another roasty pull of Brother Holding's peach and honey.

He swallowed a hearty gulp of brandy, and then two more.

Soon his head danced, eyes open or eyes at rest; but now there was merry music. Fiddles and young girls singing, giggling, calling his name to come and waltz them around a great silver ballroom of snow and ice. Cotton! Cotton! Soft words, Virginian voices of flutes and woodwinds, yet peppered with a banshee wail that hollered out an order in an abrasive Massachusetts tone:

"Shoot him, Ferris! He ain't no general! Cut him full of holes."

It took many a dizzy dance before the orchestra finally was folding its music, casing the violas, stealing off into pink and white checkerboard cottages . . . while bees buzzed, making honey from peach blossoms. And everyone was caught up in a lilt of laughter.

Later, in the night, a hand touched his face.

Without fully awakening, he brushed the hand aside, but the touch came again. Perchance a dream? He had no need to fortify his senses. Yet the touch of fingers persisted on his face, inside his shirt. In truth, a body was close to him, an intimate fragrance that was surely neither horse nor cow. Nor sheep, nor goat, hen, or wild turkey.

This was female.

Opening his eyes, he saw the blur of a face just above his own, staring down at him in the darkness. Hands were tugging at his clothing, unsuccessfully. Yet with purpose, as this was one strong female. His efforts to sit up served little use. Pushing him back onto the straw, her eager lips found his, and her body was ample; and more, she was clad in a nightgown that offered scant modesty. Its skirt was yanked up over her beefy and buttery thighs. Accidentally his hand touched the trunk of her leg and she snickered in the dark. Then she spoke, not in a woman's voice, but in the higher octave of a child.

"Don't tell," said her tiny voice.

Even though he was still clothed, her great thighs seemed to be walking on him, as a drafthorse before a plow.

"Who . . . who . . . ?" He tried to ask her who she was; but her mouth covered his, making conversation impossible.

"Promise," squeaked the elfin voice. "Promise ye won't tell nobody."

Again her hands pulled at his clothing, his shirt, his belt. Fingers anywhere and everywhere. Cotton thought his ribs would crack beneath her weight. He tried to breathe. Meanwhile, the woman panted like an uphill ox. A whale of a woman with a voice of a toddling tot. This cannot be. I am merely drunk, he thought, and this nubile nightmare was spawned from inside a brandy keg. But *who?* The Holdings had no children. And this surely was not Sister Holding, as she was leaner than a dry-spell bean.

"Ye won't tell," her voice tinkled again, into his ear and piercing his brain with a curiosity that was by no means desire.

"Please," he grunted beneath her weight, "can you stop for a moment?"

"Ye just rest, sweetsop. And I'll do."

"I . . . can't . . ."

His protest served only to spur her ardor. Up and down on his clothed person she jiggled and flounced with such enthusiasm that he feared for his own safety. Will she rupture me, this billowing buffalo, before I can toss her off?

"I seen ye," she whispered into his ear, causing him to flinch with the suddenness of her remark. "Before."

"Where?"

"Back home." She fumbled with his shirt.

"Virginia?"

Strange, but I remember no bison such as this. Am I mad? Can one brandy one's brain into such a hellish hallucination as this Princess of Peach?

"I demand to know who you are," he said, feeling as absurd as his statement. This female turns me to a fool.

"Ye don't got no beard."

"Who . . . ?"

"Well, ye can call me Love."

"Love?"

"Guess my righteous."

"Your *what?*"

"My righteous name," said the doll's voice.

"Aphrodite?"

"No. My name's Lovebreed."

"I don't believe . . ." His doubting was cut off as her full weight descended on him, snuffing out conversation as though a wee candle in a wind. He grunted in genuine pain.

"I just says it over and over."

"A comely name. Please get . . ."

"Truly be."

"Tell me your family name," he asked her, trying in desperation to prevent her hands from ripping away his blouse.

"Jack."

Her name struck his memory with the force of a brickbat. His breath stopped; and he heard naught but the rustle of straw beneath his helpless back, and the hammer of his heart as it increased tempo with every pump.

"Lovebreed Jack," she recited.

"No."

"Ye spoke to my pa."

"Yes."

"Ye gonna tell about us?"

"Never."

"Swear it." Her strong fingers grasped the soft flesh just at his hipbone, pinching and twisting and demanding. "Ye swear it, hear? Don't tell Pa."

"Yes, dear lady, I swear to you," grunted Cotton, "in the holy name of Heaven and all saints who there abide, *never* shall one word pass to Ferris Jack."

"Not *never*." Her pinching increased.

This woman, Cotton told himself, is disturbed. She is truly touched, the insane daughter of an insane man, and I do pity her fear. His fingers fought her hand, trying to release her grip on his flesh. Is she a blacksmith? Truly these are tongs that bite my body, not female fingers. I am in total pain.

"I swear it."

"Good." Her fingers relaxed.

In his eyes, water formed. He had to get out from under this mule of a maid. Her voice! Is she some sort of oversized child? Yet how could a mere heifer be so hefty?

"Please . . . get off."

"Why for?"

"I cannot breathe, or more, or even think."

"Ye gonna tell Pa?"

"No, not that. I vow to you, dear miss."

"He beats me, Pa does."

What, wondered Cotton, will Ferris Jack do to *me* when he learns of this? Need I ask? And worse, need I ask this lunatic of a lass to defend me from her papa's wrath? I must somehow free myself of this frolicsome filly so that I can defend my honor. To blazes with defending hers.

"Let's have at it," she moaned, trying to cover his lips and cheeks with wet and wandering kisses. "Right now."

A door banged open!

Lantern light flooded the stable, coming closer and closer, until the straw seemed to burn orange. Strange shadows danced on the walls as the lantern swung to and fro in a hurried hand.

"No," said Lovebreed's tiny voice.

Is it Ferris Jack? Cotton tried to twist his head to look at the approaching light, until Lovebreed pulled the skirt of her night-gown over his face. This girl, he now knew, is of unsound mind. And here I lie, innocent, and soon to be accused of forcing my attentions on a daughter with a bull's body and a pea for a brain. Brandy still churned inside his reason. Suddenly he laughed.

"Shoot me, Ferris," he tried to say.

Then, mercifully at last, the girl rolled off him and he looked up at a strange male face. The man in black clothes wore a beard, though not as full a growth as Jack's or Holding's. He held a lantern and a pistol.

"Damn ye, Lovebreed."

"Don't anger none, John."

"Anger none? How in hell do ye think ye an' me'll ever wed, if'n all ye do . . ."

"Are ye ired?" Her tiny voice was pale and pathetic, sounding contrite and confused, when all she had wanted to do was to make love in the dark with a bypassing soldier. The light in the stable bathed her face with innocence. Lovebreed had pretty features, possessed of a face that no sane person could strike.

Cotton felt strangely protective.

"Lovebreed Jack, ye would truly ire Jesus."

"Sir," said Cotton, "I realize how matters would appear . . ."

Slowly, in an iron-steady hand, the pistol moved an easy arc from Lovebreed Jack to the breast of Cotton Witty. The small black hole raised itself, eye to eye with him. How soon, he wondered, will a ball of lead smash into my head and leave me with less reason than even this poor girl who now shivers beside me in her nightrobe? Carefully, and with gentle hands, Cotton covered Lovebreed with the pink and white quilt.

"Who are ye?"

"I am Lieutenant Witty, sir, at your service."

"*My* service? At the service of my woman, more like."

Lovebreed laughed, a trill of tiny notes that seemed to come from a fallen wren, a lost mind, misunderstood and scorned; and worse, with an eager body and no doubt put upon by males of precious little compassion.

251

The young man's pistol moved from soldier to girl, back and forth, as though uncertain of its prime target. He appeared to be preparing to either discharge his weapon or hurl the lantern. Another man entered the stable.

"What happens here?" asked Glenn Holding.

"Look what I find in your barn, Cousin."

"Quiet now, John," said Glenn.

"Who's he be?"

"He is my guest. Name of Witty."

"Fetch me a knife, Cousin Glenn."

"No. Ye'll not do that no more."

"Sinner!" John hissed at Lovebreed.

The girl was crying, cuddling closer to Cotton, until he could do naught else but raise his hand and take her trembling person, still wrapped in the quilt, beneath his arm. Lovebreed Jack's pudgy hands pulled the quilt up over her mouth, so that only her weeping eyes were exposed. Below, on the straw floor, one of her white feet covered the other as though to mask her shame.

"Harlot!"

All eyes turned to the big man in the doorway, the irate sire who had yelled the one word at his daughter. He bore no gun, but his hand held a long curving sickle, with an edge which appeared to be able to decapitate an ox. "Harlot!" Again he snarled the word, slashing the night air with the blade's whistle.

"Go home, Ferris," said Glenn Holding.

"I'll nay do such until I see justice paid this night. Fetch a rope."

"Soft," said Glenn Holding, "or else I may dunk you in the horse trough." Calmly he lifted a manure fork by its long handle, holding it across his wiry body, pointing the tines at no one.

"He will hang," said Ferris Jack through narrowed eyes.

"He'll not," said Glenn Holding.

Cotton, looking at the young face of John Holding, wondered whose side in the rumpus that he'd be on. Not mine, Witty soon concluded.

Ferris Jack pointed at Witty with an accusing finger. "Never," he said, "will that there soldier leave Blandford alive."

"Go to your home, Ferris Jack, and take with ye your daughter."

"But . . . he outraged her."

"Sir, I did not."

"Liar."

"I got a disgrace on my name," said Ferris Jack. "I got me an unwed daughter near to twenty."

"And I was waiting on ye, Lovebreed," wailed John Holding. "Ye said ye was not yet sixteen."

"Ain't law," said Ferris Jack.

"What ain't?"

"Ye know our law here, Glenn Holding, and it be God's law and Canaanite law."

Canaanite law? Witty's mind raced, trying to make sense from what he heard. Dare he ask? No, he thought, I best keep silent.

"First weds," said Ferris.

"Her first man . . ." Glenn Holding paused to think.

"Was that stinking old trapper," said John.

"Hussy!" hissed Ferris Jack at Lovebreed.

"That old trapper, Duration Hatch."

Hatch? Cotton now knew why Durable had not wanted to enter Blandford on the way to Ticonderoga. The old goat.

"I was only thirteen," said Lovebreed.

"Hush your mouth."

"Her first man," said Cotton, "is one who this very night approaches and will arrive in this very settlement in a matter of days."

"Who it be?"

"A man of Verdmont," said Cotton, "name of Angus Hatch."

"That's him," said Lovebreed. "But he weren't the *first*."

"Damn his eyes!" said John Holding.

Oh, thought Cotton, I cannot wait to see Angus Hatch squirm his way out of this little trap. A wedding! Ah, what a just deserving for such a scalawag.

253

"I do know Mister Hatch," said Cotton, "and he be one who speaks of you with heartfelt longing, and respect, Sister Jack."

"Canaanite law," said Glenn Holding, "reads that the first man to lay up with a woman is to *wed* her, rightful and proper."

"Best I brand ye the letter," said Ferris Jack to his trembling daughter.

"No, she don't get no hot iron put to her," said John Holding.

Plain to see, observed Cotton, that Glenn's young cousin is more than smitten with this halfwit girl. Good, say I. For he shall love and cherish her, and not beat her. Best they wed. But first, we must hasten our old Verdmonter here to face the fruits of his philandering.

"That old trapper," John complained.

Ferris Jack sang the sickle blade as though preparing to separate Durable Hatch from the inspiration of further activity in the heart. Or the hay.

"I don't want to wed nobody," said Lovebreed, "except maybe the soldier boy, or John."

"Or that man Hatch," said Glenn.

"Law is law."

"Go home, sir," said Cotton, "for I am innocent of wrongdoing. I have not fouled your daughter. Nor would I. She is a woman who could perhaps use more understanding and less beating."

"Hatch soon comes," said Glenn Holding, "so little more can be gleaned this night. To chambers, everyone. Begone from my stable, all."

Arguing the points of their law, the four Canaanites left Cotton Mayfield Witty alone in the stable. Exhausted, he again fell into the straw, pulling the quilt snugly under his chin, hopeful that he would not be further molested. I feel sorrow for Lovebreed, he thought, even perchance my sympathy may be wasted on one who is perhaps more happy than the rest of us who more oft command our faculties.

Drifting off to sleep, Cotton thought of Durable's arrival at the settlement of Blandford, and smiled.

Chapter Twenty-Six

Leaving the settlement of Blandford became, even at the cold and early hour of their westward departure, an attraction.

Better than a score of settlers of assorted size and sex waded through the snow to wave goodbye to John Holding. He was, Cotton concluded, a well-liked young man. A food basket was suspended by John below and between his ox team, hanging from an iron hookring and swaying like a silent churchbell. I would starve en route, Cotton told himself, before he shares even one bite with me. Little matter, as Barbara Holding had his saddlebag already packed with foodstuffs for his return to the Berkshires. A belt encircled John's black coat, into which his pistol rode.

Ferris Jack was not present.

Glenn Holding brought his Holstein yoke of black and white oxen, in color and pattern much like John's, bringing the total of their livestock to four kine and Cotton's mare.

"Best ye unyoke at the wood," Glenn told John, "unless ye follow a wagon trail. If'n it be a horse path, ye'll hang up your animals on every tree, be they in yoke."

John Holding nodded, saying not a word.

Surrounding the mare, the four oxen, and the two young men, the circle of gaping Canaanites were all dressed in black. Coal on snow, thought Cotton. The men of Blandford all wore beards and black hats with wide flat brims, and appeared as stern and mirthless men, with the one exception of Glenn. Barbara smiled at the two, waving a farewell.

"Come back soon!" Lovebreed twittered. A black scarf was under her chin, up around her head, hiding her handsome hair of amber curls and causing her fair face to be cherry round. She is truly pretty, thought Cotton, plump though she be. Dare I wave goodbye to her? Perhaps it be wiser if I refrain my farewells, as her husband-to-be is both sized and surly. Ah, but big John could not despise me more than already.

As he swung his leg with grace into Mary's saddle, Cotton waved to her. "We shall see you in a few days, Lovebreed."

All heads turned black hats and blank Canaanite faces to stare at Lovebreed Jack. Only one present narrowed his eyes at Cotton Mayfield Witty, the eyes of John Holding; and beneath his eyes, the line of his mouth hardened as though his jaws had locked into raw meat.

One by one, the arm-waving children dropped back, returning down to their cabins in the clearing; tiny black specks, bedbugs on a white sheet.

At the forest edge, as Glenn Holding had earlier advised, they unhitched the oxen, roping the two yokes for back portage. Single file, they entered the great wall of green fir. Cotton led the lead ox with a rope halter, as he rode Mary. He wondered why John Holding had come on foot. He had seen few horses at Blandford. The cozy barn of Barbara and Glenn had housed only two milk cows, two oxen, and a yearling calf; all other animal heat having been so voluntarily supplied by Lovebreed Jack.

Had her first lover been Durable? Why, that rambunctious old ram! I shall, upon my return, take friend Hatch aside to instruct him in the matters of Canaanite law. A hunch haunts me that Andrew Angus Hatch, a season ago, did hie himself out of Blandford slightly out of musket range but not musket hearing. 'Twas a rich jest. Cotton laughed.

"Ye laugh at me, boy."

At his back, the five words of John Holding sounded to Cotton as if a weapon had been drawn, a knife or a pistol. John bore a pistol, but Cotton had heard no threatening click of its hammer. Turning his mare, Cotton looked back at the tall young man, whose weapon still stuffed his wide leather belt.

"I beg your pardon, John, but I was only recalling an amusing story related to me several weeks back."

"Ye turn me out a fool?"

"Nay, I do not, sir. 'Twas not I that joined your settlement to seek more than one man and four oxen. And that's all."

No more was spoken. Their column continued, moving up through the snow and trees at a slow walk.

Cotton dismounted, later on, to lead Mary through thickets of evergreen where spruce, pine, hemlock, fir, and balsam abounded. Behind the mare, John Holding led the oxen in single file; the lead ox unburdened to help to break trail, the next two toting a yoke each, and the drag ox plodding along with a fodder sack plus Love-breed Jack's basket of victuals. The basket promised a hearty noon meal and supper.

Up into the Berkshire Mountains climbed the lieutenant, mare, man, and four oxen. Up, up, up . . . heading due west, and slowly feeling the sun on their left shoulders, whenever a small clearing was bisected, to tell them they headed due west. Now they walked where the snow was not as deep, and melting.

"How come ye walk so odd?"

Could a musket ball have hit Cotton's back, between his shoulders, with as deep a stab as John Holding's question? Even as they waded through snow, the Canaanite has noticed my manner of walking. Perhaps, thought Witty, he merely wishes to create conversing to lighten our uphill load and to trim our trek.

"I am crippled, sir." Cotton stood in the snow.

"Are ye?"

"Yes, from blackfoot, which took my toes."

"Took your toes off?"

"Yes, dammit. And all twelve."

I am bored with this oaf, Cotton thought; and here I go, to stir the pot of trouble. Can I ever change? Sorrowfully for me, nay.

"Ye got twelve toes?"

"Sir, I have none."

"Ye had twelve?"

"Seven left and six right, but no longer. For now a redhide

indian wears them about his throat for necklace. As my toes had turned hard and black, and since childhood my pointed toenails were quite elongated, this indian thought them to be claws of a bear. Is it not an amusement how addled some folk are?"

Behind him he thought he heard a mutter, hardly perceptible; and then silence. And, he thought, what a dunce I be to choose a Canaanite from Blandford of Massachusetts as an audience for my wit. Ha! The joke is on Cotton Mayfield Witty, and this dolt behind me escapes unscathed from the rapiers of all repartee.

"Our day turns warm, John," he said during the noon meal, feeling the January sun seep through the wool of his greatcoat.

"It do."

"As the snow melts, our trip shortens, eh?"

John Holding nodded. "But it don't hurry no ox."

"Pity we have only one horse. With no oxen to restrain us, if were mounted, we could be joining Mister Knox's force within the afternoon. As our progress lags, we shall be laying down our weary heads in snow, with no warm stable to comfort us."

Fool! Cotton chastised himself for his slip of tongue, marking at once the face of John Holding darken. Ass that I am, I reopen his wound. Agony annoints his anger and his countenance betrays his bitterness. Then why did he agree to go with me when the request was made of him? For the money? Perhaps, as a fat purse begets a fat bride in Blandford. But, methinks Prince John the Jealous, also known as Holding the Hapless, may be a lad of deeper motivation than a few precious dollars that Knox will drop onto the manure stains of his palm.

John Holding moved slightly as he sat the stump of a fallen spruce. As he changed his position, his right hand seemed for a moment to rest on the handle of the pistol that rode his belt. Draw it, said Cotton, and I will put a neat and nimble little ball of lead into your belly. I fled from my last duel in Virginia, from a man who would easily have enjoyed his execution of me. Yet from the likes of a John Holding, I flee not. My fist has discharged a score of pistols to his every yank of a trigger. How apparent it is to me, as I watch him, that he is unsophisticated in weaponry. Note his pistol, dear Cotton. Too long for speed, too bulky for accuracy, and destined in a duel to lie cold and unfired in the clumsy hand of a lost lad who made the error of challenging the courage of Virginia. The angle of his pistol lends not to its rapid employment.

God, let me not kill him! Now nor never, as I do fervently wish to slay no one.

"John, the more I think upon what happened in Blandford, I realize that I have compromised your good name, even though it was not my intention to do so. As it was my arrival in your settlement that caused remorse among folk with whom you may sustain your residence for years, I extend to you my apology." And I would even, thought Cotton Witty, offer my hand to this wretch were he to take it in friendship. Truly I would. As I would bless his marriage to his sweet and simple lass.

Holding sighed. "Go to Hell," he said softly.

We are now headed to that very place, thought Cotton, so I shall shrug off a sluggard's insult. High time I understood how any man could shy at what John Holding endured this past night, considering the confinements of Blandford and the wag of every tongue regarding the proclivities of his sweetheart. Well, 'twill be his lot to top her and tame her, and halter her to bed. Lord, the poor lass, and only commencing to nibble at this tree or that in the orchards of Eve, so let her ramble. Unfortunate creature. How can we all behold Lovebreed Jack and her womanly weight and forget that she still be little more than a babe in the brain, born with a bent to do childish pranks?

I wonder if Durable knew her simplicity.

"Let us move on," said Cotton, rising to stand.

"Go alone then. I'm fixed to rest a spell."

"Darkness will overtake us, sir. We are barely out of hollering distance from your settlement."

"Afraid, are ye?" Holding's slight smile held no happiness.

"Yes, I confess, I am."

"Afraid of the dark."

"You are correct. I am afraid of how the havoc of a snowy night can hurt. My feet are less than whole, and I wish not a like fate to my fingers."

"We're due a thaw. I know."

"Thaw to a thick Massachusetts skin can be a dead winter to a Virginian man or mare. Thus I vote for pushing on with alacrity to the west. I shall not tarry."

"Go then. Leave us follow."

"Do you bid me to take my mare and go, leaving you with the four oxen?"

"Rightly so."

"Very well. I shall mark the route with hoofprints, and oft I shall snap branches, eye level, from tree to tree. You'll not be lost."

"Lost? Soldier boy, I hunt these hills a-plenty."

"Then I take my mare and depart."

"Leave us, then."

"Very well. Mister Knox and his purse await you, beyond the two waterfalls and into the ponds."

"I know 'em."

"God speed you, John."

Foolishly he waited for Holding's answer. None was forthcoming. Limping to Mary's left flank, his leg swung its arc over the chestnut rump onto a saddle shiny as a buckeye. His heels touched her lightly and she loped into the curtain of trees, snorting as though she too was thankful to pull ahead of an oxen pace. Behind him, he heard the bellow of an ox; he asked himself if the sound could be an omen, a warning not to forge ahead. Perhaps I am the dolt, he thought, to leave the side of a man like John Holding who hunts these hills. I do not wish, however, to sleep in his company, as to close my eyes could well mean I close my book.

As he rode zigzag through the great green nest of spruce, he aimlessly tried to wiggle his toes inside his boots. Strange, he thought; when mounted I am yet whole. Only on foot do I stagger in a gelded gait. Hell with it! Cotton Mayfield Witty was created to sit on a saddle or lie with a lass, and damn if I need toes to play either part. Again he tried to wiggle his lost toes, feeling the uncanny echo of emptiness in the hollow caves of his boots. Damn you, Hatch! I still wonder if it needed to be done. Fie upon such questioning, as I saw the fear on his face as he first beheld the blackness of my toes. And did I not smell that reek of decay? How did old Durable perform such surgery without retching?

"Andrew Angus Hatch and Lovebreed Jack. Mary," he remarked to his mare, "now there is an absurd union."

Whoa! Ahead of him, the ground was brown and bare and steaming. Hot springs? Ah, but we did not come by this spot en route to Blandford. How interesting a place. Yet I would eagerly swap it for a more familiar landmark; a tree, a rock, and a pair of waterfalls. As the mare stood, her hoof pawing the bare mud with impatience, Cotton listened for the sound of falling water. I must think, he ordered himself, and not canter on in blithe confusion, relying on dear Providence to return me to Knox.

A slight urge of his head and Mary wheeled about until mare and rider rested in a tight grove of fir trees. Each of the boughs, he noticed as he dismounted, dripped with the melt of snow. Lifting the flap of his left saddlebag, he fed Mary a handful of dry oats, feeling the softness of her lips tickle his hand. For himself, he ate one of Dame Holding's buttery biscuits, then a slab of cold cheddar, an apple, and a score of dried grapes. He offered a raisin to Mary, who fetched it up from his palm with the tip of her tongue. There were more raisins, which man and mare shared until there were no more. The taste of fruit blended well with the wet and pungent fragrance of fir and juniper.

"Shall we go?"

The air had become heavy and gray with clouds. He searched the colorless heavens for direction, and paused before mounting, feeling the breeze in his face. Looking out between a break in the greenery boughs, he saw a whitetail doe. She was upwind of him and had not heard or seen Cotton or the horse. Calmly the doe strolled from a fir thicket, followed by six other doe, three yearlings and finally a massive buck. His rack of antlers must have been, Cotton tried to count, more than twenty points. Mary watched, her ears forward. Quietly she moved through the trees, nibbling a bud from a twig and pawing the bare ground, foraging at leisure. The browsing was unhurried, unhunted; and as softly as they had come, they floated through the treetrunks and away from the hot spring.

Cotton smiled, suddenly discovering in his own mouth a partially chewed raisin, a bit of fruit suspended in his cheek as he and his mare had been totally transfixed with the stately buck and his whitetail harem. He swallowed the raisin whole, barely able to perform even that, as his eyes continued to stare at the trees into which the great brute of a buck and his entourage had disappeared.

"Mary, did you see those deer? Nothing like that at South Wind, eh?" I wish we could tell someone about the stag, he thought, or that I were an artist with the ability to quickly sketch. Small wonder our friend John Holding hunts these mountains. A herd like that could stuff the stomachs of Blandford for most of a winter. Still in awe, his leg curved upward until the cold leather of saddle held him. Walking also quietly, Mary picked her way through the fir trees, as though she knew where the column commanded by Henry Knox awaited their return.

A pistol cocked. There could be no mistaking it.

All that Witty had recently eaten rushed upward from his stomach, and again he tasted each taste of what Barbara Holding had provided. Mary stopped, her head searching side to side, ears forward and twisting. The mare did not know the full meaning of the click that had so suddenly frozen her rider.

Cotton Mayfield Witty knew.

"Ye are a dead man," he heard the voice, which came from inside the green wall of trees on his left. He waited, wondering if he should suddenly jab his heels to Mary's ribs before the voice could fire this weapon. There was no question in Cotton's mind as to whose hand had cocked back a hammer and addressed him from hiding. As his head turned, he saw the bushes move, and the man whom he expected to fire before revealing his whereabouts slowly stepped into Cotton's view.

Ferris Jack, it was.

The red-bearded Canaanite carried a black musket, as black as his clothes and hat. His eyes were dark, the tip of his nose a brighter pink; but the total image of blackness was broken only by the fire of Jack's red beard, one live ember in a clutch of unburned coal.

"Git down," said Ferris Jack.

"If you kill me, Mister Jack," said Cotton dismounting, "I have friends in your settlement of Blandford, the Holdings, who will inform the advancing column of my death and by whose hand. And you will hang, sir. You will hang."

Walking forward, Jack pushed the musket's muzzle into Cotton's belly. Again, the younger man felt the food rise up into his throat, gagging him.

"Ye shamed us," growled the Canaanite. "So I come for ye. Waited here, and heard ye circle like ye was a lost lamb."

"John Holding comes behind me, sir, and will hear your shot."

Jack slowly shook his head in denial. "Nobody'll hear. John's done gone by, whilst ye circled. He's a ridge beyond." His thumb rested on the musket hammer as though a careless flick could send it forward. The tip of the gun again poked Witty's belly.

"Henry Knox will hang you."

"Ha! Nobody hangs old Jack. Not nobody."

"Our military column advances as we now talk, Mister Jack, over these mountains and toward the settlement of Blandford and West-field. You and your crime lie directly in their path. Kill me, and my men will hunt you for execution."

"Ye fouled my girl."

"In no wise, sir."

"Dishonored my daughter."

"I say again, I am guilty of no such sin. I sought no female in your settlement . . ."

"Hush yer mouth, soldier."

"May not a dying man be granted his last words?"

"Ye can say."

I am about to puke, thought Cotton, as the front of his gun pushes against my upper belly. But I dare not flinch. Die? Die? I cannot face this. Courage, he thought. Why have I so little?

"Hear me, sir. My coming to Blandford to hire John Holding

will not only fatten his pocket with money, but also hasten his marriage to your girl. For you, this was fortunate . . ."

"Sinner. Ye will pay, sinner."

"Let me . . ."

"Now ye *die!*"

The roar of the big musket filled his ears, just as he threw himself down in the snow. A horse screamed as if in pain. Mary! The stink of exploded sulphur and saltpeter stabbed Cotton's nostrils. Wide-eyed above him, the frenzied face of Ferris Jack raged over his miss of his target. Grabbing the black barrel, raising it high over his head, the Canaanite started to bring it down, to crack the boy's back or spine. But then Ferris Jack fell forward onto Cotton, his big body kicking in the snow. His mouth roared in raw pain. Lifting his head, the fire in his bloodshot eyes matching the red of his beard, he stared at Cotton. Slowly the great head sank down again, his dying becoming death.

From behind the thick bristles of green stepped a man in deer-skin and blanket, who walked to the fallen Ferris Jack, kicking him once. His red hand slowly pulled out an arrow that was shiny with warm blood. The tip was steaming as he wiped it clean in the white snow. Trembling, Cotton looked at the slayer's savage face, and spoke his name.

"Blue Goose?"

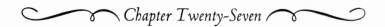

Chapter Twenty-Seven

"Blue Goose sorry."

The Huron felt relieved that he had remembered the Yengeese word for pity. He saw the hurt in the eyes of Child Face, as the boy with the yellow hair sat in the snow, holding the head of his

264

dead mare in his lap. Blue Goose knelt in the wet snow on one knee, remembering the friendship that he had seen between the boy and his horse, a bond like the one between Blue Goose and his white friend, Old Ax.

The boy could not speak.

His arms were around the neck of the animal, holding the great chestnut head against his breast, slowly rocking, a mother with a sleeping child. Child Face sang no song, and Blue Goose saw that his eyes were dry; yet he blinked quite rapidly, over and over, and when the blue eyes were open, they saw nothing. His white hand stroked the lifeless white mane.

It is hard to believe, thought Blue Goose, that a Yengeese heart bears the weight of sorrow; the face of a Yengeese is cold even in summer. He wondered if the Redcoats who burned the lodges of Wolf Eyes knew regret. Can a white heart ever wish to call back an arrow to its bow? No, he thought, for the English are the stones that walk. As a child, Blue Goose remembered when warriors returned to the camp of Wolf Eyes with a captured Britisher, his hands bound behind him around a stick across his back. Blue Goose and the other children threw pebbles at the white face, who was then kicked, and burned, and killed. The Englishman died with neither an outcry or a tear.

"Stone that walks," Wolf Eyes had said, long ago.

But old Wolf Eyes lies cold, like Sky, and Tall Face and Leaf. So now Blue Goose has come south to help Old Ax battle the soldiers with red coats. It would be a sad thing to cut the bond, he thought, between Old Ax and Blue Goose, as death has cut its gray knife between Child Face and his woman horse. The animal will not return to run.

"Horse go to God," he said to the young soldier.

The boy from the Virginia place said nothing to the Huron; but his lips, Blue Goose noticed, formed the horse's name. Mary, the white trembling lips said. Over and over the soldier rocked the head of his departed animal, repeating the name . . . Mary . . . Mary. Finally, without looking at Blue Goose, he spoke.

"I want to die with her."

"Soldier not die. Horse die."

"I can never be killed now, for my soul is dull and dry and deader than my mare."

"Mary good horse?"

"She is *my* horse. Yet no more mine than I am hers."

Blue Goose gave one nod. "Old Ax say."

"You saw Hatch?"

The Huron made a sign with his hand, holding one finger, thrown over his shoulder to indicate that he had seen Hatch yesterday. "One day. One."

"How can I bury her? She is still warm."

"No, ground like iron."

"Rightfully she should be buried in Virginia. Can you understand what I say to you? In Virginia."

"Virginia good place?" Blue Goose slowly blinked his eyes, as a sign. He thought of the village in Canada, the smoking lodges and the ill stink of burned flesh and the body of Sky. "Home gone." His hand held his heart; then pulled away in a backhanded cast.

"Your home in Canada?"

"Gone. All die."

"Even your woman?"

"Sky."

"I am sorry, Blue Goose. Your woman had a beautiful name."

"Yes, like music . . . like life." Blue Goose touched the still hoof of the motionless mare.

"I wish he'd shot me instead."

"Blue Goose know. You cry."

"Do you weep for Sky?"

"Heart cry much. And eyes. Blue Goose all broken, like Child Face."

"I am no longer a child. Perhaps not yet a man, but at least no longer a babe in swaddle."

"Blue Goose not call you Child Face." He tried to smile at the Virginian. "New name."

"No Toes?"

"Old Ax take. You sick."

"He told you."

Blue Goose grunted, pointing at Cotton's boots. "Old Ax say you get new Huron name. Blue Goose give."

"There is no need. Not now, as I am empty of heart. I am sick of lugging iron over the mountains, and watching animals die. God, if we were at the column, we might even eat . . ." His head fell forward, resting on the ear of his dead mare.

"You me go."

"I can't walk. I can barely stand."

"Blue Goose carry." He smiled at Cotton Witty, pointing at the young Virginian, and then said, "Old Ax want. Get up."

"I cannot."

"Hatch say bring. Find. Bring."

"How did Hatch know I was lost?"

"Him know many."

"Yes, I agree. Hatch is my friend now. I told him about my gun."

Blue Goose laughed. "Him got ax."

Cotton faintly smiled. "Him got Blue Goose and Child Face."

"Talk funny."

Sitting in the wet snow, Cotton's body shook.

"Cold," said Blue Goose. "You come."

"Leave me here. You can return alone."

"Hatch say bring."

"Well, you can tell Mister Hatch that you are not a dog and I am not a twig to be fetched to and fro between slobbering jaws."

Good, thought the Huron. He still has fight in him. Blue Goose had been standing motionless, arms folded inside his red blanket. Then quickly he leaped over the dead mare to behind Cotton's back. Hands under the sleeves of the greatcoat, he lifted the Virginian to his feet. "Cold here. Go."

"I . . . can't leave her." His hand touched the mare.

"Kick man."

"What?"

Drawing back his left moc, Blue Goose gave the dead face of Ferris Jack a vicious kick. So hard that he tore the nose, producing blood on the wet snow. "Kick. Kick hard. Him kill horse."

The boy rose, his face expressionless. Then he looked bitterly at the man. As Cotton kicked Ferris Jack, the Huron grunted his blessing to the ritual. He pointed at the Canaanite's gun. "You want?" The Huron squatted to empty the saddlebag of its food, ate a biscuit, and stuffed a yellow pear into the band of rawhide at his waist.

"No, I have a pistol." With his bare hands growing red from cold, Cotton started to cover Mary with snow. Blue Goose hurled the musket into the bushes, where it fell in a soft sound.

"Come. We go sundown."

"West?"

Blue Goose nodded. "You walk."

"I do not walk well."

"Blue Goose know. Hatch tell."

"It will be too far."

With a whip of his red hand, Blue Goose slapped Cotton Witty's face a stinging blow, and a crack of blood swelled from the boy's lower lip. "You walk. Blue Goose friend."

The Virginian seemed dazed by the blow. "I can't walk very fast" — Cotton started through the wet snow — "as I have no toes. No balance. No toes!" He nearly screamed the last brace of words at the Huron, and for a breath, Blue Goose hoped that Child Face would return the slap. But he only shouted. And only a fool allows another fool to holler where Mohawk hunt. His red hand covered the white mouth. "No wisdom," whispered Blue Goose. "No tell Mohawk. Sorry hit face. Walk more."

"Wait," said Cotton. Kneeling in the snow, he loosened the cinch strap of the saddle, pulling off the saddle, which he threw over a tree limb. Gently his fingers opened the teeth of the horse to remove the bit in order to slip the bridle over her ears. Using the plaid saddleblanket, he rubbed her still body, looking up at Blue Goose.

"After every ride," he said, "I must rub her down."

They walked, Blue Goose in front. As they left the small clearing, Cotton looked back once more at a mare with a light golden mane and tail, that he would ride no more. My mind remembers, thought Blue Goose, the time I saw Child Face and his horse jump over a fence, like birds. He heard the boy speak.

"Farewell, my sweet and gentle lady."

Turning his back, so that he would see no more of the wetness flow from the blue eyes, the Huron headed west. The boy's heart, he told himself, is a gray rock. How can a white man long so for an animal? White men are not red men, and a wren is not a heron. And if Old Ax were here, he would bless the wisdom of God who made not all of us herons. Nor all wrens. Tonight, I see Old Ax. Much laugh.

At his back, he heard Cotton Witty fall. Yet he did not turn round; pretending, as the opossum pretends so wisely, that he was unaware of the tumble. Tall Face had once told him that shame is a heavy burden for two, but lighter for one. So he did not turn around, slowing his pace, allowing the boy with yellow hair to rise and follow. There is, he thought, gut in the white belly. Old Ax has so spoken, a day ago, and the mouth of Old Ax sings truth. Except, smiled Blue Goose, when the old gray beard whispers into the young pink ear of a woman. Ha! Old Ax is boy.

They reached the first waterfall.

Seeing the ice formation for a second time that day, made Blue Goose recall how he had sped by it earlier, without looking, following the hoofprints of the chestnut horse. It was good to see the pretty ice at a more leisured pace. And the weather is warmer, as will the heart of Blue Goose turn warmer to see Hatch again. And eat, eat, eat.

Yesterday, thought Blue Goose, I come. But does Old Ax ask much about Canada? No. For as he knows somehow that Sky has gone to God, he sends me before sunrise to chase the boy who is now, according to Hatch, his friend. Much trouble clouded the eyes of Old Ax when he spoke of the frozen feet of Child Face. And about the Blandford place, where trouble had found us. And now Red Hair sleeps in the snow until the red foxes find him, and the crows, and until his body is covered over by the white robe of winter. Until the gentle drops of spring run from his corpse, and ants will hurry over green moss to carry Red Hair away, in bits.

I did not wish to bury my arrow in the black coat of Red Hair. But had the shaft lingered in my bow, the fox would snap the bones of Child Face. This would have painted sadness on the face of Old Ax. He did not tell me this, as he is a man who does not speak of all his thoughts or his aches. Hatch knows what it is to walk in pain, as age twists his toes instead of tearing them off. As it twists the knuckles of his hand. Old Ax wishes to refill the emptiness in the boots of Child Face, as he will refill the emptiness in the heart of Blue Goose whenever he knows that I have been alone to sing of Sky.

So he sends me to find Child Face, and I find him with a dead horse. When Old Ax tells that the Virginia boy is now our friend, I run all day to track him. We are three, said Old Ax, as he held up his three crooked fingers. One for Hatch, one for Blue Goose, and now a third for Lieutenant Witty. Ah, I can only think such a rank, as to try to say it would knot my tongue and the red of my face would deepen, which I would wish to hide.

"Three," he turned to say to Cotton.

"I beg your pardon."

"Hatch, Blue Goose, you." He smiled.

"Did . . . Durable say that?" The boy's face brightened.

"No more two. Now three."

"And our leader, Mister Knox, well deserves to join us to a foursome, I say."

"Half Hand good. Big strong."

Cotton smiled. "Yes. Old Ax and Half Hand and Child Face. Brother, you really can brand a body, but we all best not complain. *Any* name would be preferred over Blue Goose."

Cotton softly laughed, and the Huron laughed with him. I do not hear funny words; but as he feels fun, I shall also laugh. Throwing back his head, he let his hand fall on Cotton's shoulder, howling as silently as he could.

"Funny," he whispered to Witty.

For a few paces, they walked together, side by side through a pass in the trees where the snow was shallow. "You understand almost everything that people say, don't you?"

"No," said Blue Goose, which seemed to set the two of them again to a chuckle, the Huron falling down in the snow. Secretly his hand packed a snowball which he suddenly threw, striking the Virginian in the neck, sending tiny fragments of ice exploding into the air, as well as into his shirt. Giggling once more, Blue Goose rolled over in the snow, pretending to be dead. He kicked furiously and lay still. But when Cotton's ball of snow hit his exposed belly, only then did he jump up and pretend to fire back an imaginary arrow.

"Fun," he said. "Warm, like whiskey."

He got to his feet, leaping like a mad roe, kicking snow at Cotton and dancing a few steps that he remembered from many winters ago, seeing the Huron braves do; the warriors of Wolf Eyes. I will not, he thought, think more of Canada. The stink of burning hides quickly returned to his nose, from days back and many days' run to the north. Then, after helping Wolf Eyes to end his story, he had run south. Day, night, day, night . . . he ran without food or sleep, running to carry his eyes from the dead of Canada, and his nostrils from ever again smarting from the smell of his dead. He ran back to Ticonderoga, where the soldiers told him that Old Ax had gone south on the upper lake, the water that they called George. And at Fort Ticonderoga they fed him cornbread and whiskey and pork, and let him sleep near the warm cows.

He found the canoe, the one that Hatch only yesterday had jokingly accused him of stealing. And then he told Hatch that he had paddled their craft south on George, only one dip of the paddle ahead of the ice, and hid their canoe once more near Fort George at the head of the lake. Again he ate and slept. The ox trail, he told Hatch yesterday, had been so easy to follow that a blind warrior could have done so, merely by tripping over every hunk of litter that Knox and his troops dropped or discarded. And so into the Berkshire, he caught up with Old Ax and the two had danced before all eyes, as he now danced before Cotton Mayfield Witty.

"Are you mad?" asked Child Face. "Crazy?"

To answer, Blue Goose molded a ball of snow larger than the largest cannonball. Tossing the snowball into the air, he allowed it to fall and smash atop his own head. Then he fell into the snow, kicking his mocs high into the air and masking his face under the red blanket. Jumping quickly to his feet, he leaped a log as gracefully as a young hart, and raised a buckskinned arm to point westward. He forced his face to be a stone.

"Walk now."

"No Toes walk," Cotton stiffly marched forward.

"Old Ax want. Blue Goose bring."

"Enough of that. You told me a dozen times."

"Dozen good," Blue Goose said over his shoulder.

"Good? What do you talk of?"

"Blue Goose and Old Ax eat dozen. Trade one beaver for dozen at Fort Crown Point. Hatch eat half, Blue Goose eat half. Dozen all eat." He rubbed his belly.

"A dozen what? Mohawks?" asked Cotton, as he limped through the snow in the Huron's tracks.

"Buns!" said Blue Goose. "Dozen under jam. Much eat at Crown Point. Blue Goose not eat Mohawk." He spat. "Hatch laugh. Him say Mohawk too hard to clean! Funny?" Stooping down, he again threw snow in the air.

"Funny," said the Virginian, smiling.

"Friends now."

"Yes, we are friends," puffed Cotton. "Yes!"

"Mohawk not friend," Blue Goose turned around to say.

"Too dirty to eat, are they?"

"Throw Mohawk meat to dog."

"I see."

"Feed to crow. Feed ant."

"Aunt who?"

The boy with yellow hair asks strange questions. Blue Goose is foolish to try to understand a white man. Some days even Old Ax is a mystery. Old Ax not like war, and yet he now wants to make war on the Redcoats. Yengeese kill Yengeese? The Huron do not slay the Huron, nor do the Mohawk hunt themselves. And now Old Ax tells that George is no longer their chief, their King. Ha! How can that be truth, when Blue Goose rides a canoe there? George is a lake, as Champlain is a lake. One is French and one Yengeese, says Hatch. Crazy talk. Even if George is a chief of the Redcoats, he does not own the upper lake. Not even the Mohawk own George. A lake is a waterdrop in the hand of God.

Why, he thought as he walked through the snow, must the white fist reach out to take so much? No white belly is so thirsty that it must drink a lake. Blue Goose drinks and owns a swallow, and his body returns his mouthful to the earth. Not even one drink do I own, or wish to. It would be a sad thing to be born inside white skin. To my eye, white faces appear sickly. Worse, they think sickly. And talk sickly, when they want to climb a tall pine in order to reach up and own the moonlight. Or to plant a flag on a star and call it New France. Flags are strange flowers that are fed with gunpowder and watered with blood. Old Ax does not say this. Blue Goose speaks.

Old Ax is more red than white. I am sad that the hands of Wolf Eyes and Hatch never did lock in a meeting. Or share tobacco. I would like to listen to their lips and words. I wonder if Old Ax will soon be old and white, and broken, as Wolf Eyes became. Before that, I hope Hatch dies. Before that, I will take the ax from the belt of Hatch and end his life, in sorrow but with honor. When the day comes, Blue Goose will give the old man to God.

The splattering and misty roar of the second waterfall grew louder in his ears. Blue Goose waved back to Cotton to hurry along. He does not complain, thought the Huron. His bowels tighten inside his white belly and he walks his wounded feet. Limping, like a furry marten whose paws are bloodied from the iron teeth of a white man's trap; even though his toe scars are healed and do not bloody the snow. His head is not yet healed, said Hatch, and it is truth.

And now, like his toes, his Mary horse is dead.

Can he swallow the sorrow as he closes his eyes when this night comes? At the evening is when the face of Sky visits me, her eyes moving close to mine, so that I can see her beauty. Hatch says that the big iron guns must go to the Boston place to roar their fire at the Redcoats. I will help take the iron to its home, even if I become an ox in yoke. As the Yengeese who wear red coats will die, Blue Goose will laugh and spit on their beloved flag. This I do not for Old Ax, but for Sky.

Without stopping, they ate supper, wading through the starlight of a January evening, washing down their meal with fresh mouthfuls of snow.

"Oh," whispered Cotton to his back, "for a hot mug of tea."

Blue Goose smiled over his shoulder. "Tea," he smiled. "Hot gold water, and good. Burn mouth, still good."

"Or hot cider, with a cinnamon stick to stir it."

"Hot gin good. Hot wine. And hot Blue Goose."

"Are you cold?"

"Much."

"If you want, you may wear my greatcoat and I will walk awhile in your blanket."

"No. Home soon."

"Can we please rest a moment?"

"Rest bad."

"You and Durable are the most rigid people I have ever met, next to Father. An idea in your head is a rabbit in a bulldog's jaw."

"No talk. Walk."

"If I am silent, I think of my Mary. I must talk or go insane. You redhides are lucky in a way that you force yourselves not to feel things. You Hurons must be a pack of stones."

"Yes, like stones." Blue Goose was glad that he walked in front, breaking trail, so Child Face could not see his weeping. When the night wind finally dried his cheeks, he paused in the snow to lean against the rough trunk of a big bare oak. Fumbling into his shirt, his hand came forth with a tiny packet of purple velvet, presented to him by Henry Knox, the night at Ticonderoga when he had brought the deer to Half Hand. Slowly he untied the delicate yellow bow.

"Spoon," he said, "for baby."

"It's beautiful. And it's silver."

"Half Hand give, for when Sky have child." As he spoke to Cotton, he knew that his voice was unsteady, the way a mother speaks when her warrior son dies in battle. But I do not care, thought Blue Goose. I will teach Child Face as Old Ax has taught Blue Goose. Slowly his red hands bent the soft silver until the tiny spoon was a twisted snarl of metal which he handed to the soldier. As Cotton held it, his face frozen in confusion, the Huron pointed to the knot of silver.

"Spoon now like heart of Blue Goose."

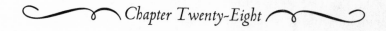

Chapter Twenty-Eight

The thick barricade of pine boughs formed almost an airtight enclosure for four tired oxen and four tired men. Fragrant branches of green had been woven to form a leanto against the great gun that the men called the Old Gray Whale.

"Good evening to you, Mister Knox," said the Shaker.

"And to you, good sir." Knox threw a friendly salute as he entered their shelter, surveying the four men that huddled on one log 'twixt the unyoked but hobbled Holsteins and the crackling fire.

"Henry, did you bring salt?" asked Durable.

"Nay, I did not. I was merely invited for venison, not knowing that I'd be charged for it."

Hatch turned the spit that middled the hindquarter, a leg of deer meat. The far end of the spit was supported by a forked maple stick, upright in the trampled snow.

The big Shaker rose, saying he knew where there was salt, at two fires back; and he departed in its direction, promising his return with the seasoning that Hatch's cookery usually demanded, along with other constant requests for assistance.

"Well," said Henry Knox, squatting his big bulk down on the beam of an ox yoke, "never again did I dare to dream the three of you, cuddled at fireside as you are, would be sharing company as well as camp."

"I always been hard up for friends," snorted Hatch. "So that's how come I get to wetnurse them two icicles here." His old head nodded to and fro to indicate Cotton and Blue Goose.

"Welcome back, Lieutenant," said Henry.

"Thank you, sir. And you may please tell Mister Hatch that he need not ask Blue Goose to shadow me from Berkshire to Boston. Though his assistance in my return is appreciated. To add, his return to our company shall be a lift to us all." Cotton's voice, Henry noted, sounded empty and alone.

Knox, remembering the knife slash on his hand, nodded to the Huron. "And to you, Blue Goose, we are fortunate that you are again among us, and already serve us with valor. Welcome."

Blue Goose nodded. A red blanket was around his shoulders; his mocs were removed, in order, Knox presumed, to toast his dirty toes closer to the orange embers than comfort or prudence would permit. Hatch sat in the middle, ignoring the two younger men, ordering which precise twig was to be added to the flame, and exactly where, so that the venison would be fit for even King George himself. Yet even as Durable snapped out his instruction, Knox detected a joy in the old man's voice that had been missing all day. For many past hours, Durable Hatch had done more than just squint eastward. He had gone on ahead, looking and hollering for the Huron or the Virginian, hoping both would hear.

"A new teamster has arrived," said Henry, "and I am reported he came with two more yoke of black and whites. You did well, Lieutenant Witty, as all five from the settlement of Blandford stand sound and willing for the morrow's task. Strong-looking animals they be, and a sturdy Jack of a lad who led them here."

The old trapper looked at him; then returned to his cookery, but not without a question: "This here fella from Blandford, he got red hair or a red beard?"

"Both," said Cotton quickly. "His name is Ferris Jack."

"Holy hollering humpback," muttered Hatch.

"Meat burn," said Blue Goose, reaching to lift the spit stick that was slipping from Durable's suddenly limp grip. The old man's shirt seemed to now irritate him, forcing a scratch.

The talk perplexed Knox. Even though it was dark, Knox mused, I do not recall the new arrival as having a red beard, but rather a black one; and I could swear on Lucy's wedband that the lad introduced himself to Sergeant Cutter's crew as John Holding. Perhaps I mistook.

"Sir, a word with you, please, outside?" asked Cotton.

"Of course," said Henry Knox, lifting up his big body.

"Military matter," said Cotton Witty to Mister Hatch, who snorted as though his mind carried other concerns. Once outside the windbreak of cut pines, Cotton Witty limped hastily to Henry's side.

"I smell a rat, Lieutenant." Placing his hammy fists on his own heavy hips, Henry looked down into the face of Cotton Mayfield Witty. The boy looked enthusiastic, and Knox wondered if it was true that he had lost his mare. Well, he thought, I shall let him tell me what he wishes. Heartbreak can manifest in strange styling.

"Sir . . . ," began Cotton, who then paused.

"A moment ago, our conversing inside led me to suspect someone of deviltry. If it is that, I wish to play no part in it." He smiled at Cotton. "However, if't be harmless mischief . . ."

"It is that, Mister Knox. I vow it."

"Methinks an explanation is due to me, if only that I be privy to the prank. The man who arrived here, shortly after you and Blue Goose, told me his Christian name, and said naught about anyone called Ferris Jack."

"Our man's name, sir, is Holding."

"Aye, so he be. Who is Jack?"

"He is dead."

277

"Dead?" And to think, Henry told himself, I was about to console him at the death of his Mary.

"Yes, sir. Quite. Blue Goose put an arrow through him."

"Blue Goose slew him? For what reason?"

"He was about to undo me, sir."

"Why?"

"Mister Jack had a daughter."

"And is *she* also killed? Good God, I let you go for two days and . . ."

"No, sir, she's alive and well. One could not hope to ever find a young lady in such condition."

Knox said the two words slowly: "What condition?"

"Health, sir. Healthy and hardy and fair."

"I begin to see, Lieutenant Witty. A daughter's health and a papa's ire can lead me only to a singular surmise. May I remind you that our journey has enough perils without your digging additional pits in our path? If I could confine you to quarters and spare the manpower, believe me, I would hasten to so do."

"Sir, please allow me to explain."

"Explain then."

"In Blandford I pursued no female, only oxen and a teamster. The daughter sought me, sir."

"You expect me to swallow such yarn?"

"No, sir, but 'tis truth. However, a year or so ago, our good friend Mister Hatch also passed through Blandford and sampled hither and yon. But he does not know that Ferris Jack is no more, so my prank is to let him think that the redbearded revenger is but a breath behind. The girl is simple, sir."

Knox scowled. "Merciful Heaven, 'tis a poor business."

"No harm will come to Mister Hatch, sir, I promise."

"You say the redbeard revenger is no more?"

"Precisely. But I will entreat the Huron not to tell Hatch about the manner of his parting, much less about the comely Lovebreed."

"Good plan. And to think that all of this started because of one little defenseless girl," said Henry.

"Just wait until you see Lovebreed, sir."

"Lovebreed?"

" 'Tis true, sir; her name is Lovebreed Jack."

A minute of mirth passed before either Knox or Witty attempted to return inside, where the old goat had drawn his hunting knife to carve the steaming venison. The big Shaker returned, and the five of them reduced the deerleg to bone. Hatch had also boiled potatoes and onions and one carrot in a black kettle. This pottage likewise disappeared.

"How did you take this deer, Durable?" asked Knox, a soiled handkerchief to his mouth, to wipe away the remnants of venison. "I am yet to see you tote a gun."

"No need," said Hatch, his mouth full. "That's why we got hunters. All I done was track her and tell the gunny fool where to stand and what direction to fire. Yer dang *hunter* couldn't smell a moose in a pisspot. What he was best at was toting her carcass back to camp."

"Well," said Knox, "soon we all shall be quartered and suppered in the fine firelight of civilization."

"Right," said Durable, "be as our next stop is Westfield."

"All in due season," said Knox. "But I have decided to bear a wee bit north, according to the map provided me, and add a stop for breath at the fair town of Blandford."

The old man stopped chewing, eyes darting from Henry to Cotton to Blue Goose, his old hands suddenly not knowing how to occupy themselves. He dropped his last hunk of venison into the pine needles.

"According to our young lieutenant here," said Knox, "the settlement of Blandford will one day become a thriving community, and already he has found the citizenry capable of a warm welcome. So I conclude that a stopover there will" — Knox pretended to search a word — "*jack* up our spirits."

"A delightful community," said Cotton.

"Out of our way," Durable snorted. "If'n I be the trail boss, which I don't claim, 'twould be my guess we best stay south and head straight for Westfield." Hatch nodded one emphatic nod with his beaver hat.

"Why keep south?" asked the Shaker.

Hatch spat into the pine needles. "Ermine," he whispered, closing one eye as if to announce the location of the royal jewels.

"Ermine, you say?"

"By the score, the hundred. White ermine so thick that they near to jump at yer knife and skin theirselfs."

"Come now, Durable."

" 'Tis the straight of it, Henry. Why, me an' Blue here, we was through that pass and we could hardly walk 'twixt two trees and not tread on ermine. Thick as mayflies. And big! Why one a them ermines was so doggone dimensional you'd a throwed a saddle on the varmint. Whiter than snow, except for the tips of them tails, which is black."

"I have seen a pelt, of course," said Cotton Witty, "but never a live ermine."

"Nor I," said Henry, "and it be my understanding that in summer they are brown or grayish tan."

"True," hollered Durable, now voluble on the subject of the furry beasts. "Come spring an ermine'll coat up brown as mud. Then he ain't no ermine no more."

"What is he?" asked Knox.

"Stoat."

"A stoat?"

"Yup, a plain and browny little weasel's all he be."

"Well," said Knox, "it would be folly to digress to observe naught more than a brown pack of common weasels, or stoats."

"But it's winter, now," Hatch almost leaped to his feet, "and they be all white. Whiter'n innocence."

"Innocence," said Knox. "Now there is a subject to charm every ear, worthy of considering by every firelight philosopher."

"Aye," the big Shaker agreed.

Once again, the back of Andrew Angus Hatch seemed to be suddenly beset upon by gnawing lice. His old hand scratched away, chasing his livestock to fresher pasture. Watching him, Knox wondered how many weeks, or years, had gone by since the old trapper's last bath. Or would his next bathing be his first? Our young Witty observes him now with a blend of deviltry and yet devotion. I must become, thought Knox, better acquainted with this silvery senior, as I am curious to learn what there be in him that so inspires men as opposed as Blue Goose and Cotton. Our friend Hatch is more, mused Henry Knox, than an unwashed larder for lice. Before me sit a red Huron and a fair Virginian; yet both our young men look at this old hickory knot with a fervent fellowship that borders on worship.

Cotton's face grew sober, and Knox tried to guess his thoughts. His mare, methinks. I truly pity the lad. Best I not bring it up. And best the boy stays busy with boyish business. Aye, we surely are in need of some foolish fun, if meant in good humor.

Knox studied the face of Durable Hatch. The poor wee girl was no doubt helplessly seduced by this old Verdmonter. Ah, I suppose the ages of hillbilly ladies and their customs of the chamber vary somewhat to ladies of Boston.

"Honest," said Hatch, holding up his hands as if to measure a fish, "them ermine to the south run in packs, like wolves . . . and to hear their hoofbeats trot through the timber's enough to scare off my skin. You'd swear they was elk."

"Large as an elk, Mister Hatch?" asked Henry.

"Well now," said the trapper, "perhaps a foot or so on the smaller side. But if you never seen ermine, enough of 'em at your feet to do a robe for King George, be a pity to miss. Yessir, me boys, be a tribulation to waste eyesight on a plain old settlement like Blandford when we can see all them ermine."

"Are they white as snow?" asked Cotton.

"Whiter," snuffed Durable.

"Alas," sighed Cotton. "For with so many white ermine on so much white snow, it would be my guess that our untrained eyes would see naught but a white blur. Be it up to me, Mister Knox," said Cotton sternly, "I cast my vote to take our cannon the more northerly route, continuing due east, and where the warm hospitality of Blandford will come running to meet us."

Knox saw Durable Hatch swallow. Oh, he thought, this is indeed a priceless jest, one which the old bear well deserves. I hope it

281

all be harmless hokum, as this would not be the first or the last sporting to slip out of hand into a tryst of trouble.

"Ah," said Henry aloud, "I can picture our welcome. The men of Blandford coming forth to meet us, bearing torches, to help guide us and our weary convoy to their homes and hearths."

"And bringing rope," Cotton added.

"Rope?" asked Hatch.

"Of course, to aid our hauling, sir."

"What type of people reside there?" asked Henry.

"They are plain people," said Cotton, "and I am told their religion calls them Canaanite."

"Ah," the big Shaker said with a nod of his brown beard, "I know the sect. Vengeful practitioners they be, who worship a wrathful God."

"True," said Cotton. "While in their midst, I learned much concerning their beliefs, which they call Canaanite law. For example, the first man to lie with a maiden, by their law, becomes her husband."

"That is true," said the Shaker, almost as though he were a player upon a stage and had taken his cue from the young Virginian.

This, thought Knox, is a worthy episode for the book I must write. I shall relate this incident to Lucy; and upon my joining General Washington, lighten his spirits with an accurate accounting of it to the best of my recalling. Knowing our general, he will find much sport in the story.

Later, in his own quarters, Knox shared the story with his brother William. And such was their levity that Sergeant Cutter appeared at their shelter to inquire as to the cause. So he also had to be told, along with a warning that Andrew Angus Hatch would be allowed to sustain his suffering until the column advanced to the settlement of Blandford.

"Before I retire," Henry told Sergeant Cutter, "I will prepare my usual report to General Washington as to our progress, plus a hurried note to my wife. Please appoint a horse and rider to be ready at sunup, to ride easterly with these papers of dispatch. We want General Washington to know of our determinations, do we not?"

"We do, sir," agreed Cutter.

"I bid you goodnight, Sergeant. Sleep warm."

"If we can, sir. This thaw is our blessing."

"Indeed it is. We shall endeavor to reach Blandford in less than two days."

"And soon we'll travel on a wagon road, Mister Knox, instead of a path of our own hewing."

"Aye, and not soon enough."

"These old Berkshires," the soldier shook his head, "were surely planted in our path by Satan."

"True," said Henry. "Yet our strength to conquer them, and haul our iron through the damnedest they strew in our way, our resolution was planted in us by the Almighty." He smiled at Sergeant Cutter.

"Henry," said William, after Sergeant Cutter had left, "have you ever held any doubts?"

"I had none, Brother. And you?"

"None."

"None at all, William?"

"To be honest, when the barge sank, some fears did overtake me. But when we waded into that icy Lake George water and raised up that brass, then I knew that Lucifer himself could not arrest this artillery."

"I recall. We left three men at Fort George with their lungs weak with pleurisy. Our men have since been broken and our oxen die of pure exhaustion, yet onward we trudge."

" 'Twould be my guess," yawned William Knox, "that our adversary in Boston would not believe his English eyes were he to see what obstacles we have bested en route to confront him."

"Aye, he would not."

"Did you look to all the men?" asked Henry.

William nodded. "All snug. And no talk of rebellion. I suppered with the fifth squad, Tupper's group, to finish the last of the pork. Can we hold out until we are free of these hills?"

Henry said, "We can and we will. We must."

"How fares the man with the crushed leg?"

"Better. We shall leave him in Blandford where he can rest in warmth and with some decent cookery to nurse his belly as well as knit the bone."

"Grief, what a winter," sighed William. He had pulled off a big boot and was massaging the toes of his left foot. "I had some misgivings about our ability to traverse our merry motions through these cussed ledges."

Knox smiled and spoke softly. "William! My ears do shock at such a pause. Are we Scottish Presbyterian or are we not?"

"We are."

"Then surely we shall persevere. And to the east, our tall and stately Virginian awaits his artillery, for without it he is hogtied. 'Twill be another Bunker Hill, only on a grander scale."

"No, good Brother. No more Bunkers."

"Right, as this time forthcoming, dear William, it shall be we who charge at them. Can't you envision our Gray Whale, her big belly well wadded with powder and a giant sphere of lead in her teeth? And then! She spits at Billy Howe with a roar that will jump him and his Lobsters right back into the salt of Boston harbor."

William Knox cracked the nest of pine boughs beneath him as he tucked his big body under a mound of quilts and blankets. "Turn thyself in, Henry. The chilly morn comes early."

"Aye. I'll just poke up our fire a mite, and ink out a letter. I have much to report to the general concerning our progress. And I would be remiss not to speak, as well, of the lad."

"Our young Cotton?"

Henry nodded. "Yes. He is still a lad in many ways, yet he has performed with energy and fervence and has more than pulled his weight. His mission of late was exemplary."

"I heard about his feet."

Little more was spoken between William Knox and Henry.

Lighting the stub of a candle from the campfire, Knox scribbled a fond note to Lucy. His letter to Washington was longer:

to G. Washington   12 January 1776
Cambridge (by messenger)

Sir,
    Your requested merchandise is well en route, so that you may take full possession of it by February. Our going soon eases, but the impossible climbing of these mountains has been almost more than to which human will could aspire. A miracle that people so laden should be able to get up and down such hills.

    With loads below them, our oxen back down each slope, while our men brace each inch of the sledding with logs and stone. Gravity has taught us a bitter and costly learning, that such items are more weighty going down than up.

    A personal remark: Be pleased to inform your dear neighbor in Virginia that his young son performs with dedication, endures hardship, and assists with valor. Ignoring his own peril, he accomplished an advance mission through a wilderness inhabited by savages and wild beasts, yet executing my orders to the letter.

285

Although he has not given his life, he has made more than one personal sacrifice. And each instance alone was enough nearly to defeat even the most stalwart soldier. Atop all this, he maintains wit, and has also managed to earn the friendship and respect of older fellows, few of which have backgrounds comparable to his own; yet they accept him for what he has become, a worthy officer.

Lieutenant Witty merits his rank.

H. Knox

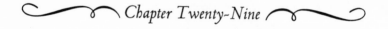 Chapter Twenty-Nine

Durable Hatch spat.

Narrowing his eyes so that the bright glare of sunlight on snow would allow him a more clear picture of the settlement of Blandford, Massachusetts, he saw a citizen running toward them through the drifts. I wonder, he asked himself, just who this might be. Too distant to mark a speck.

For most of the day before, he had thought of little else than remembering a man from Blandford whose name was Ferris Jack. Was it a year or less ago, or longer? Lucky I be still alive. She near to killed me. He felt himself smile. There be worse deaths than to die doing.

Durable's eyes shifted from one cabin to another, brown freckles on a white cheek, seeing little more than a distant blur. Eyesight's as poorly as my hands and knees, Hatch confessed to himself. But that there is the hamlet of Blandford, sure enough, and it be a location for mad folk, if you ask for my study of the place. Canaanites!

Dang it! If'n her pa . . .

An ox snorted, causing Hatch to turn suddenly to face the noise.

"Jumpy this morning, Durable?" asked Cotton.

"If I be, it ain't yer business. Fetch me a pry-pole, on account I got a runner near to stuck on my side. Hold them oxen!"

The Huron shrugged his blanketed shoulders, saying nothing. He seemed to Hatch to be making an effort to be sober. The damn goose. Why didn't he stay up in Canada and look for other villages of his people? Well, I don't guess Blue will tell me until he's a mind to. So best I don't ask. His gaze switched to the smiling face of Cotton Mayfield Witty.

"What makes you so confound comical?" hollered Hatch.

"Nothing, nothing at all."

Them two, Blue and Cotton, a brace of fine friends they be. Here I am trudging through snow that's been halfway up to my arse end, on the way to what may well be my demise at the hand of that redbearded butcher who sired a daughter with more buttocks than brains, and my two sidekicks don't neither know nor care what's about to befall old Durable. I wonder if Blandford's got a proper cemetery. Here lie Andrew Angus Hatch, born in the year . . . doggone if I know and nobody else does either, as my poor old Ma is long put away and rested. So here lies A. A. Hatch, who knows the wilderness of Adirondack and Verdmont better than the mysteries of a mistress mind. Maybe I'll let our Gray Whale go down this here meadow by her lonesome, whilst I retreat to the tail of our column.

"Hoo!"

Again he squinted at the person who was wading to meet them, cabin to his back, and yelling something at them. Who could that be, wondered Hatch. A big fellow, from the size I make him out, but no red beard on his face, which is six kinds of a Sunday blessing. I swear, if I ever make it alive to the town of Westfield, I'll be tempted to join the cloth.

Hearing a giggle, he turned to face its maker. Cotton Mayfield Witty seemed also to turn, busying himself with a pole in order to lever the left runner of their lead sledge away from a tree stump that had been hidden beneath a snowdrift. The stump was a good sign, Hatch told himself, as they had hauled iron for many miles without a sign of the ax of civilization. And here it be, Blandford. Dang, he thought, I ought be joyful. But that's a mite hard when yer time's about to snip. Cuss that gal! Why don't Ferris Jack keep a closer count of his kinder? No, he just lets the girls run loose and lay in the livery with any innocent trapper who happens to pass through and expects no more than to snore away the nocturnal in a friendly barn.

Grunting forward, the double yoke of oxen pushed their mighty chests through a drift of deep snow, kicking up an explosion of white powder. Behind them, the Old Gray Whale rested snugly in her wooden cradle atop the silvery steel of the runners. To the rear came the rest of the entire column. Not one piece of artillery had been left behind to perish in their battle against the Berkshires.

"Every dang one," Hatch nodded.

"Sir?" Cotton looked up from the snow.

"We brung 'em, Lieutenant. We ain't there yet, and not by a dang sight, but the Hell of it is near to behind us."

Allowing the oxen to pass him by, Hatch knelt down on one knee into the snow, squinting at the oncoming figure that was now less than a quarter mile from where they were, atop a gentle rise above the settlement. "Quick now, lad, and tell me who's coming."

He studied Cotton's face as the boy shaded his eyes with his mitten in order to squint along the winter quilt of almost a blinding white that was also gilded with shiny silver specks of reflected sunlight.

"Who is it?" he asked Cotton.

"Alas, I cannot make him out. Too far away."

"The cuss is yelling at us in high pitch," said Durable.

"So he is."

"Got a gun?" asked Hatch, standing up to see more clearly.

"Yes, sir, I do. If you wish to borrow . . ."

"No, ya lop-eared lump of lard, not you. *Him!*"

"You wish me to lend him my gun?"

Hatch didn't answer. Instead, he worked himself around behind the Old Gray Whale, as the great sled plowed slowly forward toward Blandford. Again he heard what stabbed his ear like a strange voice, even though the person yelling seemed familiar. *What is that durn fool hollering? Sounds like gun to me. Or maybe Tom.*

"Who's he be?" Hatch demanded of Cotton, as the old man ducked down behind the cargo.

"Well, as I see now, good sir . . ."

"Yeah?"

"It is a person I met while in Blandford," said Cotton.

"Who? What name?"

"Jack."

Hatch swallowed his tobacco. "Did you say Jack?"

"Yes. Do you know such a person?"

"Me? Never heard of nobody by that name. And if he says I know him, he's a liar, on account that I may of run into a member or two of his tribe in my travels. Can't recall every soul I meet. So probable I don't know the man."

"I never said, sir, that the one who now approaches us is a man. To the contrary, she is a female."

"Did you say . . . *she?*"

" 'Tis obvious a woman. A friend of yours, perhaps. And as I can now perceive her face, she seems to be hailing us."

Durable hunched his shoulders as low as he was able. He coughed. *Then it's true. All that much ado on Canaanite law. Golly be, my old heart is like a host of hammers, and it sure ain't that I'm lovesick. Never did get wedded and I ain't about to settle down in this pigsty of a place. Do this and fetch that and take a bath. And shave!* Durable Hatch felt a shudder rattle the links of his suddenly cold spine.

"Marriage," he said aloud. "I'd sooner get drownded in sheep-dip." Time to act. Just then the oxen paused for a breather, and quickly Hatch slid himself feet-first under the cold iron barrel of their biggest piece of artillery. I'm sure thankful to be lean, he told himself, as he lay beneath the belly of the Old Gray Whale.

"I see others," said Cotton, "afar off."

"With guns?"

"Not that I can clearly see."

"A rope?"

"No, nor that. Yet at such a distance . . ."

"Aye, I know. Ya can't see much."

"Hello! Hello!" It was surely female voice who was much closer now to the first team, and asking "Where is he?"

"Good morrow, Miss Jack," said Cotton.

She ain't spotted me yet, said Hatch to himself, and if I just keep this Gray Whale 'twixt us, it be possible I can slip out and go back into the timberline and leave this here place to its lonesome.

"Thank you for coming to welcome us, Miss Jack," he heard the young Virginian say to her. "Do you seek someone here?"

"Surely I do."

"Then I shall presume you will find him."

There was a pause. Hiding under the cannon barrel, Durable Hatch waited for her next words.

"Everyone," he heard her say to Cotton, "talks of ye and the guns. My stars! What a big gun. Really does it shoot?"

"Yes, Mistress Jack, it doth truly shoot. But only at British Red-coats and not intended for all you kind folk at Blandford."

"Is he Mohawk?" she asked.

"This man is Blue Goose," Cotton told her, "a loyal Huron and a friend."

"I remember ye," she said.

"Me?" asked Cotton.

"Him."

"You and Blue Goose have previously met?"

"Year ago. Him and his trapper friend come through Blandford."

"Did they now?"

"Surely did. I won't forget."

Dang this girl! What in the name of Old Harry does she want? I'm finished, and I might as well face up. One way or another. Either I be dead or wed in a matter of hours. Soon as her old pa can ram his musket, muster his kinfolk, and drag me to my destiny. I wonder where the old boy is keeping himself. Lord save me, but this iron is cold. And hard.

"Do ye stop at Blandford?"

"Yes, we plan to."

"I guess ye sweet remember Lovebreed Jack?"

"For certain," Hatch heard Cotton tell her.

Something is afoot. I smell it. A ruse is at work. Soft, soft now, as my brain is going a mite fast. But by jungles, you can tell a-plenty from the way a woman's voice speaks to a man.

"Surely," he heard Cotton remark, "I remember you."

"Pa's missing."

"Is he?"

"Gone two days. Ever since John and ye left, and before that. I hope he don't come back, not never."

The sled bumped over a rock, cracking the head of Andrew Angus Hatch, against the iron. Irate, he muffled his oath, swearing into his hat.

"Bear you no love for your father?" asked Cotton.

"He's mean as a boar-hog. Beats on everybody. And he'll come back, soon enough, and boil grief."

They were silent for a while, as Hatch waited for the next outburst of information, and then he heard her ask another question.

"Where do ye take all them guns?"

"Eastward."

"How many guns in all?"

"Sooner we will enter your community and you will be able to take your own count. I would guess well over a ton."

Ha! Good lad, thought Durable. Tell her little, my boy, as her lips might be well as loose as her loins. The fewer folk who know our strength, in both head count and firepower, the happier I be.

But I ain't overjoyed at the prospect of a stopover in Blandford. You don't suppose old Ferris Jack come looking for us and got lost? Stranger things happen.

"I never see such a big gun."

"Quite frankly," said Cotton, "nor have I."

"We set off a powder charge once, in Blandford, and the roar of it near to busted open our ears."

"Is that so?"

Lovebreed Jack's next question to Cotton nearly straightened Hatch erect:

"Where's your horse?"

A natural question, Hatch nodded to himself, as to see Cotton Mayfield Witty afoot and missing his mare was like to look at a lid with no jar beneath. A spire with no church. I do want to hear the lad's answer.

"My mare is dead."

"What was her name?"

"Mary."

"A sweet name. Was she always yours?"

"Father allowed that very spring that I could have my pick of the new foals, and probably he assumed that my selection would be a colt. But no. She was the only animal that I ever held the desire to say . . . she is my very own."

"Why did ye call her Mary?"

"From a song."

"Which song was it be?"

" 'Sweet Mary.' "

"Sing it."

"As far as I know, no lyric was written. Only a tune."

"Hum it then, please."

"I cannot. I used to whistle it, back home."

"Why do ye walk so strange?"

"I am crippled."

"How?"

"Without toes. I contracted blackfoot."

"I am sorry."

"Don't be. Sorrow will not regrow my feet."

"May I be sorry for Mary?"

"If you wish." Cotton's voice sounded kindly, to Hatch's ear, as if the lad spoke to a wee child on his knee.

"I like to hear ye talk of her . . . of Mary."

And do I, thought Hatch.

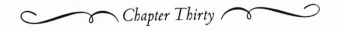

Chapter Thirty

Blandford greeted them.

As Henry Knox jumped down from Major's saddle, ebon-clad Canaanites slowly converged on the front of his column from all directions. Looking back up the distant meadow, Henry saw the drag crew, last in the long column, emerge from the timberline of the Berkshires. This, he thought, is our first cleared land in how many days? Eastward from here, according to our dear Hatch, wagon roads link the towns, thank the Almighty.

Henry Knox patted his steaming horse.

"Major," he told the burly brown gelding, "come this night you shall stand in a barn. Oats for you and corn for me, which may thaw us both into a more clement condition."

Someone fired off a musket!

Shouts of hail and hello filled the air. Children danced around in the snow, pointing at the Old Gray Whale. Never, thought Henry, had I seen so prodigious a piece of artillery, and think how near godly our Gray Whale must appear to a toddler's eyes. Loosening the cinch strap on Major's saddle, he leaned his brow upon the animal's silky shoulder.

"There! Feel better, boy?"

Ox by ox, yoke upon yoke, each and every crew lumbered and

limped into the settlement, horses and oxen puffing their plumes of vapor into the cold air. All about them, the citizens of Blandford stared at each gun of brass and iron, and at every mortar. A sober lot, thought Knox. Earlier have I read books on the plain people, sects scattered here and yon, devoted to leading the unfrilled life. Well, we now stand among them, ready to test both their hospitality and their patriotism.

Soft, he warned himself.

Blandford is yet a far cry from Boston. Expect not these people who have been unbruised by battle to share the sympathies of their besieged fellows to the eastward. Nay, we best not. The smarting cause of Bunker Hill is not the cause of Berkshire, even though it may become so. Billy Howe could easily march from Boston, to Albany, and perhaps that is his plan, come April. Sir William, if you have any inkling to cross those peaks, with or without the burdens of brass, may I advise you to seek a saner route. Enemy though you be, General Howe, I could not wish such an expedition on a dead dog, even though this force of worthy men and I have just accomplished such a trek. Truly do I believe, and with fervent thanks, that we are the only heroes (or fools) who could do so. Aye, but once, and nary again. Not for Washington, or Schuyler, not for Samuel Adams or John Hancock or even King George, do I ever cross those canyons a second time. By damn, he thought, but our American ox can surely stand up proudly against even the British lion.

Henry looked at one of the oxen. "Well done, friend."

"Blandford, sir," said Lieutenant Cotton Witty. "And there's merriment to be had."

Why, asked Henry Knox to himself, that when I behold a grin on this yellow chick's face am I so charmed by him; and yet does my bowel behave with slight trembling, as though I am about to be duped by either damnation or delight? Yea, this golden lad is not unlike our able and most august Virginian, as about both there lurks an aura of elegant grace to disarm the most vehement of doubters. A gift bestowed perchance by the schoolmasters of

Virginia to all her scholars — that tidy talent of being able to fascinate or fool. And are we fools, all of us, who are both charmed and chaffed? Perchance we are, yet willingly. For my world and my war would indeed be dull were I disallowed the honor to soldier at the side of Virginians.

"Where," he asked Cotton, "is our friend Durable?"

"Still hidden, sir," the lad whispered.

"Hidden, you say. Where abouts?"

Without talking, Cotton Mayfield Witty rolled his eyes of bright blue toward their giant of a gun, punctuating his glance with a precise nod of his head, flouncing the black bow that adorned his corny hair. Following his gaze, Henry still saw naught but the big belly of the Old Gray Whale. Knox felt his eyes squint as he puzzled for a moment.

"Underneath," whispered Cotton with a wink.

"Ha!" The laugh erupted from somewhere deep in Henry, an errant emotion determined to tweak his face into a grin. "Excellent," he told the young officer, "so there he rests, snug as a fly in a bottle. Or under one."

"Quite so, sir."

"May I presume you to guess my next inquiry?"

A brief look of confusion shadowed the Virginian's face. Then his smile returned, like sunlight. "Oh," he said to Knox, "I do believe you wish, sir, to behold that lovely landmark of a lass who has been the hostess of our humor." Cotton paused.

"Lovebreed Jack," said Henry, shaking his head slowly.

Lieutenant Witty seemed to be searching for the child, but it became obvious to Henry Knox that she was beyond location. The poor little thing, Henry was saying to himself, is probably also hidden, too shy a young maid to come forward and face the crusty old Verdmonter who had serviced her undoing. More and more Canaanites arrived, folk of all ages.

"Hello!"

"Hello to you, Glenn Holding," said Cotton Witty.

Cotton was shaking his hand, and claps of camaraderie upon

both shoulders were pleasantly exchanged. Like many of the other mature males of Blandford, noticed Henry, the fellow displayed a full beard as well as the now familiar black clothing.

"Colonel Knox," said Cotton Witty, "I have the honor to present one of the elders of Blandford, who, along with his good wife, took me in as a stranger to warm me with a supper and a robust dram of his superb peach brandy. Sir, this is Glenn Holding."

"Pleased, good sir," said Knox. They shook hands. "We are in your debt. And may I conclude that you are akin to our newest teamster, John Holding?"

"He is cousin to me, Colonel Knox. He arrives with ye safely?"

"Aye, he does, as we be all present."

"And will ye not sup with us, Colonel, as my lady has ways with a skillet that would oft make friends of strangers."

"Done," said Henry. "I see, Brother Holding, that your eye did not overlook my girth. You conclude rightly. I be an eater, for true."

"Ye be also a partaker?" Holding made a gesture, as though to wipe his lips with the back of a hand.

"Spirits?" asked Knox.

"Think us not topers, Colonel Knox. We are farmers and workers who give thanks to the Giver to bless our bounty. Yet when the yield is in, and the glean slumbers in a November barn, ye'll not think us daft to drink to the harvest until spring doctors us with her own dose of salts, will ye?"

"Nay, kind sir. My brother William and I were both raised in a large Scottish family and in the Presbyterian faith. And there were few in the taverns of Boston who could match us in fist, or filling."

"Fist, ye say?"

"Aye, but not in anger. Little more than a scuffle, I wager, and among friends."

"Ye mention the word . . . wager?"

"Only in passing, sir."

"Henry Knox, ye carry a fighter's fist, as one handshake told me. Pity how I would loathe to see our own sweet Shirley put ye down."

"Shirley?"

"How about a drink and a wager, and then a smile of a scrap 'twixt ye and Shirley, just as a lark? Do your lads good to toast their throats with Blandford rum, and behold their leader humbled or bested."

"Sir, I'll not as much as arm-twist a woman, as 'twould go against my principle."

Glenn Holding did not answer. He only smiled, gently nodding his head as he looked Knox up and down as if to weigh him for butchering. "Nay," he said at last, "ye'll not stand up to a woman. I do promise ye that."

"Nor do I wager my own fist, sir. Perhaps near a decade ago, yet only as a lad. But now I am wedlocked to my own sweet Lucy, who has extracted from me my vow to abstain from chancing, not only on the Sabbath but on all days, so 'twould be unfit for me to gamble."

"Little of note happens here," said Glenn Holding, as his eye left the face of Henry Knox to examine the Old Gray Whale. "So please forgive me, if ye will be so kind, for a dip of my spoon to stir things up."

"No pardon needed," said Henry. "I see you admire our Gray Whale."

Glenn nodded. "That I do. What's her weight?"

"Our guess is over five thousand, closer to three ton than two."

The Canaanite walked closer, resting his hand on the great flank of her cold barrel. The sled that held the great gun was at rest and a long iron cam protruded from the basket of the sled which had oft been employed en route as a pry pole. Lifting the crowbar up easily with the strength of a farmer's arm yet with no apparent reason, Glenn Holding smote the big barrel one clank of a clanging blow. The great gun rang louder than the loudest churchbell, thought Knox, in all Creation.

Out he tumbled!

Durable Hatch, hands over his ears, yelling abusive words that would have painted a red blush of shame on the cheek of Boston's most unruly harlot. Holding dropped the cam rod in dismay, looking at Andrew Angus Hatch as though he had flushed out from under a bridge a most treacherous troll. With his hands over his ringing ears, Hatch continued his savory swearing for nearly a half-minute, not once having to repeat any floral phrase or tangy epithet, impressing all who were privy to hear his lesson in vocabulary.

Oxen were unhitched, barned, and fed. Men ate.

A keg of rum was rolled through the snow, and a mallet pounded loose the bung, replaced (neatly and with little spillage) by a spigot that turned constantly by thirsty hands holding hungry vessels. Pewter tankards clanked together as teamsters, soldiers, farmers, Virginian or Canaanite or Presbyterian, saluted. Some sang, as others danced in the snow, drunker than nobles. Together they fought and fell down in a swirling stupor that hollered for naught but more hilarity, begging to wipe the memory of beaten oxen from their bloodshot eyes. The animals that had survived were hugged and kissed, knighted and ordained. There were no colonels, nor privates; only soldiers and singers and sots.

One of the Blandford families was gifted in music, and produced three fiddlers, a basswood fife which was early-on borrowed by Durable Hatch, a drum that was lent to the thumping hands of Blue Goose, plus a lute that bore only three strings. No one seemed to care. Time and again, Hatch tried to sing "Yankee Doodle" while blowing the fife. Rum or ale had been sloshed by an untidy celebrant, causing the fife to gargle a bit as Hatch's musical accomplishments strained to hit the higher notes.

A bear came.

The big black animal had been declawed, and was also muzzled, making her "safe" for wrestling. Although she was obviously a pet, a few swallows of rum turned her playful and then warlike. A teamster from the nearby settlement of Otis was first to face her in the ring. Before the man's brawny arms could purchase a hold on the black fur, the she-bear presented the big teamster with a clout on the ear, sending him sprawling into the gray slush. His valor in trying to best a bear, however, was rewarded with a stout swallow of brandy. In like manner, the bear was rewarded, having established herself earlier as just one more participant among many who would swallow any and all beverages offered.

"Never," remarked Henry Knox to William, "have I seen such an animal. A battling bear. Care to give her a round, just to show the lads what a Knox is cut from?"

In the lantern light, the brothers were leaning against the side of a wagon, in order to witness what activity unfolded in the clearing among the houses that could best be described as Blandford's village square. Or green, had it not been shin-deep in snow.

"Shame," said William, "but if I try to walk even from this place over to that, surely I shall fall forward and burst my poor pate. My head spins, yet do I retain a modicum of reason to warn me that best I not best a bear." Turning, he gave Henry a silly smile.

"Good jesting?"

"How about you, Hank?"

"Me?"

"Are you to this Canaan, or whatever this pot of a place is, to deem that their beast can undo a Presbyterian?"

"Already," said Henry, "I am near daft with drink. Think you I should, Brother?"

"Think me you should," said William slowly.

"Very well," said Henry, "hold my mug."

"Ah, but if you cannot hold your own liquor, how must I?"

Henry laughed. "Come on," he said, "before my courage melts." He stripped off the coat of his uniform.

Despite every plea for a confrontation with Henry, the bear would pay him no attention until her thirst drained a bucket of ale. Then, as Henry faced her, she stood fully up in order to snarl her muzzled snarl, advancing toward Henry with uncertain steps. She walks, Henry told himself, the way I feel. As she came closer, the bear slowly raised up on hind feet, causing Henry Knox to assess her height. As tall as I, he thought, yet twice my weight. Inside the muzzle strap, Henry caught a glimpse of her fangs. Were that thong to snap, my throat would instantly be pulp. Knox smelled her breath, a pungent stench.

Dropping low, then quickly rearing high, the she-bear swung a paw as if to cuff Henry's head. Ducking, he lunged under the black pads of that great paw, thrusting his shoulder into her as his hands sought the stiff black fur for a purchase. His charge staggered her balance, as though she had expected to be the sole attacker. Few men, Henry only a moment earlier had surmised, would take immediate offensive upon such a brute. Down they went, the bear grunting as Henry landed atop her middle. The great grunt spewing forth with a breath so bad that Henry feared it would arouse his supper.

Up, and down. Twisting, he landed hip-first on the bear's black chest, trying to hold one foreleg with his two arms, to spin and pin. Five hundred pounds is no ball to be freely juggled. His hold was broken as though his might was made of smoke. Opening her great jaws, even only for half an inch, caused the thick leather straps of her muzzle to crack loudly. Henry prayed the hide would hold. He was aware that men and women were both cheering and jeering; his teamsters rooting for him, while the Canaanites supported their pet.

"Hug him, Shirley!"

"Squeeze him!"

"Press him like an apple, ye will!"

So, this, he wanted to laugh, is Mistress Shirley. Then the sudden blow to his belly was more than fun. Stunned, and fearful of another from any one of four big paws, Henry tried to rise. He could not. Massive limbs of black fur (that upholstered what had to be lead or iron) encircled his chest, locked, and applied pressure. My bowels, thought Henry Knox, are sure to move. Somehow his big hands found the leather strap, part of the muzzle that encircled the great black neck. Locking the hams of his hands into fists, he twisted his wrists to shut off her air. Again and again she kicked at him, but the foul grunts of her rummy breath came shorter and shorter. Her gasps choked to a wheeze, then to silence.

Shirley lay still. Many fists were then required to pry loose his cramped fingers from the leather thongs, where they had nearly knotted into the black fur beneath her chin. Gasping for air, the bear rolled slowly from her back to hip, nearly lying still. Henry was aware only that strong arms hauled him erect, holding his right hand high as a sign of victory. William embraced him. Somewhere in the crowd, the crusty voice of Andrew Angus Hatch proclaimed a championship for the Continental Army.

Recovering quickly, Shirley drank ale.

Nine wagonloads of Welsh settlers had arrived during Henry's match with the bear. They were bound for new lands, west of Otis, and were at once invited to stay the night in Blandford. Not by the Canaanites; but by his soldiers and teamsters, Colonel Knox noted. Especially as each wagonload folk seemed to be preponderantly female.

"Welshers!" another man spoke with hostility.

"What matter?" said Henry. "As they we all be easterly bound, as sure as their wagons are headed west. They'll not block our way."

"Is not this wilderness vast enough for us all?" William Knox wanted to know.

"Already it is not," said Henry, "absurdly though it hits our ear. So let the Welsh folk be. Tell the men. No fisting and no spooning."

"Soft," said William, "as our dear lads have seen neither liquor nor a leggy lass for many a mile. Rest is a recipe of more than a suppered sleep."

"I am corrected, Brother Will, but nay do we court trouble this eve. Mark me, I'll not turn a decent community into a rapery."

A woman laughed from somewhere in the darkness. More rum was offered, to any mouth that was thirsty, male or female, Welsh or Canaanite, soldier or civilian. A stout Welsh lad volunteered for a bout with Shirley, and lost with good nature, endearing him and his bruises to Canaanite hearts. The lad, who announced after his trouncing that his name was Hoel Griffith, was offered more than one slug of brandy or rum by the Blandfordites. And then, Henry Knox noticed, Hoel's ear seemed to be promised a more personal gift from the lusty lips of a rather enormous Canaanite female. As she whispered what could have been a preview of her rewarding ribaldry, Griffith's young face flushed with sudden color, his entire countenance brightening with anticipation; as though, Henry Knox thought, a peasant had been promised a princess.

"Ye be challenged, Hoel!"

Almost every tongue was stilled by the sudden shout. Turning, as did all heads, Knox saw the angry face of their newest teamster, John Holding, and it was apparent that a rush of jealousy had overtaken his reason.

"Claim her, John!" a voice hollered.

There were shouts, in Welsh, in English; even a grunt from Blue Goose that could have meant anything at all. A fist caught a jaw. In less than a breath of time, the rum and brandy and whiskey twisted smiles into drunken scowls; fingers into fists, brotherhood into a brawl. As the Canaanites were strong men, things looked grim for the newcomers; plus the fact that it was difficult for Henry and William to determine which side was being taken by his troops and teamsters.

Blue Goose giggled.

Despite the kicks and punches, fiddlers fiddled and fifers fifed. An earthenware jug was smashed over Glenn Holding's head, causing his eyes to roll and his mouth to go slack. Several voices tittered as though greatly amused: high pretty laughter of lasses, or lovers. The fighting stopped as suddenly as it had started, allowing the drink again to flow, and flow. Knox was trying to stand up long enough to witness what seemed to be, of all things, a wedding. As there appeared to be no father of the bride, the one who served in the capacity of giving the lass away was no less than Durable Hatch. Henry's eyes were a blur, yet there was Cotton Witty as best man. The groom was John Holding, standing beside his enormous bride. Wearing a black Canaanite bonnet, a red blanket and a wide grin, Blue Goose seemed to think himself the maid of honor. My head swims, thought Henry. The ceremony was brief, yet final.

"Who," Henry asked Cotton, "was that broth of a bride?"

Cotton smiled. "Lovebreed Jack . . . sir."

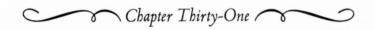

Chapter Thirty-One

In his hand, the wisp of hay rustled dry and coarse; and yet a sweet remembrance of Augusts past. So long ago.

With his fingers stretched out flat, General Washington allowed the strands of dry timothy tangled with clover to rest on his palm, as a soft gray nose discovered the silage, lips gently popping in possession. The hay slowly worked its way into the quiet mouth of his new white mare.

"Lady," he whispered to her. "For I shall name you Lady, provided such a calling merits your worthy approval."

Inhaling the rich smell of the Cambridge barn, Washington slowly let the breath escape his lungs, holding it for as long as comfort would allow. This fragrance, he then thought, is so like any well-found barn, be it in Virginia or here. So clean and so pure that indeed I must rest my eyes to breathe in all its reverence.

His hand stroked the mare's grayish-white jaw. "So very animal, like you. And there, my quiet friend, lies a barn's soul. No stink of man, his passions and his hostilities; his ruthless ambitions are absent among the dung and fodder. Posies, the both, by a comparison to politics."

Finding a remnant of brown burdock in her mane, his fingers worked to remove it; carefully and without pulling her hair.

"John Hancock was here today, Lady. John Hancock and John Adams; a cock and a rock, if you will permit a gentle jest. God Almighty alone knows how they each refer to their commanding general. My guess 'twould be that each be too clever, too sly, to share my nickname of what-ever-it-be with the other. Too polite, Lady. Too poised and too polished. Ah, too unbarnly, be there such a word. They do mistrust my actions."

Nay, thought Washington, best I correct that statement. What old John and old John mistrust is my inaction. How they pressed me this day to attack Sir William. Had they their way, the two of them would surely have seized pitchforks to prod our green lads down those hills and onto red steel.

Washington sighed.

I wonder where you are at this moment, young Knox, you and your tons of ordnance. I want that iron. When it arrives, as it blessedly shall, I will hold a twelve-pound ball in my hand, and ask the Lord to hallow it, like the holy orb of a monarch. Billy Howe, rest ye well this wintry eve; for soon you shall cast your eyes to the westward and to the south (stand you in Boston Common) and see naught else but a row of black holes. Cannon mouths, dark and sooty, a garland of black pearls to throttle your neck, Sir Billy.

"How rests such a taunt with you, Lady?"

Too much bravado and yet lacking in courage, is that your assessment? Well, my girl, you be right. My military acumen tells me that 'twill be more than the King's iron needed to scat away the King's lancers. And you, Sir William Howe, are indeed a sovereign's soldier.

"You know, Lady, that I have no desire to slaughter his lads, forbid he undo mine. None do I have. Ah, to send them packing 'twould be a tasty trick, one I shall relish in reality when the time comes. Yet when does it come? Hancock demands to know where the cannon is, and so does Adams; but I'll not betray Henry's position. The fewer who know, the safer you are, big fellow. Truly, I cannot fault John or John this day for pushing me, as others press them. I can close my eyes and hear the tongues:

"Remove that Virginian," they say.

"Rip the rank from his tunic."

"We need a commanding general who can oversee more than a withdrawal from confrontation."

"Whither hides Washington?"

Lady, my dear, we shall not let them spook us. Mice! So will we be, like a wee mouse who secrets himself beneath a fallen birch leaf, his tiny ears of gray fur bristling as he hears the hoot of the great horned owl and its attempts to flush out the quarry. Soft, dear horse. Let them screech, for you and I and our untried lads do not flush as readily.

Whose side are you on, Hancock? Are you Sir Billy's bird dog, quartering a field like a well-bred spaniel, until Washington flutters up before the gun? Then if our feeble attack fails, what next, Hancock? Do you carry my fallen and feathery form in your mouth to drop it like a faithful springer at the huntsman's boot?

Forgive them, Father, for they know not what they do!

Politics, dear horse. Lucky be you that in thy sweet meadow lurks no such weed. Very good thought, sad though it be. Yet well put. Avon's bard could nary have said it the better. If only I were a poet this night, instead of a solitary soldier. I thank God that Martha is finally here.

Lady, never were there a sentry as alone or more forsaken than a commanding general. Be there ever, Providence forbid, a hostility among horses, take my advice and seek not stars for your shoulder. Oh, how I do pity myself. Fie on it! Best I attend my mail.

Remembering, his hand slowly sought the pocket of his buff-colored breeches, until the tips of his fingers touched the letter. Crackling the dry paper, he unhurriedly withdrew it, slowly unfolding it. There was no necessity to read the words, as he had done so again and again, perhaps because the letter had been put to ink in Virginia. It had come from Thomas Witty, his neighbor. Looking at the unfolded paper, General Washington raised it slowly to his nose. No fragrance. Strange! But when first I opened it, there came forth a waft of Virginian evening, or did I imagine? Naught, they say, beclouds more a man's reason than war or love.

Hah! My horse, it must be war that robs my reason, as 'tis my guess there is too little loving in Massachusetts to steal away the sense even of a shrew.

My dear George . . .

Having no need to reread the letter, Washington refolded its worn seams and tucked it away once again into the dark depths of his pocket. Already he had cheered his spirit with the news.

Thomas Witty and Loring Stowe, both gentlemen his neighbors, were now en route to Cambridge; to see for themselves, so the letter said, how the war was progressing.

"I know why," Washington whispered to the mare. Then, suddenly laughing, he looked about. " 'Twill not do, my girl, to have our troops see their general conversing with a horse." Shaking his head, again he laughed, but quietly.

Lifting a discarded scrap of saddle blanket up from the straw beneath her belly, he slowly rubbed her back with the wool. Along her spine, withers to croup, he worked the woolly rag. Then down her legs, checking as he did so pastern and hock and stifle, lifting each hoof to satisfy his personal curiosity, finding her sound.

"To cheer me, Lady. And more, I do surely know the purpose of Thomas Witty. No journey, even in winter, could be too distant when one's only son is the prize."

Gently he slapped her satiny rump. Well, I shall surely keep my opinions locked inside my lips. Regardless of what I heard that one time from Colonel Knox, this lad of his was more to me an ache than an aide-of-camp. As though the pup expected all of us, senior officers or not, to attend him. Now there, from what precious little I did manage to see of Cotton, is a youngster who has much to absorb. However, how does one tell a neighbor such a rancid report concerning his only issue?

Thomas, shall I say, I see you have come to fetch home that brat of a boy? Why in the name of Lucifer I ever consented to write that corn-haired cub a commission I will ne'er understand. All persons have occasional lapses of reason, and truly this was one of mine. Or, should I confess, one of my many; another being my talking to a horse.

So shall I begin . . . Thomas, concerning your son . . . Hell! 'Twas an error on my part never to have the Wittys at least done the courtesy of informing them that young Cotton was no longer with me. In my command, yes, nay not at my side. All this time, Thomas perhaps pictured his whelp safely ascamper in Cambridge and under my wing. Damn, I should have given Knox orders to employ the lad with special handling! Too late. Before I knew it,

Knox had sent the lad off to Ticonderoga in the company of a redhide Huron and some old codger from the north territory. Verdmont, I believe. A place beset with heathen and hoarfrost, unfit for residency, and totally uninhabitable by anything Christian. So be Verdmont.

The epistle I received from Knox a week or so back, I read as both credit and debit. A warning, between his words, that all is not wholesome with young Witty. The note touches on his loss. Personal, he said. God, is the lad blind? When ordnance is not properly fitted prior to fire, mishaps occur.

As he is precious little more than a child, I hold myself responsible for young Witty's safe return.

Not that he was entrusted to my care and protection; yet as he is the sole son of a man who is in every way a compatriot, I cannot absolve my own person from authority. Were the boot on the other foot, and had I a son, no man on this planet would tender more his ward than Thomas Witty. I pray thankful that Cotton is now with Knox. Yet even years ago, this youth was handing heartbreak to his mother. What was the rumor I heard?

About a horse?

Lady gently tossed her head, as though wanting to learn more. Her action, albeit no more than coincident, urged George Washington to a slight smile.

Thomas Witty sired his heir. I have sired none.

Enough of this. Thomas and Loring Stowe will soon arrive. Knowing their prompt natures as I do, they will be with us well before the arrival of the ordnance. 'Twould be politic, dear horse, if both could witness the King's iron and its regal entrance into Cambridge. And when Thomas and Loring wend homeward, I would not be opposed if Virginian ears by the scores heard about our artillery. If this Continental Army is to survive this winter, somehow we must stuff our military magazine with more than chatter.

Hell! Most of us prance in uniforms we design for ourselves and yet we lack as much as a pea-shooter to train on Sir Billy. Make haste, Henry, for the likes of Hancock and John Adams have already found their target, and it is George Washington of Virginia.

May I blame them? Nay, for I am no better than they. Only a more seasoned soldier I be. All three of us know that. All I have to do, whenever John Hancock is wont to strap on his silver saber (in fact or in fancy) is to account the battle I fought with Braddock. With eyes open and chins closed, they listen, for they know they are not soldiers, no matter how many silver sabers they trip over. God, but that sword of Hancock's must be worth the dowry of a duke's daughter. Yet he is not a soldier.

Braddock was, rest his soul.

More bowel than brain; and I should wager, from all I study and hear, that Billy Howe is cut from the same bolt. Braddock would have picked a scrap with Satan. Yet 'twill not be men of his stamp to wage and win a war in an American forest. I daresay that's the answer. The vast woodland of this continent was a wilderness to Braddock in divers ways. Our geography turned him askew. Braddock lost his base, his arbitrary points of attack. Formerly his enemies were before him; not on all sides, the way the French and the savages positioned. What old General Braddock demanded was a direct confrontation, which is, I should imagine, the like that Billy Howe covets with Washington.

Much can be favored with discovering that which one's enemy desires, only cautiously to skirt it. This will fan the fires of frustration in you, Sir Billy, and then you will commit yourself. Charge out of Boston and up the hills at us? And again, as we did at Bunker, we shall roll boulders at you, or kegs on either end of an ox chain. For that, my dear Billy, is all we have.

"And so" — Washington pressed his face to Lady's warm neck — "we shall make General Howe sweat with our delay. If such inertia causes the others to sweat also, then let them all be awash with perspiring."

Washington gave the mare a final pat, leaving the barn, walking slowly through the mud toward the house that quartered Martha and himself. Mud, he thought. The thaw will be both pleasure and pain for Knox.

"All we shall do here in Cambridge is await you, Henry. Verily, we shall abide," Washington looked upward to tell a winter sky.

Using the bootscraper at the front doorway, General Washington removed the patty of brown clay from each heel. The soldier at entry presented his musket.

"Good day, soldier."

"Aye, sir!"

"Well, we are near through January, eh? Perhaps the worst of winter is behind us."

"Pardon me saying, sir, but this be but a thaw."

"Is it not yet spring?" Washington smiled, lifting his brows in order to mock amazement.

"Not yet, General."

"Where is your home?"

"New Hampshire, sir."

"A proud place, I'm told."

The soldier was young, no more than nineteen, and his smile allowed his pleasure to speak about home.

"I weren't born in New Hampshire, sir." The boy seemed desperate to continue their conversation.

"No? Then where?"

"In the territory of Maine, to the east'ard."

"Are your people farmers?"

"Oh no, sir. We are fishers."

"Fishermen?"

"We be, sir, and builders of vessels, too."

"And one day you'll hunt whales."

"Aye, that I will, General."

"Ever been to sea?"

"Once, for cod and halibut. I was near signed for a whaling voyage, but instead my brother and I enlisted."

"But now you fish for Lobsterbacks."

The lad smiled, eyes sparkling. "Yes, sir, if we ever do. To confess, I ain't much as seen a Redcoat since my service began. When will we attack them, sir? If you don't bother my asking. I mean no disrespect, sir."

"No bother. 'Tis a pondering I oft ask of myself, soldier, so I take no umbrage. When, you ask? The answer lies as much with patience as in patriotism. A good Whig like yourself will come to understand that."

"Sir, my brother and I signed up to fight."

Outspoken young rascal, thought Washington. Well, bless him for it, as that is our purpose . . . to be heard. How can I ask King George to harken unless I listen to a shipwright's son from Hampshire?

"So you volunteered to be soldier, not sentry."

"Aye, I did truly, sir."

"Likewise did I. How long have you and your bud been soldiers?"

"Going on eleven weeks, sir."

"And not as much" — Washington lifted his leg to rest a boot on the porch railing, leaning his elbow to his knee — "as even once smelled the burnt powder from your musket's discharge, except to train."

"We're itched to fight them, General. All of us."

"So be I. May I please ask your name?"

"Wilk, sir. I am Joshua Wilk. And my brother is Bertram, a year younger than myself, although near to my growth."

"There are Wilks in Virginia."

"Are there?"

"Indeed. A merchant of tobacco, and a sheeper. Are there perchance Washingtons up in Maine?"

"None I met, sir."

"Tell me, Joshua . . . do you ever study about the French War?"

"I have heard tales, sir."

"Have you heard of General Braddock?"

Even the freckles on the boy's face seemed puzzled by the question. Strange, he thought, how isolation doth breed apathy to replace a bloody war with naught but dreams.

"No . . . no, sir. Is he on *our* side?"

"Hardly. Our friend Braddock is dead."

"God rest him, sir, if he was your friend."

"Ha! Some said that Braddock was no one's friend. But by damn,

310

he surely was every man's general. Yet he made a mistake. Pardon me if I bore you to a yawning with tales of my expeditions.

Yet there is a lesson here. We attacked too quickly, Braddock and I. Our advance under British colors was not well thought, more rush than reason. 'Twould be my guess, soldier, that General Braddock died and went to Heaven knowing not how imprudently he lunged."

"Who beat him, sir?"

" 'Twas the trees."

The boy's mouth suddenly showed a row of white teeth as his lips slowly opened in total dismay. "Trees?"

Washington nodded. "Oaks do not move, Joshua; they only wait. When the tempest whips their branches, they bend and sway, to give way a bit. In other words, an oak branch knows when to retreat and let the wind slip by, to dash itself to death in the unknown beyond."

"So we may be wise to wait, sir. Until the Redcoats come to us and stumble."

General Washington bowed slightly. "With lads like you, and Bertram, I surely do pity Billy Howe if he dares come our way."

Joshua Wilk smiled.

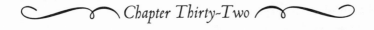

Chapter Thirty-Two

Henry Knox held his breath.

Because of the constant creak of wagon wheels, he heard no hoofbeats from the oncoming horse. The animal was coal black, all but the left foreleg, which was white nearly up to the chest. Stocking, he had been aptly named by his rider, Lucy Knox.

As their column was nearing Worcester, Henry Knox knew that

at any moment Lucy would come. There would be no holding her, not by rain or snow or any kind of tempest that might rattle the bones of even the most adventurous horseman. Lucy, he surely knew, would appear. At a gallop, waving to him as he now wanted to wave to her, had his entire body not suddenly frozen with the joy of seeing his wife. He tried to shout her name, but the choke in his throat and the wetness in his eyes seemed to forbid language. Closer, closer, closer . . . until Stocking's white leg had nearly run him down. Up went his hands in time to catch her as she literally flew from the saddle, her arms encircling his neck, her feet never touching the brown earth of the wagon road.

"Henry . . . Henry . . . Henry . . ."

Again and again she whispered his name. Knox heard all the music and felt all the magic that marriage to Lucy gave him in such full bounty.

Lucy! Lucy! Oh, I shall never go to Ticonderoga again. Even if His Majesty, King George, attends me there and awaits to do battle with all the brigades of Christendom.

"Every day," she spoke into his arms. "I would throw the tack on Stocking before anyone was stirring, and we would canter westward, hoping . . ."

"I know, I know . . ."

"Hoping to see your advance riders, or scout, or whatever you call it. Henry, let me look at you." Up and down her eyes traveled.

"Well?" he waited.

"You be a stranger to shears and soap. Yet you be also a knave if you think I much care."

"For sure I need razor and tub."

"Henry, sweet mountain, no man nor beast on this earth could smell worse than you do to me. Or better." Her sudden laugh bubbled out, a happy fiddle of fun that promised so much that his chest wanted to burst with his own joy. The rediscovery of her is more, he thought, than I can contain. Surely I overflow.

She noticed the knife scar on the palm of his hand, allowing him to explain that he had sworn an oath to a Huron savage at midnight, in exchange for a slain buck. And then he told her about Sky and Blue Goose and the tiny spoon for a babe. He talked and she talked, at once, wishing to tell each other all.

Together they stood, as cannon upon cannon rolled slowly by. On mud-splattered wagons now, as the unseasonable thaw had turned white to brown. No snow was about, except for a thin white blanket deep in the spotty stands of evergreen. Below the leafless hardwoods lay only a brown carpet of fallen foliage, damp and dark as chocolate. Each wagon wheel was thickly frosted with heavy layers of clay, dripping from the rains. Legs of oxen were mired brown; also their bellies, from places where the hauling was deep and with little footing.

"Brown," said Henry. "We are brown with mud, even our souls. All of us. Soldiers, teamsters, horses, brass and iron. And our noble oxen. I tell you, Lucy, if America ever requires an animal as a symbol, as England has her lion, then I shall be proud to nominate our worthy ox, rampant on a field of mud."

"Your oxen seem near death."

"Indeed, as they truly be. Some have already died and several of those you see now straining before us will also fall. The men, too."

"You all need a rest."

"Aye, that we do, my dearest. Half our teamsters returned homeward to the west, back to New York towns to tend their own farms and families. Many of their oxen went with them. No amount of persuasion nor promises of money could induce them to continue with us beyond Springfield. We are hungry and dirty and all but defeated."

"Dear Colonel. My dearest Colonel."

"Nay, Lucy, not yet, for I am still a civilian."

"Wrong you be. The Congress hath approved your rank. General Washington sent word to me, asking if I would savor the pleasure of announcing the commission."

"And," he smiled, "is that your pleasure?"

"My pleasure, sir, awaits you," she said.

Slowly, as if in pain, the column limped into the community of Worcester. Lucy had prepared the townsfolk for the arrival. Hardly a woman had refused to bake and roast. Almost every oven blistered forth the aroma of buns and biscuits, pies or potatoes or pudding that tortured every nostril in the entire company. The men of Worcester, excepting only Tories, turned out to unhitch the oxen, removing the heavy oaken yokes and rubbing balms of lard ointment on sores to help heal their grievances.

Beds were turned down or made up; and children were cramped and crowded into more than one loft to allow a tick of cornhusk to rest a teamster, or some of the soldiers who had labored the entire way from Fort Ticonderoga. All found a friendly haven. Hatch, Blue Goose, and Lieutenant Witty were taken in by Mistress Wakeman, who was, according to Lucy, the undisputed best at cookery in Worcester. Tubs of soapy water were afforded those who asked for bathing. Their tattered garb was burned, or buried, and fresh clothing supplied where washing would have done little more than cleanse worn rags. Boots were donated. A team of honey-colored mules was brought down from a farm southwest of the settlement of Marlboro.

"Your faces," said Lucy to her husband in the kitchen.

"What of our faces, pet?"

"Your beards are so filthy with grease, and your cheeks so raw, that you remind me of ghosts. All of you have that look. And when I saw the whip marks on the oxen I nearly became ill."

"We pushed them. God forgive us for driving them even harder than we drove ourselves. Yet we are here, wife. I found few clothes en route to fit me, even though some were offered. My girth was a difficulty."

"I sewed you a fresh uniform. Now, undress, and I shall prepare your tub. Oh, my big muffin, you were so dearly missed and longed for."

"Was I?"

Together they rolled the immense beechwood washtub into the center of the kitchen floor and near the great black stove and its three teakettles of steaming water. Henry's nose touched hers. I am alive, he thought. Alive! And home again.

"Where is Cousin?"

"Out," she said. "And a-shoo for the afternoon, knowing full well how the two of us wish to be alone."

Knox smiled. What need for words?

"But," Lucy said, "pray tell me what befell your Virginian lieutenant."

"In what wise, sweet?" He pulled off a rancid boot.

"When he departed that day, in the company of Mister Hatch and the Huron, young Witty was a graceful dove. The way he sat that chestnut mare of his was a portrait in gentility."

"You saw him this day?"

"Not at first. Only later did I see a limping wretch, a scarecrow in rotted rags, or near to, with no uniform and no horse."

"And no toes."

"No!"

"Yes, dear Lucy, yes." Henry's voice became softer. "It was blackfoot."

"His toes fell off?"

"Hatch did it."

"Did what?" Her voice said she was almost afraid to ask.

"Durable removed the lad's toes, with tongs."

"God." She spoke His name in piety.

"Lucy, you will never know what our boys and beasts have done these past weeks. More than human flesh ought be capable of doing. Wife, it was as though we were clamped helpless in the vise 'twixt war and winter."

"I knew you'd do it."

"We did. William and I and all of us, as one."

"He looked as poorly as you."

"William had less padding to sustain him," he said without mirth.

"Ghosts. I could not believe how you all appeared. As though you had returned from the grave, where your eyes had shared abuses too extreme for sanity to endure."

315

Knox worked off a soiled and sour stocking, noticing how it had a hole in both heel and toe. Between his toes was a crust resembling charcoal, and the stench of what was near to stale vinegar filled the kitchen.

"Be not ashamed."

"Nay, for I be too weary. But do not let me collapse now. For 'tis true we have forty miles to go 'twixt here and Boston."

"The mud is worse," she said, "from here to Framingham."

"How do you learn this?"

"Asking a waggoner. Each day I try to glean us bits of information to assist your mission. Little they be, but perhaps some of what I can uncover will prove valiant to my husband, and to our cause."

Once he had eased his bull body into the enormous tub of hot soapy water, he leaned his head back into Lucy's arms, closing his eyes, feeling Lucy's fingertips explore his hair. With a heavy sponge that oozed a white lather, she bathed his hair, his face and neck, scrubbing wherever a mere rinse was inadequate to scrape away the scurf and the grime of three hundred winter miles. The entire kitchen seemed to swim around him, making him dizzy in the relaxing warmth. Giddy, in fact.

"Father was here," she whispered.

"Was he?"

"Yes, and he plans to go to England."

"Did he inquire?"

"Slightly. But only in a family sense, not as a Tory, if that is what you contemplate."

"I didn't mean that."

"Didn't you?"

"Well, perhaps. In a family sense," he smiled, opening his mouth to laugh, only to receive a hot mouthful of soapy suds from a playfully quick squeeze of her sponge.

"Lucy!" he sputtered.

"You deserve it."

"How so?"

"Suspecting my father of acting as a spy."

"Nay, I do not."

316

"You cannot dupe *me,* Henry."

"No, I cannot. Nor do I wish to."

"Best you never try, sir."

"Nary again, as I swallow too much soap." He spat.

"Oh, my sweet, sweet Henry." Although wetting the sleeves of her pink and white dress, her arms were around his neck as she knelt on the floor behind him. "How, in this old world, was I ever so fortunate as to find a sugarlump like you?"

"Home," he sighed.

"We'll be back in Boston one day."

"Indeed we shall."

"All because of you, dear soldier. Because you plus William and all the rest had the entrails . . ."

"Lucy!"

"Guts, then! The courage to grunt the King's iron for three hundred miles."

"Thank the oxen, not myself."

"Perhaps I should be soaping an ox."

"If this tub would hold him."

"Hah! If a tub would hold you, husband, it would surely accommodate an ox."

Turning in the tub, he pretended as though to splash her. Quick as a shrew, she nearly pushed his head under, causing him to laugh and sputter all in a breath.

"My," she said, "what a temper."

"What a wife."

"Poor you." She flicked a large soapy bubble at his cheek.

Gently she rinsed off his shoulders. "There! You're clean as a cat and as slippery as a wet seed. Ready to retire?"

"So I am, as these January afternoons become dark and dreary, with little to do but slumber." He waited for her to react.

Turning about, he caught the wisdom of her smile, hearing the chimes of her chuckling mingle with his. Home! Wherever you are, dear wife, shall be my castle.

"Lucy, you are some wife."

"And you are some soldier, Colonel."

317

Not until now did he notice that Lucy had hung his pale yellow dressing-gown near the kitchen stove, to be warm for him as he stood up dripping in his tub. The towel she handed him was also warm against his skin.

"This is more a tent than a garment," she observed.

"Every warrior warrants a tent."

"What you warrant is a big soft bed."

"And" — he held her — "a little wife."

Later, in the great bed, Henry could not sleep. Instead he lay motionless on his back, his arm around Lucy, holding her gently. In his ears he heard the constant rumble of wagons and oxcarts, even though all the ordnance was now at rest in the roads of Worcester. Still the noise of his caravan haunted him, and he wanted to stem the sound of oxen breathing heavily, laboring and straining, and being urged on by men too exhausted to beat their animals for even one more furlong.

"Can't you sleep?" asked Lucy.

"Nay, not yet."

"Do you still travel?"

"Indeed. My mind cannot halt our hauling. It be as though my conscience is a wagon wheel, struggling through some portage of mystical mire, unable to progress. Yet around it spins, a millwheel in place, no closer to either reality or to General Howe."

"Sleep, sweet mountain."

Colonel Henry Knox slowly lowered his eyelids, allowing the rumble of cannon wagons to retreat into stillness, forgetting the welts of his winter and his war.

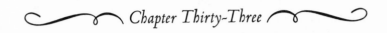

Chapter Thirty-Three

Durable scratched himself.

He and Blue Goose were afoot, a mile ahead of the first yoke of oxen, as the column left Framingham, headed due east for Roxbury. This close to Boston, thought Hatch, it usual makes my old heart leap. What a tankard of a town. And to think them rotty Regulars closed down Nell's place, and sent Britchie and all them doxies packing. How could anyone be so dogblame heartless? Boarding up Nell's is like to a law against laughter.

"Bad," said Blue Goose, his mouth close to Hatch's ear.

"Ya dang tooter it's bad. Or worse."

Blue Goose frowned, placing a red hand over Hatch's mouth. "No talk."

"What's up? It is them three again?" Durable's eyes searched the thick spruce that lined the road, great silent walls of green.

Blue Goose gave the old man a solitary nod of his head. Side by side they slipped off the trail. I am red once more, thought Hatch. We ain't to Nell's yet, nor to Boston, so best I tread a moc instead of a boot.

"Where?"

Slowly the Huron raised his buckskin covered arm to the ridge on their left. Squinting, the old Verdmonter saw nothing and smelled nothing except the spruce trees that crowded the narrow wagon trail on both sides. Little to hear but the whisper of a wandering wind.

"Where they headed?"

Blue Goose told him, his eyes looking silently back toward

Colonel Knox's column. Hatch still wondered if it was the same three that had shadowed them yesterday and the day before. Although the trio of white men had chosen to walk through the bush and not down on the trail, keeping up with the column should have been no task for them. Not in all this mud. Progress from Worcester, where that portly widow had taken him in for the night, had been snailish.

Dang it, Durable Hatch thought!

We lug that iron from Ti to just behind us, and then we leave half of it mired in mud back yonder in Framingham. And when Henry Knox told that Virginny cub that the Old Gray Whale weren't to go a grunt further, I won't forget the look on that kid's face. I sure thought old Cotton was fixing to weep. But she was up to her hubs in it. Bellies of oxen resting in the mud with no footing. Couldn't wedge a pry-beam under the axle; and by damn, I weren't about to lash them critters even half a lick more. Get somebody else to whip a dying animal, and don't ask Andrew Angus Hatch. Even that there Shaker fella quit and went west; back home to his kith, I cogitate. Good riddance. He was gettin' to smell worse'n me. Need it or no, a man ought to allow himself a bath ever year.

Again, the Huron pointed.

I don't see a fool thing, Hatch told himself. Nevertheless, he nodded to Blue Goose as if he himself had spotted the men. Holding up three fingers he gestured to Blue Goose that he had even taken a headcount. A brief shrug of his shoulder suggested that the two of them move in behind the three and do a bit of spying.

"Go west," whispered the Huron. "Go see cannon?"

"Reckon they will. I believe they be Tory."

The expression of the face of the warrior told him that the word was new to him. "Bad?" he asked Hatch. "Tory?" His eyes turned cold.

"Friends of the English and friends to the stinking Mohawk, that's for certain."

Hatch was remembering the Huron's face when they had to leave some of the cannon deep in Framingham mud. "No kill Redcoat now," Blue had said as they left the Gray Whale, his red cheeks painted with sorrow.

Together they were now silently sliding through the low boughs of spruce. Ahead they could hear the voices of the three who continued west, unmindful that Hatch and Blue Goose had doubled back and were now behind them. The trio conversed casually and not like pursued men. Whites never learn, thought Durable, not about staying alive nor about much else. Had me a druther, I don't guess I'd pick white to hang out among, nary from the little I see of French or English or Dutch. Either alone or with maybe one another, just to work the other paddle when the wind's against your face. Somebody like good old Blue, on account he knows lots and speaks little, which makes him out to be a right rare bird. With most folks, it be t'other way round.

Feeling the grit bite into his hands, Durable pressed his belly to a shelf of gray rock, cold and hard. Again Blue Goose pointed with his eyes at a gap in the spruce where the three men were walking. Were they armed; and if so, with what? Hatch squinted to learn the answer, seeing little more than three soft-edged shapes of gray. Against his cheek, the rock was still damp from the dew of morning. Like his body, the stone was stiff and cold from a long night. Mornings were the worst, thought Hatch, and the only solution is to limp all day and pay no mind to the malady. This nigh to Boston overshadows a stiff knee and knitted knuckles.

"Same three," snorted Durable Hatch.

Blue Goose blinked a silent agreement. Looking at Hatch, he seemed to be asking what the old man packed in store for the men whose voices were now fading as they continued west, back toward the first cannon crew.

"Way I got it figured, them three is fixing to watch Henry. So if it be all the same to you, best we tag along behind, as I don't cotton to the smell of it. Not a whit."

Blue Goose grunted.

As the two of them slid off the rock, dropping without sound onto a green bed of moss, it was plain to Hatch that the trio was in no hot rush. They walked steadily westward, conversing among themselves. Speech without words. Only a muffled mumble of sound, as though the dense stand of spruce was partisan enough to strain away their intent.

"Tories, them three."

"Bad people."

"Some are. Depends to which side you be."

"Not with Redcoat."

Until recent, you only hated the Mohawk, enemy of the Huron of Canada, thought Durable; but now you crouch for revenge. Sky is no longer alive. Dead for sure. Not that he told me, on account of it ain't Blue's way, yet I'm aware of it. His laugh is hollow compared to what it once was. Damn them British. Snakes, that's what. Nothing more'n a den of rattlers. Well, is she dead, your Sky? I'll never ask it, Blue, and ya never need tell.

At his side, as they moved quietly forward in the shadow of the spruces, the red hand rested on the handle of a knife. Blue Goose thirsts for blood.

"We kill?"

The Huron's voice was less a question to Durable's ear, and more of a threat, an announcement of his intention. Wish I hadn't told Blue all that there stuff about all them Tory people. Shut your mealy mouth, you old fool. Else you just could get a young fool toppled into the hot porridge. Aye, he be starved for a scrap with anything that reeks of the Union Jack, and I won't be able to stop it once he tastes the gore and swallows it down as glory. His belt aches to sport a British scalp.

The three men were climbing now, atop a bluff of granite that commanded a clear view of the wagon trail, the twin ruts of brown on a narrow ribbon of early grass. Soon weeds would spring up to whip their heads along the bellies of oxen, and the bins of wagons. Now it was too soon for weed.

It was a long climb. Hatch's legs hurt.

Inching upward, their mocs kissing both moss and boulder, whispering only to the yielding cushion of tan spruce needles, Hatch and the Huron drew close enough to see the three. Within arrow range, Durable told himself what Blue now knew. One man was taller than the rest, taller and leaner, with a long horse face. His hair was part black and part gray, from what Hatch could make out. The second man wore a faded yellow shirt, although a light jacket was strapped around his waist in case the warm weather turned to cold once more. The third man was in white. Durable studied the white britches and shirt, and younger than the other two. Can't see the lad's face, but by dang, I can read the crouch of his frame. He motions easy. A spring brook 'twixt two pebbles. Don't appear he fits them other two. Horse Face and Yellowback were on either side, as the three lay on their stomachs, pointing down at the trail below them.

Hatch breathed deeply from the climb. Worth it, though, as he and Blue were slightly above the trio of men. White Pants, as he had labeled the youngest of the three, wore his blond hair tied back neatly in a bow, while Horse Face and Yellowback sported unkempt locks beneath their tricornes. Something strange was cooking in this pot, Hatch warned himself, and I sure would like to learn what.

"Redcoat!"

Blue Goose spoke only one word, hardly more than a controlled sigh, yet the warrior's single word chilled his body into a clam. His spine felt cold and crawly, like some doggone dangerous thing was fixed to take place and he didn't have an inkling. Nary a hint? Fie to all of that. Hints usual come traipsing out like a spooked rabbit. Well, best we wait, until the bud busts to blooming. It'll unfold. Them three sure ain't up here for scenery's sake, and Blue Goose is mistook.

"You daft? I don't see no Lobsterback."

Blue Goose pointed. "See coat."

Squinting, the Verdmonter suddenly saw. Folded neatly into the back of his black belt, Hatch saw a quick flash of red, like a warning. Tunic for sure and redder than Lucifer's arse. The man in white, Hatch saw, was a British soldier. More than that, an officer.

"Officer," he breathed at Blue Goose.

"And two Tory."

"Right. He's a brass-ass for dang sure. I can smell a British officer from ridge to neighbor, and that there chappy is one of 'em. No mistake."

"No musket."

Durable squinted. The Huron was right, no guns. Well, what about it? Officers don't lug muskets over the lace of their shoulders and strain their finery.

"You see any pistols on them three?"

Blue Goose nodded. "All."

"Can you hear anything, Blue?"

"Yes, hear Half Hand." Blue Goose put a finger to his own lips. Listening, the trapper heard the familiar rumble of the wagons, coming their way. He could hear the iron rims of the wheels grind into the gritty gravel of the road ruts.

"Half Hand come. Men speak."

"What they say?"

"Half Hand. I hear Knox."

"Maybe we best slip back to alarm Henry."

Frowning, the Huron shook his head. "Men talk."

"Men always talk. About what?"

"Horse."

Durable snorted. "Horse?"

Blue Goose held up three fingers.

"Three horses?"

"Uh," grunted Blue Goose.

"Where they at?"

The Huron shook his head. "Men got."

Well, thought Hatch, we cornered three jacks and three pistols and three horses. What next?

"Him write."

"Who?"

"Redcoat mark paper."

Eyes straining, Durable could faintly see that the young British officer in white was working a feather. Below, the rumble of moving wagons was stronger, and closer.

"He's counting out our ordnance," said Hatch.

"No. Him write."

"I know that, ya pesky redhide pup. That there fella is marking what artillery we got on his wee paper. Next thing be, off he goes on his horse to spout it all to Billy Howe!"

"Who?"

"General Howe, the chief of the Redcoats."

"Where him camp?"

"Boston, I reckon."

"We go?"

"Someday. Not today, laddie, and leastwise not now."

"Soon."

"Sooner than you think. Right now, we got other matters to tend. That there officer is to put down all the brass we got, all the iron, and oxen, and even the flint."

"We tell Half Hand. Men tell chief. No good."

"Aye, no good. Well?" Hatch waited. "Out with it. What we best do, Blue?"

"Kill." The warrior spoke the word softly. "Take cannon back Ticonderoga place . . . or kill."

"They got three to our two." Hatch tried to study the Yellowback and Horse Face as they watched the British officer work the tip of his quill into a tiny well of ink, as though witnessing the miracle of penmanship (or any literate practice) for the very first time.

"Two are weak. One strong."

"Ya marked that, eh?"

Blue Goose nodded, slowly removing his bow from his shoulder, and withdrawing an arrow from the bundle of five at his back. Hatch noticed by the cruel design of the stone that the arrowhead was not for hunting meat. This was Blue's war arrow. Gracefully he stood, bending the wooden bow until the deergut bowstring cut the tip of his red nose. Without relaxing the pull, he looked down at Andrew Angus Hatch, his face asking the silent question.

Hatch nodded.

There was sharp crack as the released deergut slapped the bow's wood, a whisper of the hissing shaft, a thud, a scream. Blue Goose had missed his intended target. For as he released his war arrow, Horse Face leaned behind the whiteclad back of the officer, catching the arrow through his neck, which became, in less than a breath of time, a red freshet.

Horse Face screamed again, a tortured and gargling cry of a man about to drown in his own blood. His long hands tore at his throat in an effort to rip out the arrow. He stared with widening eyes that would not close. Drawing his pistol, Yellowback discharged it with improper aiming, yet the ball creased the flesh of Hatch's upper arm. The sudden heat made the old man aware of the passing lead. Without hesitation, his opposite hand rose to his left shoulder as though to cover the minor wound.

The British officer did not panic, even though Yellowback jumped to his feet, yelling foul words at Hatch and Blue Goose. Instead, the Englishman folded the ordnance report, stuffing it inside his lacy blouse, yet smoothly drawing his small pistol with his free hand. Tumbling from the shelf of granite, Horse Face rolled and kicked at the agony of dying. Crimson beads freckled the gray stone.

But as Yellowback stared at Horse Face, his own mouth open in a silent howl, the British officer ignored his fallen comrade. Sharply he issued an order to Yellowback, the latter too dulled by near death to respond. The officer jumped to his feet, presenting the unguarded rump of Yellowback a stout kick.

"Reload!"

To Hatch's ear, the Britisher's terse command cut sharp and crisp, the bark of a fox to his mate. Dang it! Blue should of made sure to cut down the youngster first, as he was the spine of the lot. With him gone, Horse Face and Yellow would a been a brace of easy quail, pistols or no.

"Let's git!" hollered Hatch.

Blue Goose and Andrew Angus Hatch melted into spruce as silently as they had arrived. Yet it did require a more-than-gentle shove by a Verdmonter's arm to persuade a Huron that an arrow was a poor match against the precise pistolry of a British officer.

They trotted westward. Knowing that their two enemies would at once turn toward their escape to the east, and to Sir William Howe, Hatch figured as he ran. He stopped, so quickly that Blue Goose nearly trampled him.

"Give them pair a start," he wheezed.

Blue Goose's face asked the question and so Hatch scratched himself, leaning against the lower limb of a spruce before giving the Huron his due reply.

"Right about now," Hatch shook a bony finger, "that pair o' pilgrims is hightailed due east. And probable lost. Best they find them horses, if I be any judge of what thoughts they might conjure up."

"Chase."

"Ya dang wager. Aye, we'll give chase for certain, soon's we let that Britisher think that he run us off like a papa boots off a penniless swain. And you don't understand one whiff of what I'm telling, do ya? Ya dumb redfoot. Well, I don't guess we stand here all day. I'll catch my breath while I run. So best we have at it."

Sure enough, ahead of them even Hatch could hear the yelps of Yellowback complaining to the British officer that Horse Face was dead, or dying, and the three of them should stay together, plus an added gripe that the British officer's pace was not to his liking. Somewhere beyond the curtain of trees, a polished British boot once again found a Tory behind, and Yellowback yelped his protest until he was silenced with a stinging slap.

Now in circles, wondered Hatch. That young smartpants forgot which way to Billy Howe and he don't know lost from lonesome.

"They go north," said Blue Goose.

"Aye."

"Find horses."

"Not 'less they tethered in Hampshire."

"Tell old chief?"

"Not thataway. They won't tell nobody 'twixt here and the Arctic. But that there pup of a Britisher ain't no fool. He's mean as a lash and bright as Christmas. Aye, he'll find his horses like a priest finds his pound."

"We find first."

"Best we do, Blue, best we do. Else it'll be a handsome run for you and old Hatch."

Together they trotted due east. At last the nicker of an excited horse halted them. It came from close on; very near, thought Durable Hatch. Again the horse made its noise, turning Durable and Blue Goose in one step. Over a rise in the forest they saw the three horses, two bays and a brown, tied in a clump of white birch. Yellowback and Britisher were already there, swinging their legs onto saddles, trying to control their plunging mounts. Them horses, Durable told himself, must of smelled something gone awry.

As the two horses plunged off into the thickets of brush, Hatch's face darkened. Dang it! Never catch them two birds now. Out of breath, he sank to a fallen birch log to replenish his laboring lungs with air. Without warning, a pair of strong red hands, gripping his body under his arms like turkey talons, swung him up into the air. Suddenly he was in the saddle of the brown gelding, the third mount that had obviously belonged to unfortunate Horse Face.

"Ride! Blue Goose run."

Ahead of him on the panicky horse, Hatch admired the uncanny speed of Blue Goose. Lighter than a roe, he leaped fallen logs, his mocs seeming to barely touch the leaves still dark and wet with winter. Although each stride of the horse tortured the muscles of his body, somehow Durable hung on. A sudden bound of the gelding caused him to drop one of the reins, yet this sudden lapse of guidance affected the gelding not in the least. The horse seemed determined to pursue the galloping Blue Goose, who ran faster than Durable had dreamed was humanly possible.

Aye! Look at them red legs run. With his attention on Blue Goose, he was momentarily relieved of dwelling upon his personal agony astride the gelding. It was all the horse could do to keep Blue Goose in sight.

"Slow down, ya cussed heathen! I'm too old to run and too lame to ride."

Beyond a wall of pines, the two bay horses had hit soft ground. Hatch saw Blue Goose run by the Yellowback's horse, gaining upon the mount of the officer. Up he leaped, his buckskin arms encircling the neck of white lace. Off they both fell, and Hatch leaped for Yellowback. The man had drawn his pistol. Now Hatch's back pressed into the ground mire, the pistol barrel stabbing his belly. Durable's knife came up fast, yet too late to nip the pull of the trigger. Hatch heard a click! His belly tightened, prepared to take the ball of lead, and then remembering that Yellowback had enjoyed little or no chance to reload.

In less than a second, Yellowback's wet intestines spilled out over Hatch's knife, and he smelled the stink of the man's breakfast.

Durable heard the same laugh that had tickled his humor for many a trap run and for countless dips of a dripping canoe paddle. Then he heard the British pistol, loud and sharp; and saw Blue Goose clutch his own belly, and scream, doubling in a helpless pain.

"Old . . . Ax . . ."

As if in some strange slumber, Hatch's hand threw his tomahawk, its small, knifelike edge embedding in white lace. The young British face stared at him. Slowly sinking his satiny knees into the muddy earth, the Britisher looked no more than a dying child. His hand tried to touch the ax handle that protruded from his bleeding breast.

"Who . . . who are you, sir?"

"My name's Hatch."

Falling forward, the lad's head splashed into a puddle of brackish water and did not rise, or move. Hatch turned to care for his fallen friend.

Chapter Thirty-Four

With oxen, they forded the Charles River.

Instead of following the north bank to Cambridge, it had been the decision of Henry Knox to cross ten miles west of Boston, then to bear a few degrees southward and head for Roxbury. Finally the last wheel rolled out of the river, shaking itself free of water like a wet dog.

"We're over," whooped Lieutenant Witty.

Wheeling the gray gelding that he now rode, he spurred the animal forward to report to Colonel Knox. "Sir, the last crew is ashore."

"Excellent," said Knox.

"Praise the Lord." Knox shifted his big bulk on Major's saddle. Henry's face became slightly distressed. "How fares Blue Goose?"

"Bleeding a bit, but alive, sir. Thriving with care. In a litter, as he and Mister Hatch insist on staying with our column.

"I understand that Durable's grace with needle and thread had much to do with our red friend's recovery."

"Yes, sir. Mister Hatch . . . is rather gifted."

"And you also, Lieutenant Witty."

"I did little, sir."

"You saw both dead men."

"A British officer and, according to Mister Hatch, a Tory. A third was also reported dead by an arrow from Blue Goose. I did not myself inspect him."

Remnants of food in Cotton's stomach turned suddenly sour as he remembered the exposed headbone and torn brow. The sway of the gray horse sickened him, and it took a moment before he answered Colonel Knox's question:

"Sir . . . their heads . . ."

"What about their heads?"

"Cut away, sir. The hair was gone."

"Aye, by Blue Goose, I presume." Knox looked at the scar on his own hand.

"I found no blood on the Huron's knife. Only on Durable's. I tell you this only because you and I both understand their friendship."

"We do, Cotton."

"Sir, I feel that it was . . . necessary for Mister Hatch to cut the scalps, as though one was for Blue Goose, even though he did not quite die, and the other . . ."

"The other," said Henry, "was for a woman called Sky."

As their horses stood at roadside flank to flank, a gray and a brown, the two men watched the column clatter by them. Ox after ox, pulling the brass and the iron behind them, with footsore teamsters trudging at their sides.

"How oft," said Henry quietly, "I do desire to salute them all as they pass me by, time upon time, along our endless way. I want golden trumpets to herald the coming of the King's iron."

"Comes the seventh crew, sir," said Cotton.

"Aye, and Blue Goose bumping along as a protesting patient, as he lies betwixt two howitzers."

"While our good Mister Hatch screams at the oxen for every bump in the road."

"Your brother, sir. William comes."

"Aye, and you are all our brothers now. And" — Henry exchanged a tired wave with William — "I know that William expresses a like sentiment. Now, sir, what is that object Blue Goose holds as he comes riding along?"

"A British drum, sir, of their military."

"A drum?"

"Yes, sir."

"Where on earth did he get it?"

"From me, sir."

"And where did . . . ?"

"A farmer had it, sir, who had stolen it. So I traded him for the drum."

"What did you render up for it?"

"My pistol, sir."

Knox slowly raised his right hand, displaying a scar across its palm. "Lieutenant, as my left hand is partially gone, my right is the only good hand still at my disposal. Because of your pistol, Blue Goose did this to me, and if you ever endeavor to possess another, I will avenge myself upon you personally. Do we understand each other?"

"Very good, sir."

"And now, Lieutenant, I have a surprise for you this day, and possibly even within the hour."

"A surprise?" Cotton nearly blushed at the boyhood in his own voice.

"Indeed. He will arrive any moment, I suspect."

"General Washington! Here?"

"He comes to accept the King's iron. And, if I know your Virginian neighbor, he comes forth also to beg us to accept his gratitude. Just before you rode forward to report that our drag's crossing was complete, a courier arrived and departed, saying only that he was en route."

In his breast, Cotton Mayfield Witty became aware of his own heart. *Washington is meeting our exhausted column!* "Sir, best we slick the men up a bit?"

He saw Henry's face brighten. "Aye! Some spit and polish will give us all a boost, a lift of our spirits. Not every day do our lads pass in review before the commanding general of the Continental Army, so best we gussy up. Hand out some wadding to wipe the topsoil off our oxen."

"Very good, sir."

"Oh, and Cotton . . ."

"Sir?"

"In Worcester, my dear Lucy provided us with a canteen of brass polish. Please set the men to work, buffing those barrels. See that the oxen get a breather as well as a rubdown and a scratch behind the ears. Stoveblack their hoofs. Dab some dubbing or lard on the leather if you can, to give it a glow. Or use cheese."

"And we'll oil the chain, sir."

"Aye. Now please to halt the train and inform the entire company that we await the commanding general."

In less than an hour, every iron barrel turned ebony with fresh blacking. Each brass piece of ordnance was yellow with polishing. Copper fittings gleamed in the late February sunlight. Saddles were soaped as thoroughly as the men soaped their own necks and the sweatstained collars of their uniforms. Andrew Angus Hatch considered a wash and a shave; but then, reason prevailing, turned to the cleansing of artillery.

"Lieutenant Witty!" yelled Knox.

"Sir!"

"Something is amiss." Knox wiped his perspiring face with a handful of artillery wad.

"Pray what, sir?"

"Music."

"Blue Goose has a drum, sir."

"I know. Can he play it, with drumsticks?"

Cotton smiled. "Even without sticks, sir, he is the finest Huron drummer east of the Berkshires."

"Fair enough. Have we a fife or two?"

"Mister Hatch has one, sir, which he borrowed from its former owner."

"Who was that?"

"A citizen of Blandford, sir."

"I hope he borrowed little else from . . . what was the name of the incredible wench?"

"Lovebreed, sir."

Knox chuckled, his hand to his side. "Oh dear," he said in a weak voice, "I must confess how fortunate I am to have kept a diary of our trek. Are there any more instruments of music?"

"There are, sir."

"And what?"

"Our cherubic voices, Colonel Knox."

Cotton threw the saddle that he had been soaping once again over the gray gelding, waiting for Henry Knox to reply, watching the slow smile spread over the great moon of his face.

"Aye, an anthem."

"Sir?"

"A hymn, by good Heaven! A ditty we can march to."

"But we have halted our march, sir, as we be now unyoked."

"No matter," said Henry Knox. "If our feet and hoofs do not stomp to its rhythm, then our hearts and souls and spirits will dance along in place."

"Understood, sir."

"What about 'Yankee Doodle'?"

Cotton hesitated.

"Well," demanded Henry, "what gives you pause?"

"Sir, it's just that 'Yankee Doodle' gets trilled by every trooper in the Continental Army."

"So?"

"As I see it, Colonel, we deserve our own tune."

"Aye, that we do," agreed Henry.

As they talked, Andrew Angus Hatch joined them. " 'S matter?"

"We are in need of a song, Mister Hatch," said Henry.

"I got one," Durable's face brightened.

"Its title?"

" 'Yankee Doodle'!"

"Mister Hatch," said Cotton Witty, "we are somewhat familiar with that ditty. Yet I believe that you are, my good sir, the master of a melody that you and I together could profess to our comrades in arms."

"What be that?"

Cotton sang three words: "Brown eye Susan . . ."

A wide smile captured the old face. "What a song! I knowed a Susan one time, back in Verdmont. Legs like twin loafs of fresh bread!" Announcing only that he was off in search of his fife,

Hatch shuffled away in the direction of Blue Goose, who still kept his arms around the British drum, as though it were his most valued chattel.

Cotton drew up the cinch strap under the saddle and gazed across the shiny seat of leather to the road ahead. Just then, around the bend came cavalry. Leading the force was a mare whiter than virtue, and astride her sat a man who belonged on a saddle, wearing a uniform with a flowing cape and a white wig. A blue tunic modestly trimmed in red. Breeches of buff and polished boots.

"Uncle George!" he wanted to yell out.

Yet he did not holler or break ranks. Instead, leading his gray gelding, he took his place near Hatch and Blue Goose, watching Colonel Knox ride alone to meet his general. In the distance, he watched Knox salute, a greeting smartly returned by Washington and all his staff of officers. Two only did not salute. Side by side, the two civilians sat at ease upon their mounts. They were men of importance, Cotton sensed. And gentlemen of substance, by their garb.

"Sure glad this here trip is over," snorted Durable, still fumbling among some kegs and flints seeking a fife. " 'Twas either the end of this trip or the end of Andrew Angus Hatch."

"What plans have you now, sir?" asked Cotton.

"Me an' Blue, we're to head to the northwest, to Ontario. I heard tell they got beaver up yonder stocky enough to pull an uphill plow. You want to come along, boy?"

Cotton swallowed. "Sir, do you really mean you'd invite me?"

"You and me and old Blue. That's all, as I sure won't have nobody else. I don't guess you gotta be told that Blue and me don't harness up with just everybody."

Cotton tried to speak. His throat was suddenly dry. "I would not be able to keep up."

"Ain't no walkin' to it. The whole durn business is by canoe. You be welcome, lad, if you're of a mind."

Blue Goose hit the drum one hollow thump with the flat of his hand. BUM!

"Sing!" ordered Hatch.

335

"Why must I?" asked Cotton.

"On account of Blue Goose don't know all them Susan words, on account of I got to flute the fife, and account of if'n you don't, ya cussed whelp, I'll boot yer ornery Virginny arse from Hell to breakfast. Sing, dang it!"

Cotton sang. Phrase by phrase, the other men joined. At first, only with the chorus:

> Brown eye Susan
> Brown and sparky eye
> I hope I hug my Susan
> Once more before I die.

Several of the men knew the verses, while others struggled along; even the teamsters and soldiers who were ungifted in voice began softly to hum as a background to the drumbeats of Blue Goose, the shrill and shattering squeaks and squawks from Durable's tinny fife, and Cotton's tenor.

Close came the mounted officers, Washington and Knox in lead, their horses assuming a martial highstep. Sergeant Cutter's curt command snapped the men to attention, as they presented arms by hand salutes to General Washington. Still they sang, repeating "Brown Eye Susan" verse upon chorus, as though to say, *We are here, General, what little is left of us. We are still on our feet. And we bring you the King's iron.*

How elegantly, Cotton thought, our general staff is uniformed compared to our own borrowed and raveled rags. Behind Washington rode a young aide, perhaps also from Virginia and also a lieutenant. His uniform was faultlessly tailored. Never, thought Lieutenant Witty, would I exchange my humble company for yours.

Cotton saw his father.

Thomas Witty and Loring Stowe, the two civilians, rode quietly behind the officers. As they passed by, Cotton forced himself to stare ahead, as though he sang only to empty air and the silent forest. May I be allowed to hope, he silently asked, that my father

336

sees his son. I shall not beg your forgiveness, sire, nor will I extend to you mine.

Down the line of saluting and singing men they rode, allowing Cotton to see the straight back of his father's suit of brown velvet, atrim at collar and cuff with a lace of light cream. How proudly my father sits his mount. Yet he did not halt his horse to address me. On he rides in his finery as brown as a buck's eye. *Come back, Father. Come back.*

Voice by voice, the singing finally stopped.

Turning their mounts, the general staff executed a half-circle, to face the center of the column who faced them. All dismounted. A senior officer read from a scroll; and, according to his words, General Washington had created a Medal of Honor. At the conclusion of the oral citation, General Washington hung a disc of gold and a ribbon of light blue around the neck of Colonel Henry Knox.

Men applauded. Some lofted their hats at the sky. Henry Knox saluted, accepting the hearty handshake that General Washington offered him. Turning toward his men, Knox spoke:

"Fellows and comrades, be it here known that it is not I who receive this citation, for of all this column, I am perhaps least worthy to wear it."

"Nay! Nay!" a few men shouted in good humor.

Knox continued. "So, only does my neck accept this honor on behalf of us all . . . each horse and mule, every ox, and each man jack of us."

The men cheered.

"An oddity though it appear," said Henry, "another medallion was prepared for me whilst I rested briefly with my wife in Worcester." From his tunic pocket, he withdrew a wee star of bronze, suspended by a crimson cord. With little ceremony Knox handed the medal to Thomas Witty.

"Gentlemen," said Henry, "it now is my privilege to allow Mister Thomas Witty of Virginia to award this distinction to one of us and from us all." He paused to clear his throat. "Will you please come forward and receive your due, for service and sacrifice, for duty and honor and for your country, on behalf of this noble company and by the grace of God. . . . I now order you to step forward, Lieutenant Cotton Mayfield Witty."

Cotton felt his legs pegged into the earth, aware that rough faces about were smiling, turning his way. The only thing that started him forward was a well-intended yet healthy kick on his behind by the moc of Durable Hatch.

"Git going, ya lumphead cuss!" Only a whisper, and yet the men nearby hooted their appreciation.

Although the ground was uneven, he stumbled only once. Walking forward, he tried to parade erectly and to carry himself in the manner of a soldier. Looking straight ahead, his face frozen into sobriety, he did his best not to limp and to stride directly until he faced General Washington, Colonel Henry Knox, and his father. He saluted.

Thomas Witty cleared his throat, yet even so, his usually silver voice was now hoarse and he spoke with a tremble of the chin:

"Lieutenant Witty, for valor and in victory . . . I do now decorate you as a distinguished soldier and officer. Along with a Discharge of Honor, a promotion to the rank of captain, I place around your neck this Star of Bronze as our tribute of loyalty . . . and devotion."

Suddenly there were two long arms of brown velvet around him, and pressed against his face a cheek as wet as his. He felt his own hands embrace the back of his father, feeling for the first time in ever so long a soft touch of velvet and Virginia. Like the mouth of a mare, said his heart.

"Come back, Cotton."

"Yes, I will . . . Father."

"Come home to South Wind."

THE END

338

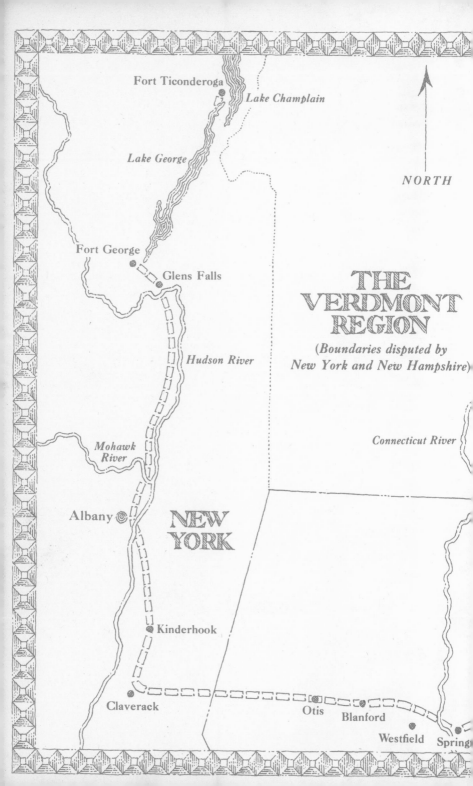